The Angel Asrael
and
Other Legendary Tales

FROM THE SAME AUTHORS

Martyrs of Science and Other Victims of Devilry and Destiny
ISBN 978-1-61227-229-0

The Angel Asrael
and
Other Legendary Tales

by
S. Henry Berthoud

Translated, annotated and introduced by
Brian Stableford

A Black Coat Press Book

English adaptation and introduction Copyright © 2017 by Brian Stableford.

Cover illustration Copyright © 2017 by Aurélien Maccarelli.

Visit our website at www.blackcoatpress.com

TABLE OF CONTENTS

Introduction

Asrael et Nephta, Histoire de Province by S. Henry Berthoud, here translated as "The Angel Asrael," was first published in Paris in 1832 by the Widow Charles-Béchet. The 1842 bibliography of *La Littérature Française Contemporaine*, edited by J.-M. Quérard, records that copies of the book also exist bearing what was presumably its original title, *L'Ange et le Démon, ou Asrael*. I have taken that variation as a license to amend the title again; while the original one carried the false implication that the angel and the demon to which it refers are two individuals rather than one, the belated substitute affords Nephta a parallel status that is unwarranted.

Asrael et Nephta was the author's first novel, although it is perhaps a little too short to warrant that title and might be better regarded as a novella. It was his fifth publication in volume form. Its first predecessor had been a pamphlet version of a poem that had won a prize in 1823 awarded by the Societé d'émulation de Cambrai, published by that author's father, the printer Samuel Berthoud (who used that signature on his own books, obliging his similarly-named son to employ his second name in his own signature, anglicizing it as an affectation). That had been followed by two short story collections, *Chroniques et traditions surnaturelles de la Flandre* (1831), published in Paris by Charles Lemesle, but printed by the Widow Charles-Béchet, and *Contes misanthropiques* (1831; tr. as *Misanthropic Tales*), similarly under the aegis of Lemesle but printed by Wedret.

In the same year as *Asrael et Nephta*, Berthoud also published another novel. *La Soeur de lait du vicaire* [The Curate's foster-sister], issued in Paris by Charles Vimont, which is listed ahead of *Asrael et Nephta* in the 1842 bibliography, but

7

was certainly written later, even if it was published earlier. The four volumes issued in 1831-2 marked the beginning of what was to become a long and prolific, if somewhat checkered, literary career that reached its culmination, and its most successful economic phase, in the 1860s, by which time the author, born on 19 January 1804, was beginning to grow old.

The brief biography attached to Berthoud's entry in the 1842 bibliography records that in 1817 he received a bursary to enter the Royal College of Douai, which he left in August 1822. He subsequently became the literary editor of a local periodical, the *Journal de l'arrondissement de Cambrai*, and in 1828 founded *La Gazette de Cambrai*, in which he published much of his early short fiction, some of which was pirated by Parisian and other provincial periodicals, and even by periodicals in England, America and Germany. That experience led to his recruitment by the pioneering Parisian journalist Émile Girardin, who employed him on the editorial staff of *La Mode* and *La Presse*, and he also worked for *La Revue de Deux Mondes* and *La Revue de Paris*—then the two central organs of the burgeoning Romantic Movement—as well as *La Silhouette* and *L'Artiste* before he was entrusted by Girardin, first with the sole editorship of the revamped *Mercure de France*, and then that of the pioneering "family magazine" *Le Musée des Familles*.

The 1842 biography makes no mention of Berthoud ever having attended university or having lived in Paris prior to relocating there permanently in the early 1830s, but there seems to be little doubt that his close friendship with Honoré de Balzac was initially formed some years before then, and it is possible that he spent some time as a student in Paris during the early 1820s, which he later erased from his biography, perhaps because he failed to take a degree. In the late 1820s and early 1830s, however, he certainly became an important person in Cambrai, not merely for his editorial endeavors but also working in local government, primarily in public education—he organized free courses in hygiene, anatomy, geometry, literature and the arts—and subsequently as the administrator of the local hospitals during the great cholera epidemic of 1830-31, during which, according to the biographer, the public health precautions he introduced allowed the epidemic to be attenuated more effectively in Cambrai than any other city in France.

Berthoud was still in Cambrai—and the cholera epidemic was still raging—when he wrote *Asrael et Nephta*. Once he had taken up permanent residence in Paris, however, he devoted himself entirely to editorial work and authorship, on a prolific scale. In the former capacity, at least, he became one of the lynch-pins of the French Romantic Movement, and did a great deal to stimulate its prose component, especially the imaginative fraction of that component.

Berthoud seems to have remained devout throughout his life, unlike most members of the Romantic Movement, and also gives the appearance to a political agnosticism that was similarly atypical, but there is something odd about the quality of his devotion, as the stories collected in the present volume, especially *Asrael et Nephta*, clearly illustrate. The other stories included here all come from the 1831 collection, the somewhat misleadingly-titled *Chroniques et traditions surnaturelles de la Flandre*. It does seem, however, that the collection in question was always envisaged as the first part of a larger work; it was reissued in 1834 as the first of three volumes, the second and third of which do indeed consist almost entirely of historical narratives and supernatural vignettes set in Flanders, whereas the first volume concludes with a number of contemporary documents, some of which would not have been out of place in *Contes misanthropiques*, Berthoud's pioneering collection of what would later become known as *contes cruels*.

It appears from his autobiographical comments that Berthoud did have the ambition at one time to become a genuine folklorist, traveling through Flanders on foot collecting local folktales from the indigenes, but he confessed ruefully that blistered feet soon cured him of the ambition and sent him home. Only a tiny minority of the stories in to *Chroniques et*

9

traditions even maintain a shallow pretence of being reported folklore, therefore, the great majority are manifestly literary works. This is more particularly true of the stories included in the present volume, because I have omitted nine that I translated previously for the showcase anthology of Berthoud's works, *Martyrs of Science and Other Victims of Devilry and Destiny*,[1] to wit: "La partie d'échecs du diable" (tr. as "The Devil's Chess Game"), Le Trou d'enfer" (tr. as "The Mouth of Hell"), "L'Archet du sabbat" (tr. as "The Sabbat Bow"), "La Bague antique" (tr. as "The Antique Ring"), "La Dame aux froids baisers" (tr. as "The Lady of the Cold Kisses"), "La Grange de Montecouvez" (tr. as "The Barn in Montecouvez"), "La Noce de Cavron-Saint-Martin" (tr. as "The Wedding in Cavron-Saint-Martin") "Le Sire aux armes brisées" (tr. as "The Sire with the Broken Armor") and "Saint Mathias l'Ermite" (tr. as "Saint Mathias the Hermit"). Most of those stories at least pretend to be accounts of Satan's interference with human affairs reflective of the role typically attributed to him by popular folklore. The stories in the present volume sometimes begin from the same perspective, but they move in several different directions therefrom, sometimes very dramatically, most conspicuously and most strikingly in the title story and the two stories from the earlier collection that are evident precursors of it, "L'Âme du Purgatoire" (tr. as "The Soul in Purgatory") and "Le Séminariste" (tr. as "The Seminarian").

It is blatantly obvious from the pattern of Berthoud's early works that he suffered some deep disillusionment during the 1820s, which left him, as he says in "Le Séminariste," in which he employs himself as the narrator, "indolent, skeptical and disenchanted." The annotation of *La Soeur de lait du vicaire* in the 1842 bibliography observes that "This novel was initially entitled *Bah!* By that title, the author said, he wanted to express the derisory insouciance with which the passions and their consequences are envisaged today. The author's friends assembled extraordinarily and, it appears, found *Bah!*

---

[1] Black Coat Press 2013, q.v.

too pretentious and too affected a title." If that is what happened—the anecdote was presumably supplied by Berthoud—one can hardly blame his friends for thinking that, but it is significant that Berthoud's initial impulse was so aggressively contemptuous.

It is difficult, in reading Berthoud's early work, to avoid drawing the inference that he had suffered at least one deep and injurious amorous disappointment, and probably more than one, whose culminating impact was permanent—he never married, and a biographical sketch of him published in the early 1860s found him living alone in Paris, save for his dog Maître Flock and a pet lemur he called Mademoiselle Mine. That disillusionment, as the note observes, was not merely personal, but colored his view of everything that was happening around him, encouraging him to call his second story collection—without his friends intervening—*Contes misanthropiques*. As to the exact nature of his amorous disappointments, we can only speculate, although his obsession with the theme of doomed love, in various versions, including several in which it terminates, and a few in which it even originates, in eternal damnation, certainly seems to reflect an ease of identification and a fervor of protest.

The 1842 biography, naturally, has nothing to say about intimate matters, but if its details were supplied by Berthoud the fact that it refers to his personal situation at all, albeit very diplomatically, might be regarded as significant. The sketch in question concludes with the observation that:

"In addition to a certain talent that distinguishes him as a man of letters, Monsieur Berthoud possesses special qualities that render his relations precious and which have acquired him numerous friends, among whom one remarks Madame Desbordes-Valmore, whose disciple he is. Endowed with a meditative mind and a great tact as an observer, he is particularly attached to the study of the human heart, and he has obtained a noble profit from that science."

The reference to the Douai-born poet and actress Marceline Desbordes-Valmore (1786-1859), whom Berthoud pre-

11

sumably first encountered when he was at school in Douai, is at least significant in identifying the esthetic and philosophical position Berthoud took up in affiliating himself to the Romantic Movement, and it might well have been her who recommended him to Émile Girardin and secured him the editorial work on which his long-term financial stability was built.

After her father, an armorial painter, was ruined by the Revolution, Marceline Desbordes had been taken by her mother to Guadeloupe, but when her mother died of yellow fever she returned to France, still in her teens, and began a career as an actress in Douai. After a passionate liaison with the writer Henri de Latouche in 1810-12—although its aftermath dragged on for thirty years, during which Latouche became one of the severest critics of the Romantic Movement— she married her second husband, the actor Prosper Lanchantin-Valmore, in 1817, and published the first of her six volumes of elegiac poetry in 1819 before retiring from the stage in 1823; her poetry became increasingly lachrymose as her life progressed, and all her children died one by one.

As well as adopting Berthoud as a protégé, Madame Desbordes-Valmore became a good friend of Balzac, who once named her as the model for *Cousin Bette* (1846), although that nomination, if true, is far from complimentary. She is, however, obviously the model for more than one of the tragic women featured in Berthoud's *Contes misanthropiques*, several of which feature tormented actresses, sometimes with a predilection for her favorite role, Rosine, in Beaumarchais' *Barbier de Séville*. Greatly admired by Charles-Augustin Sainte-Beuve and Charles Baudelaire, she was the only female writer included in Paul Verlaine's famous study of *Les Poètes maudits* (1884), and the noted Naturalist writer Lucien Descaves wrote the most exhaustive of several memoirs of her life, *La Vie douloureuse de Marceline Desbordes-Valmore* (1910).

Along with Sophie Gay and the latter's daughter Delphine, who married Émile Girardin, Marceline Desbordes-Valmore became one of the women who played key roles at the heart of the French Romantic Movement, somewhat underestimated by history, and the fact that Berthoud knew her well before going to Paris—after which he became a steadfast member of Delphine Girardin's salon—evidently had a considerable influence on his attitude to his work, and to life. Although his principal case-study in his philosophical analysis of the works of the human heart was his own, hers must have been the second, and Balzac the third. Although he eventually followed Balzac's policy in devoting himself almost exclusively to naturalistic fiction, his early fiction, almost all of which is historical or supernatural, undoubtedly owes more to his first and most dominant muse.

Although Berthoud soon abandoned, or at least greatly modified, the love of reckless fantasy that is conspicuous in many of his early works in order to concentrate on the disenchanted naturalism exhibited to the full in the *Contes misanthropiques* and almost all of his many novels, it is highly probably that that development of his work was impelled by market forces. The Devil never entirely disappeared from his work, and kept cropping up occasionally, rarely but insistently, even in the 1860s, when almost all of his work was aimed at a juvenile audience and very carefully sanitized. There are, however, good grounds for considering *Asrael et Nephta* to be the most personal, the most heartfelt and perhaps the most revealing of all his works, precisely because it is the purest of his fantasies, the one that looks back at the perverse and unsatisfactory operations of the human heart from the remotest hypothetical standpoint.

The novella is a significant early contribution to what was eventually to become a great Romantic and Symbolist tradition of "literary satanism," in which writers deliberately adopted a stance removed from orthodox Christianity in order to reappraise the character of Satan and the role of the diabolical in human affairs. By no means all such works were sympathetic to Satan, although some were wholeheartedly so, including Charles Baudelaire's "Les Litanies de Satan" (1857; tr. as "the Litanies of Satan") and Anatole France's "L'Humaine

13

Tragédie" (1895; tr. as "The Human Tragedy"), the precursor to the subgenre's second great prose masterpiece, *La Révolte des anges* (1923; tr. as *The Revolt of the Angels*). The subgenre's first poetic masterpiece, Alphonse de Lamartine's *La chute d'un ange* (1838) was broadly if diplomatically sympathetic, but its first prose masterpiece, Gustave Flaubert's *La Tentation de Saint Antoine* (tr. as *The Temptation of Saint Anthony*), was far more ambivalent—and very uneasily so, having gone through two earlier versions before its eventual publication in 1874, and building upon several precursors among the author's juvenilia, written in the late 1830s.

Only two subgeneric works of considerable significance were however, available as examples to Berthoud when he began to work within it: Jacques Cazotte's pioneering novella *Le diable amoureux* (1772; tr. as *The Devil in Love*), and Alfred de Vigny's long poem "Éloa, ou La Soeur des anges" (1824; tr. as "Eloa"). Both are obvious influences on *Asrael et Nephta* and its precursors; "Le Séminariste" is an intensely focused readaptation of the theme of the former and the "chatelaine of Hell" featured in one of the "ballads" interpolated in the novella appears to be Éloa, although she is not named.

As might be expected of a devout writer, Berthoud shows no sympathy at all for Satan, who remains an archetype of vitriolic nastiness, but in his characterization of the rebel, like John Milton before him, Berthoud cannot help reflecting a certain admiration for his overweening pride and vaulting ambition. What is more remarkable about Berthoud's Satan, however, is his representation of God, whom he regards as a peer essentially exchangeable with himself, who owes his status not to any intrinsic virtue but merely to his victory in the War in Heaven, which Satan unhesitatingly attributes to chance. And it has to be admitted that, setting piety aside, God really does come out of Berthoud's clinical accounts of his actions and policies extremely badly: perverse, stingy and, most of all, uncaring; the small modicum of sympathy he does show to the many souls bound for Hell who really do not deserve to be there by any sane and reasonable standard of jus-

14

tice is not attributed to his own benignity so much as the intercession of the Holy Virgin, who can sometimes soften his harshness.

The other forceful indictment of God uttered in *Asrael and Nephta* is the one credited to Astaroth, who mocks the manner in which God conspicuously fails to reward his most ardent supporters. As with Satan's own tirade, the reader is free to discount that as a diabolical argument, but the fact remains that the specific charges that Astaroth brings are correct. It is therefore, perhaps unsurprising that—apart from the Holy Virgin, upon whom no aspersions whatsoever are ever cast in Berthoud's work—the true exemplars and sources of virtue in Berthoud's satanic fantasies are those condemned to Hell or Purgatory who really ought not to be there: Béatrix in "L'Âme du Purgatoire," Jeanne de Beaumetz in *Asrael et Nephta*, Asraelle in "Le Séminariste" and, of course, foremost and quintessentially, Asrael himself, the fallen angel with whom the reader is invited and expected to sympathize, in the main if not quite wholeheartedly.

Asraelle is perhaps only interesting because we are carefully not told how she came to be a demon in the first place—i.e., the reason for which she joined Satan's revolt—and it is perhaps that absence, from a story too short to accommodate such a speculation, that led the author to follow it up with a much more considerable companion-piece in which her masculine equivalent is provided with both an elaborate backstory and an extraordinary quest to undertake. The form and impetus of that quest, in search of a minimal palliative that might make Hell slightly more bearable for him, via a human amour that is established by the fundamental parameters of the story as a weak and shabby reflection of the ideal love that can only exist in Paradise, is an original and fascinating literary invention.

Given that "Éloa" is such a tentative work, featuring a heroine who is so innocent that she does not even realize that the angel with whom she has fallen in love is Lucifer until he drags her down to Hell with him, and that Cazotte's account of

15

a female demon smitten with a handsome human eventually takes refuge in surreal confusion rather than attempting any kind of moral denouement, there is some justification for regarding *Asrael et Nephta* as the first literary work really to grasp the moral nettle in trying to address the questions it raises, in a remarkable alloy of allegorical and naturalistic terms. Whether the reader will find the eventual resolution genuinely satisfying will necessarily depend on the reader's own ethical standpoint, but the story certainly does not shirk the issue; there is nothing vague or evasive about it...except, perhaps, for the question, neglected and left dangling, of what will happen to poor Jeanne, left devoid of support for eternity soon after the beginning of the story by Asrael's initial defection from Hell.

Berthoud did contrive to reprint *Asrael et Nephta* during the phase of his belated popularity, by slipping it surreptitiously into an 1862 volume of *Légendes et traditions surnaturelles des Flandres* (sic), which reprinted almost all of the contents of the 1831 volume (but not "Le Séminariste"), a set of linked tales from the second volume of the 1834 collection, and a dozen or so similar items written after 1834. The novella remained, however, one of his more obscure works, too far from the orthodox to win much praise from critics of readers. Like *Contes misanthropiques*, however, it is an important early contribution to a subgenre that was to become increasingly important as the nineteenth century went on, and, as such, was one of many significant signposts Berthoud planted that anticipated not merely the direction that Romantic prose would take, but also the evolution of the Decadent and Symbolist movements that followed it.

Although the translation of *Asrael et Nephta* is undoubtedly the most important story in the present collection, it is not the only one that can be seen with the aid of hindsight to have been far ahead if its time. Another of the stories from the 1831 collection dropped from the 1862 collection, "La Délation" (tr. as "Delation"), can now be appreciated as a remarkable early study of personality dissociation and experimental exploration of "stream-of-consciousness" narration. In combination with the other narratives from the 1831 collection, *Contes misanthropiques* and *Asrael et Nephta*, it helps to demonstrate what a truly ground-breaking author Berthoud was in that era, and how amply deserving he is of a modern reappraisal of his achievements.

The translation of "Asrael et Nephta" was made from the text in the version of the 1862 version of *Légendes et traditions surnaturelles des Flandres* reproduced on Google Books. The translations of the stories from the 1831 collection were made from the version of the 1834 reprint reproduced on the Bibliothèque Nationale's gallica website.

Brian Stableford

BEAUDUIN BRAS-DE-FER

871

> There still exist, in Flemish dialect,
> songs full of originality, which must
> date back to the remotest epochs.
> Such, among others, is that of
> Beauduin Bras-de-Fer.
> (Le Carpentier, *Histoire de Cambrai.*)[2]

I

"Flanders to the rescue! Beware the iron hand!" Such was the war-cry of Comte Beauduin Bas-de-Fer.

II

When that cry was heard in the fiercest part of the battle, you could be sure that it would immediately open a wide passage, for death was inevitable for anyone who did not flee before the great sword of Beauduin Bras-de-Fer.

---

[2] I have retained Berthoud's spelling of this name, although it is more usually rendered as Baudouin (Baldwin in English). Baudouin I, nicknamed Bras-de-Fer, was Comte de Flandres in the second half of the 9th century, before dying in 879; he leapt to historical prominence when he eloped with Judith, the daughter of the King of France, Charles the Bold, and widow of both Aethelwulf and Aethelbald, Kings of Wessex, in 861, as celebrated in this "ballad." Jean Le Carpentier's *Histoire de Cambrai et de Cambrésis* (1664) is one of the principal sources from which Berthoud drew inspiration for his historical fantasies

III

If the warriors, by night, around a large fire, recounted the prowess of a knight, striking their coats of arms and saying "Our Lady protect him, for no one has a better right to the name of knight," you can be certain that they were talking about Beauduin Bras-de-Fer.

IV

One day, he stood at the entrance of his tent, had the clarion sounded, and started crying himself, and having his heralds repeat it: "Come all, come hear your lord and master, Comte Beauduin Bras-de-Fer."

V

"Men of war and faithful companions," he said, "Flanders is the most beautiful of comtés."

All the soldiers immediately replied: "And the bravest of comtes is Comte Beauduin Bras-de-Fer."

VI

"My companions," he continued, "who seems to you to be worthy of becoming Comtesse de Flandre and to be put in the bed of your lord and master, Comte Beauduin Bras-de-Fer?"

VII

There was a long murmur among all the men-at-arms, each enquiring of his neighbor and saying: "By the salvation of my soul, there's only one woman worthy of being put in the bed of Beauduin Bras-de-Fer."

VIII

"There is indeed only one!" cried Beauduin. "She is young, she is beautiful, she is fecund; she is so nobly born that one could not ask for better; she wears the bonnet of a queen. Isn't that the one that Comte Beauduin Bras-de-Fer must have?

IX

"The daughter of King Charles of France, the widow of King Edward of England, Madame Judith, whom everyone calls the beautiful widow, is coming back from overseas to go to her father. Four thousand lances escort her; she has eighteen carts full of gold. She will pass by Mons in a little while. Would you like her for your Comtesse, for the wife of Beauduin Bras-de-Fer?"

X

"Yes! Yes! We want that!" That was what the army howled, in a voice like an angry sea. "Yes, yes! We want the beautiful widow, for Comtesse de Flandre, for the wife of Comte Beauduin Bras-de-Fer."

XI

"Then tighten the buckles of your armor, bestride your chargers, and come to conquer a Comtesse for Flanders with the points of your lances, a wife for Beauduin Bras-de-Fer."

XII

"To arms! To arms!"

An hour later, there remained not one man-at-arms of the four thousand English lances.

A knight covered in blood opened the litter of Madame Judith, the beautiful widow, and said to her, courteously: "Noble lady, here comes a husband for you, the Comte de Flandre, Comte Beauduin Bras-de-Fer."

THE DEAD

1136

The Priest. Requiescat in Pace.
The Deacon. Amen.

"It is sad to see that the clergy, in that still
disordered century, like a great nation, had
its populace as it has its nobility, its
ignorant and its criminals as well as its
scholars and virtuous prelates. Since that
time, what remained to it of barbarism
has been polished by the reign of Louis
XIV, and what it had of corruption was
washed away in the blood of the martyrs it
offered to the Revolution. Thus, by a very
particular Destiny, perfected by the
monarchy and the Republic, softened by one
and chastised by the other, it has arrived that
today, it is austere and rarely vicious.
(Alfred de Vigny, *Cinq-Mars*, chapter II.)[3]

Gilles-Amalric Delavigne, squire of Sire Gérard de
Saint-Aubert,[4] was returning in all haste. "Blessed be Monsei-

[3] Alfred de Vigny's novel historical novel set in the seven-
teenth century during the reign of Louis XIII, *Cinq-Mars*
(1826), was very recent when this story was written. It became
a significant model for the historical fiction at the heart of the
Romantic Movement, especially the novels of Alexandre Dumas.
[4] There was a Gérard de Saint-Aubert, nicknamed Maufilatre,
who was castellan of the château of that name in the late
twelfth century, but it was half a century after the date at-

gneur Liétard!" he thought." Even more blessed be the worthy provost of the church, Messire Nicolas de Chièvres, by whose intercession the bishop of Cambrai has deigned to accord me a dispensation to set forth today, the great festival of All Saints! Without that dispensation, I would not have been able to see my lovely wife Gertrude until tomorrow. By Saint Gilles my patron, since the Monseigneur betrothed me to Gertrude personally, and endowed her so richly, a vespers has appeared to me to be as long as a Christmas Eve when one is awaiting the midnight mass.

"She will be very surprised, she will be very joyful, soon, when she sees me return. When I left Saint-Aubert to go to Cambrai, she said to me in an agreeable and sad fashion: 'Oh, how endless the time will seem to poor Gertrude during those two long days of absence!'

"She does not expect me until tomorrow, and here I am on the road to Saint-Aubert. In half an hour I will be embracing her."

Those thoughts caused the man-at-arms to give his mount a thrust of the spur, immediately changing its gait to a fast trot. Besides which, in addition to the desire to see his wife, anyone else in Amalric's place would have preferred a manor to the muddy and difficult road that led to Saint-Aubert. The north wind was blowing violently; the rain was falling in torrents, and it was the hour when the souls of the dead, covered in long white shrouds, come to tap with a desiccated finger on the doors of their relatives and friends, in order to recommend themselves to their prayers.

Then again, everyone knows that anyone who passes from life to death by murder on All Saints' Day never reposes tranquilly in his bier before having punished the one who has caused his death. Frightful and marvelous things are related on that subject.

---

tributed to the story by Berthoud, and the other biographical details known—including the names of his wives—are not consonant with the present story.

Now, the worthy squire Gilles-Amalric had made war more than once on that day of ill-renown, notably the previous year, when Monseigneur Gérard was so terribly punished for having profaned the sanctity of a great feast. For he had been beaten and taken prisoner, with his men, by the Franks, at the moment when he was emerging from the fortress of Hugues d'Oisy, his father-in-law, in order to go an surprise the manor of Cambrai while vespers was being said for the dead.

God and the Holy Virgin alone know how much it had cost Monseigneur Gérard to redeem himself. This was the fifth time that he, Gilles-Amalric, had taken to Bishop Liétard a heavy bag of a hundred silver marks, not to mention all the domains gained lance in hand, which it had been necessary to return. After that, the worst of all: a damned garrison of a hundred men-at-arms more insolent than sires of high lineage, and who, for six long months, came to lodge and gorge themselves at the Château de Saint-Aubert. Thanks to Our Lady, they had been gone since the feast of Saint Anne, ninety-eight days before.

While these thoughts were causing a blush to rise to the face of the worthy man-at-arms, and, mechanically, he gripped the shaft of his lance more tightly, he perceived in the distance, through the trees, a light whose aspect suddenly changed the course of his ideas.

"God be praised!" he said, breathing more easily. "It's the Château de Saint-Aubert! That light is shining in the tower that flanks the manor's left wing. It's a true pharos of amour, for it announces to me that my Gertrude is awake in the tower only inhabited by the two of us. As a good Christian and a faithful spouse, she is surely saying some prayer to Saint Julien for the poor voyager Amalric."

As he concluded that mental monologue, the feet of his good Norman horse slid over the large sandstone blocks on which the drawbridge came to pose, presently raised in accordance with the custom over every evening. Taking his horse back a few strides he sounded the horn.

The drawbridge lowered and a sentinel came to recognize the newcomer. "Enter, Master Squire," he said.

A few paces away stood a man with a venerable face, clad in a robe of black camlet, with a silver carcan suspended around his neck. That was Master Wirembault Delavigne, the steward of Gérard de Saint-Aubert's house and Amalric's brother.

"Jesus my savior!" he said, making the sign of the cross. "Is that really you, my brother? Holy Virgin! You have dared, scorning the commandments of the Church, to set forth on a feast day like this! If no misfortune has happened to you for such a great sin, you're assuredly luckier than you are wise!"

"Reassure yourself, my devout brother; a truce on your remonstrations. I obtained a dispensation from Monseigneur the Bishop of Cambrai to travel today. Thanks to that blessed parchment, I have encountered nothing nasty, neither goblins not ghosts. It's true to say, however, that I, who would never recoil before a ballista loaded with stones, believed that I saw incessantly appearing the skeletal visage of some man-at-arms slain by me a year ago to the day...

"Hola! Hey, varlet!" he shouted, interrupting a passing groom. "Take my horse to the stable and give him good provender, for he has come from the manor of Cambrai, where chargers have litter up to their knees and the steward is not stingy, like some of my acquaintance, for a bale of straw and a handful of oats."

While speaking, Amalric had dismounted from the horse and had thrown the reins to the varlet. Then traversing the long corridor, he went into an immense and solitary hall.

The walls were decked with brilliant armor, while reflected the light of a lamp suspended from the ceiling. Further on, heaps of various instruments of war, ballistas, etc., were visible.

Amalric deposited his lance and buckler some distance from his master's arms. Then he took off large boots of a sort in flexible iron mesh, lined inside with thick leather. After that he took off a camisole similarly woven of little steel rings, the end of whose sleeves enclosed the hand in a glove devoid of fingers. The glove was split under the palm in order to allow a sword to be gripped and reins to be manipulated. At the height of the shoulders, the iron tunic terminated in a hood of the same fabric as the rest, which was pulled down over the face in combat. Three holes larger than the rest allowed the eyes to see and the mouth to breathe. That bag of sorts, its round form maintained by a leather lining, was the only kind of helmet then in use.

Disencumbered to such a heavy accoutrement of war, Amalric remained in a deer-hide doublet, a narrow garment that outlined his thin and wiry figure. Then he started climbing, briskly, the spiral stairway leading to the bedroom that he and his wife occupied in the château. On the way, he had the idea of giving Gertrude a joyous fright by coming to her at a stealthy pace, for which his soft and flexible deerskin shoes would serve marvelously.

So here he goes, climbing each step with precaution, having trouble not bursting out laughing; he opens the door by a crack...

O rage!

Gertrude is in Gérard's arms!

He seeks his dagger; he is unarmed...

They have not seen him, no...oh, his vengeance will only be deferred...

And in the most frightful despair that ever struck an unfortunate with vertigo, he tries to descend to the armory...

He mistakes the corridor; it is on the platform of the tower that he is marching...

He takes one more step. Suddenly, the water of the deep moat resounds with a dull sound. Amalric has just fallen into it.

A few moments later, the hour for evening prayers was heard to chime. The men-at-arms, the varlets, the ladies of the bedchamber, went into the chapel and knelt down there. Dame Gertrude, her complexion animated by a slight blush, took her place among the latter, bedside the prie-dieu of the beautiful and unhappy Ermangarde d'Oisy, Gérard's wife.

Neglected, continually a victim of the castellan's ill-humor, Ermangarde opposed to the harshest treatment an angelic resignation. Spending all day in prayer, she had only one pastime, that of going to console the suffering, and there was no lack of them at Saint-Aubert. She administered balm to some, and gave rich alms to others. All were comforted by the benevolent words of her mild voice. Those worthy people, when they emerged from their cottages, said to one another, shaking their heads sadly: "Our poor lady is very pale and very ill. Weary! What will become of us if she ever dies?—may the Holy Virgin preserve us from it! Who will intercede with the Monseigneur for our mercy? Who will cure us when we fall ill? Who will console us when we are afflicted?"

After the almoner had recited all his paternosters and everyone had responded *amen*, men-at-arms, varlets, ladies of the bedchamber and the rest went away, some to stand guard and the others to sleep tranquilly. Master Delavigne, one of the last to emerge, came gravely to accost his beautiful sister-in-law, who was talking to Gérard.

"You ought to admonish your spouse, Dame Gertrude, in order that he does not abstain thus from the common prayer on the Holy Day of All Saints."

"Master Delavigne," she replied, in a playful tone, "I assume that Amalric has acquitted his Christian duties devotedly. As if one would fail in the precepts of devotion in the house of a bishop!"

"That pretence is not appropriate," the steward put in, ill-humoredly. "The first person to see my brother a little while ago was me."

Gertrude went pale, and Gérard appeared to experience some embarrassment. Delavigne, convinced by Gertrude's solemn tone, and even more by her sharp emotion, put his hands together in astonishment.

"What has become of him, then?" he asked, in an inexpressible anxiety. "He cannot have left the château; the drawbridge is raised and the portcullis lowered. May this mystery not hide some great misfortune!"

And while Gertrude, shedding tears, went to her mistress in order to carry out her duties as a lady of the bedchamber, Master Delavigne, escorted by two varlets, ran all over the château, calling to his brother in a loud voice.

Day was beginning to break, and he had not yet found anything.

Wirembault had explored the ramparts ten times over. Nevertheless, the sentinel charged with watching the draw-bridge perceived the unfortunate steward going along them again, although he knew in advance the futility of that further search.

"Hubert," said the old man-at-arms to his comrade, who was warming himself by a large fire nearby, half-asleep, "it's necessary to agree that the disappearance of the squire Amalric is very strange!"

"Squire Amalric?" asked the latter, yawning.

"What! You don't know that he came back yesterday shortly before the evening prayer, and that no one knows what has become of him since?"

"Pardieu! I might be able to tell you, for the news you're giving me explains the strange sound that I heard yesterday, when I was on guard beside the tower, next to the moat. Amalric has drowned."

"What are you staying? How do you know?" demanded the old man, drawing nearer to his comrade, curiously.

"It was diabolically cold, and I was wrapped in my cloak, half asleep..."

"Damned idler! Going to sleep when one is on sentry du-ty!" muttered the guardian of the drawbridge.

"Well, there's no great fault in drowsing at the foot of a tower defended by thirty feet of water! Suddenly, I heard a cry, and then something like an enormous mass hitting the water. The night was one of the blackest, as you know; I couldn't distinguish anything. But if the squire has disap-peared, there's scarcely any doubt about it; it was him who precipitated himself from the top of the tower where he resides alone with his wide."

"And what could have driven him to such an act of despair?"

The soldier's voice then became lower and more mysterious.

"Monseigneur Gérard loves Dame Gertrude. I saw him yesterday morning embracing her tenderly, and, by the salvation of my soul, she lent herself to it with pleasure. It's a good means to get rid of a jealous husband...by night...from the top of a tower... Gérard, nicknamed Maufilâtre because some say that he poisoned his father in order to be castellan of Saint-Aubert sooner..."

"Silence! silence! Such words, Hubert, might be worth the gibbet to you...and yet, alas, I'm only too tempted to believe what you're saying. Yesterday evening, when Master Delavigne mentioned his brother, Monseigneur started. Gertrude went pale. May God have pity on us! If it's thus, woe to our master! Yesterday was All Saints' Day; whoever is slain on that day only rests in peace in the tomb after having punished his murderer."

The two soldiers shuddered suddenly. A shrill cry was heard at the drawbridge.

"That's Amalric's voice!"

"So, imbecile, he was drowned in the moat of the high tower? You've had a bad dream. That's what a sentinel gets for going to sleep at his post. Come and help me lower the bridge."

Both of them laughing at their somber conjectures, went to introduce the squire. At the sight of Amalric, they exchanged a glance of terror and signed themselves. Mercy! He resembled a cadaver more than a living man. His cheeks were pale and hollow, his gaze dull and fixed. When he spoke, his white lips could hardly be seen to move, and when his hand gripped the hands of the men-at-arms, it appeared to them to be as cold and stiff as that of a dead man.

"My brother! My brother!"

It was Delavigne who was running, full of joy. At the sight of the strange change that had taken place in Amalric's features, he stopped suddenly, and let the arms that he was holding out in order to embrace his brother fall back.

Amalric, seemingly unsurprised by the terror produced by his appearance, marched in silence. He finally showed a sign of emotion; that was when he suddenly encountered Sire Gérard.

His pale face became paler still; no disinterred cadaver ever appeared so livid.

Gérard seemed no less stupefied than all the others, but he disguised his disturbance beneath an expression of severity and discontentment.

"Where are you coming from at such an hour, Amalric, without arms and dripping wet, as if you'd swum across the château's moat? You arrived yesterday; Delavigne told me so; why didn't you come immediately to tell me how you had carried out my orders with regard to the Bishop of Cambrai? Why have you left the château?"

Amalric replied in a hoarse and slow voice that bore no resemblance to his habitual manner of speaking: "I perceived that I had lost something precious…the parchment remitted for you by the bishop, the receipt for the ransom that you owed him. I scaled the postern in order to go in search of the document: here it is."

"And in what disposition did you find that old drunkard the bishop?"

"He does not want for anything in the world to lift the excommunication launched against Your Lordship. If I were you, I would take no account of his excommunications; I would take my revenge on him; I would recuperate my ten thousand silver marks. The manor is poorly guarded; the repair work that is being carried out there renders its defense impossible. In addition, the Bishop is leaving tomorrow to go and see the Emperor; the canons have served him well with regard that Prince. He is taking half the garrison as an escort:

31

two hundred men-at-arms could easily take possession of that rich fortress without encountering any resistance."

"What are you saying, Gilles?"

"Yes, their sense of security will cost them dear if you are able to take advantage of it."

Then the seigneur and the squire became to talk in even lower voices, and headed for the castellan's apartment together.

Half an hour later, the greatest agitation reigned in the courtyard of the Château de Saint-Aubert; four hundred men-at-arms were equipping their horses and donning their battle-dress; Gérard was going from one to the next in order to hurry them up.

Standing on the perron, the pale Amalric contemplated the scene with a gaze the sight of which made one feel ill.

While the animated tableau that he had before him seemed to absorb him entirely, a small white hand came to pose gently on his shoulder.

"Amalric! Amalric! After the sad anguish you caused me last night, you're going to depart without having said a word to me, without having seen me! Amalric, you no longer love me; I can see that clearly!"

He turned his livid face slowly toward her, and began to smile horribly. Poor Gertrude shivered in all her limbs.

"I appreciate your tenderness for what it is worth; I'll prove it to you, Gertrude." And, seizing her hand, he dragged her toward the tower where they lived.

"Amalric! Everyone is on horseback; you alone are un-armed! Cursed be the newly married! They think more about wiping away women's tears than putting on a coat of mail."

"A few moments' respite will suffice, Monseigneur. Grant them to me; I'll catch up with you before you've reached the end of the avenue."

The men-at-arms immediately set forth on the march. Amalric remained alone with Gertrude.

He attached a gaze to her that she could not support; but, forcefully shaking the arm that he gripped in his gauntlet, he obliged Gertrude to raise her head.

"You are a faithful spouse," he said, finally, with an indescribable smile.

Gertrude fell in a faint.

Amalric, standing without making a movement, waited until she came round.

When she opened her eyes again, the inexorable Amalric was still there; the infernal smile on his lips had not been effaced.

"Mercy! Mercy!"

Without proffering a word, he lifted her up with a wiry and icy arm, went up rapidly to the platform of the tower, and showed her with his finger the abyss open beneath her feet.

"At least have pity on the salvation of my soul!" she cried, in despair.

"Be saved then, you…but your seducer will be damned."

She started to beg: "Amalric! Amalric! Mercy! Mercy!"

He did not reply, seized Gertrude by the hair, held her for a few moments suspended above the abyss as if to prolong her execrable agony…and then it was done.

The aspect of Cambrai in 1136 was very different from the one it presents today; the town extended, narrow and compact, from the Château de Selles to the foot of the Mont-du-Boeufs; there, it suddenly extended two immense wings, which covered the hill; a church under the invocation of Saint Médard and Saint Cloud dominated that vast amphitheater.

The town was therefore formed of two quite distinct parts, one black and inhabited by poor people, the other the more becoming abode of the nobility and the well-to-do townspeople. Those two parts were only held together by a sort of isthmus that formed a square surrounded by palisades. That was the warren of prostitutes, the Ruelle des Bellottes, and the dwelling of the executioner. One could not be mistaken about that, on seeing wretched women, half-dressed and wearing faded cheap jewelry, wandering in that muddy enclo-sure. As for the executioner's house, it was even less unmis-takable; in front of the threshold a gibbet rose up between two enormous stakes; the stake to the right was covered with the ears of thieves; from the one to the right hung, at the end of a long iron chain, the narrow pointed dagger that was made red hot in order to pierce the tongue of blasphemers. The place was named then, as it still is today, Coupe-Oreille.

At the other extremity of the town, not far from the Porte de Selles, or Saint-Jean, in the middle of angular fortifications, the bell-tower of the Episcopal palace, the Abbaye de Saint-Aubert, surged forth, and the semi-ruined towers of the cathe-dral.

The numerous workmen who were laboring to repair that immense edifice, to which Gérard Maufilâtre had set fire a year before, were mostly vassals of the Seigneurs du Cambrésis, sent by their suzerains to undertake that pious chore.

Dusk was beginning to fall; the workmen emerged in or-der to return in troops to their villages, for the roads were not safe then. If some imprudent individual had dared the leave the town alone and unarmed, he would infallibly have been robbed by the brigands that infested the region. Besides which, by gathering thus, they were dispensed of the toll levied by each seigneur on the travelers who traversed his domain. Re-lief from that toll was accorded to the workmen in favor of the Christian motives that had sent them to Cambrai.

Each of the workmen doffed his cap respectfully before Messire Nicolas de Chiêvre, the provost of the church, stand-ing on the drawbridge of Bon-Secours. He counted them as they passed before him; that was to make sure that none of them had remained in the château. In doing that he was ful-filling the duties of his charge, duties prescribed by the suspi-cious prudence of those times of war and strife.

Messire de Chiêvre's garments were those of the laymen of the twelfth century: a long robe, brown in color, descended all the way to his feet, the soft gray leather shoes of which were cropped above the ankle. Above that robe he wore a narrow mantle that allowed the sight of a large chaplet placed around his shoulders, and which fell back over to his breast; that; that mantle, lined with miniver, partly covered the satchel attached to the left-hand side of his belt, the usage of which was the same as out present-day pockets. But the most singular object of his costume was incontrovertibly the headgear, a bonnet of brown cloth terminated by a long point; that point wound twice around the head and came to fall as a narrow cord above the forehead.

Messire Nicolas might have been thirty years old; his pale and regular physiognomy offered a mixture of firmness and melancholy that was not devoid of grace; his distracted gaze and vague smile gave rise to the thought that he had suffered the long chagrins that time softens but does not efface, the chagrins that are the deadly privilege of an ardent and sensitive soul.

While the individual whose portrait we have just traced was occupied in counting the workmen, he saw a man-at-arms approaching at the gallop. Such as the manner in which he was pressing his horse that the bridge resounded under him before anyone had had time o think about stopping him. The unknown man threw a scroll of parchment at Messire Nicolas' feet, and, making his charger execute an abrupt about-turn, he vanished like an apparition, without anyone being able to ascertain where he had come from, or where he had gone.

This is the tenor of the said parchment:

Inform Monseigneur Liétard that Gérard, known as Maufilâtre, suzerain of Saint-Aubert, has left his domain with four hundred men-at-arms in order to surprise, set ablaze and pillage the episcopal manor at nightfall.

"Raise the drawbridge of Bon-Secours and let down the portcullises!

"Workmen, let none of you leave. Go up on to the rampart; load the ballistas with stones; assemble your companies; let every archer have a good sack full of arrows with him.

"As for the men-at-arms, seneschal, let them don their coats of mail, and let the horses, fully barded, be maintained ready to be mounted.

"As for you, Messires the canons, while we fight for the Lord's house, go pray in the church with the intention of those who will receive martyrdom today, and implore for our holy cause the protection of Jesus Christ and the immaculate virgin."

The crowd that the strange apparition of the man-at-arms, the news of which had immediately spread through the manor, had caused to assemble around Messire de Chiêvre was suddenly seen to disperse. A few moments sufficed to carry out the prudent measures ordered by the provost. All the more urgency was put into it because several people had already recounted that they had seen the mysterious messenger evaporate into the air. Others went even further; they had been dazzled by the luminous aureole that scintillated around his head; they had seen him deploy his two great white wings. The most credulous had no doubt that it was the blessed archangel Saint Michael, send by the intercession of Our Lady in order to preserve the cathedral church of Cambrai from ruination.

A year had gone by.

Night was beginning to fall. Messire Nicolas de Chiêvre was standing on the drawbridge of Bon-Secours; as usual, he was counting the workmen who were coming out when Master Delavigne, clad in black, approached the provost, who extended his hand to him affectionately.

"May Our Lady aid you, Master Wirembault Delavigne. Be welcome! A few more moments and I'm all yours. Raise the drawbridge, men-at-arms; the workmen have gone. Let no one enter or leave unless they say the password.

"Now," he added, turning to Delavigne, "tell me, Master, what earns me the honor of your visit at such a late hour."

Delavigne, leaning on one of the pillars of the draw-bridge, had plunged into a profound reverie. In order to extract him from it, it was necessary to address him for a second time.

"I desire to speak to Monseigneur Liétard immediately," he replied, finally, "and I have come to implore you to intro-duce me to his presence right away."[5]

That request evidently embarrassed the man to whom it was addressed. Liétard was at supper at that moment, and, as he scarcely had the custom of drinking soberly and was almost always tottering when he got up from the table, the provost of the church was reluctant to let him be seen in such a state. Offering, in consequence, a few excuses, he engaged Delavigne to defer his interview with the prelate until the fol-lowing day.

"Oh, no, it's necessary that I see him immediately. The salvation of my soul depends on it; the slightest delay might damn me for eternity."

The warmth with which the old man expressed himself caused Nicolas de Chièvre to yield, although regretfully; he took Delavigne to the vast hall where Liétard was. At the sight of the provost the coarse merriment painted on the trivial and pedantic face of the prelate gave way to the serious constraint of a schoolboy caught at fault by his regent.

Liétard readjusted his soutane precipitately, which was undone over his breast, and sat up straight in the large arm-chair in which he was sprawled. "Oh! Here's our worthy provost! *Benedicto tibi!* In the ear of a stout canon sitting to his right he added: "*Vade retro, Satanas!* He could surely have

---

[5] This is slightly anachronistic; the bishop of Cambrai named Liétard—who left behind a reputation for dissolution and ava-rice—occupied that position from 1131 to 1135; the bishop in 1136 was, in fact, Nicolas de Chièvres, who fulfilled the role for more than thirty years, but is here relegated to the status of steward.

left us to sup in peace." He went on: "By my miter, here's the rich treasurer Master Wirembault Delavigne! Oh, I understand—you've come to reclaim the four hundred silver marks you had so much trouble lending us, in spite of the guarantees we gave you. You've picked a bad time, Master, we've been chastised by iron and fire. The servants of Notre-Dame-de-Grace are very poor, for the accursed Maufilâtre has destroyed the Lord's house from top to bottom, and if the Archangel Michael hadn't struck him down a year ago..."

"That's not the reason..."

"Then speak freely...but, one moment... Hola! Cup-bearer, two goblets and another bottrine[6] of wine."

"Monseigneur," de Chiêvre, interrupted, in a tone that was simultaneously respectful and severe, "Master Delavigne wants to speak to you privately."

"Privately? Doubtless you have some advantageous loan to propose to me? Messire de Chiêvre, always vigilant for the interests of the church, and who knows its needs, has been able to arrange its affairs; we're grateful to him for that, the worthy provost. Let's see, don't be too demanding, Master Delavigne, and we'll arrange that *inter pocula*."

"In the name of the salvation of your soul," cried the old man, putting his hands together, "deign to listen to me with no other witness than Messire de Chiêvre!"

"Go away, then, Messires the canons, and please excuse our incivility. You can see that the crosier of a bishop is heavier than people think; the duties of our ministry overwhelm us even after supper, while it one remain for you to digest peacefully and lie down in a good bed...

---

[6] A bottrine was a leather flagon containing about two pints of wine; the term is used in Walter Scott's *Quentin Durward* (1823; Fr. tr. 1827), which was extremely popular in France because of its French setting in the late fifteenth century, and became an important stimulus to French historical fiction; Alfred de Vigny and Berthoud probably both read it and took some inspiration from it.

"Now we're alone, Master Delavigne...but, one more moment...two clean goblets. Pour, and fill mine... Now speak, Master; we're listening to you."

A silence of a few minutes went by before Delavigne, collecting his ideas, began to explain the motives that had brought him. Perhaps he was also waiting until Liétard had finished filing his goblet and arranging himself comfortably in his armchair.

"I have come," he finally said, in a slow voice, "to beg you to permit me, Wirembault Delavigne, and Marie Dauvilliers, my legitimate wife, to make a vow of continence between your hands, my will being to consecrate to pious foundations all that I possess and to retire to the Hôpital Saint-Julien, to spent the rest of my days in the service of the sick; to beg you humbly to receive in the Abbaye de Saint-Aubert my two sons, Luc and Guillaume; and finally, to employ you to request the Archbishop of Rheims to admit my daughter Berthe to a religious community; all in the hope of obtaining from the Divine Redeemer the forgiveness of our family's sins, and particularly those of my late brother Gilles-Amalric Delavigne."

"That's a worthy, a praiseworthy and a pious design!" exclaimed Liétard, trembling with joy and rubbing his hands. "We receive with gratitude the gift that you're making us. On the epitaph that will be place in the choir of the cathedral when you are no more—for you shall be buried in the crypt of our church—it will be engraved that you consecrated your wealth to the re-edification of the dwelling of your bishop, persecuted by heretics. Our provost, Messire Nicolas de Chiêvre, who yields nothing to any rubricator for writing, will draw up the deed immediately."

"But in the name of our holy patron," the provost asked, anxiously, "what can have inspired you to such a grave resolution. I saw you two days ago; you appeared disposed to live as a good Christian, as you have done to this day, but not to deprive yourself and your family of all patrimony."

During this speech by Nicolas the bishop darted angry glances at him, and sought to impose silence on him.

"It's the soul of my brother, which appeared to me yesterday at Vespers in the church of the Carmelites."

"You saw your brother's soul yesterday?" asked the bishop, signing himself. "*Requiescat in pace!* May Heaven preserve me from such visions!" With the interest that an old woman takes in a tale told to frighten and amuse her, he added: "You saw him? Really saw?"

"Alas, it's not the first time, Monseigneur. If you'll permit, I'll tell you the story of my brother's misfortunes and his incomprehensible adventures..."

"I'd like that; never in my life have I heard tell of such a marvelous story as the one you describe, Master Delavigne. But before then, let's kneel down and recite, devoutly, a *de profundis* for the dead."

All three knelt down, and when they got up again:

"You'll recall that on the day of the dead last year, the episcopal manor was besieged by the late Monseigneur Gérard de Saint-Aubert..."

"Holy Virgin! Yes, I remember! If I were tempted to forget, the ruins of the church and my own palace, and the large sums that it has cost me to rebuild them would enable me to remember only to bitterly! Without the prudence of Messire de Chiêvre—for we were not at Cambrai in those days of desolation—and without the miraculous protection of the benevolent Archangel Saint Michael, it would have been the end of our treasures forever. For Maufilâtre scarcely respected the sacred vases and holy vessels any more than if they belonged to the most wretched Jew."

"Monseigneur Gérard had quit the manor of Saint-Aubert scarcely an hour before in order to surprise the Episcopal manor when the cadaver of my sister-in-law Gertrude was found in the moat of the tower. You have heard tell that a soldier had seen her unfortunate husband, my brother Amalric, fall the previous night, and that the dead man's soul came the following day to give Monseigneur the fatal advice to attack the manor. We have discovered since that Dame Gertrude had committed the sin of adultery with Monseigneur Gérard..."

"You see? I recognize him well in that, the joyous companion, the most brazen friend I ever encountered in my life!"

"Doubtless the unfortunate Amalric, who returned to Saint-Aubert without being expected there, discovered the infidelity of his culpable spouse, and, in despair, precipitated himself into the tower moat. Now, it was the feast of the dead, and you know that the body of whomsoever perished violently on that day can only remain peacefully in his bier after being avenged on the person who has caused his death.

"On the news of the fatal accident that had happened to her lady of the bedchamber, Madame Ermangarde experienced such horrible convulsions that the physician declared that she only had an hour to live. I mounted a horse immediately and ran in all haste to inform Monseigneur of that terrible news.

"When I succeeded in reaching him, he was approaching Cambrai, and my brother had only just joined him, which surprised me greatly, for he had left the château only a few minutes after Monseigneur—and yet he had galloped all along the route, for his horse was bathed in sweat.

"After having acquitted my sad duty toward my master, who scarcely appeared to care and continued to hasten his men-at-arms, I approached my brother, not knowing what precaution to take in order to announce the terrible death of his wife.

"'Gertrude...Gertrude...!' The sobs cut off my voice, and I could only proffer that name.

"'Well?' he said, fixing his immobile eyes upon me, and without moving is blanched lips.'

"'Her cadaver had been found in the tower moat.'

"He started to laugh—to laugh at such news! I hastened to draw away, for his laughter was frightful, as the Devil's must be.

"My heart horribly constricted, for I could see only too well, alas, that it was not my brother but a revenant that was there, I accosted Monseigneur in order to take my leave of him and to enquire as to what orders he had to give me for Saint-Aubert.

"'None,' he said to me. 'Come with me to Cambrai; I have need of you. You'll know for what reason in a little while.'

"Night had fallen in the meantime.

"When we arrived under the walls of the bishopric, the greatest silence reigned around us. Ladders were set up; men filled the ditch and got ready to assault the defenseless manor, all of whose inhabitants were asleep...

"You know the rest. A terrible discharge of arrows and stones crushed the besiegers and an ambush of two hundred men-at-arms hidden nearby came to attack them from the rear. No carnage was ever as prompt or as frightful.

"For myself, I was wandering in the dark, in the midst of stones and arrows that were whistling all around. I was leading a fresh horse in order to give it to Monseigneur Gérard, for nothing remained to him but to take flight. Alas, I found him mortally wounded, calling loudly for a priest. After having bandaged his large wound as best I could I was about to set off to find a priest I had seen a few paces away, confessing the wounded, when a glacial hand endowed with a supernatural force seized me and stopped me. It was my brother's soul! This time, there was no doubt about it. No living man ever had such a visage and such a gaze.

"'A priest!' he said. 'A priest! You, Gérard? No. You're damned. Your father's murderer, your wife's torturer, Gertrude's seducer, you'll be damned, damned for all eternity.'

"At the same moment, the hand that retained me let go. An enormous stone had just broken Monseigneur's head, and my brother's soul disappeared.

"Yesterday evening, after having heard the office for the dead at the episcopal church, I was passing the convent of the Carmelites. I had the idea of going there to make a station in the chapel, which was deserted. I had scarcely recited half of a *de profundis*, than I saw a phantom coming directly toward me. He was waving his arms despairingly and utterly inarticulate groans, Oh, Holy Virgin, it was my brother Amalric! I saw him as I see you. My strength abandoned me...

"When I recovered consciousness, the church was deserted again.

"On returning home, to which I retired with great difficulty, everyone was frightened by my pallor and my agitation. My distress was so great that I could not say a word about my frightful adventure; it was necessary to put me to bed incontinently. Fever shook my limbs in such a fashion as to render me an object of pity for the most hardened.

"After a long sleepless night of delirium, I became drowsy at daybreak approached.

"Suddenly, an icy hand weighed upon my breast; it was stifling me; I wanted to cry out, to struggle, but I could not utter a word or make a movement. My brother's soul was there again.

"'Pray for me, pray for me, from matins until vespers. I am burning in the fires of purgatory. Save my soul! It requires more *de profundis* to redeem it than there are souls in Hell.'

"No mouth pronounced those words, and yet I heard them very distinctly, three different times. After that, the hand was removed from my breast and I fell into a profound sleep, until midday.

"When I awoke, I assembled my family and I set about telling them what had happened to me since the previous evening. Then, Monseigneur, all of a common accord, we resolve to consecrate the rest of our lives to redeeming my brother's soul from purgatory. I told you just now in what place each of us desires to be cloistered.

"Of the wealth I have acquired I shall make three parts. One will serve to reestablish the church of Our Lady, the second to endow the hospital of Saint Julien where I count in ending my days in the service of the sick, and with the third I shall redeem the toll established at the Porte de Selles. Each traveler will no longer have to give either an obol or a measure of oats, provided that he recites a *de profundis* with the intention of my late brother, Amalric Delavigne."

"Those are strange adventures," said Nicolas de Chiêvre, with a pensive expression.

"Yes, very strange adventures," continued Liétard. "But you have taken a sage and holy resolution, Master Delavigne. We approve of it greatly, and it only remains for us to execute it rapidly.

"We will take responsibility for redeeming from Sire Fulcard the toll at the Porte de Selles, which Madame Hildeberge his wife gave him as a dowry. In our consideration and in favor of your pious motive, he will give us a good price.

"Now, Messire Nicolas, go draw up the deed of donation of all his wealth that that Master Delavigne is making to the church of Our Lady and the hospital of Saint Julien. Put there: *Perturbatores precipitentur in infernum cum Dathan et Abiron; conservatores aeternae beatiuidinis gadio donentur.* Add that he will report to our wisdom for the division."

"Such a determination," hazarded the provost, "requires to be ripened sagely for a few days."

"Holy Virgin! When Heaven has spoken, to want to prevent obedience of its orders! Go, Messire Nicolas, obey promptly what we command, or fear incurring our disgrace."

The provost obeyed, although with evident reluctance, Master Wirembault Delavigne signed at the bottom of the parchment, which was sealed with the great seal of the cathedral church.

"Master," said Liétard, when all was concluded, "Tomorrow you will be received among the religious hospitalers of Saint Julien. As for the rest of your will, it will be observed like that of a father on his deathbed. We will do more; we will join our prayers with yours for the repose of the soul of Gilles-Amalric Delavigne, squire while alive. Tomorrow, a solemn office will be celebrated with his intention.

"Now, receive our benediction and go in peace, full of confidence in the Lord's mercy."

The following morning, Liétard was still sleeping profoundly and calmly when someone came to tell him that the

44

superior of the Carmelites was asking insistently to speak to him without delay. After a few bitter complaints on the prelate's part regarding the fatigues of his ministry, the monk was introduced.

"Monseigneur," he said, after kneeling down to receive Liétard's benediction, I came about a year ago to consult you relative to the request of a stranger to make a rich gift to our convent, provided that he was admitted as a novice without enquiring as to his name."

"Well? I gave you permission, as I remember."

"That man exercised the cruelest austerities on his body; he spent the night moaning, never quitting his cilice, and rent himself with atrocious mortification. To judge by the rigor of his penitence, he must have committed very great sins.

"This morning he was found dying in the choir of the chapel. I tried to encourage him in his final moments; nothing could calm his remorse. He rendered his last sigh despairing of God's mercy, accusing himself of the murder of his wife and the damnation of Seigneur Gérard Saint-Aubert..."

At those words, Liétard raised himself precipitately into a sitting position.

"Under pain of mortal sin, Brother Superior," he exclaimed, troubled by an emotion that was not customary to him, "yes, under pain or mortal sin, I forbid you ever to say a word about all this, particularly to the provost of our church, Master Nicolas de Chiêvre. Think hard, Brother Superior, under pain of mortal sin!

"Now go; have the dead man buried immediately, with a hood pulled down over his face. That is for the greatest mark of humility. Pray, you and your monks, that he rest in peace. The Lord's mercy is infinite.

"The extent of the repentance testified by the novice will doubtless find him mercy before God. The assistance of our episcopal prayers will aid him as much as their feeble merit can. *Requiescat in pace*, my brother!"

"Amen," responded the Carmelite, and he went away.

THE COOK'S SON[7]
1219

Rien ne m'est plus, plus ne m'est rien.
(The motto of Valentine of Milan.)[8]

In 1205, in the month of March, under the episcopacy of Monseigneur Jean de Béthune of Hainaut, the king of the guild, or brotherhood, of mulquiniers, rendered up his soul.[9]

After long negotiations and endless discussions, for among the merchants and dressers of batiste thread there was more than one rich bourgeois desirous of a similar dignity, they elected for the dead man's successor Master Eustache

---

[7] This was one of several of Berthoud's early stories pirated in English translation, by the Irish novelist Thomas Colley Grattan, who entitled his plagiarism "The Orphan of Cambray" (1832).

[8] Valentina Visconti, Duchesse d'Orléans (1371-1408) adopted the motto in question in 1407 following the murder of her husband. A rough translation would be "I no longer care about anything; nothing any longer means anything to me."

[9] I have left the term mulquinier untranslated because it does not have a precise equivalent in English; it pertains to the manufacture, preparation and marketing of fine thread for weaving, but it would be oversimplified to describe the mulquiniers simply as "spinners" or "weavers." The initial industrialization of that craft was very closely associated with Cambrésis, which was its first great center in Medieval Europe. Although I have translated the French *serment* as "guild," it is also worth bearing in mind that French industrial corporations of that kind were more highly-organized and elaborately structured than their English equivalents, and their "kings" were individuals of great importance—hence their possession of their own "court jesters."

Dinault, who was a good companion, of sage advice and jovial humor.

You will understand, moreover, what celebrations followed, and for more than seven weeks.

First of all, the king of the mulquiniers, in honor of the three holy persons of the trinity, fed for three days in succession, in three different places, all the members of the guild, not to mention his relatives, his allies, his friends and his acquaintances. Thus the statutes of the guilds required.

On the other hand, and as custom made it a duty for them, the richest members of the guild took it to heart to entertain in an appropriate manner, and each in his turn, the man who had been elected as the head of their brotherhood.

Nothing is as impossible, in my view, as to determine how much was expended in the purchase of victuals, nor the number of wine-casks, which as the jovial expression of the making of mulquiniers put it, "lost their soul" on that occasion.

It is better to write quite simply that the mulquiniers placed themselves side by side at table at the hour of vespers and departed at dead of night, and only when the bell in the tower chimed the curfew; and everyone moaned "Already!" when the clear, slow sound began to ring.

It was at a similar hour, and a few days after the festival of Easter, that one of the most honorable members of the corporation of mulquiniers, Master Bartholomé Le Baudain bid farewell to his guests.

There was no longer anyone in the great banqueting hall but him and two very different individuals; one was the canon Nicolas Watremetz; the second an individual clad in a multicolored doublet covered in little bells, whose silvery tinkle sounded at the slightest movement. For the time being, it was necessary to hasten the canon's servants, who were striving to saddle their master's mule, which they were not able to do very quickly, because they had clinked glasses with such fervor in honor of Master Eustache Dinault that their hands had difficulty knotting the girth-straps.

Seeing that, Master Le Bauduin enjoined the man with the bells, whose name was Nicolas Parigault and who was the *sot-seuris* or court jester of the guild of mulquiniers, to accompany Messire the canon as far as his lodgings, or the Episcopal manor. He also recommended him, many times over, to walk in front of the canon's mule, torch in hand—a necessary precaution for arriving without encumbrance on the far side of the "accursed warren" that was located half-way along the route.

The area known by the name was the assemblage of the Rue des Juifs, the crossroads of the Coup-Oreille and the Ruelle des Belottes, places haunted by miscreants, thieves and prostitutes. The executioner's dwelling, with its scaffold and gibbet, stood in that place of ill-repute, like a perpetual and salubrious reminder of the chastisement reserved for people of such evil species.

Master Le Baudain had a house on the most elevated part of the Mont-des-Boeufs, next to the church of Saint Peter and Saint Paul. The journey to the Episcopal manor becoming, in consequence, long in duration, the sot-seuris thought it his duty, on the way, to cheer up the rich canon, a favorite of Monseigneur the Bishop, who would assuredly not fail to remunerate him appropriately for his joviality and quips.

To that end, the jester set about imitating, grotesquely, the drunkenness of varlets and telling ludicrous stories. The worthy canon uttered busts of laughter, and, put in a good humor by that encouragement, the man with the bells redoubled the jokes and mocked the entire company of Messire Watremetz to excess.

"Brother," he said, passing his arm beneath that of a stout varlet who could hardly stand up so often had he raised his elbow during the evening, "worthy and gallant friend, you do well to cross yourself in that fashion at the noises and clamors coming from the accursed warren. Cross yourself again, for God help us, the Devil comes in person to hold a sabbat in the region we are traversing. He has for society the hanged men that he unhooks from the gibbet and the Jews, those miscreants whose greatest feast is the flesh of a Christian child. I get gooseflesh just thinking about it.

"By Saint Touch-me-Not, can you hear? What black figures are stirring over there in the shadows? One can hear nothing more now, one can see nothing more. Don't believe that the debauchees have taken flight at the sight of us; I tell you, my brother, we have well and truly seen pale revenants, infernal devils, and, God preserve us, perhaps worse things still."

While he was making mock in this fashion, to the great pleasure of the canon, the sot-seuris, stumbling unexpectedly, fell face down on the ground and uttered a cry of distress. This time, it was not feigned, but a plaint in good faith: can you imagine that two hairy hands were running through his hair, and that sharp teeth were biting his face and ears?

"Messire Canon," he cried, piteously, Messire Canon, I am, as a punishment for my heretical mockeries, at grips with the infernal Devil!"

"Shut up, I order you," replied Messire Watremetz, in an angry tone. "A truce on such remarks. I don't regard it as prudent to stop in such a place and awaken the debauchees of this accursed quarter; it might cost you, Master Jester, to have extinguished the torch in your ill-timed frolics."

"My Heaven have pity on my soul," continued the poor sot-seuris, struggling against his strange adversary; it's not a pretence, Monsieur Canon; say an exorcism and I'll be liberated from the Devil."

"March ahead," Messire Watremetz ordered his varlets. "March, and leave this clown who picks such a bad time to laugh here."

At that order, the sot-seuris testified so much despair that the canon finally understood that the poor fellow's terror was not simulated. Dismounting, for none of is servants dared approach, he picked up the torch and succeeded in relighting it. Then, drawing nearer to the place where the sot-seuris was lying, he was only slightly astonished to see him lying next to the bloody cadaver of a woman and at grips with a large monkey, which, at the sight of the torch, abandoned the contest and went to take refuge on a roof.

Chilled by fear, Messire Watremetz, was getting ready to continue on his way, firstly to get out of such a den of cut-throats, and secondly to advise the provost that a murder had been committed, when the wailing of an infant made itself heard beneath the very feet of his mule. Apparently having fallen from the arms of the slain woman, the poor thing had doubtless rolled that far.

Moved to compassion by the sight of the innocent crea-ture, Messire Watremetz wrapped it in his cloak and took it home with him, where his first concern was to wake up an aged sister named Berthe, who had been living with him for twenty years.

After having first complained at being abruptly awak-ened during her first sleep, and after having asked her brother, with a quinquegenarian bitterness, what he expected her to do with a child; after having enumerated the difficulties, fatigues, cares and late nights that the education of his protegé would infallible accumulate, the respectable lady commenced to care for it as the most tender mother would have done.

"It's a charming little girl," she said to Mademoiselle Cunégonde, her chambermaid and confidante; "she's as pale, see, as the alabaster columns in the chapel of the Virgin. Go and fetch some milk, quickly, for the poor child is crying and dying of hunger... Oh, how slow you are! Jesus my gentle sav-ior, I would already have been and come back at least twice... God be praised! Finally, here's what I need. Here, look how the dear little one throws herself on the nourishment!

"Now that she's finished, there she is, going to sleep. I want to keep her next to my bed, in order that her first whim-per will wake me up and warn me that she needs help."

The little girl, however, did not wake Madame Berthe up all night, and when, the day after Nones, her brother came to enquire about her, Mademoiselle Cunégonde responded that her mistress was still sound asleep.

On his return, the canon found Madame Berthe rocking the little girl on her knees, clad in clean and becoming linen.

After having listened patiently to his sister's long dissertations on the manner of raising children, and the superiority of her knowledge of such matters, Messire Watremetz, in his turn, found a means of recounting the results of the investigation mounted by the provost with regard to the previous evening's murder.

To judge by her dark complexion and strange garments, the woman slain in the accursed warren was a gypsy who exhibited a monkey and made it dance to earn her living. A few debauchees of the accursed quarter, where she had come to lodge cheaply, had seen her imprudently showing an adequately-stuffed purse; it had not required any more than that or thieves to put her to death. In any case, her ears, from which the ear-rings had been torn away, left no doubt as to the motive for the crime.

But where did the woman come from? Was she the mother of the foundling little girl? No one knew. Her wretched belongings, which were not worth four patards, except for a silver medallion attached to the infant's neck,[10] gave no indication as to that.

"In any case," Dame Berthe interjected, who doubtless felt that it had been a long time since she had said anything, "Yes, Messire Watremetz, in any case, we won't abandon her to the piteous fate in which she was left.

"First of all, it's necessary to have her baptized, for her miscreant of a mother will not have done that, I'm sure. Such an idea hasn't occurred to you, my brother, I know that for certain, even though you're a priest, and what's more, a canon."

---

[10] Berthoud did not invent this narrative device, which was to become the hoariest of the clichés of popular, mocked by Paul Féval as "her mother's cross," but this is one of its earlier uses in prose fiction.

Messire Watremetz did not contradict Madame Berthe, who looked at him with a triumphant expression.

"Indeed, my sister, indeed; you'll hold her over the baptismal font, and I've found a godfather."

"I don't want him!" exclaimed Madame Berthe, shrilly. "Myself, I've chosen the provost of the church, and I certainly won't depart from my choice."

"I'll go and inform Monseigneur the Bishop, then, that you refuse to be his co-mother," the canon continued, with a smile of satisfaction, conceit and malice; and he pretended to leave.

"Monseigneur the Bishop! Monseigneur the Bishop, my brother! He would deign? How did you do that? How did he come to offer? For, I'm sure that you haven't asked him for such a favor; in your eyes, any villain would have been a co-father good enough for me. Of, the worthy Bishop! I recognize him by that action!"

Messire Watremetz allowed that eruption of his sister's joy to exhale, after which he resumed speaking in these terms:

"I told Monseigneur about my adventure yesterday evening, and he immediately said that he wanted to hold the little orphan over the baptismal font, and associate himself in that fashion with our good work. You can imagine that I refrained from refusing. The provost won't take offence, and it will be better..."

Madame Berthe tried to form a smile of good humor, a smile so unaccustomed to her old and sullen physiognomy that all her efforts were unable to produce anything more than an equivocal grimace.

A few days later the baptism took place in the Episcopal church, with a pomp that redressed by the height of at least two inches the somewhat curbed stature of Madame Berthe. The child was given the name Lydorie.

An ostentatious feast was held after the baptism in the bishop's house.

Canon Watremetz being a great lover of good wine, and above all of beautifully-organized meals, went to visit the kitchens beforehand As he arrived there he heard a child crying bitterly, while the voice of Master Magalouffe, the bishop's chief cook was scolding the poor thing with an extreme anger.

Messire Watremetz thought highly of Magalouffe, and, as the latter was glad to return the compliment, honored him with a familiar bounty. When he arrived he found the cook shouting at the top of his voice and striking his son, aged six or seven, furiously, with a roast peacock that he was holding in his hand. The bird's neck formed, in human's hand the shaft of a long pliant whip, which, although not very redoubtable, was nevertheless causing the little fellow the greatest alarm.

"Hay, hey, Magalouffe," asked the canon, interposing himself between the beater and the beaten, "whence comes such wrath against little Séverin?"

"Messire Canon," the cook replied, "if I weren't choking with range, I'd be weeping with despair. By my divine patron Sainte Marthe, it's as if my arms were broken, and for the first time I've come to curse the noble profession of cook.

"See whether I'm not right! Was ever a more beautiful, fatter and magnificent peacock ever spoiled in a culinary laboratory?

"Yesterday, at vespers, the scullions, the cutlery valets, the boiler-heaters and the sauce-makers were working hard on today's feast. One couldn't imagine, Messire Canon, a wiser and more worthy menu for a repast!

"In order only to cite the most admirable, for vanity, thank God, is not one of my traits, examine these thin slices of fried deer-antler, this roasted suckling-pig, buttered and embalmed by aromatic herbs, Tours plums and Greek grapes.

"Look, above all, at this gilded soup; assuredly, I don't say it out of conceit, but there are only two cooks in the world capable of fabricating one like it, to wit, Taillavant, head chef of His Majesty the King of France and me, Jacques Magalouffe, who invented it with him in the times when I was in the royal kitchens in Paris. Few other hands than his or mine are able to cut slices of prime bread in that fashion, imbibe them in a layer of honey, white wine and egg-yolks, and then fry them in soft lard and make them float without sinking to the bottom, in a juice of rose-water sprinkled with saffron and impalpable flecks of gold."

During that long digression, Magalouffe's ire had cooled, but it boiled over again at the sight of a new peacock that was brought to him to replace the one with which he had thrashed little Séverin.

"A feast with such a menu ought to earn me the praise of everyone!" he added, trembling with indignation and raising his voice to the maximum possible. Malediction! This little reprobate has plunged me into an abyss of confusion and opprobrium. It only remains for me to throw away my white baton of Episcopal cook and go to hide myself humbly behind the poorest housewife, who puts a cheap smoked duck to cook in an earthenware pot once a week, on Sunday.

"I plucked the skin of the peacock you see at my feet without a scraper, without missing a feather; after which, enveloping its delicate neck with thin bandages, I put the noble bird on the spit with my own hands, not without instructing Séverin to dampen the bandages from time to time with cold water, in order that the plumage and the rich down of the peacock were not caught by the flames... Sainte Marthe give me patience! The miscreant started studying I don't know what fragment of parchment that would even have confused Monseigneur's chaplain. When I thought I would be able to dress my peacock and recover its skin, I saw—what infamy!—I saw, Messire the Canon, that its neck and its down were as hot and black as coals!"

"You know how to read, then, Séverin?" the canon asked the weeping child.

"Alas, yes, Master Watremetz," replied the poor boy, finally emerging from the corner in which he had crouched.

"Read!" cried Magalouffe. "Read! Where will that take him? I ask you!"

"To be a canon," said Séverin. "The chaplain told me so."

"Canon? Canon? Oh, for a start, he's losing his mind. I'll..."

"Calm down, my dear Magalouffe, and forgive Séverin—come on, out of amity for me."

Magalouffe bowed, and replaced his hat on his bald head.

"Since your son has fortunate dispositions for study, I want to cultivate them myself, and we'll make him, if not a canon, at least a chaplain with some good benefit."

"Alas," sighed Magalouffe, "A stranger, someone other than my son, will therefore receive the white baton of the episcopal cook from my dying hand!"

And with tears in his eyes and a heart constricted by a profound sadness, he set about preparing a new peacock. This time, he sprinkled the down and the neck himself, in order that the recent misadventure was not renewed.

So much care did not remain unfruitful, and a murmur of admiration went up among the guests when Magalouffe served the beautiful bird, reclad in its gilded plumage, the tail deployed and the neck dressed, as if it were still alive on the perch.

Messire Watremetz kept the promise that he had made faithfully, and Séverin, from the very next day onwards, became his assiduous disciple.

*

Let us allow fourteen years to go by now, and return to the episcopacy of Monsieur Godefroi de Fontaine in 1233.

Séverin had become a mild and laborious young man. The good Canon Watremetz, so joyous a companion himself at eighteen, marveled to see his pupil studying the scarcely attractive science of theology with an extreme ardor and perseverance. Séverin's fervent piety and the ardent desire, the obsession, that it inspired in him of entering holy orders, smoothed out the harsh difficulties of an ingrate labor for the young man.

The only relaxation that Séverin had was spending two or three hours every day copying missals and manuscripts and coloring capital letters and illustrations. He had even attained an extraordinary perfection in that kind of work, of which the most renowned rubricators would have been proud. Messire Watremetz owed to that talent of Séverin's a library of fourteen volumes, a veritable phenomenon, a rich literary treasure in the epoch we are attempting to depict.

We have omitted to say that four years previously, Madame Berthe had left her brother's home in order to go and live with another old and infirm relative, who resided in the castellany of Marcoing. The worthy lady had taken Lydorie with her; she was only rarely seen in Cambrai, although her amity for Messire Watremetz, bitter as it was but very sincere, had not suffered any deterioration. When his sister departed, Messire Watremetz had persuaded Séverin's father to let him come to live with him.

When Dame Berthe's aged relative had rendered her soul and she returned to live in Messire Watremetz's house, Séverin was awaiting the moment when it would be granted to him to receive orders—an epoch for which he sighed impatiently, as if after the object of his entire life's desire.

Oh, he thought, emotionally, at every moment, *blessed by my savior, blessed be Our Lady his immaculate mother, who, in her mercy, has granted it to me to spend the rest of my days amid the holy duties and mild jubilations of the clergy! To aid sufferers, reconcile sinners with heaven and themselves, encourage the dying, console the afflicted and find one's heart beating more rapidly after having completed a work agreeable to the Lord. And then to accomplish the sublime mysteries of a God who, under the appearances of bread and wine, descends from Heaven at the voice of a humble priest—that's the life that awaits me on earth.*

As for the rest of the time, far from the perils of the world, I shall spend it in the peaceful frolics of study and the work of rubrication, striving to testify to my dear benefactor, Messire Canon Watremetz, how fortunate he has been for me, and to prove my gratitude to him.

Madame Berthe's pupil, thanks to the gusts of contradiction and tenderness, bitterness and exaggerated kindness of the woman who had educated her, was far from possessing the quietude of tastes and mildness of Séverin. A veritable little demon, by turns whimsical, docile, noisy, taciturn, foolish, tender, and enthusiastic, she was always pleasing, because it was impossible for such a lovely creature to displease anyone. Messire the Canon was infatuated with Lydorie; Madame Berthe scolded her twenty times between matins and vespers and embraced her as many times.

Lydorie was dressed as richly as a townswoman of quality. No one complained about it; no young woman with large bright eyes had ever put on with so much style and grace two brightly colored dresses and bonnet, which designed such palpitating forms so well.

Everyone in the house yielded to her slightest caprices: the varlets, Messire the Canon, Madame Berthe and Séverin, like everyone else.

One day when she chanced to see the young man painting a beautiful missal, she had a sudden whim to become a rubricator herself; and immediately, it was necessary for Séverin to teach her to extend colors and put gold on blank vellum.

During that lesson it became necessary more than once for Séverin to guide Lydorie's scantly docile fingers; playful and laughing, she rejoiced in the professor's long admonitions, and out of malice, took pleasure in spreading large patches of red or black in the middle of the white margin, which spoiled it horribly. But she did not care a jot, and reveled in recommencing, not without having promised beforehand to be attentive and careful, and having feigned a magisterial gravity.

When Séverin went back to his bedroom, he started praying. Without wanting to, all his thoughts gradually became memories of the recent lesson; he could not think about anything else.

First he was afflicted by that, as a mortal sin, and he promised himself that he would not risk such a peril again. But

Lydorie came to beg him in a fashion so coquettish and so polite not to abandon such a hopeful pupil, and she became so joyously annoyed by his scowls of refusal, that he could not keep it up, and it was necessary for him to give in.

From that moment on, thoughts very different from thoughts of devotion and the clergy took possession of his imagination. The life of a priest began to appear to him severe and isolated, and when he saw some townsman out for a walk with his wife, while a little boy rode a stick beside them, Séverin's heart was constricted; he experienced a vague sadness, and the need for I know not what good fortune—but he felt at least that it could not be possessed all alone and in the recollection of study.

For her part, Lydorie always found the lessons in rubrication too short, and the frolicsome young woman, mocking and childish, became thoughtful and more serious. Sitting next to Séverin, she took pleasure in meekly doing what he told her to do; or, he read to her aloud some beautiful story from the Holy Bible, and the voice of the clerk became tremulous, and Lydorie's eyes filled with tears when he read the page that recounted the amours of Jacob and Rachel.

Now, almost every day Séverin opened the book at that touching place.

Meanwhile, the feast of Trinity had come, and the epoch when Séverin was to receive the first orders of the clergy was arriving rapidly, for it was set for the day of the Nativity.

The poor young man shed bitter tears at the idea of that day, of which he had once dreamed with ardent desire.

In the thirteenth century the feast of the Trinity was celebrated in Cambrésis by a pompous procession. Old authors even claim that it is necessary to see in that custom the origin of the procession of Cambrai that, until 1682, did indeed take place on the Monday of Trinity.

All the guilds of the town took part in that procession, and, trumpets at the head and ensigns deployed, marched clad in their distinctive doublets.

After the ceremony the guilds went to escort with honor, back to the residence of their kings, the statuettes to the benevolent patrons they invoked: Sainte Pélagie for the weavers and mercers; Saint Sébastien for the archers; Saint Maur for the bakers and Notre-Dame-du-Mont-Carmel for the mulquiniers.

In the year 1233, on the Monday of Trinity, after the procession had made a tour of the town, Monseigneur the Bishop went back to the Episcopal Manor, not without giving his blessing beforehand to the guides from the drawbridge. Then there was a great racket of trumpets and viols, and the cries of the corporations were heard to repeat from all directions: "Saint Antoine! Saint Maur! Sainte Pélagie!" etc.

Dominating all the others, the cry of the mulquiniers rose up: "Notre-Dame! Notre-Dame!" for there was no guild in Cambrai richer and more numerous than theirs, given that the preparation and sale of fine thread obtained large profits, and it required a great many individual tasks to get them to bobbins fit for the weaving

Incontrovertibly, the individual who strutted most conspicuously with the importance of that corporation was our old acquaintance Nicolas Parigault, the mulquiniers' sot-seuris.

His waist encased in a little wooden horse on which one might have thought that he was veritably perched—for a cloth trailing on the ground did not allow it to be seen whether Parigault's legs were beneath it or those of a wooden hack—the sot-seuris ran around all the passers-by and had no shortage of quips and licentious jokes, inspired by many draughts of wine. The mulquiniers welcomed the lewd merriment with bursts of laughter and applause, and as you can imagine such encouragement only emboldened and exited him.

Not far from the drawbridge of the manor, Madame Berthe and Lydorie, accompanied by Séverin, were watching the animated spectacle offered by the immense crowd, previously concentrated, which was now beginning to scatter in all directions. The sot-seuris recognized the canon's sister, and came to gambol around her in order to be gratified by a few copper coins. But it was a complete waste of time making his charger leap and prance, and saluting over and over with his wooden sword; Madame Berthe did not give him a patard. The fact is that the lady had forgotten to pick up her satchel before leaving the house.

The sot-seuris, whose head, as we have said, had been warmed up by excessive draughts of wine, then began to tease the canon's sister in improper terms.

Séverin enjoined him to be more circumspect.

"Saint Touch-me-Not, my patron!" cried Parigault, giving the young man a slap with his wooden sword. "Saint Touch-me-Not! My son, you have impugned my honor and stained my escutcheon with filth. It's necessary for us to fight a duel. You take for a helmet one of your father's old cooking-pots, and a kiss from that pretty gypsy will be granted to the victor."

At those uncouth words Lydorie's face turned red, and she could not hold back her tears, for there was a large crowd there, in which some rejoiced in that insult, because Madame Berthe protégée deluded herself somewhat and sometimes spoke ill of people of low birth.

In any case, the townspeople were, most of the time, openly hostile to the canons because of their privileges, which the Chapter always wanted to diminish, while they sought, on the contrary, to increase them. You can imagine, therefore, how the little people rejoiced in seeing the sister and the intimates of a canon mocked.

Séverin, wanting to put an end to the discourteous negotiation, tried to cleave a path through the crowd to get back to the manor, but, instead of making way for him, it tightened its ranks, and the sot-seuris, supported in that fashion, put his multicolored arms around Lydorie's waist, and made a gross kiss resonate on the poor child's cheeks.

At that final insult, Severin struck the buffoon with a terrible blow, who fell silent, his face rudely bloodied.

If you had heard the clamors that rose up from all parts when the beloved sot-seuris fell, you would have gone pale with dread. All those who were there, without taking into account that Parigault had merited it, started shouting: "Aie! Aie! We're being murdered, guildsmen rally!" and rushed Séverin. On the other hand, the archers guarding the drawbridge ran to help the young man, and a frightful melee ensued.

But the townsmen, who had no weapons, found themselves at a disadvantage in the battle, for the archers' daggers thrust at them good and hard, while they could only render in exchange blows with closed fists or staves—which, to tell the truth, they delivered rudely.

During the disorder of the brawl, Séverin was able to get Madame Berthe and Lydorie back inside. That was not easy, given that one of them was lying in a faint in the poor clerk's arm and the other seemed almost to have lost her reason.

The archers then decided to beat a retreat, for more guildsmen were arriving at every moment to attack them. Thanks to their good discipline they got out of it with a few bruises and succeeded in returning to the manor and raising the drawbridge without leaving any of their companions at the mercy of the townspeople.

The people of Cambrai, seeing at least thirty guildsmen rudely covered in wounds, went to take possession of the town barriers in spite of the commands and admonitions of the high bailiff; others ran to Saint-Géry and the Magdelaine to sound the tocsin there and rouse the rest of the lower orders.

In less than no time, four thousand fanatics were under arms. They took possession of the Château de Selles, which Robert, the bailiff of the chapter, did not have the courage to defend, and imprisoned the senior curate, a relative of Messire Watremetz, who, thinking no evil, was returning peacefully from the castellany of Marcoing.

Pillages and extortions were carried out in the various quarters of Cambrai. A freeman who had taken refuge in the Abbaye de Saint-Aubert was taken out by force and only released in return for a large ransom. Finally, the houses of the archdeacon of Brussels and several canons who were living in the town were broken into and looted.

Everyone in the Episcopal manor was in consternation. The Bishop held a council to decide what to do in such difficult circumstances, and no one proffered any good advice but many heaped abuse—more than was appropriate to clergymen—upon poor Séverin, the innocent cause of the revolt.

Meanwhile, the townsmen brought strong ladders in order to scale the walls, and there was scarcely any means of resisting their assault, for the men-at-arms were small in number at the Episcopal manor and the capture of the fortress of Selles by the assailants rendered its defense almost impossible.

But it would not have made any difference; they only had food for two days, and after that time it would have been necessary to surrender, unless the seigneurs of the Bishop's fiefs came to attack the townsmen. Unfortunately, there was little aid to be expected from those pretty suzerains, more likely to make common cause with the rebels than to attack them and reckon with them.

Nevertheless, the aspect of things suddenly changed, without anyone anticipating it.

The sot-seuris Parigault—who was thought to be half-dead, although he had only been stunned by the blow struck by Séverin, and the unconsciousness that gripped him was three-quarters due to drunkenness—had been carried to his home. When his wife's cares had brought him round and he learned what had happened, the wily companion reflected seriously on the big risk that he was taking by letting things continue at the momentum with which they had begun.

It will be necessary for the guildsmen to make honorable amends in any case, he thought, *for the emperor will shake their shoulders rudely for the villainous manner in which they've just treated the bishop. The bigwigs will extract a good deal of gold in exchange. But I, the cause of all this, will pay with my skin; and it could be that I'll be seen prancing at the top of the high scaffold of the Coupe-Oreille. Oh, my throat tightens just thinking about it!*

Quickly mounting his wooden horse, Parigault ran to the manor, where everyone was very surprised and glad to see him. Aping a general then, he performed so many buffooneries that the townsmen forgot to deploy their ladders and press ahead with the assault.

It is necessary to say that the wisest and richest among the, including Master Le Beaudin and Master Eustache Dinault, only watched the revolt with a sullen frown; they calculated that their savings would be depleted when the emperor came to avenge his bishop, which would not fail to happen, given that he had sworn on his share of paradise to do so during the last riot.

They therefore saw with contentment the diversion brought by the presence of the sot-seuris, and were already seeking to tell him in secret to try to bring the great stir to an end, when hazard and the malicious skill of the Fool came to serve them marvelously in their desire for peace.

Having no suspicion of that had happened, and supposing that the feast of Trinity alone had assembled the immense crowd in the quarters surrounding the episcopal manor by which they were encumbered, Magalouffe was returning tranquilly at the walking pace of his mule. Two scullions were marching behind him, holding the bridles of four horses laden with provisions of which the savant cook had been in quest himself in the places where the best was to be found. Then too, he was meditating the important question of how it was necessary to cook a magnificent salmon trout that he was carrying behind him, not having wanted to confide the fish in question—the most beautiful that had been fished out of the Escaut in living memory—to the care of anyone else.

He had just taken the resolution to serve the trout with a bitter almond sauce, old wine and grape juice when he suddenly found himself stopped by the sot-seuris, who shouted to him at the top of his voice: "Bonjour, well met, be welcome, brother ambassador of the Bishop."

Magalouffe rebuffed the buffoon disdainfully, but the latter, redoubling his frolics, found a means of making people

63

believe that Magalouffe was listening to him, when, to tell the truth, the cook was only grumbling and cursing wholehearted-ly.

Then, raising his voice, as if he were about to announce the result of the conference, the jester proclaimed: "Oyez, bourgeois, oyez; Monseigneur the Bishop, in order to com-plete the good and joyful pleasantry that we have commenced, has sent his cook to negotiate with your sot-seuris, not without rich presents, such as you see on these two horses.

"Monseigneur deems that things have perhaps become a little more facetious than they should have done, but, in favor of the feast of Trinity, no more account will be taken by him of the events of today than if they had not happened; the mat-ter has been settled between us two sage clerks."

With these words he threw himself into Magalouffe's arms, who, falling from a height, was preparing to reply; but the sot-seuris caught him in such a fashion and gripped him so forcefully, that he could not utter an audible word.

"Now, all of you go home," Parigault continued, "in or-der that the Sire d'Esnes men-at-arms, so well equipped, who will soon arrive, do not take it into their heads to believe that you are out of control. Go, I give you my blessing."

With those words he made parody of blessing the towns-people, raising and lowering his fool's baton.

"He's right! He's right! Long live Monseigneur Godefroi!" was shouted in all directions. And then everyone went home rapidly, having more desire to close his door with solid bars of wood than to take the Episcopal manor by storm.

In the meantime, Magalouffe, brought up to date by Ni-colas Parigault, succeeded, not without difficulty, in having the drawbridge of the episcopal manor lowered, and explained what had just happened to the bishop and the canons, amazed to see the populace going away peacefully, having previously been intent on revolt and carnage.

We shall say right away that a deputation of guildsmen came the following day to beg the bishop for mercy. Monsei-gneur Godefroi de Fontaine, after more than one remonstration, granted them their pardon under the following conditions:

That the procurator of the town, in the presence of the magistrate and forty bourgeois, would make solemn restitution of everything that had been stolen from each place where the damage had been caused;

That they would pay two thousand livres for the things that had been destroyed and other losses, for which ten guildsmen would stand surety;

That a hundred townsmen in chemises would come to make honorable amends in the Episcopal church;

That in order to prevent the townsmen from recidivism, it would be very severely prohibited for anyone to appear with the town standards without an express order from the magistrate;

And finally, that the bell of the Magdelaine, which had been rung to rouse the people, would be removed.

As several lords rallying to the bishop had arrived with companies of men-at-arms, the townspeople were obliged to obey those conditions, harsh as they appeared to them.

*

Among the talents and qualities that recommended Magalouffe among cooks of great renown, people admired most of all that at the first sound of the horn he was always ready, along with his scullions, to serve a feast on time; he had never—absolutely never—caused the delay of a single *ave*.

And if the steward took it into his head to enquire: "Where are we, Master Cook?" Magalouffe would have made, with irritated pride, the following response: "Never has it happened that people have had to wait for dinner or supper since I have had the good fortunate of being the episcopal cook. It never will happen, as long as it pleases Monseigneur to keep me in that employ and the good God to keep me alive."

Now, four days after the events that I have just recounted, the varlets sounded the horn; Monseigneur had just sat down at table, and the surprise was great, for there were not yet any dishes there, except for the bread-baskets, which had been prepared the evening before.

Rapidly, as you can imagine, the steward, as flustered as one can be, started running excitedly to the episcopal kitchens.

Magalouffe, as if struck by the fire of heaven, was standing silent and immobile, while the scullions were making every effort, not without amazement at the languor of their chief. They could be heard enquiring of one another, in low voices, what great chagrin might have depressed Magalouffe in that fashion—they said "great" because grief had not caused him to omit the duties of his office, even for a single second, when he had lost his wife, of whom he was nevertheless very fond.

At the voice of the steward, he emerged from his reverie with a start, and commanded everyone so rapidly and so well that supper was ready immediately. After which, he returned to his chagrin, and started weeping with a bitterness that could scarcely be believed.

"That's too much self-affliction for a delayed supper," said the steward. "Once is not a habitual sin. In any case, as Monseigneur often says, quoting the Holy Scriptures, it's written that a sage stumbles seven times a day."

"Oh, I'm exceedingly mournful, and I have every reason to be. By Sainte Marthe! If I knew, in the entire principality of Cambrésis, anyone who was in a fit state to hold, as I hold it, the white baton of Episcopal cook, I'd give it to him, I swear it, and I'd go to fulfill the wretched métier of brother-cook in some Carmelite convent, where they only eat boiled roots."

The steward tried once again to console Magalouffe, but the poor man exclaimed, more pitifully still:

"Why did Our Lord, in his mercy, not deign to conserve in my soul the desire that I once nourished of instructing my son in the noble science that has earned me such renown? Instructed by Magalouffe, he would have been lauded, like me, as one of the finest practitioners of his art; he would have become Episcopal cook.

"Now tell me, in good conscience, whether there is, throughout Cambrésis, any finer and more highly-esteemed title than that of Episcopal cook, which proves a rank among the twenty-four free-fiefs and grants the power of administering law and knowing feudal, civil, criminal and other affairs in the jurisdiction of Monseigneur the Bishop?

"Accursed be the benefits of Messire Watremetz! Monseigneur the Bishop has humiliated me just now with regard to my son; he has called him by the vile names of quarrelsome and discourteous; he has added that if he does not mend his ways, he will be forced to refuse him the orders of the clergy. Yes, he said all that to me—to me, Magalouffe, who had reached the age of sixty-four without ever having hung his head or heard a reprimand, either for myself or my own!

"Oh, if Messire Watremetz had not taken Séverin out of the kitchen, he would not have instructed himself in foolish sciences and I would not have shivered in all my limbs at such harsh words from Monseigneur; the name of Magalouffe would still be stainless!

"I could not hold back my tears, and Monseigneur, having allowed himself to be softened, and remembering my long service, ended up granting me pardon for my son and promising that he will give him the first orders of the clergy the day after tomorrow. Thanks be rendered to him, but he made me feel ill, and I shall never recover from the great blow that he has struck me!"

The steward comforted Magalouffe as best he could, said fine words to him at length, and then went away to where his duty summoned him.

Magalouffe was beginning to recover somewhat when Séverin, of whom he had sent someone in quest, arrived, pale and distraught. Kneeling down at first, in accordance with custom, he asked for his father's blessing; then he waited modestly, his eyes lowered, for the latter to acquaint him with the reasons for which he had summoned him.

Master Magalouffe collected himself for a few moments. Then he began to list, with an anguished complaisance the misdeeds of his son that the bishop had previously recited with so much bitterness.

His voice, which he tried at first to render dignified, low and slow, gradually became shrill and screeching; it was as high as possible when, by virtue of a sudden reversal, it fell back to a graver tone, exactly like the voice of a preacher who, after having striven to bark a description of Hell, concludes his sermon with the word Paradise, adding in a level voice, the customary: "That's the happiness that I desire."

Now, that mutation of voice was to announce that Monseigneur, in his benignity, had granted the pardon of such gross faults, and had consented to confer on Séverin, two days hence, the first orders of the clergy.

"I can't be a priest," the young man replied, in a tremulous voice.

As he pronounced those bold words, he raised his eyes; and that glance emboldened him, for Magalouffe's face did not express anger.

"I can't, I don't want to be a priest," he repeated, more firmly.

At each of Séverin's words an inexpressible joy refreshed Magalouffe's blood. *Oh*, he thought, *Sainte Marthe has taken pity on the troubles of her unworthy servant, and she had deigned to put into my son's soul the thrice-blessed desire to be a cook, like his father! He's already a little old, but no matter; I shall put all my cares into it, and within four years, he'll be the second cook in Cambrésis.*

"I'm in love with a young woman," Séverin continued, "and we've promised one another fidelity in love in this world and the next."

"You're getting married, you're getting married! Oh, my son, my Séverin, what would I not do, in the contentment that you have given me, on seeing you renounce your foolish sciences, to see you become a cook!"

"You're mistaken, Father; there's no need for me to be a cook to earn an honest living. Apart from the benefits of Messire Watremetz, my work as a rubricator will give me a means to live comfortably when I have the woman I love for a wife, Lydorie..."

As Séverin spoke, Magalouffe saw all the illusions he had created vanish. At the name of Lydorie he uttered a cry of despair and anger.

"Lydorie! Lydorie! A bastard! A gypsy! The daughter of a prostitute, reproved by God and the saints…!

"Listen! If you mention this infamous design to me again; if you mention once more the name of…the name that is killing me…I will give you my malediction!"

Neither the tears, nor the supplications not the despair of the poor young man, nor anything he could say, could succeed in bending the pitiless old man. Exasperated by the resistance that his son opposed to him, he even ended up chasing him away without mercy, forbidding him ever to reappear before his eyes."

His heart gripped by a mortal sadness, Séverin returned to Messire Watremetz's house.

On seeing him, the young woman understood the sad news that he was going to announce, and fell unconscious.

Then, when Séverin's cares, although he was almost in the same state as her, had recalled her to life, she dissolved in tears.

There was in that frightful moment of despair an ineffable sweetness for Séverin, for Lydorie, for the first time, called him by the most affectionate names and lavished the most tender caresses upon him.

Her feeble head rested on Séverin's shoulder, and her hand gripped her friend's hand gently; and the rest of the day went by like that.

It was finally necessary to separate.

On returning to his room, Séverin allowed himself to fall into the greatest depression. It was necessary for him to leave the house of Messire the Canon; it was necessary for him not to see Lydorie again—and to live without seeing her seemed harsher than dying.

Dying! At that idea, a culpable desire, a burning and frightful vertigo, took hold of the unfortunate fellow; he seized a dagger, plunged it into his breast, and fell, uttering a loud cry.

When he came round, Madame Berthe, Messire Watremetz and Lydorie were surrounding his bed and weeping, for they believed him to be dead, having found him unconscious and bathed in his own blood.

Messire Watremetz, who had some knowledge of the curative arts, examined his wound attentively. He announced that it did not seem dangerous, and that within a week nothing would remain to the invalid but a great weakness caused by the loss of blood.

Lydorie was so good that she remained on vigil that night beside Séverin.

In the morning, before quitting him, she put a silver ring on his finger and said to him: "As long as that ring remains, dear beloved, Lydorie will be yours and will love you truly and endlessly."

The patient tried to answer those sweet words with a few of his own, but she fled.

The canon's prognostications with regard to Séverin's wound did not take long to be verified, and it healed promptly.

Séverin had attributed his wound to an accident, improvised as best he could, and as the canon and his sister, good people, simple and without deviation, had no suspicion of the tenderness of the two lovers, Lydorie spent the greater part of the day in the bedroom of her brother—which was what she called Séverin.

Once, however, evening arrived without him having seen her; he was drawing the saddest and most disquieting conjectures from that, when Messire Watremetz appeared and sat down beside the convalescent.

"Now then," he said, with kindness, "I know everything, Séverin. Your father has told me about your amour, and I understand now what hand and what determination caused your wound. But if the mercy of God has permitted that you did not bring such a crime to a conclusion, it is not for me, a sinner like you, to show myself more severe than Him.

"Listen, my child; I have made vain attempts to soften your father; I have not been able to have any effect on him. On the other hand, Monseigneur the Bishop is irritated by your refusal to receive orders. In addition, I cannot favor an amour that is illicit, since your father reproves it. It is necessary for you, my dear child, to arm yourself with courage; accept in a spirit of penitence the chagrins that are overwhelming you, and put your consolations and your hope in the infinite mercy of the Lord.

"Here are thirty gold coins; hold on to them carefully. Tomorrow you will depart with my brother the chief curate when he goes, by order of Monseigneur the Bishop to the city of Rheims, to the archbishopric. My brother will find you protectors in that city, and you will lead a comfortable existence there thanks to your great talent as a rubricator, until we can succeed in bending your father, which I dare not hope for soon.

"Go, then, my child, and keep a good remembrance of those who have brought you up, who love you, and who will doubtless never see you again, for they are very advanced in age and God will not be long delayed in calling them to him. May His Holy Will be done!

"Go, dear Séverin, and for lack of your father's blessing, that of an old man will accompany you."

With those words, tears ran down the venerable canon's cheeks, and he hugged Séverin to his breast for a long time, who had thrown himself into his arms.

The next day, at daybreak, as Séverin was departing sadly from the canon's house, and while passing under Lydorie's windows, he raised his eyes to see, once more, at least, the place where she was, a little scroll of parchment thrown through the bared window fell at the young man's feet.

He picked it up, with some emotion, as you will understand, and read the words said to Séverin in his bedroom on the day that he had tried to kill himself: *As long as that ring remains, dear beloved, Lydorie will be yours and will love you truly and endlessly.*

71

The pupil of Messire Watremetz arrived without encumbrance in Rheims, where he soon became the favorite of the archbishop, a great lover of beautiful manuscripts and missal-paintings.

"Séverin, my friend," said the prelate, every time he saw him, "Séverin, do you not want to enter the clergy? Come the end of the year and you will be my chaplain, with rich benefits, the best that depend on my pleasure."

Séverin, smiling sadly, thanked the archbishop and replied that he could not offer the Lord a heart full of a mortal object.

Two years after Séverin's departure, Lydorie, sitting in the embrasure of a large window, remembered the events of her life and wept.

The orphan of a gypsy, picked up out of charity, perhaps obliged to live poorly on the labor of her hands when her benefactors were no more; and then, without hope, not merely of belonging to the man she loved so much, about, alas, even of seeing him again, one more time!

What young woman in the world has more to mourn than her? If Master Magalouffe could only allow himself to be softened at last! If he could only take pity on the exile of his son and Lydorie's dolor!

But no; nothing can overcome his pride or his disdain; for he is rich, and if he does not come from a noble lineage, at least, alas, he has nothing at which to blush in his mother.

Why had God not granted her great treasures and noble birth? Oh, no, she would not sacrifice to vanity placid good fortune devoid of desire! She would live the rest of her days with Séverin, with her beloved friend. Amour is worth more than grandeur—and then, it is so sweet to be able to enrich the person one loves!

While she was delivering herself to such thoughts, someone came to tell her that Madame Berthe was summoning her urgently. She obeyed that order, quickly wiping her eyes, reddened by tears, and went down into the big room, where she found with the worthy dame and Messire Watremetz a stranger clad in the scalloped mantle and hood of a pilgrim. The pale face, hollow eyes, unkempt gray beard and long, fleshless hand of the unknown man inspired a vague fear in Lydorie, which caused her to draw nearer to the canon.

The physiognomies of Madame Berthe and her brother expressed a great emotion. The stranger was shedding tears, sobbing and striking himself on the breast, repeating: "Lord have pity on me!"

After a time, he raised piercing eyes upon Lydorie, at whom he stared fixedly. "It's her! There's no doubt about it; it's her. Yes, even if that silver medal around her neck did not attest the fact, it would only be necessary to see her; she's the portrait of her mother."

At those words of the pilgrim, an icy shiver ran through all Lydorie's limbs, and it was necessary to support her, for her knees were giving way.

Woe! Woe! she thought. *This pilgrim is my father; it's the gypsy's husband!*

And the mild leisure and wellbeing of the canon's house seemed already to have quit her, to give way to the miserable life of a beggar.

The pilgrim asked: "Show me the black mark that she ought to bear on her right hand."

After having seen it, he knelt down, and, striking the floor with his forehead, he said: "Noble Comtesse de Coucy, I pledge allegiance between your hands, and I promise, by the merits of the Holy Cross, to do everything for you, for life, until death, a faithful vassal, as my duty requires.

"I am very culpable in your regard, but grant me mercy, not because of me—I only merit opprobrium—but for the honor of our family. In the name of Jesus Christ, who died on the cross of Calvary pardoning his murderers; in the name of the merits of Our Lady, have mercy on me!"

What she was seeing and hearing appeared to Lydorie to be a dream, assuredly very pleasant, but to which the slightest sound might put an end.

And while she remained in such doubt, the canon told her by what divine ways all that had come about. The kneeling pilgrim was the Sire de Montroche, Lydorie's uncle. On the death of his brother he had had his baby niece abducted, and a gypsy woman had been charged, in èxchange for a considerable sum, to take her so far away that no mention of her would ever be heard. A piece of wood was put in a coffin in her stead, to create the belief that she had died suddenly. That crime put the great wealth of the Comte de Coucy in the possession of her brother, the Sire de Montroche.

But he did not enjoy them for long without remorse. Having lost sleep, and sensing himself close to his end by a malady of languor, he confessed his crime to a hermit. The holy man enjoined him to set forth in search of his niece, to restore her domains to her and to implore her mercy—after which, he ought to retire to a solitary place to spend the rest of his life in harsh penitence.

He had not had to carry out long research to find his niece, for he had heard mention of the orphan of Cambrai, and had then conceived the suspicion that she was his niece.

Lydorie lifted her uncle to his feet and granted him pardon, after which the penitent withdrew, his soul delivered from a great weight, promising to return to find Lydorie in two days' time to take her to her domains and have her recognized by her vassals as their lady and legitimate Comtesse.

Left alone Lydorie surrendered to intoxicating thought.

A Comtesse! A Comtesse! Rich! Vast domains! Men-at-arms who watched over the walls of her château! Ladies of the bedchamber! Sparkling adornments of precious stones! The place of honor at tourneys!

Oh, why was Séverin, instead of being a clerk in sciences, not a knight expert in delivering great blows of a lance? How happy she would have been to give him the prize or a tourney with her own hands!

Those ideas kept her awake all night.

When it was known in the town of Cambrai that Lydorie had become a noble lady and one of the richest heiresses of the Vermandois, everyone hastened to come to congratulate her and strive to please her.

Magalouffe followed the example of everyone else, rejoicing privately in having for a daughter-in-law a comtesse of high lineage. However, it is necessary to say that he held his own profession of Episcopal cook in such high esteem that such a marriage appeared to him very fortunate, but not unexpected and unmerited, and not entirely a misalliance.

Decked out in his finest robe, therefore, he came to inform Lydorie that he gave his consent to her marriage to Séverin.

It would be better, he thought, *incontrovertibly, it would be better, to wait for the request to be addressed by her. But I treated her so badly once that she might never dare to mention it to me now. Perhaps also, a misplaced pride and the resentment of my former disdain might prevent them from doing so. Let us therefore do something for the poor children, toward whom, after all, I have shown a great deal of severity.*

When Magalouffe came in, Lydorie was talking to Monseigneur the Bishop, and the prelate's nephew, Sire Eustache de Lens, a handsome fellow of commanding appearance.

The rather small patrimony of that knight was adjacent to the Comté of Coucy; now, to combine the two domains into one and surmount his escutcheon with a comtal crown would suit him so well that he had taken no repose before his uncle had introduced him to Lydorie.

Dame Berthe's pupil had never heard the flowery and perfumed words of sires of high lineage, so the poor girl allowed herself to be gripped immediately by the honeyed words of Sire Eustache and did not take long to make, without meaning to, a comparison between him and Séverin—who, alas, was far from speaking with such fluency and grace.

None of the progress that he was making in the favorable opinion of Lydorie escaped Sire Eustache, and the sweet talker ended up entangling the child in vanity and foolishness, her head being too feeble to support such a strong and unusual odor of incense without spinning. To believe him, it was not

75

today that he had begun to suspect Lydorie's noble origin; the first time he had seen her—and he had only arrived at the manor the day before yesterday—he had enquired the name of the chatelaine that he had been amazed to see at Messire Watremetz's window.

With a smile on her lips and red cheeks, therefore, Lydorie was taking pleasure in such base flattery, taking it for good and sound currency of the bishopric, when Magalouffe came to salute her.

At the sight of the noble seigneurs who were surrounding his future daughter-in-law, the inventor of gilded soup felt slightly embarrassed, but he tried to disguise his disturbance under a casual manner.

"Séverin will be delighted, Madame Lydorie," he said, taking off his cap, "for at the present moment there is no long-er any obstacle to his betrothal. For what day should I instruct him to be ready? In the haste that I have to tell him such joyful news, I shall send a faithful messenger immediately. It will cost me two gold coins, but come All Saints, and we're only at Saint Remy, the man I send will see the bell-towers of Rheims. Then again, I don't fear any inconvenience for him; it's Polycarpe, one of my scullions, and more cunning than any page of his sort.

"You would do well, Master Magalouffe," replied Lydorie. A sigh followed those words, for she thought: *Why is Séverin's father this unpleasant fellow?*

"Who is the coarse bumpkin talking about?" asked Sire Eustache, with a mocking smile.

"My childhood friend," replied Lydorie. She had not dared to say "my lover."

Magalouffe, attributing his future daughter-in-law's cold welcome to the rancor she retained from the past, drew closer and asked in a low voice:

"Is it necessary to instruct Séverin to make haste, so that by Christmas, or before, if he wishes, the marriage can take place?"

"Marriage! Marriage!" Sire Eustache interrupted, whose keen hearing was on the alert. "By the three ermines of my escutcheon, I divine it! You're going to marry the son of this cook to one of your chambermaids!"

Lydorie formed a smile that seemed to let the knight believe that his suspicion was correct. Alas, she was blushing at Séverin's amour!

In order that Magalouffe should not see her lie in that fashion, she had turned her back on him. The episcopal cook, indignant at that discourteous reception, departed shaking his head, taking Sainte Marthe as his witness that the Comtesse de Coucy would not marry Séverin and more than he had married the gypsy's daughter.

Already swollen with anger at that humiliation, he flew into an extraordinary fury when he went into the Episcopal kitchens. In his absence, the scullions had been fighting, and three roasts were so black and hard that a manual laborer would not have had the heart to serve them on his table if he had only invited the goose-drover.

At that sight, Magalouffe made a terrible sign, tried to speak, and, unable to do it, fell down, stiff and inert. By the time anyone came to his aid, he had rendered his soul.

Meanwhile, the thoughts of Séverin were returning night and day to the pleasant land of Cambrai.

Having become rich and the favorite of the Archbishop of Rheims, he thought that the intervention of his protector might succeed in vanquishing his father's perverse refusal. But if he could not succeeded by that means, he would go so far as to brave his wrath, and would take advantage of an archepiscopal dispensation that granted his the right to be united in marriage in spite of the paternal hindrance.

Oh, how much it would cost him to cause his father such dolor—but he was resolved to do it for love of Lydorie, whom he cherished even more than his father.

Monseigneur the Archbishop of Rheims had so much desire to preserve his favorite Séverin from misfortune that he gave him two men-at-arms to defend him during the journey, against highwaymen and other perils.

Séverin departed, therefore, and rode for days, although it was the middle of winter, but he was going to see Lydorie again, and snow, frost and ice mattered little to him.

After twenty days of travel, he arrived in the town of Saint Quentin. It was a Sunday; his first concern was, devoutly, to go to hear holy mass at the principal church.

Now, a marriage was being celebrated, and Séverin's heart beat faster at that sight, for he thought that he would soon see his pretty and beloved Lydorie in a bridal gown.

Jesus, my Savior, how he bride resembles her! If it were not for those garments of velvet and silk, and that that with golden points, a veritable Comtesse's crown, he could believe that he was seeing Lydorie!

In his trouble he cleaved through the crowd and advanced as far as the altar. The men-at-arms guarding the choir, judging by his determined stride that he was one of their master's officers—for he was dressed in the rich livery of the rubricator of the Archbishop of Rheims—let him pass freely.

Oh! It was Lydorie! There could be no doubt about it.

In the most poignant anguish that ever gripped a Christian on earth, he was gazing at the spectacle, which appeared to him to be a bad dream, when the priest celebrating the office dropped the nuptial ring.

Séverin launched himself forward impetuously to pick it up, and anticipated all the others.

He found the means, while he was getting up, to replace it with the annealed silver ring that he had once received from Lydorie, and as the celebrant placed it on the finger of the bride Séverin recited in a loud voice, of mocking bitterness:

"As long as that ring remains, Lydorie will be yours and will love you truly and endlessly."

At the first words, Lydorie had raised her head, and, weeping hot tears, had hidden her face against the shoulder of Sire Eustache.

"Well said, handsome clerk of the Archbishop of Rheims," said Sire Eustache, who had recognized the livery. "What recompense do you require for that diction? I will grant it to you, on the salvation of my soul."

But Séverin drew away without listening, and no one gave him any further thought, for the vassals of the two spouses uttered cries of joy, and Sire Eustache de Lens squeezed Lydorie's hand gently, who could not turn her languid and amorous eyes away from him.

One can still see, among the epitaphs of the canons of the church of Rheims, a stone that bears the name of Séverin Magalouffe, canon, died in his twenty-fifth year, six months after having received the canonical ermine.

THE RUBRICATOR

1325

> The lady settled on that advice,
> gathered her possessions as coyly and
> as finely as she could, and left Paris
> with her young son and the Earl of
> Kent and marched toward Hainaut.
> (*Froissart*, vol. 1. ch. XII)[11]

The curfew bell had finished tolling; it was the darkest of nights. Without the torches lit outside the house of pillars, it would not have been possible to see the low columns and Gothic arches of the palace of Prince Philippe de Valois, although it was built in an apparent place on the highest part of the strand, a sandy extent that descended in a steep slope all the way to the bed of the Seine.

A young man emerged from one of the houses adjacent to the palace. Throwing a section of his large cloak over his right shoulder, doubtless in order to be able to make free use of the iron-tipped staff he was holding in his hand, he started walking rapidly. Having gone along the river bank he passed opposite the convent and the Rue d'Hières, and went along the entire length of the Quai des Ormes, of which the Rue du Paon Blanc and the Rue de Frosgier-l'Anier formed the two limits.

There he finally slowed down and, out of breath, clapped his hands together twice.

---

[11] This reference is false, Froissart's *Chronicle* makes no reference the incident involving the Earl of Kent and the English Queen featured in the story, which does not appear to have any historical basis.

The door of a house that was in front of him opened cautiously, and a young woman slipped out enveloped in a long mantilla; she advanced toward the young man and held out a tremulous hand to him.

"Henryot," she said, in a faint voice, after a long silence, "my Henryot, this rendezvous is the last; it's necessary for you to leave tomorrow, forever, for another country...for our love is no longer innocent and pure, as in the days of our childhood; it has become...Holy Virgin take pity on me! It has become adulterous!"

The young man proffered an inarticulate groan.

"Alas! Yes, my sweet Henryot, it's necessary for us to quit one another for life...it's necessary that henceforth, you expel from your mind the memory of Marguerite, as one rejects a bad thought of the evil spirit. Adieu, then! Adieu, adieu, Henryot!"

Until then he had stood there as if annihilated by despair, but when he saw her take a step to draw away he straightened up abruptly, and seized the hand that had just quit his own again.

"No!" he cried, "No, you belong to me! It's me that you have espoused. In the time of my childhood, when we slept in the same cradle, did not our parents discuss quietly the project of our marriage? Did they not smile, shaking their head, when I would only allow my playthings to be agitated by the hand of my little Marguerite? When I left for Flanders in order to earn money as a painter of missals, was it not agreed that in four years' time, on my return, our marriage would be celebrated? Did I not sense, in giving you the kiss of departure, your cheeks moist with large tears, your hand grip mine convulsively? And when you dreamed of me...then... Oh, they have broken their promise! They have forced you, poor and defenseless, to bow down to their parental power, in order to marry you, weeping, to a coarse mercenary. Holy Virgin, is the oath that binds you to him more sacred than the oath that binds you to me? Yes, you belong to me! Come, then! Come, then! Come, let's flee! We'll find a refuge in Hainaut were no one will be able to disturb us."

Marguerite wept bitterly, and did not reply.

"Come...let's go!" he added, impetuously.

She raised her head, which she had hidden in her hands and folded her arms across her chest. "Henryot," she said, "is it really you who are saying such things to me? You, who told me—in happier times, alas, that: 'True love is nothing but pure and holy virtue; outside of duty, no amour,' Henryot, if I listened to your insensate pleas, how much time would go by before you looked at me with scorn, before my presence became for a you a heavy burden, a remorse, a chastisement of our sin? No, my friend, it's necessary for us to part...for ever. Adieu! Adieu! Adieu!"

She drew away rapidly; and he watched her go with a stupid gaze, watched her draw away without proffering a single word, without making a single movement to retain her.

He was still there, immobile, with death in his heart, when a cry of distress extracted him from that frightful torpor. By a mechanical instinct of defense, he straightened up and took hold of his iron-tipped staff. The cries became more distinct, and he perceived, in the moonlight, a man who was defending himself against two others. Henryot ran to help the one who was being attacked in that cowardly fashion, but when he arrived one of the assassins was lying on the ground and the other took flight at the sight of the new assailant.

"May Saint George be your aid!" said the stranger, with a very pronounced English accent. "But for you they'd have done for me; but let's make haste to get away. I fear that the fugitive might have gone for reinforcements to do me a bad turn that might rebound on you. Finish your good work by letting me lean on your arm as far as my dwelling, which isn't far away, for the blood I'm losing is weakening me to the point that I can't support myself... But what are you looking for there, near the cadaver?"

"My hat."

"By God! Let's decamp quickly, without delay! There are several people coming over there, and we might well find their arrival bad. Come...I'll give you a thousand hats in exchange for that one..."

And, leaning on Henryot's arm, the two of them drew away.

After a few moments' march, Henryot and the stranger arrived at a door that the latter opened with precaution, and closed with no less care. After that they traversed a small courtyard and several large apartments, where complete darkness reigned. They finally found themselves in a room richly hung with tapestries, beneath the high fireplace of which a lady was standing whose physiognomy and bearing were full of nobility and melancholy.

At the sight of the pale stranger, weak and covered in blood, she uttered a loud scream, ran to him in extreme distress, with the least equivocal testaments of tenderness and despair.

"It's nothing, Isabelle; my wound isn't dangerous," said Henryot's companion, in English.

"Aymond, Aymond! What wretch could have tried to take your life?"

"Your brother the King of France, or at least, men-at-arms of his household. Two men bearing his livery attacked me unexpectedly. One of them made the acquaintance of my dagger; the other took flight, thanks to the aid that this young man gave me."

The Queen darted an emotional glance at Henryot, which expressed a keen gratitude.

"The danger I've escaped," the stranger continued, still in English, "isn't the only one that awaits us today. Frightened by the threats and won over by the gold of our mortal enemy, the minister Hugh Spencer, your brother Charles le Bel had just signed a treaty by which he surrenders you tomorrow to the vengeance of Edward II. You know what fate the hateful King of England has reserved for the spouse that has insulted him. As for me, this wound ought to tell you that they do not

83

intend to take me with you to England, and that they're in haste to inherit my earldom of Kent."

"And how are we to escape such a danger?"

"Only one means remains, and even that is very risky. It's necessary to flee tonight and try to reach Flanders. My faithful Harrys is waiting for me a short distance from Paris with fifteen or twenty armed Englishmen as devoted as he is. He took the initiative of assembling those brave men, whom fearful suspicion of your brother caused to lodge outside the walls of Paris. Once with them we're safe; we'll reach the court of the Comte de Hainaut without fear, where we can expect benevolence, aid and protection.

"Harrys had given me a guide to lead me through the streets of Paris to the place where the escort is waiting, but the wretch ran away at the sight of the assassins who attacked me."

As he finished speaking, the Earl of Kent turned to Henryot and asked him in French whether he knew the streets of Paris well enough to guide them rapidly and reliably to the road to Flanders. "I'll pay you well," he added.

"I don't need any recompense. I'll take you quickly and reliably, as you request."

"En route, then! And may God and Saint George aid us! You, Madame, go fetch your son and the richest of your jewels; I'll go saddle a hack, and two horses."

A few moments later, the Earl of Kent came back to announce that everything was ready. The Queen, who was carrying her son in her arms, followed him with Henryot, and all three of them set forth, at first slowly and with precaution, and then, shortly afterwards, at a gallop, at the top speed of their horses.

Day began to break when they had not yet begun to reduce the rapidity of their pace. Preoccupied by their chagrins or their perils, none of the three had proffered a word. As for the child, he continued to sleep profoundly.

The Queen was the first to interrupt the bleak silence. It was Henryot to whom she addressed herself.

"Now that we're on the right road and doubtless close to our escort, it would be prudent for you to retrace your steps, for if anyone knew that you had favored our escape, it might cost you your life."

"Life is no longer anything to me, Madame; I've lost forever that which could have made my happiness."

"So young and unhappy, without hope! How can that be?"

Briefly, Henryot recounted his sad amour for Marguerite. The story made a profound impression on the Queen. That modest and ingenuous tenderness was a bitter reproach for her, whom passion had led astray to the extent of rendering two kingdoms witness to her culpable affection for her husband's bother, Aymond, Earl of Kent.

And, her heart dolorously oppressed, she turned her tearful eyes to the man for love of whom she has lost repose, happiness, a throne, conscience and renown. She searched for some allegiance in the sight of that cherished lover...

Kent's lips were contracted by a mocking smile, and he jeered at Henryot for the extreme tenderness that had made him prefer to quit Marguerite for life rather than cause her the remorse and the shame of having fled her husband's roof.

On seeing the irony of his gaze and hearing the bitterness of his pleasantries, a frightful doubt took possession of the unfortunate Princess for the first time. She wondered if the Earl of Kent really loved her, whether the tenderness that had drawn his victim into so much shame and woe might not be a cold and ambitious calculation. Alas, she dared not deepen that dolorous examination; she turned her head in order not to see a sudden, horrible verity that was offered to her for the first time. Oh, she cruelly expiated then the sin that she had committed!

At that moment the travelers reached the escort that was waiting for them. The Queen gave Henryot a valuable ring, which she begged him to keep for love of her. The Earl of Kent took him gravely to one side. "Young man," he said, "in coming to our aid you have done more for us than you think. I do not believe it prudent as yet to tell you who we are; but if Our Lady and Saint George aid us and do not abandon us, you will remember this day."

With those words he rejoined the escort and Henryot took the road to Paris again.

In the epoch in which the events we are recounting occurred—in 1325—under the reign of King Charles IV, nicknamed le Bel because he was, one chronicler says, a man of commanding appearance and had a great appetite for amour. Painters limited themselves to a scrupulous, cold and gauche imitation of nature.

What is lacking most of all in the very small number of paintings made in that epoch is movement. None of the faces is animated; a glacial impassivity is spread over the regular features, perfect but soulless. The artist has tried to reproduce life, but death is imprinted everywhere; he has sought to make his subjects active, but they have remained stiff and compassed beneath his brush. Curbed, leaning forward, the gaze fixed and dull, one might think them figures of wax, which resemble death all the more because the artist has applied himself to imitating life, or those seated Egyptian statues, which, with their hands on their knees, sustain with their heads the slender shaft of a tall column.

In the fourteenth century, painters were only employed, most of the time, in the embellishment of manuscripts. In that sort of miniature, the patience and skill of the rubricator produce results that attained a truly marvelous point of perfection. When one leafs through the precious and rare volumes that remain to us from that epoch, one is astonished by the rich ornaments that extend over the margin, scintillating on the capital letters, surrounding them with a sort of gauze of gold and azure, extending between the two columns of the page and terminating in sharp *culs-de-lampe*. The most vivid colors are married there with tints that, although not as bright, nevertheless cast a sort of reflection that modern painting does not reproduce; finally, the dazzled gaze would be wounded by so much glare if it did not have for repose the spacious margins of a blank vellum.

Ordinarily, the artist puts at the head of each of the chapters a miniature that represents some pious subject or one related to the seigneur by whose orders he is confecting the manuscript. Sometimes, it is a saint whose head is surrounded by an aureole produced by a gilded layer that would be difficult to imitate now; or one sees a tourney, with its knights, its field-judges, its ladies, its banners and its lists. In other places, the rubricator has painted the author of the book; with both knees on the ground, he is presenting his work to a pope with a benign face, who is giving him his benediction with two fingers raised. There are some in which it is a suzerain with long straight hair with a short robe quartered with his arms and motto, receives the homage of scholastic labors while his fool, with a jay on his wrist in the guise of a falcon is standing behind the feudal armchair among the officers and varlets, of whom not one has been omitted.

But in the same way that the faces in the paintings lack life, the groups offer nothing picturesque or true, and the faces there are immobile and stupid. Finally, men-at-arms, châteaux, the sky and rivers, nothing is detached by the magic of perspective; all the objects are crowded together on the parchment, where they are stacked grotesquely.

A manuscript was a precious treasure. Sixty-five years after the time of which we speak, Charles VI only possessed six volumes in his library. A double lock prevented them from being opened, and when some sire of high lineage came to the King's court, he obtained the favor of seeing the precious volumes. He waxed ecstatic before the wooden cover surmounted by silver figures and enriched with topazes and emeralds. Then, on returning to his feudal manor, he recounted to his amazed chatelaine how a price of gold had been paid for the work of some obscure serf or monk, embellished by so many riches, which he, a noble and powerful seigneur, would have blushed at being unable to read.

The profession of rubricator was very lucrative, given that in the fourteenth century a man who knew how to read passed for a scholar, and it was only given to him after long and serious study to be able to trace with perfection the paintings of manuscripts.

A few moments after returning home, Henryot had sat down at a large table on which were disposed brushes, colors, little plates of copper and all the utensils necessary to his profession. But he tried to work in vain; the memory of the strange events that had happened to him since the previous day had taken possession of his imagination and held him plunged in the most profound reverie when the cries of a large crowd assembled outside his door finally extracted him from it. At the same moment, archers threw themselves upon him, bound him tightly, and he was taken to prison, in the midst of the insults and outrages of a furious population, who were calling him wretch and murderer.

And as the doors of the prison closed upon him, and he was dragged into a cell, they reopened with a great racket and a redoubling of the imprecations of the populace.

It was Marguerite who was being brought, her hands bound, unconscious in the arms of a man-at-arms.

For about three months the rubricator lay in the cell where he had been thrown, and no other human face was offered to his gaze but the sinister physiognomy of his jailer, a harsh man from whom he had never been able to obtain a word, nor had he discovered for what reason he had been deprived of his liberty. He formed a thousand conjectures on that subject without knowing on which to settle. If the stranger whose flight he had favored was the cause of his captivity, why had Marguerite been implicated in an affair in which she had played no part, even indirectly? Why those cries of the populace that still seemed to resound in his ears: Assassin! Murderer!

It was a labyrinth in which the imagination of the poor young man went astray, and the uncertainty that agitated him was perhaps a torture more atrocious to him than the cold cell in which he lay semi-naked on a little damp straw.

One morning, four men came in, and after having made sure scrupulously that his irons were in good condition, they took him away.

It was then the beautiful season of spring; the air was pure and mild, the sky luminous and blue. On emerging from the dark and noxious place where he had lain for such a long time, a delightful frisson ran through his limbs and warmed them. An indescribable wellbeing took possession of each of his faculties, and that sensation, entirely physical, made him forget his cruel chagrins momentarily, and the strange situation in which he found himself.

The voices of those surrounding him and the order to march forward soon rendered him entirely to the horror of his position.

They traversed several streets and conducted him into a vast hall where judges were gathered and a vast crowd of people. At Henryot's entrance a murmur of indignation spread through all the spectators, and redoubled when, at the sight of Marguerite, he uttered a heart-rending cry and tried to advance toward her.

He was made to sit down on a bench opposite the one where Marguerite was enchained.

The chief judge then said:

"Henryot Mahu, you are the murderer of Pierre de Maurepas, when alive a man-at-arms of the household of his Majesty the King of France. You have treasonously slain him at night, by ambush, in his own house, and dragged him outside with the aid of Marguerite Beaumin his wife, to whom you had given a rendezvous that night, with the aim of putting to death the said Maurepas. The King's justice, on having the cadaver removed, found not far away this hat, in the folds of which a tiny scroll of parchment was hidden containing the words: 'This evening, Henryot, when the curfew tolls, for the last time.' It is written by Marguerite, for she had foolishly been taught the science of writing, which only befits monks for reading and conserving the holy books, and men of law for interpreting them. It would have been more prudent to leave her in the sage ignorance that befits a woman raised in the fear of God and the observation of the duties of her estate.

"Henryot Mahu, what have you to respond?"

Overwhelmed by the weight of a terrible accusation, the fatal appearances of which did not permit him to justify himself, could only say, in a hoarse and inarticulate voice: "She is innocent."

"And you, Marguerite Beaumin?"

The young woman stood up and said: "Heaven is my witness that I am innocent, and Henryot also."

Cries of indignation rose up from all parts and prevented her from finishing. She sat down again calmly.

Henryot, recovered from his initial emotion, then tried to explain by what succession of events he found himself the victim of appearances, but the judge listened to him with an air of incredulity, and the spectators repeated in all directions: "They're guilty! It's necessary to avenge Pierre Maurepas, so wickedly slain!"

The judge got up to read the sentence; it condemned Henryot Mahu and Marguerite Beaumin as murders and adulterers: "to be punished in three manners, to wit: to be dragged on a hurdle, to the sound of trumpets, though the city from street to street, and then taken to the house of the said Marguerite Beaumin; in that place to be bound to a ladder so high that the everyone, short or tall, could see them; and a large fire would be made in the said place. When they were bound, their right and left hands would be cut off, their tongues torn out and their eyes punctured. After which, they would be thrown in the fire to burn, and after that their hearts would be taken from their bodies and thrown in the fire. After the said Henryot Mahu and Marguerite Beaumin had been thus dressed, their heads would be cut off and they would be cut into four quarters, and sent to the four best streets of the city of Paris."

The Hôtel Saint-Paul, when was also known as the "solemn house of great enjoyments," stood on the bank of the Seine not far from the place where the initial events of this chronicle were set. It was a large complex formed of numerous buildings bought at different times and which, in combination, formed a rather irregular whole.

In the remotest part of the Hôtel Saint-Paul was a large courtyard planted with trees, in the middle of which was a fountain; grilles carefully closed the windows overlooking that courtyard in order that the pigeons, pheasants and other birds nourished within the enclosure of the palace did not penetrate into the apartments, the rich tapestries of which they would have soiled.

It was at the extremity of that courtyard, in a sort of little turret, that King Charles le Bel was still sleeping profoundly and peacefully, although the rays of the midday sum had been reflected for some time on the thick curtains of gold brocade that enveloped the royal bed.

Suddenly, the sound of heavy and firm footsteps resonated on the marble flagstones of the antechamber, and although semi-stifled by the thick rush mats of the bedroom, they were heard approaching closer and closer, and stopping beside the king's bed.

"By my patron saint," the monarch demanded ill-humoredly, although he had recognized the grave march and dry cough of his cousin, Comte Philippe de Valois, "By Saint Charles, is it not given to me to sleep in peace? Are my chamberlains standing at my door, halberds in hand, only to leave me at the mercy of the first comer?"

"I am bringing Your Majesty news that will wake him up entirely now, and even prevent him from sleeping for more than one night," replied the Comte de Valois, with severity. "A messenger has arrived from Hainaut, which recounts matters not calculated for rejoicing. Messire Jean de Hainaut and his men-at-arms, on disembarking in England with the Queen, have found a good welcome among the barons of that country; the majority of them have immediately raised the banners for

91

the Queen. King Edward II and his minister Spencer have been besieged in Bristol, taken prisoner and bailed to the Seigneur de Berkley, who is keeping the former under close and faithful guard in his fortress. As for the other, he was decapitated immediately and unceremoniously. Finally, the Queen—which is to say her lover, the Earl of Kent, for she only does what he wishes—has been elected regent of the kingdom in replacement for the King, declared unworthy of the throne. Now, Earl Aymond of Kent bears in his left side the mark of the dagger of a man-at-arms of your household, and is proposing to make a pilgrimage to Notre-Dame de Paris, who has preserved him from such great peril. Thirty thousand pikes of thirty thousand men-at-arms will serve him as candles for that procession."

"And all that has been done without my having any suspicion of it?" demanded the King, pale and beside himself.

"Six weeks have sufficed that damned soul Jean de Hainaut; he disembarked in England on the twenty-fourth of December, and the act of dispossession of King Edward II, of which here is a copy, bears the date of the fourteenth of January."

The King made no response, and after a moment's silence, Philippe de Valois went on:

"And what forces will you oppose to such a terrible enemy, who has never forgiven? The finances are exhausted; you can put Lombards and tax-farmers to the torture, but they'll let themselves be flayed and hanged rather than let go of a single doubloon, as witness Gérard de Guette and many others.

"As for the aid of the great vassals and feudal subjects, it's necessary not to count on them. English gold has won the majority; as for the rest, they're too busy battling against one another to think of defending you.

"Nothing remains to you but the amity and intercession of your sister, who loves you in spite of your harsh and discourteous conduct in her regard. They will be lost to your forever today, for a man will soon be executed who, without knowing it, saved the life of her dear Aymond on the night when you had him assassinated to please Hugh Spencer. I've just heard what I'm telling you from a worthy priest, who has prepared the man to die and came to beg me to save an innocent man. Here, for proof, is a ring your sister Isabelle gave her liberator by way of thanks."

Then, on the King's demand, the Comte entered into the greatest detail, and told him what our readers have read at the beginning of this chronicle.

"There's still a means of obtaining an advantage from this," said the King, after a moment of reflection, "and accommodate this event to the mad ideas of my sister, so amorous of the marvelous. Help me, Philippe, and all will be for the best. Go and order that this man be taken to the church of Notre-Dame in an hour, to make honorable amends, and to be taken from there to execution."

The Comte looked at the monarch with astonishment, who repeated the order he had just given him.

"Do as you're commanded, cousin," he added, with more dignity than he usually showed. And to forestall the observations that Philippe de Valois was about to make, he summoned his chamberlains and gave them the order to dress him promptly.

At the moment when the confessor had entered the cell to prepare the patient for death, he had found him in the state of great depression produced by a great injustice and the presence of an inevitable disaster. But when he had heard Henryot's confession and the story of his adventures, the old priest had told him what important persons whose flight he had favored; when he had shown him an almost assured means of salvation, a means of proving his innocence and Marguerite's, a troubled and bitter joy took possession of the condemned man. A poignant anxiety produced within him an impatience and agitation that tended to delirium.

It was in that mental situation that he spent the rest of the day, all night and a part of the following morning.

Finally, the door of his cell opened; the old priest reappeared; his pallor and his tears announced that no more hope remained.

Then a sudden despair and a horrible rage gripped Henryot. He started pacing back and forth in his prison, striking his head against the wall, uttering frightful howls and bruising himself with his irons. Neither the friendly voice of the old priest nor the robust efforts of the hailer who came running in response to his cries could calm the furious man. It was only long afterwards that he fell, bloody and exhausted, at his confessor's feet.

"Oh, my son, my son!" the man of God said to him then, "if human justice strikes us wrongly, is not the justice of Heaven there to recompense us for our sufferings down here? Accept with resignation of crown of thorns of this world, in order to receive a better one, the crown of the blissful. Offer your torments to Jesus Christ in expiation of your sins."

"And her? What of her! What sin has she committed, whose purity equals the angels? And she's going to be torn apart before a crowd that will rejoice in every one of her screams, which will applaud every shred of flesh torn away by the executioner! Leave me alone! There's no justice either on earth or in Heaven!"

At that blasphemy, the saintly old man crossed himself devoutly, and promised a novena to Our Lady of Mercy if, by her powerful intercession, she contrived to distance Henryot from such a horrible despair.

"Oh, my child," he said, emotionally, "don't die a miscreant! Don't reject the divine palm that the angels are preparing for you. The virgins are preparing to celebrate your celestial hymen with Marguerite; they are unfolding the nuptial robe that will be purified by the martyrdom, by the martyrdom that will sanctify what your amour has of the terrestrial. Don't die thus! For your death would be, for me—for me who has sustained and consoled you—a subject of endless tears and despair."

"Oh, forgive me…forgive me, Father…but it's so frightful to think about! If I were dying alone…but her! Her…!"

The priest finally succeeded in rendering Henryot a little calm, and when the executioners came to fetch the unfortunate rubricator, they found him kneeling before the old priest, who was standing up, blessing him and weeping.

Following the custom of those barbaric times, the patient was thrown on to a hurdle and dragged thus, in the midst of the insults of the populace, to the church of Notre-Dame, where he was to make honorable amends.

An immense crowd filled the church and, contrary to custom, Henryot was taken into the choir, where a large black curtain was extended, as if to add to the lugubrious aspect of the tragic scene.

While Henryot was made to kneel down, that curtain was lifted, and Marguerite, ornamented as a bride, came to throw herself into her lover's arms, who fell unconscious.

When he came round, Marguerite was still there; she was still sustaining his head; richly clad individuals still surrounded him, as well as ladies of noble appearance, who were smiling and weeping at what they saw…

It was not a dream…no.

The King took in that scene the interest that the author of a mystery play takes in the representation of his work while the Brotherhood of the Passion perform it.

"Let's go, Messire Bishop," he finally said to a priest in pontifical garb. "Celebrate the marriage; the time has come.

"This is the dowry that we give with our royal hand to Marguerite, and here is another for Henryot Mahu. The latter is in the name of our cherished sister the Queen of England. For you should know that the said Henryot saved that beloved relative from the greatest peril, when our wrath had been treacherously excited against her.

"But such is the fate of princes of the earth," he continued, affecting a sigh, "that wicked advice too often causes them to march on false paths!

"Messire Robert d'Artois," he added, turning toward a young Prince placed to his left, "it is assuredly not from you that this villainous advice came; you have always spoken to us in favor of our sister; even the fear of our royal and redoubtable anger has not retained you. Tell all this to Isabelle, and how we have recompensed the brave and faithful Henryot. Here, return this ring to the groom, which has served us to uncover the mystery that nearly doomed this young fellow; let it be the nuptial ring; let a devoted servant of my sister take it from a devoted friend."

The marriage was celebrated, after which the monarch went away with his entire court. The populace, who had previously heaped poor Henryot with imprecations, carried him home in triumph, felling the scaffold on the way, jeering and nearly rending into pieces one of the judges who had condemned the innocent man the day before, whom curiosity had drawn to the window of his lodgings.

THE SHEPHERD'S CLOCK

In the southern casement of the church,
near the chapel of the crucifix,
a clock can be seen that excites
the admiration of the curious.
(Le Glay, *Research on the metropolitan
church of Cambrai*, ch. VII)[12]

I remember that in my childhood I was given for a maid a young Fleming named Tréa, who was cheerful, with big blue eyes, white teeth, and fresh and rosy cheeks. When Tréa appeared in her Sunday clothes, it was a genuine pleasure to see her, becoming and neat, with large pendants in her ears, her arms bare in accordance with Flanders custom, and her slightly plump waist designed by a very narrow corset, whose red color stood out over a blue woolen skirt with white stripes. On those days, she put coquetry into putting a shoe on a foot that did not lack smallness or elegance. So people asked, smiling, as they saw her pass by: "Who is that pretty creature leading a child by the hand?"

And in my vanity of a little boy of six years, I rejoiced, proud of the flattering attention given to my guide. Yes, the days when we went for a walk together were true feast days for me, awaited and calculated with impatience.

It is necessary to say more; to the attraction of my satisfied childish vanity a second was added, no less keen; every Sunday, the objective of our walk was the smoky room of an

---

[12] Joseph Le Glay (1785-1863) was a physician and antiquarian who became archivist of Cambrai in 1822 and the city's librarian four years later; Berthoud knew him well and was also a friend of his son Edward Le Glay (1814-1894), the author of a *Histoire des Comtes de Flandres* (1843).

old blind woman, the mother of a handsome boy of timid character, of whom Tréa was very fond. As soon as we arrived, there were two kisses for Tréa and some treat for me. I can still see the two lovers going hastily to sit in the embrasure of a window with little square panes, and drawing their two wicker chairs as close to one another as they could. They talked for a long time in low voices, forming endless projects, the kind of projects of which one dreams when one is young, and which a happy carelessness, a mild confidence in the future only surrounds with pure and delicate images by means of the imagination.

In the meantime, the old blind woman set about telling me some story. I shall live a long time yet and will still remember her gray hair, enclosed in a white headscarf, her dull and immobile eyes, her features full of amiability, her thin and suntanned arms emerging half-naked from beneath a big red kerchief.

She talked about marvelous apparitions, fantastic legends, infernal adventures and touching traditions. When she reached the point of the catastrophe she straightened her curbed stature; her thin voice took on a firmer one, and her two long hands rose into the air and fell back on her knees. Sitting in front of her on a little stool, I listened to her, motionless, hardly breathing, my eyes staring and my cheeks burning. When she stopped speaking, my chagrin became inexpressible, and I would have given anything in the world to hear her continue.

Among those curious legends, that of the Shepherd's Clock produced a particularly profound impression on me.

"My child," the good woman said to me, "there was once in Cambrai a beautiful church that can no longer be seen there now. Nothing as beautiful has ever been encountered. One could have spent an entire year—yes, an entire year—examining it, and there would still have been many things to see. But the most precious thing it contained—there was only one voice as to that, my child—was the clock, the clock that I often spent hours admiring when I was no bigger than you, when I went to school with my little basket under my arm and I had, alas, two good eyes.

"That beautiful clock was bigger—oh, much bigger—than my bedroom. It was like a little church with its profound portal and its pointed bell-tower. At the tip of the steeple there was an angel who, when the hour was about to chime, put his trumpet to his mouth and played a fanfare. Then the angel Gabriel, placed to the left of the clock, waved a lily branch, as if to say *Ave Maria* to the Holy Virgin, who was on the other side. She, kneeling on her prie-dieu, joined her hands and nodded her head, as if she were responding; 'The Lord's will be done.'

"Afterwards, the doors of two niches opened, on which death's-heads could be seen, and then a book whose pages turned of their own accord to allow devotional thoughts to be read. After which a marvelously soft and plaintive carillon started to ring, and one saw passing on a sort of little gallery the entire passion of Our Lord, from the moment when Judas betrayed him so villainously to the one when Jesus' head bowed and he rendered his soul to God the Father.

"The angel blew the trumpet again; then everything went back in, everything closed up, everything became motionless and silent.

"Is it not true, my child, that that was a spectacle worthy of admiration, of which you would have loved to be the witness?

"Now I shall tell you on what occasion the church of Notre-Dame de Cambrai was gratified with such a rich present.

"Many years ago, a Prince came to lay siege to Cambrai, but in spite of all his armies, in spite of the great wooden towers from which enormous stones, arrows and flaming torches sprang forth, he could do nothing against the town. A miraculous cloud extended around the walls, like a second rampart, and Our Lady and the angels appeared in the middle of that cloud and rejected the stones, the arrows and the flaming torches among the besiegers, where they caused great damage.

99

"The enemy Prince, furious at that miraculous protection, blasphemed hideously against the patron saint of Cambrai. He was punished for that in a terrible manner; he lost his sight. Then he humiliated himself beneath the hand that had struck him, lifted the siege, and promised that, if he could recover the usage of his eyes, he would give the church of Our Lady of Grace a golden crown in which his horse could easily turn.

"His repentance found grace with the mother of the Savior; his eyes were opened again, and he came to make honorable amends in the church, with a yellow wax candle in his hand. You can understand his joy, my child. Would you not have a great deal to complain about if, like mine, your eyes no longer saw anything but a dismal obscurity? No more lovely blue sky, no more clouds flying like birds, no more green trees, no more lowers of a thousand colors. Not daring to take a step without the fear of bumping into something, remaining sadly seated all day long...and then, no longer to see one's children! Night, night, always night! Oh, my little monsieur, one has a great deal to complain about, believe me, when one finds oneself blind!

"The Prince I am telling you about, in the transports of his delight, said aloud that he wanted to offer the church a second present as rare as the first was rich. At those words, a young shepherd from Rome emerged from the crowd, who said, boldly: 'I will make it. Give me a thousand écus, grant me fourteen years, and I will build you a clock of which people will talk everywhere as one of the seven wonders of the world. Yes, I make an oath on the salvation of my soul! It will be called the marvel of Cambrésis.'

"He was paid the thousand gold pieces; he worked day and night for fourteen years, and he made the beautiful clock that you know. After which he came to see Monseigneur the Bishop and said; 'Now I am going back to my homeland to join my poor and good mother, whom I have not embraced for fourteen years. I have enclosed in this staff the thousand gold pieces that I have received as a salary. God and the blessed virgin be praised. As long as my guardian angel protects my on the way, I shall bring back to the worthy woman enough to no longer fear poverty.'

"The Bishop of that time was not a God-fearing man. He said to himself: 'The shepherd is going away to other countries; he might perhaps fabricate another clock more marvelous than this one; ours would lose its renown, not to mention that pilgrims would no longer come to make their devotion in a town where they can be amazed before such pilgrims before such a unique miracle of art. He therefore tried to retain the savant shepherd in Cambrésis; but to each seductive promise the young man replied: 'All that is not worth as much as my aged mother.'

"'We'll send someone to fetch her for you,' the Bishop said.

"'Oh, no,' replied the shepherd. 'She'd die under your damp and cold sky. My mother lives in the beautiful city of Rome, and even if she could support the fatigue of such a journey, would she want to leave the city of the Pope, the Pope whose encounter every day is worth an indulgence to her?'

"The Bishop then wanted to have the shepherd arrested as a sorcerer and a heretic, but he feared seeing the townspeople revolt at such an indignity.

"He contented himself with sending bad men, with neither faith nor law, to wait for the shepherd as he left the town. The shepherd defended himself bravely, and they were only able to take possession of his staff, which contained the thousand gold pieces. 'I've become poor again,' he cried, after having escaped from their ferocious hands, but I still have my eyes and my fingers, and I'll be able to earn a thousand gold pieces a second time.'

"The evil Bishop, to whom the shepherd's words were reported, then made a resolution inspired by the Devil in person; he had the shepherd's eyes put out with a red hot iron, and the fingers were cut off both his hands.

"The poor young man died many years afterwards, wandering in the town of Cambrai, where he begged for his bread from door to door. He never saw either the papal city or his mother again."

At that moment I shivered at a slight sound; it was the farewell that Tréa was giving to her lover. The young woman stood up, took me by the hand, and we came back to the house. All night long, in my dreams, I heard the voice of the blind shepherd weeping and calling for his mother, and in the morning, when I woke up, I thought I saw a pale and mutilated phantom drawing away from my bed.

The clock on which that legend reposes was commenced in 1338 under the episcopacy of Guy de Collemède; it was finished in 1397. Pierre d'Ailly had it improved toward 1400 and it was restored again in 1542 and 1602. Finally, the mechanism of the clock was almost entirely renewed in 1765.

The dial indicated the days of the week, the succession of the months, the signs of the zodiac, the phases of the moon and the various aspects of the sun.

SIMON THE ACCURSED
Lord of Cagnicourt
1137

Guillaume de Cagnicourt made the plaint
that the eagle made in Julien's emblem:
"Was it necessary to produce plumage
to give velocity to the iron that has pierced my body?
Was it necessary to engender a child
to give me the death-blow?"
(Jean Le Carpentier,
History of Cambrai and Cambrésis,
Cagnicourt Family.)

The daughter of Monseigneur Guy, sire de Villers-Outreaux, had almost passed from life to death during an illness that had held her enfevered from the Sunday of Laetare to the feast of Pentecost.

The lovely Alix had only been brought back by dint of prayers and the vow sworn by her noble father to take the cross and go to the Holy Land to make war against the miscreants, conjointly with the King of France Louis VII.

This is the place to say, if I am not to be at fault, that the King of France had undertaken that crusade in order to expiate a profanation of holy places, having burned thirteen hundred people in a church during the sack of Vitry in Pertois.

The good God had mercy on the paternal dolor of the sire de Villers-Outreaux, and rendered Alix to his fervent intercessions.

When the fever of the adolescent had departed, the roses of health were seen to return to her cheeks instead of blanched thinness, the sire de Villers-Outreaux thought of fulfilling his enterprise in Christian loyalty. He sold to the sire de

Gonnelieu, in exchange for a large sum, the beautiful wood of twenty muids that he had near his château, and in the middle of which was the farm of Revelon. He reserved, however one muid, of which he made a gift to the Abbaye de Vaucelles.

With that large sum, which was the equivalent of about half his patrimony, Monseigneur Guy armed eight men-at-arms suitably and confided his daughter to the old chaplain Pierre Beaumetz, a man of saintly renown and faithful to any proof. After that he departed to go to join the King of France, not without turning his tearful eyes more than once toward the towers of his domain and not without saying internally, with hash anguish: *Adieu forever; alas, never to see my lovely little Alix again! Alas, never to see again the place where the relics of my ancestors lie in peace!*

Monseigneur Guy de Villers-Outreaux had already been a crusader for four years, and no one knew anything yet about the good or ill fortune that had overtaken the old knight.

Meanwhile, things had not gone well in his castellany. Among the neighboring lords there were some who pillaged, shamelessly and gradually, the domains of an absentee and an orphan—or, at least the equivalent thereof.

The chaplain protested loudly to Monseigneur Alard; the good prelate of Cambrai swore to chastise the felons as was their due, but old age can make sage designs without the arm being able to put them into execution, and taking no notice of the admonitions of the Bishop, the pillaging castellans continued nevertheless to take from Alix's domain everything that they pleased. Now, almost everything pleased them.

Despairing of keeping for his lord the little that remained to him of his castellany, the chaplain resolved to put Alix under the protection of the loyal and powerful Guillaume, sire de Cagnicourt, an old friend and brother-in-arms of the sire de Villers-Outreaux.

Guillaume de Cagnicourt, after having made war for some time in the company of sovereign emperor Frederick I, had returned to Cambrésis less than a month before; otherwise, the chaplain would not have expected to wait until then to have recourse to such a protector.

One morning, therefore, Pierre Beaumetz arrived at the Château de Cagnicourt and implored Monseigneur Guillaume to come to the aid of the daughter of his former brother-in-arms. At the priest's first words, the brave sire, moved to compassion, ordered him to bring the young forsaken orphan to the Château de Cagnicourt immediately.

"For the salvation of my soul," he swore, "I shall make sure that the domains of a crusader are not ravaged thus, and I shall put the point of my sword so forcefully to the throat of these pillagers that they will cough up in full what they have devoured in detail.

"Go fetch your demoiselle, good and worthy priest. Our virtuous and sapient spouse Isabelle de Béthencourt will educate her as befits a daughter of high rank whose father is fighting in the Holy Land. May I be deemed a coward and an oath-breaker if I do not treat her as well as I would my own daughter!"

Chaplain Pierre Beaumetz, understandably joyful, went swiftly to give this good news to his good lady, who set out immediately for Cagnicourt, so anxious was she to find herself in a safe and decorous place.

She was riding gracefully on a white hack, with her veil raised, as much because of the hat as in order to listen better to the wise words and prudent admonitions of the chaplain relative to the conduct it as appropriate to maintain in the manor of Cagnicourt, when two men suddenly appeared at the end of the causeway.

As a well-educated damoiselle, Alix de Villers-Outreaux lowered her veil and covered her face.

The two strangers stopped short in order to watch them pass at their ease. One of them, still young, appeared to be of high lineage, to judge by his silver spurs, and of irregular mores to judge by his drink-reddened face. The other wore the livery of a hunter

Not content with that insult, they set about speaking discourteous words, such as wine puts on the lips, in loud voices.

The chaplain reprimanded them, as befit and old man and a priest.

In spite of the fact that Pierre Beaumetz had done so mildly and without wishing to offend, the face of the young man went red with anger, and the hunter demanded to know since when had uncouth clerics taken to preaching on the highway to seigneurs of noble rank.

The chaplain judged it necessary to end the dangerous conversation as rapidly as possible, and spurred his horse in order to continue his route.

"Corbleu!" said the hunter, then. "If I were a sire of high lineage, that girl wouldn't go away without paying the ransom of a kiss on the lips."

It did not require as much to excite his brutal master. To seize the bridle of the hack and swearing that neither the lady nor the priest would take another step without being ransomed at the price demanded was the affair of a moment, and he set about taking the unseemly ransom by force.

Alix uttered screams of terror.

The chaplain tried to come to her aid and leapt off his horse, but his foot caught in the stirrup and his aggressor, giving the frightened animal a mighty stroke of the whip, sent it galloping across the fields.

The plaints of Pierre Beaumetz were audible for a few moments; after that, nothing was heard but the gallop of the horse and the dull sound of the cadaver bumping continually against a stone or a tree.

Alix had fallen unconscious in the young sire's arms; he contemplated her with sparkling eyes and then carried her off the road, aided by his hunter, who was manifesting an execrable joy.

Damoiselle Alix's vassals, having learned of her abrupt departure, had wanted to see the good and tender mistress who had so often aided them in their misery one last time; they assembled to escort her as befit a noble lady, and set off diligently in order to catch up with her before her arrival at the manor of Cagnicourt.

Imagine what they experienced at the sight of the chaplain lying in shreds in the middle of the road.

While they were gazing at the piteous spectacle in a silence of terror and despair they heard feeble stifled cries. It was the voice of demoiselle Alix.

They ran in the direction from which the cries were coming. At the sight of the crowd, two men remounted the horses and take flight, leaving poor Alix de Villers-Outreaux there, bruised and dishonored.

While a few men set off in pursuit of the guilty men, the rest hasten around her; they lavish cares upon her; she opens her eyes, pronounces the name of the Holy Virgin, utters a great sigh and renders her soul.

"Vengeance! Come on! Come on! Let them be slain!" Such are the clamors that rise up on all sides; some run to fetch weapons, others join those who are already pursuing the murderers.

On the way they encountered one of those whose horse had fallen. "I know those who have wickedly kill out mistress and the chaplain," he shouted at a distance as he saw them coming.

"Say! Say! Let them be slain!" they repeated from all sides.

"It's young Simon de Cagnicourt and his infernal hunter Amalric."

"Let them be slain! Let them be slain!" To the Château de Cagnicourt!"

Those cries of vengeance reached the culpable individuals, who, pale and half-dead with fear, only opposed flight to the small number of peasants who had caught up with them, covering them with mud and throwing stones at them.

They escaped them in the end toward nightfall and reached the Château de Cagnicourt, of which they had the drawbridge lowered and the portcullis closed immediately.

Surprised by the clamors that he heard around his manor, Monseigneur Guillaume went up on to the rampart and enquired as to where such a mob had come from.

He learned only too quickly at the sight of cadavers carried on a stretcher by men carrying torches, as if to excite vengeance more effectively by displaying Simon's two victims.

Monseigneur Guillaume, stricken by a mortal dolor, had the drawbridge lowered, and bareheaded and unarmed, as pale as a corpse, advanced among the men of Villers-Outreaux. Each of them, at the sight of him, fell back to open a route and maintained a profound silence.

The unfortunate father had great difficulty forming his words, which were interrupted more than once by bitter sobs.

"He has committed a great crime; I shall punish him, oath of a knight! Yes, justice will be done, exemplary and satisfying justice. Depart, worthy people, and leave me to act."

Then Monseigneur Guillaume went back into his manor, and the people of Villers-Outreaux went away in procession, carrying the two cadavers and reciting prayers for the repose of their souls. No one had any doubt that the honest Seigneur Guillaume would keep his promise faithfully, and that he would punish his son as was his due. Monseigneur Guillaume had never told a lie in his life, and he was also known to be as severe an administrator of justice for veritable crimes as he was merciful to venial faults.

Monseigneur Guillaume, having gone back into the manor through the postern, had his son summoned. On the advice of his hunter, Simon, in order to put on a brave face and to numb himself with regard to his recent actions, had drunk a large bottrine of wine.

Amalric followed him, and hid behind a stout pillar.

Monseigneur Guillaume maintained silence for a moment; then, extending his arms, he said in a low and solemn tone:

"Murderer and oath-breaker, coward who only has valor for slaying priests and raping women, who flees like a veritable coward before a mob of peasants, take off your knight's spurs, have your head shaved and retire to a convent of austere rule, to spend the rest of your days in penitence. I make you a gift of all my property at the Abbaye de Vaucelles, in order that you can recite prayers night and day with the intention of demoiselle Alix and her chaplain. Go; I give you my malediction in this world and the next."

Emboldened by drunkenness, Simon marched toward his father and said to him, boldly: "You will do nothing."

The old man, irritated by such effrontery, struck Simon's face violently with his gauntlet.

Beside himself, the young man drew his dagger and delivered an ill-assured thrust. Monseigneur Guillaume fell nevertheless, although not dangerously wounded.

But he was not yet on the ground before the hunter Amalric leapt forward with a single bound and split his skull with a blow of an ax. Then, leaning on the bloody weapon, he asked: "Now what do we do, Sire de Cagnicourt?"

Simon thought he was struggling in a horrible dream.

"The night is black," the hunter continued. "No one, except one sentinel of whom I will take charge, has seen your father reenter. Let's go throw this carrion in the external ditch, and tomorrow, we'll say that it was the men of Villers-Outreaux who have killed him."

"Let's do that, let's do that," replied Simon, with a stupid expression.

Amalric loaded the cadaver on to his shoulders, and Simon followed him.

They crossed the first bridge, from which Amalric had taken care to send away the sentinel, and when they arrived close to the gulf underneath the second drawbridge they threw the cadaver into the water.

But instead of sinking, Monseigneur Guillaume's body remained upright, his arms extended, as if he were cursing his son again.

Simon wanted to flee and launched himself on to the bridge, but scarcely had he crossed it than, without understanding how it had happened, he found himself on the edge of the pavement before the terrible cadaver.

The same thing happened at each of his numerous attempts.

When day broke, he was found, pale, his hair standing on end, fixing his haggard eyes on the cadaver of his father, who was still cursing him.

Everyone fled the château at the sight of that terrible marvel, and it remained uninhabited for two hundred years.

Long after the events contained in that veridical legend, when it was scarcely remembered, the castellany of Cagnicourt fell by succession to sire Jacques Le Baudoin de Villers, hereditary chamberlain of Cambrésis. Curious to know what basis there was to the tales that were told about the abandoned manor, he went into it in the company of the prior of the Abbaye de Vaucelles.

They saw very distinctly, in the middle of a pond that had almost become a marsh, the skeleton of a man standing upright, holding his arms extended.

From the height of the rampart another skeleton seemed to be considering it in an attitude of distress.

The prior of Vaucelles recited prayer for the repose of the soul of Monseigneur Guillaume de Cagnicourt. After that he sprinkled the two skeletons with holy water.

They fell into dust.

GILES THE HIDEOUS
Seigneur de Marcoing
1338

Assuredly, the poor devil said to me, it is not difficult
for you to remain virtuous, you who are young, noble,
handsome, rich and likeable. Take my beggar's wallet,
my hump, my sixty years and my hunger, and we'll see
in a while whether you'll be as honest as me.
(Maître Haller,[13] plea in favor of a man accused of theft).

*Confiteor... quia peccavi... Verbo et opre, mea culpa,
mea culpa, mea maxima culpa. Ideo precor.
(Confiteor.)*

The evening office in the cathedral church of Cambrai
had finished a long time ago. The religious chants and the confused buzz of the departure of the multitude had been succeeded by the most profound silence. Only the footsteps of
one of the faithful emerging from the confessional could be
heard from time to time, brushing the marble pave of the nave
like a whisper and gradually dying away beneath the profound
arcades of the vast edifice.

The dead silence of the Christian temple borrowed,
moreover, something lugubrious from the great obscurity that
reigned among its ogival vaults and its heavy columns, stout
and squat. One scarcely saw the reflection of the ruddy flame
of a dying lamp gleaming on the golden feet of some statuette
of the blessed, or the vacillating reflection of a lantern that an

---

[13] Presumably the Swiss jurist Karl Ludwig von Haller (1768-
1854).

old sacristan was parading from chapel to chapel designing a yellow and indecisive angle on the flagstones.

It was the eve of Pentecost, and the church had been left open to the faithful later than was customary, in order that they could approach the sacrament of penitence, but numerous patrols were circulating around the edifice, and a contingent of men-at-arms, spears in hand, were on guard at the portal. Such precautions were necessary to prevent the townspeople, always ready to revolt against the bishop, from taking possession of the Episcopal château by means of a surprise attack.

The last person that Monseigneur Guy d'Auvergnac believed to be in the church finally came out; it was none less than the respectable wife of the town treasurer, Messire Eustache Panseron. She had murmured at length into the ear of the good bishop a list of sins of which the worst were doubtless some petty slanders that the worthy treasurer's wife did not believe to be false. Duly sermonized and absolved, she was going away contrite with a repentance that would not prevail for long against the force of habit.

Finally liberated from such rude labor, the prelate was preparing to return to his palace, and had already started to recite a final prayer, when a man of tall stature—whom Guy d'Auvergnac had not perceived until then because he was standing with his back to a column enveloped in a large cloak—approached abruptly.

"Worthy fellow," the prelate said to him, mopping his sweat-covered brow, "we're too tired to hear you in confession today; come back tomorrow."

The stranger replied in a strong and vehement voice; "I can't wait another moment. If I die without confession, I'm damned. May my damnation fall back on you!"

A vague terror took possession of the man of God, but he calmed himself with a mental prayer, sat down resignedly in the confessional, and made the stranger a sign to commence.

"I am Giles de Marcoing, Giles the Hideous," the stranger murmured, without kneeling down. My mother died on the day of my birth; my father gave me, three months

112

thereafter, a pitiless stepmother. No one, therefore, ever loved Giles the Hideous, for his repulsive appearance made those whom his miseries might have moved to pity turn their heads away.

"My brothers were handsome; they were the children of a second bed, and, in consequence, my father only had tenderness for them and aversion for me, paltry and deformed. Neglected by him, maltreated by his wife, outraged by her children, turned to derision by my own family's varlets—that is how lived until the age of twenty, desiccated by anguish and despair, damaged, burning a with thirst for vengeance.

"Eventually my father died. Without mercy, I threw his widow and her children out of my domain personally. After that I made all those who had become my vassals expiate harshly the cruel derisions of before; my gibbets were covered in cadavers. My extortions brought need and tears into my eight villages, Marcoing, Villers-Plouich, Paluisel, Pronville, Brebières, Flesquières, Mésengarbe and Rouveroy. How many of the young women who once mocked my red hair, my haggard eyes and my sharp teeth I have made to enter my bed by force! Several have died of it. Well, I was unable to change my insupportable nickname. I believed that they would call me, like Simon de Cagnicourt, the Pitiless or the Accursed, but no! Always the Hideous; always, always Giles the Hideous.

"One day it was announced to me be a herald-of-arms that a tourney was to be held a few days hence in the vicinity of Cambrai; it was the young nephew of Bishop Pierre de Mirepoix, Hugues de Levis, the only son of Maréchal de la Foi, who was assembling five hundred knights for breaking lances in honor of ladies.

"At that news, a thousand merry thoughts, pleasant and unfamiliar, came to refresh my blood. 'I'll go!' I cried. 'Yes. I'll go. My armor will be magnificent, and I'll keep my visor constantly lowered. Oh, if I could perform prowesses! If I could hear good wishes formed from all directions for the unknown night! If I could perceive young woman smiling at me! If I could hear mention of me with praise and benevolence!'

113

"If I were to be fortune enough for things to happen in that fashion, I would not say that I was Giles de Marcoing. I would disappear when the heralds came to proclaim the victor; I would be called and sought in vain; but when I reappeared at other tourneys people would cry: 'There's the unknown knight! There's the knight who flees triumphs as others seek them!' And perhaps some lady of rare beauty and high lineage, deceived by the attraction of the mystery with which I would be surrounded, would take a vague and tender interest in me; perhaps her heart would beat faster with emotion when I encountered my adversary in the arena, and when the swirls of dust did not allow her to see which of two would be lying in the arena.

"The day of the tourney came; it came and twelve knights fell, disarmed by me. Messire Le Borge de Mauny, the rude jouster who had just maltreated so badly young Hugues de Levis that he died of it subsequently, yes, Messire Le Borge de Mauny, found me unshakable in my stirrups, and was tipped over by my lance all the way to his horse's rump.

"Never had I struck a blow so rude! Oh, that was because I saw curls of fine black hair escaping from his helmet, it was because people had clapped their hands when he had raised his visor on his entry into the arena and displayed his mild, pure and charming features.

"I was proclaimed the best performer of the day The clamors of the heralds, the cries of joy, the enthusiasm of an entire crowd, the ladies who saluted me while waving their scarves and applauding me with their delicate hands, the knights who surrounded me, congratulating me, shaking my hand—all of that stunned me, troubled me and intoxicated me.

"I no longer knew what I was doing…a thousand different sensations swelled my chest, took away the use of my reason…I allowed myself to be dragged to the feet of the queen of the fête, Mahaut d'Apremont, the fiancée of sire Georges de Quiévraing. My visor was raised...

"Mahaut fell in a faint at my hideous aspect, and a cry of horror and disgust went up from all direction, and then execrable bursts of laughter.

"In an inexpressible despair, I launched myself on to my steed and went to hide in my castellany of Marcoing.

"Would you believe it? The image of that pale woman, fainting at the sight of my hideous features, the image of that woman only reopening her eyes to turn them away in terror, yes, that image no longer quit my imagination; it intoxicated me with a cruel sensuality, a bizarre ecstasy, a mixture of despair and amour. A bitter fire was consuming me; I roared, prey to insensate desires and transports of rage; I wept, I prayed to God, I blasphemed! Oh, what sufferings were mine!

"To see her, to see her once again, and die! That idea did not quit me. On the day of the wedding I put on the clothes of a varlet, I put a dagger in my belt; with my face covered by my cloak and after having prowled around the manor of Quiévraing for a long time, I succeeded, at nightfall, in penetrating as far as the nuptial chamber; the disorder of the celebrations served me in that. I hid behind great brocade curtains. *When the guests bring the newlyweds*, I said to myself, *it will be easy for me to slip out without being recognized. I shall have seen her one last time, and I shall die less unhappy*.

"But a magical power enchained me to the place where I was hiding. They remained alone. They exchanged words of love; they said delirious things; I heard their lips meet…and then I launched myself forward, furiously…

"After that, I don't know what happened. I only remember having struck two blows with my dagger, and finding myself the following day in my domain of Marcoing.

"What had happened to me the day before seemed to be a bad dream; I could not believe it. A summons to appear before the bishop, my suzerain, informed me only too clearly of the reality of my crime: Godefroi d'Apremont had accused me before Monseigneur Pierre de Mirepoix of having wickedly and treacherously killed his brother-in-law the sire de Quiévraing and his own sister Mahaut d'Apremont.

"My first impulse was to refuse to obey the bishop's summons; but, held in horror by all my vassals, who among them would have wanted to defend me even if a bull would not have struck with excommunication anyone who opposed resistance to the bishop's orders? I therefore followed the prelate's provost and his numerous men-at-arms with apparent docility.

"As you can imagine, what I suffered on the way is not something that human words can describe.

"The fate that unfailingly awaited me held me breathless with horror and despair. My head shaved, my escutcheon broken and covered with mud, heralds who proclaimed me a villain, my head cut off by the executioner, my cadaver on the gibbet! The hairs still stand up on my head when I think about it.

"And no compassion, no pity. Who would cry mercy? Who would even say: 'Poor young man,' on seeing Giles de Marcoing, the murderer, the Hideous, led to the scaffold? Doubtless people would be moved to pity by the sad end of a young sire with a handsome face, with long black hair, even if he had, as I had, slain in a jealous rage a rival and mistress! But Giles the Hideous? 'To the scaffold! To the scaffold! The monster! Well done!' Yes, that is how they would have been moved to pity by my fate!

"You know the rest. I appeared before the bishop. Sire d'Apremont's accusation only reposed on vague indications. I was about to be sent away absolved, and I was already making a vow to Our Lady to give the holy church all my domains and retire to some austere convent where I would spend the rest of my life in hard penitence—alas, she too turned her head in order not to listen to me, and perhaps it was in horror of my ugly face and hoarse and ill-sounding voice.

"'I demand the judgment of God!' cried the Sire d'Apremont.

"'What you demand is granted to you,' replied the Bishop, after having consulted the peers of Cambrésis.

"And the day of the combat was designated for a week hence.

"If you knew what it is to go to an arena, when one dare not invoke either the Holy Virgin, nor one's good angel, nor one's patron saint, because one is going to fight for a bad cause! In order not to become guilty of a further crime, I had formed the design to allow myself to be struck by d'Apremont, without assailing him with my battle-ax, without opposing my shield to the cutting edge of his. I would let one and the other fall, as if by fortuitous ill-fortune and the disfavor of fate. Slain by a single blow, I would have been spared the anguish of a dolorous death, and the humiliation of hearing my crime proclaimed in a loud voice. Perhaps also, I said to myself, Our Lord Jesus Christ would take that voluntary and expiatory death into account in his mercy and for the remission of my sins.

"But when I advanced into the arena to swear an oath on the Gospel that I was not bearing either any enchanted weapon or any talisman, it was necessary to raise my visor. My face had its effect, and from all directions people shouted jeers and insults 'Down with Giles the Hideous!' A rage that I cannot describe troubled my reason; it changed my good thoughts into a thirst for blood. The heralds had scarcely cried 'Begin!' than the Sire d'Apremont rendered his soul, his head broken by an ax-blow.

"Then I felt myself shiver with a fiery joy and a heretical delirium.

"I had triumphed, and I was the guilty party. *The executioner will suspend the cadaver of the innocent from the gibbet; there is no God, there is no Hell!* I said to myself. And I laughed, and I went back to my domain without thanking God for my victory and repeating: 'There is no Hell, for there is no God; I will therefore not be damned.'

"For fifteen years I have not set foot in a church once, observing neither vigils nor fasts, cursing with a glad heart, laughing at oaths sworn on relics and delivering myself to all sorts of evil actions; for I said to myself in memory of the

117

judgment of the God of Cambrai: 'There is no God, nor any Hell.'

"Alas, I have learned only too well, in the last month, how insensate such blasphemies were.

"Three phantoms never quit me, day or night.

"They hold one another by the hand; they circle around me incessantly.

"One of them has a bloody head, each of the other two a large wound in the breast. They laugh in bursts, they exchange mocking glances between them that they then direct at me; and then they cry out, as they recommence their execrable dance: 'He will not be damned! He will not be damned!'

"They quit me for the first time since then when I entered the church. Ensure Monseigneur, ensure that I do not fall back into their power, and I promise to give all my property to the church; I promise you to go barefoot to the Holy Land if necessary; but do not let me fall back into their power—oh, no!"

Bishop Guy d'Auvergne dared not give absolution to such a great sinner. He engaged him, however, not to despair of divine mercy, and enjoined him to come back in two days in order that he would be able to reflect maturely as to what remedies it was necessary to bring to a soul sick in that fashion, whose salvation appeared so desperate."

But Giles the Hideous never reappeared at the church of Our Lady or the manor of Marcoing.

He was robbed and slain by thieves as he was returning to his domain.

Peasants found his cadaver the following day, stabbed by two dagger-blows, with his head broken by a battle-ax.

Day began to break during that encounter, and the good people thought they saw three phantoms disappearing, and heard voices repeating ironically: "Oh, there is no Hell! Oh, you will not be damned!"

THE *DE PROFUNDIS*

Manuscript of an old Monk
1343

"If I live I shall pray for you,"
Those were your last words;
Alas, alas!
I never hear your prayers;
I listen, but you are not praying.
(Casimir Delavigne, *The Soul in Purgatory*.)[14]

At the commencement of every endeavor, every Christian ought to invoke the name of the Lord, without whose mercy nothing can be brought to a successful conclusion.

And as we, humble sinners, can obtain nothing from God, except by the intercession and merits of the holy Virgin Mary, the immaculate mother of the savior of the world, I intend to commence the veridical history you are about to read by presenting to that celestial queen the august salutation that the angel Gabriel brought her from the heights of Heaven: *Ave Maria*; begging and imploring all those who see the present book to recite that prayer, in order better to understand the great information and good examples contained herein.

My name is Raoul Beaugenin, presently in religion, in the order of Minims, under that of Père Berthe. I am the legitimate son of Bartholomé de Beaugenin, vassal and squire of the noble and powerful Seigneur Enguerrand Le Portier, Sire

---

[14] The poet Casimir Delavigne (1793-1843) became enormously successful following the publication of the impassioned patriotic poems he published after the Battle of Waterloo; he subsequently became the royal librarian. "L'Âme du Purgatoire" was published in the *Revue de Paris* in 1829.

de Marigny, treasurer of the King of France. My very honored mother Anne-Marguerite Bonvouloir, brought me up in dread of sin and the love of God, until the age of sixteen.

Now, one evening, after having recited the prayers of my rosary, I had just requested her blessing on my knees, when she started weeping bitterly and hugging me for a long time to her bosom, agitated by a great emotion. Finally, through many sobs and lamentation, he told me that Sire Enguerrand, for love of my father, was sending me in the quality of page to the house of his brother, Monseigneur Philippe de Marigny, bishop of Cambrai in Cambrésis.

"He is," she said, "a venerable prelate, and you will find in his house edification and good examples. Now then, dear child," she added, redoubling her tears, "hold yourself ready tomorrow, after having heard a mass in honor of Saint Julien, patron of travelers, to depart under the escort of Messire Jacques Marly, canon of the chapter of Our Lady of Mercy. That worthy priest has been sent to our suzerain by the prelate of Cambrai, and is returning, after having terminated affairs of great importance to everyone's satisfaction."

For myself, I was weeping too, for the sight of my mother's sadness had afflicted me. But a childish merriment soon brought me consolation. Nevertheless, I scarcely slept, turning in a hundred fashions in my bed. I was breathless with joy merely in thinking of making such a long journey riding a fine hack.

So, I was the first one standing when the hour sounded for the mass said with my intention. Afterwards, I soon perceived that I was not the only one who had spent a sleepless night, for no one ever saw a woman paler and more mournful than my mother. Without proffering a word, so heartsick was she, she put around my neck a reliquary on beautiful golden chain, containing a fragment of the true cross, and then she hugged me in her tremulous arms. Suddenly, she let herself become inert, her head on my shoulder.

Finally, my father, who was standing there, trying to be firm—although, in spite of his efforts, large tears were flowing down his cheeks into his beard—recommended me in an emotional voice to be a good Christian, devoted to the Holy Virgin and loyal to my new sovereign. After that, he gave me his blessing, and it was necessary to extract me from my mother's arms. I departed in an indescribable sadness and bitterness. Alas, an anguish far more poignant would have squeezed my heart if it had been given to me to foresee events to come: if I had known that my father would be struck by death defending his master Sire Enguerrand; if I had been told that my mother would die suddenly of the grief.

After a month of risky travel, during which we were fortunate to have twelve of the King of France's men-at-arms riding before and after Messire Jacques Marly's litter, we arrived at Monseigneur Philippe de Marigny's Episcopal manor on the eleventh day of the month of May in the thirteen hundred and twelfth year of the world's salvation.

Monseigneur Philippe was a charitable and pacific prelate, who had set his heart on reestablishing peace between messires the canons and the townspeople—which was not, truth to tell, an easy thing, for the people of Cambrai, proud and jealous of their franchises, rioted continually under the pretext of defending them; and for their part, the canons, seeing those franchises with envy, never wearied of contesting their rights and privileges.

While discord and contention were thus seen to rein in the town, peace and honor took refuge in the Episcopal manor. How could they not be brought there by the angel of bounty and grace who had made her abode there, the beautiful and pious Berthe de Marigny, the prelate's young sister? A coarse manual laborer or a brutal mercenary would have felt a desire for courtesy at the sight of her welcoming smile and her pensive expression; and even had they been as hard of heart as the enemy of humankind—God preserve me from his ambushes!—and deprived of the light of Heaven, it would have been necessary for them to yield to the soft speech of her suave voice.

For myself, when I saw her, I stood motionless, as if dazzled by such marvelous beauty. A week later, I made a vow to the Holy Virgin never to love any other lady. However, I knew only too well that I would never be permitted to confess my respectful tenderness, much less to think of obtaining any in return.

Three years when by rapidly for me, in a kind of sad and ineffable happiness, for Madame Berthe had taken me in affection. She was kind enough to praise my zeal; she sometimes cited me as an example to the other pages. She was far from having any suspicion of the motive that made me act. Nevertheless, a benevolent word from her, such as "handsome page" or "faithful varlet," caused me to shiver with a frisson that I cannot express, and caused me as much joy as pain. I surprised myself by repeating it aloud. While I was at prayer, she caused me a sin of distraction.

Alas, today, when I am ninety-one years old, that memory still causes me a great disturbance, and causes tears to flow from my desiccated eyes.

In the times of Bishop Guy de Collemède, there had arisen between him and Robert, Comte d'Artois, a grave difference on the subject of a jurisdiction that the officers of the comté arrogated over the villages situated between the two towns of Cambrai and Arras. Belatedly convinced of the injustice of his pretentions, the Comte d'Artois had renounced it. But when he was dead, his widow, Comtesse Mahaud, revived that iniquitous quarrel and had the lands of Cambrésis within easy range of Artois ravaged by her men-at-arms. It was necessary to use reprisals; endless wars ensued, which cost many lives.

As Bishop Philippe was greatly afflicted by such a state of affairs, he proposed to his enemy that they resort to the arbitration of the King of France. In that, he gave proof of a rare prudence, because the Comtesse Mahaud, being a vassal of the monarch, could not refuse the arbitration of the prince; then, when a sentence was rendered, she would be obliged to submit to it or incur the wrath of a powerful suzerain. Now, convinced of the evidence of his right, Monsieur Philippe had no doubt that the decision of the King of France would be favorable to him; thus the war would be infallibly terminated and there would be an end to the unjust pretentions of the Artesian Comtesse.

It was his own brother, Prince Charles de Valois, whom the King of France chose to arbitrate in the dispute.[15] Monseigneur Charles de Valois thus arrived in Cambrai on the twenty-eighth day of the month of May in the year thirteen hundred and thirteen.

The first days were spent in feasting and hunting, but soon, the Prince, who had initially seemed so ardent for those pleasures, began to make eulogies to repose and retreat, which the prized above all if it was necessary to believe him. Men-at-arms had sounded the trumpet, dogs barked and hunting-horns delivered fanfares in vain; he paid no heed to them at all.

In the morning he was seen to arrive in Madame Berthe's oratory, and always with some rare gift to offer her; sometimes it was a popinjay that talked and laughed in bursts like an old woman; sometimes it was some rare flower bought at a great price, or one of those rich knickknacks opened by long and difficult work.

Those gifts, at which Madame Berthe never failed to marvel, were seen to be followed by gallant words that were prolonged considerably. As the objects came from France, Italy or Germany, the Prince de Valois took the opportunity therefrom to narrate the travels he had made in those distant lands.

---

[15] Charles de Valois (1270-1325), the third son of Philippe III and younger brother of Philippe de Bel, quarreled with the latter's chamberlain, Enguerrand de Marigny (1260-1315) in 1311 and pursued a relentless vendetta against him thereafter, eventually framing him with various false charges and having him executed for sorcery, following an evil example set by his brother's destruction of the Templars.

He never said anything about the high destiny that he would infallibly have had in the last-named country, without the scheming of Pope Boniface; for, on the assassination of the Emperor Albert, killed near Reinfeld by the Duke of Swabia, the electors wanted to give the crown to the Duke de Valois, but the pope made sure that nothing came of it. In that he was following his hatred against the King of France, with whom he had had grave quarrels.

In spite of his modest silence with regard to the above, however, the name of Germany pronounced by Monseigneur Charles gave sufficient pause for thought, and caused to shine on his person a reflection of illustrious misfortune that moved Madame Berthe to a respectful commiseration.

"Oh," he said, "how I would like now to spend my life in these peaceful and pleasant lands, far from grandeurs that are heavy and tormenting. Will it never be given to me to have no other care that to obtain, by dint of submission and amour, a smile such as you sometimes form?"

And Madame Berthe, moved, formed a smile that filled me with despair, and lowered her eyelids in order to hide the disturbance in her gaze.

Gradually, with the Prince arrived, Madame Berthe acquired the habit of sending her pages and ladies of the bedchamber to the antechamber. She had, according to her, important affairs on the subject of peace to disentangle with Prince Charles. She therefore remained alone with him, and many a time when the hour or supper sounded, it was necessary to warn them that Monseigneur the Bishop was waiting for them to commence the benediction of the table.

While I had death in my heart, everyone around me rejoiced; the most discreet nodded their heads mysteriously and talked in whispers about marriage; others, less reserved, said aloud that the sister of the rich and noble treasurer of the King of France might well become Comtesse de Valois—for, according to them, nothing was too worthy of a lady who combined high lineage, marvelous beauty, angelic virtue and immense wealth. Finally, it was continually repeated that:

"Comtesse Mahaud surely will not win her case, and Monseigneur the Bishop is certain to recover his good lands of Cambrésis."

Those rumors, at first confided to the manor, were soon known to the townspeople and arrived in Arras. Comtesse Mahaud, who, in order to delay the verdict, had pretended to be seriously ill, then made a sudden decision. Trusting in her rare beauty and diabolical cunning, for all means were good to her to achieve her ends, she was seen one evening, without her being expected there, to arrive at the Episcopal manse, escorted by a rich and numerous retinue.

"Now then, Monseigneur de Valois," she said, in a treacherously polite and agreeable fashion, "here I am, come to beg you and ready to ask you for mercy, barefoot and with a rope around my neck, because for four long months a dolorous fever has retained me in a sickbed and rendered me poor and paltry, while those two beautiful eyes, I see, have won Messire the Bishop's case. They have also, I'm sure, more than was necessary, irritated the brother of the King of France against a humble and sad window."

In concluding those bold words, at which Madame Berthe blushed deeply, the Comtesse d'Artois made as if to kneel down. The Prince did not let her do so, and lifted her up with the most gracious urgency.

Then, leaning on the Prince's hand, she started whispering in his ear, turning to ridicule the virtuous simplicity and naïve grace of Madame Berthe, so effectively that Monseigneur de Valois, circumvented by her perfidious speech, began to be ashamed of what had at first, rightly, charmed him so much.

From then on, the merriment and confidence in which the Episcopal manse had been frolicking became sadness and discouragement.

Prince Charles, from that day on, no longer had any other care but pleasing Comtesse Mahaud, and scarcely gave a thought henceforth to the sad Madame Berthe. To the detriment of the endless conversations in the oratory, falcons and lances resumed favor; nothing was heard but charger snorting and hunters playing fanfares; everyone whetted lances to run to the field of combat. Finally, at the demand and insistence of the Comtesse d'Artois, a solemn contest of arms was proclaimed for the ninth of the month of November. Prince Charles put off until the same day the proclamation of the verdict relative to the argument that he had to judge.

The following day, the second of September and the day of the fête of Notre-Dames-de-Anges, Monseigneur the Bishop enjoined me to depart with a herald of arms to carry messages to the knights of the land inviting them to come and take part in the jousting.

We were to return on the eve of the tournament, the eighth of November.

In spite of the great urgency I put into it, it was not granted to me to appear before my noble mistress either on the day of my arrival nor even the following morning. It was necessary, therefore, as my duties as a page enjoined me, to remain at the foot of the velvet tent erected in the place of honor to receive the noblest ladies, the bishop, the judges of the lists and messieurs the canons.

How eager I was to see Madame Berthe arrive, the pleasant sight of whom her not been permitted to me for two months and seven days. She finally appeared, escorted by Messire Le Borge de Mauny and marching behind the bishop, who was giving his hand to Comtesse Mahaud.

Holy Virgin! The piteous state of my noble and unhappy mistress informed me only too well that frightful chagrins had caused her distress; she had become pale and timid; already there was I know not what skeletal appearance in his thin, but still beautiful, features; an imperceptible nuance of indecisive pink and blue surrounded her eyelids, and made her eyes seem larger. Finally, a dry cough continually escaped her throat, whistling.

At that sight, it became impossible for me to retain a cry of surprise and despair. She heard it, she understood it, and she darted a glance at me. Oh, it desolated my soul!

After a few moments of expectation, the trumpets played the fanfares and the knights entered the lists. The Prince de Valois was wearing the colors of the Comtesse de Mahaud.

I cannot relate here the prowesses of that day; my gaze was scarcely directed toward the field of combat; it was fixed on a dearer and more dolorous object. I shall therefore say briefly that Monseigneur Charles, Prince de Valois, remained the champion of the day.

It was Madame Berthe, as the sister of Monseigneur the Bishop Philippe de Marigny, who had to give the victor the prize of the tourney, to wit, a golden chain with an emerald of great value in each link, and a well-tempered sword in the pommel of which a relic of the blessed Saint Géry had been enclosed.

The Prince therefore came to kneel before Madame Berthe; but as she came forward, the courage of my mistress failed, and she fell unconscious. While all the ladies hastened around her, shaking her with great emotion and careless of everything else, the Comtesse d'Artois—I was told subsequently; I was in too dolorous a panic to see—picked up the chain and passed it graciously around her lover's neck; for she no longer hid that fact; she even took vanity in granting the Prince the gift of amorous thanks.

Would one believe that it as in the midst of the disturbance of such an accident that Prince Charles de Valois had his verdict on the difference between Cambrésis and Artois proclaimed?

That verdict condemned "the city of Cambrai to pay compensation of thirty-two thousand livres in sound coin, four thousand each semester until the entire payment." It only enjoined the Comtesse to "restore the items stolen to the villages belonging to the Chapter and in the contested places, which were evidently within the jurisdiction of Cambrésis."

How to describe the night that followed? The townsmen of Cambrai, outraged by the injustice of the verdict, gathered in mobs here and there in the town, vociferating and ready to assail the wing of the manse where Monseigneur Charles was lodged. The Prince's men-at-arms were alert, spears in hand, in fear of an attack, and the varlets made hasty preparations for the departure. Their master had announced to the Bishop that he would leave the manse at dawn the next day. It was easy to recognize in such a lack of courtesy the advice of the Comtesse d'Artois. It was said, at least, that the Prince had only made that impolite decision after much hesitation; seeing that the wicked woman that he loved had declared that she would depart alone and never see him again as long as she lived if he did not consent to escort her the following day. Such was the power she exercised over him that it was necessary to concede.

At daybreak, therefore, a great noise of hoofbeats was heard. Madame Berthe enquired as to where it was coming from. Monseigneur Philippe, who had sent the night at his sister's bedside, replied frankly: "It's the Prince de Valois and Comtesse Mahaud who are leaving the manse without warning. They are going together, like husband and wife, to the court of King Philippe."

Madame Berthe put her hands together, emotionally, tried to proffer a few words, but could only murmur a feeble cry. It was her last.

For more than seven weeks I lay abed, overwhelmed by fever and delirium, calling loudly for Madame Berthe, having not yet been able to shed a single tear. Everyone around me marveled at that sudden illness, and I was told afterwards that Monseigneur the Bishop exclaimed one day: "By Saint Philippe"—that was his blessed patron—"I'd give a thousand livres of sound money to whomever could cure this poor page in such great peril of dying for regret of his mistress. Nowadays, it is not in dozens that varlets so faithful are counted!"

He should have said lovers so heartbroken.

One night, when I was able to become drowsy, unusually, I suddenly heard my name being called: "Raoul! Page Raoul!"

Jesus my savior! It was the soft voice of Madame Berthe. She was there, the unfortunate woman, standing next to me, as mournful as on the last day that it had been given to me to see her. At the sight of her, I sensed a mortal sadness, liked Our Lord Jesus Christ in the Garden of Olives. Since that moment, no Christian has seen me smile even once.

"Raoul, Page Raoul," she said, "I have come to request from you the end of my pain, from you to whom I have caused so much—without knowing it, however, for you carefully hid your fervent and dolorous tenderness, Raoul…" At that point I thought I saw an imperceptible blush color the pale cheeks of the soul. "Raoul, I have sinned! The Prince de Valois... As a punishment for that sin I am retained in Purgatory until the moment when the man who made me sin has recited a *de profundis* in my intention.

"Alas, he has not yet given me a thought—me, who died because of him, and who is suffering so much in Purgatory because I loved him too much!

"And yet, Raoul, God and the Holy Virgin are my witnesses that I would gladly have consented to remain a thousand more years in this place of darkness and tears, if he had only said, at the news that I had died: 'Poor Berthe!'

"Go, then, Raoul, to Messire de Valois; tell him that Berthe's soul is in pain in Purgatory, and that if he will only recite one *de profundis*, the angels will take her to Paradise. He will not refuse you, Raoul; I hope so, at least—for is there a Christian harsh enough to refuse a *de profundis*, even if it were a matter of saving the soul of a Jew?"

That apparition returned me to life as if by a miracle; from that moment on the fever and delirious transports departed, and within two months, by the grace of God, I was in a state to undertake the journey that Madame Berthe had requested of me.

In order to complete that expedition, it was necessary for me to obtain leave from Monseigneur Bishop Philippe; I therefore went to him, and begged him to hear my confession, to which he consented. The marvelous vision that I had had and the duty to which Madame Berthe had commanded me were related faithfully by me, except that I did not allow myself the

129

shame of daring to confess the hopeless amour that I had nourished for the departed. Nevertheless, I was not making a bad
confession in that, for that amour, so chaste and so secret,
could not be a sin.

Monseigneur Philippe listened to me in silence. Finally,
he said: "These are supernatural things, and it is necessary not
to lend credence to them too easily. Perhaps it was a hollow
dream of malady and feverish transport. In any case, my son,
there are hundreds of obstacles that are opposed to the accomplishment of your pious design; great and sad events have occurred in our house."

Then he set about telling me how the King of France,
Philippe le Bel, had died. His son Louis X, had succeeded
him; under the new King the Prince de Valois had become all-
powerful at the court, and, driven by the wicked Comtesse
Mahaud, had done disservice to Monseigneur Enguerrand, and
had accused him in full council of dissipating the State treas-
ury, requiring him to say how he had employed the large contributions levied on Flanders. Now, they had been paid by the
lord treasurer into the hands of the Prince de Valois himself

Messire Enguerrand therefore replied frankly: "I have
given the greater part of them to you, Monseigneur, as is prov-
en by regulation parchments sealed with your seal."

"Parchments that lie!" cried the Prince.

"Monseigneur, if there is a lie, it is not on the part of
those parchments, but you," the Lord Treasurer interrupted,
justly indignant at such an outrage. The Prince de Valois drew
his sword; he would have struck Messire Enguerrand, but the
prudent men of the council held him back. He went out then,
swearing by the living God that he would not come back from
the Louvre without having taken bloody vengeance against the
high treasurer.

"Since the time when my brother sent me this news himself by way of a faithful bodyguard," the Bishop went on, "I
have been in great anxiety and painful doubt as to what has
happened. The Comte de Valois will not rest until he has had

Enguerrand hanged. Judge, my son, whether he is in a disposition to pray for Berthe's soul.

"Go in peace, then, Raoul. Tomorrow, we shall celebrate a solemn mass to the intention of the mistress of whom you are showing yourself such a faithful servant. As for your design, it is necessary to renounce it, as hazardous and recklessly conceived."

It was necessary for me to obey. But on the very night that followed that conversation, I was woken up by a plaintive groan; Madame Berthe was there again, joining her hands in a sign of distress and prayer. I resolved to go and see Monseigneur the Bishop again, but as I was preparing to go to him, a varlet came on his behalf to summon me.

"Raoul," Monseigneur said to me, "my sister's soul appeared to me last night, plaintive and suffering. There is no longer any doubt that I was wrong to deflect you from your pious design. Go then, my son, and may the benediction of Our Savior and that of an old man accompany you!"

While saying those words he extended his venerable hands over my forehead, gave me a purse full of gold coins, and told me that the provost of his house had orders to let me choose the best horse there was in the manor's stables.

I set forth the following day, the tenth of March in the year of grace thirteen fourteen, when the church was celebrating the festival of the forty blessed martyrs.

I arrived in the city of Paris after a week of travel without incident. My first concern was to go to the palace of the lord treasurer. How rapidly my heart beat when I saw its high towers, its sculpted walls and its multicolored windows! Three times, with a tremulous hand, I made the iron hammer at the enormous door resonate in order to summon an usher, but although the hammer resounded with a great noise, no one came to open the door to me.

Then I had a prescience of the fatal news that I was about to learn.

While I was standing there, darting glances of uncertainty and anxiety around me, an old man surreptitiously made me a sign to follow him, and led me into a solitary street where his lodgings were.

When he had looked around, fearful that someone might be listening, he asked: "Have you so much desire to be hanged that you're walking in Paris clad in the colors of the Bishop of Cambrai? Do you not know that Messire de Marigny is in disgrace, that he's a prisoner in the tower of the Louvre, for having cast spells against the person of the King? In addition, he's accused of having treacherously dissipated the royal treasures.

"The Palais de Marigny has been closed by the King's seals. The varlets, pages and squires have been ignominiously expelled—those at least, who, like me, did not have the good fortune to be slain defending our master."

"And my father? In the name of Heaven, my father, Sire Bartholomé Beaugenin? Give me news of him…"

"*Requiescat in pace*," replied the old man. "He's in a better world than this one, along with the venerable lady his legitimate wife; one dead of a dagger-thrust, the other of seizure and grief."

Taking pity on my distress and despair, the old man, who was one of the Lord Treasurer's squires and a friend of my father's, kept me in his lodgings, and comforted me with pious exhortations.

During the three days that I remained in his home, God and the Holy Virgin did me the grace of awakening in my soul a pious design that they had already put there several times; but I had always set it aside, for it would have required, in order to accomplish it, separating myself forever from Madame Berthe. That design was to enter into religion, and consecrate myself to the service of God for the rest of my life.

Well, what would I have been able to do in the world, when those who had made my joy there had died? What love, except divine love, could fill the void that Madame Berthe's death had left in my soul?

But before entering the cloister, it was necessary for me to accomplish a great and holy duty. I therefore went to the Louvre, where the Prince de Valois resided.

The seneschal, of whom I enquired as to how to obtain an audience with his seigneur, asked me my name and qualities.

"Raoul de Beaugenin, page of Messire Philippe de Marigny, Bishop of Cambrai."

He looked at me with an expression of surprise, went away, and came back a few moments later to introduce me.

When I found myself alone with the King's uncle, I felt my heart hammering and my knees buckled.

Finally, trying to pull myself together as best I could, I told him about the vision I had had, how I had undertaken such a long and difficult journey, in order to extract Madame Berthe's soul from Purgatory, and why that only required a *de profundis* recited by Monseigneur Charles de Valois.

The Prince, while I told my story with a compunction calculated to move a heart of stone, continually turned his gaze toward a crimson curtain that closed a large window. Suddenly, a burst of laughter departed from behind that curtain. The Comtesse d'Artois appeared, and drew me on to the balcony.

"There!" she cried. "Those are the prayers that one recites for the Marignys!"

Holy Virgin! The Lord Treasurer, with a rope around his neck, was being taken from the tower of the Louvre to the gibbet of Montfaucon!"

Two years later, I had been to aid in his final hour a poor sick man who dwelt in the vicinity of the Louvre and was returning to my convent of Minims when two varlets came to me and said: "Revered Father, in the name of Jesus Christ, come; our master is about to die without confession if he is not heard immediately by you; our almoner cannot be found." And they took me away, without telling me where they were taking me.

Imagine my surprise when I found myself taken in to the Palais de Valois, to the bedside of Monseigneur Charles!

At the sight of me he uttered a terrible cry.

"God is just, Raoul! My crimes are very heavy, at this hour of punishment! Will Jesus Christ pardon me, who caused the innocent Marigny to perish for vengeance? Will the Holy Virgin intercede for me, when I have left in Purgatory an unfortunate woman whose death I caused, when it only required a *de profundis* to extract her from pain? O, despair! O terrible wrath! I'm damned!"

I attempted to return to the sinner some confidence in divine mercy, but nothing could give him hope of salvation, and he rendered his soul in my arms, repeating: "I'm damned!"

That same night, the soul of Madame Berthe appeared to me with a crown of light on her head. Two angels of marvelous beauty were taking her to Paradise.

Thus was delivered from Purgatory the soul of Madame Berthe, which was suffering for having sinned by amour.

She is now in the abode of the blissful, glorifying the Lord forever.

Let it be given to us, by the infinite mercy of God, and the intercession of the Holy Virgin, the unique source of all good, to live piously, in order that in the hour of our death we can, by means of our good works and our sincere actions, find ourselves with Madame Berthe and the elect in eternal glory.

So might it be.

THE PACT

1554

> May I hold her in my arms for a day,
> an hour, an instant; then you can kill me.
> (Owen.)[16]

Everything presaged a terrible and imminent storm: black and heavy clouds covered the sky; there was only warm air to be respired; and the only objects that could be distinguished in the profound obscurity were the lights shining in the windows on the Château d'Anet.

A pale young man whose gaze had something wild was marching precipitately across country, following the left bank of the Eure. He stopped in front of a cottage built by the riverside, and knocked on the door twice, impatiently. It was only at the third blow, however, that the broken and sullen voice of an old man replied.

"Open up, Mathias, open up!" shouted the young man.

"Tell me who you are."

"Henriot Maurepain, the Fleming.

"Henriot Maurepain! What are you doing at poor Mathias' door so late? Is it to say to him, as you did three months ago: 'Dog of a sorcerer, I'll denounce you to the high provost, for you merit hanging and the pyre?'"

"Malediction! Open this door, or I'll break it down and break your head!"

As he spoke those words, Henriot shook the door and get ready to put his threat into execution.

---

[16] The author presumably has the Welsh epigrammatist John Owen (1564-c1625) in mind, but the quotation is fictitious.

The old man finally gave in and let the young man into his cottage. While the latter marched precipitately back and forth in the narrow enclosure, he considered him in silence. In order to do so more easily, he extended a hand behind the lamp he was holding; the light of the lamp was reflected, ruddy and vacillating, from the wrinkled forehead and little eyes of Mathias, giving his physiognomy, which was scarcely attractive anyway, a truly odious expression.

"Why have you come so late to trouble a poor man's repose? Is it to run around before him like a madman, as you're doing?"

"Listen, Mathias," the young man interrupted, seizing him by the arm and speaking in a distressed voice, "listen... You know how one can make a pact with the Devil; tell me, and this purse, the only wealth I possess in the world, is yours!"

The old man tried to recoil, but the young man's arm was gripping him too vigorously for that. The result of the attempt was a simple movement on the spot, which Henriot did not even seem to perceive.

"Let me go. I'm sure of it—you've come to make me say something indiscreet, and to deliver me to the Lord Provost, who'll have me burned as a heretic and a sorcerer. There are men there, hidden behind the door. But the Devil take me if you get another word out of my mouth. You're doing vile work there, young man!"

Henriot stamped his foot impatiently. "Have no fear," he said. "Look, I'm alone. You must know, in any case, that I wouldn't do what you fear for anything in the world.

"Marie...you know that I've loved her since I quit my homeland of Flanders to come and live here; you know that for a year, everyone in the village has been talking about our amour. Well, her father has refused her to me, because my cousin Grégoire Bonneau is the sole heir of my uncle's wealth. I ought to have half that succession, but the accursed cantor has been able to flatter our old uncle so well that he's left everything to him alone. There's even talk of giving Marie's hand to some rich miller in a neighboring hamlet. She'll die of it! And me! No, no; it's necessary that I have her, if only for a year, a day, an hour!

"I want to sell my soul to the Devil. Let him give me a thousand *écus au soleil*, and in a year, I'll belong to him body and soul. Give me the means to make that pact, and take this purse."

The old man started to laugh, picked up the money, and after having stowed it away carefully in his jerkin, he said: "you think, my handsome young man, that Satan will give a thousand *écus au soleil* for your soul? I very much fear that he'll find the price excessively dear, for more than three-quarters of it already belongs to the Evil Spirit when one has bloodshot eyes, an unsteady gait, a body shaken by frissons and a forehead covered in cold sweat. In good conscience, even if I knew the means to enable you to conclude such a bargain, I believe it would be futile to tell you what they are."

Henriot drew his dagger and put it to Mathias' breast.

"Speak! Speak, or you're dead!"

"Well, I can see that you're appropriately resolute. All of that was to test you. Listen, then:

"Begin by stealing a black pullet. There are some very fine ones in the home of my neighbor Bartholomé Giron. After the theft...good! Now he's trembling at the mere thought of a petty larceny! Fine delicacy, in truth, in a man who wants to sell himself to the Devil! After the theft, you go to the cross-roads in the forest; there you trace a circle with this wand.

"It's made of hazel-wood; I cut it on the first Wednesday of the moon; I needed a new knife for that. I hid my wand furtively on an alter at which a priest was about to celebrate mass; I engraved at the stout end the mysterious *agla*, in the middle *cor*, and at the thin extremity, *tetragrammaton*; a cross surmounts each word.

"Once your circle is traced, you bare your left leg, and you stand in the circle naked. Then, cutting the pullet's throat, it's necessary to cry: 'Silver of the blood of my black beast! I

137

want a thousand *écus au soleil* for it.' Then, if the Devil wants you, he'll appear to you.

"But Henriot, make haste, for midnight is approaching, and after that hour, Lucifer becomes invisible."

As he finished speaking, he extracted himself abruptly from Henriot's grip and, shoving him outside, closed the door behind him.

The young man remained pensive for a few moments. Then, suddenly starting marching like a man taking a desperate resolution from which he fears he might retreat, he went to the farm that Mathias had mentioned to him, scaled a low wall, seized a black pullet and plunged into the forest.

Meanwhile, the storm had commenced. Large raindrops were falling on the foliage, and a violent tempest was engulfed in the trees with a frightful roaring. Lightning was flashing continually, and detonations of thunder following rapidly.

Henriot, sustained by the frenzy of despair, ran rather than walked to the crossroads. There he accomplished the mysterious rites that Mathias had taught him:

"Silver of the blood of my black beast! I want a thousand *écus au soleil* for it."

A frightful clap of thunder resounded at that moment, and a white phantom, and then a squat black figure, appeared through the trees.

Henriot fell in a faint.

Day was beginning to break when he recovered consciousness.

Directing bewildered glances around him, he had to collect himself for a few minutes before being able to recall distinctly his despair, his criminal projects and the fatal apparition of the previous night.

But perhaps that apparition, he thought, *was the effect of my trouble imagination. Oh, yes, I need that idea. To think that I'm forever—for eternal life—the property of the demon would be too frightful! Come on—it's nothing!*

He got to his feet, not without difficulty, and dragged himself slowly as far as he path to the hamlet.

A few more steps, and he was about to emerge from the forest, when he tripped over a cadaver lying across the path. Marcy! It was that of his cousin, Grégoire Bonneau.

Henriot uttered a cry of despair.

"It's done, then! I belong to the Demon, body and soul! He's struck my cousin with lightning. That's how he's paying me the thousand *écus au soleil*."

He was still speaking when soldiers seized him and bound his arms.

"By Saint Hubert!" said their leader; "this is a good prize that will be worth a big reward. You heard him. One, two, four, six, ten witnesses: he's sold himself to the Devil on condition that he would kill this poor cantor. God be praised! We were there to catch a poacher, and it's a sorcerer we're bringing back.

"It's necessary to leave the cadaver here; it's up to the bailiff to collect it; we simple forest wardens don't have the right. Let's go, comrades, let's take this man to Messire the Lord Provost, who's at the château now among the King's retinue."

They set forth on the march, and the crowd that Henriot's arrest had gathered recoiled precipitately and opened a wide path, so fearful were people of touching even the garment of a scoundrel sold to the Devil."

A few moments later the bailiff came to have the corpse taken away. There was no longer anything there. He crossed himself, trembling; as did, the hirelings and the peasants who were accompanying him—for who could doubt that the Devil had taken away the cadaver, in order that no evidence should remain against the sorcerer?

An hour later, the Lord Provost judged the poor young man; firstly, that was to attest to his activity and his zeal; secondly, he encountered sorcerers to burn too rarely for him not to put some urgency into the matter.

The people who had been unable to get into the hall of the tribunal were gathered outside the door, conversing between themselves about the strange event, whose denouement they were awaiting impatiently.

A short, fat, red-faced man clad in black approached one of the groups and enquired as to the reasons for such a gathering.

"A sorcerer!"

"A man who has given himself to the Devil!"

"He'll be hanged!"

"He'll be burned!"

The exclamations came from all directions.

A tall peasant, who surpassed the little man by at least a head, started recounting the affair at length. His listener was no less attentive; he interrupted incessantly to ask some ludicrous question, laughed in everyone's faced in the most unceremonious fashion, and then, plating himself without listening to the end of the interminable story, and shoved his elbows to the right and left with the intention of penetrating into the tribunal.

That project nearly proved unfortunate for the little man, however. His discourteous interruptions and bursts of laughter had offended many people; the discontent increased further on seeing the casual fashion in which he was bumping into everyone. But the indignation peaked, and cries and threats rose up from everywhere when he took a pretty young girl by the chin, and kissed her gaily on the lips.

He might perhaps have received a few solid slaps in recompense, if two pages who happened to be standing on the threshold of the tribunal had not perceived him in the middle of the crowd.

"Hey! What are you doing there?" they demanded of him. "By God! Make room bumpkins! Back, rabble, or it will cost more than one of you a rib or a backbone! Come in, Master François Rabelais."

In the left wing of the Château d'Anet was an apartment from whose windows one discovered a delightful view. The hangings and the furniture were of an extreme richness, laden with the monograms of Diane de Poitiers and Henri II. Everywhere, the needle had embroidered, everywhere, the brush had reproduced the silver crescent of the duchesse and the golden fleurs-de-lis of the monarch.

There, sprawled on velvet cushions, completely naked, was a woman. Her slim figure, the admirable contours of a voluptuous breast, the whiteness of her skin, the regularity of her teeth, and above all hr long black way hair, could only belong to the beautiful Duchesse de Valentinois; it was, in fact, Diane.

It was that celebrated woman, whose supernatural beauty seemed to have been spared by time, and who conserved at the age of forty-seven the freshness and seductive forms of adolescence; she was "the incomparable Phoebe" in memory of whom Brantôme ecstasizes in his *Dames galantes*: "Six months before her death, I saw her still so beautiful that I know of no heart of stone that would not have been moved by her… Her beauty, her grace and her beautiful appearance were all similar to what they had always been."

The King's old sculptor, Jean Goujon, dressed as people were in the time of François I, was placidly modeling the beautiful creature who was offering herself to his gaze without the slightest veil. He could have been working from a bronze statue and would not have struck his chisel with a more impassive calm.

"Now then," growled the sculptor, in a surly tone, "if Your Majesty does not put an end to her transports, I shall be forced to leave my statue imperfect, for these continual movements are rendering my work impossible."

The King, accustomed to the old artist's abruptness, smiled and replied: "I believe he's complaining! The man who can contemplate at his ease the most marvelous beauty on earth, and acquire an everlasting renown by reproducing such attractions in marble! Besides which, Master Goujon, your statue is too advanced for you to leave it there; you'd lose too much entitlement to glory and effort."

In fact, the beautiful production of statuary was almost complete. Goujon, in giving Diane all the emblems of the hunt, had represented her, in order to satisfy the King, in the state of nature that custom attributes preferentially to Venus. Moreover, there was nothing antique and very little of the ideal in the stature; the features, the coiffure and the proportions offered as exact an image as possible of the Duchesse de Valentinois.

The sculptor, forgetting his discontentment, had picked up the chisel that he had thrown away, and the King had sat down in his armchair again, when the door opened abruptly and Rabelais hurtled into the room.

Diane uttered a scream, and enveloped herself in haste, as best she could, in the kind's mantle. A sudden blush spread over her face, all the way to a breast imperfectly veiled by the short mantle.

Undisconcerted, Rabelais seized an end of the mantle, and Jean Goujon was forced to release the importunate, every movement of whom uncovered one of Diane's charms. As for the King, against whom the Duchesse was pressing, he could not help the sculptor in any way to throw Rabelais out.

"Sire, by the bottrine, I swear that I won't let go of this mantle until I've obtained mercy for a poor devil who has just been condemned to be burned by the Lord Provost."

As he finished speaking he tugged the mantle gently.

"Grant him that," demanded the Duchesse, half-annoyed and doing her best to hide herself, but still rather ineffectively, from Rabelais' brazen gaze.

"It shall be as you desire, beautiful friend...but you get out, boor."

"I need one more mercy," Master François continued, evidently taking pleasure in gazing at the attractive Diane in her voluptuous accoutrement.

"What mercy? Speak..."

"Mine, Sire."

"You have that too... Get out, then!"

"Here, sign: that's all that's necessary…good…and now your seal…."

Rabelais finally withdrew.

About two hours later, a page came to tell him that he had been summoned by the King. The historian of Pantagruel obeyed immediately, and the page led him into a vast room where the entire court was united, arranged in a semicircle.

In the center of that semicircle, next to Diane, the King was sitting, the physiognomy of whom, rendered even more striking by a black beard, displayed an expression of melancholy and harshness.

On seeing the indiscreet individual who had surprised her in such a singular situation a little while before, the Duchesse lowered her head and veiled her face with her fan of plumes.

"Your ladies-in-waiting have done what they can to spoil nature," Rabelais said in a low voice, "you were much better adorned this morning."

The Duchesse did not reply, but through the fan of plumes, Rabelais' piercing gaze seemed to perceive a smile and a gaze that did not express too much anger.

The King ordered Rabelais to explain the reasons for which he had taken such a keen interest in the wretch for whom he had requested mercy that morning. The Curé of Meudon commenced immediately, without having to be begged.

"The fever of thirst—thirst for wine, I mean—started burning my throat yesterday at vespers. 'Quick and soon my remedy!' I exclaimed: 'sudden goblets to fill and bottles to clink.'

"Now, when the good evil arrived, I had with me Grégoire Bonneau, cantor of the royal chapel. Since then, I have fallen into the suspicion that I, François Rabelais, might well have caught the fever of thirst from him, for it torments the poor man night and day.

"Whether the contagious fever came from him or me, I care little; let anyone make of it what they will: I only know that both of us began to shiver with it. Pressing evil, prompt remedy! There we were, both shouting as loudly as we could: 'Valet, pour, pour, pour, out without pure water, and fill the glass up to the brim, but without spilling any, it's too precious a liquid for a single drop to go to waste... Oh, false fever, won't you go away? Look, here's another glass; then another, and then that one...By my faith, old woman, you're soaked, doomed, not to say banged up!'

"So much was poured and repoured, drunk and redrunk, that the fever departed and took with it, arm in arm, reason, equilibrium and continence. Grégoire went off, I know full well to whose house, and I went for a walk in the woods where, waiting for me, was a certain..."

An old seigneur, a friend of Rabelais, tugged his sleeve gently, as a mute warning to restrain the intemperance of is language; for Henri II was of a serious and reserved character. His romantic passion for Diane and the fidelity that he maintained to his mistress added further to the aversion he had for debauchery and lewdness.

The adroit Duchesse de Valentinois, to render even greater the empire that she exercised over the monarch, flattered that ostentation of grave mores; she gave to everyone that surrounded her a character of reserve that contrasted singularly with the dissolute court of Catherine de Medicis. There, there was nothing but licentious talk, amorous and public intrigues. Thus, by a strange bizarrerie, there was in the house of the concubine a decency full of dignity, and in that of the legitimate wife a brazen profligacy.

All those ideas presented themselves to Rabelais rapidly, and made him understand how good the secret admonition of the old seigneur was. The King had been able to pardon him for that morning's escapade; no one had seen it; but he would infallibly be annoyed by obscene words spoken in front of his entire court. Rabelais therefore interrupted himself briefly, substituting an equivocal gesture and a smile full of finesse for reticence he was making, and continued as follows:

"The bells of the château were chiming midnight when we were still lost in the wood. In the end, though, the rain reminded us to decamp, and, thanks to the patron saint of sinners…and sinneresses…it was given to us to arrive at the hamlet without mishap and without having been seen by anyone, except for one man, as he will tell you later. The mystery of our stroll rejoiced my companion greatly…I shan't say where it as a he or a she...

"Today, at nones, drunkenness and dizziness departing from my head, reason returned to it. Now, it had never seemed to me to be so gross and so weighty; it was lolling about in my brain so much that the poor thing was swelling up, quite painfully. Fresh air was called to the rescue.

"When I went past the bailiff's house there was a horde of merciful people who were rejoining in some good news: to wit, that a sorcerer as being judged, who would doubtless be hanged and burnt. Justice is sometimes ludicrous and hilarious. I sat down in the place of honor behind the Lord Provost Trinquamelle.

"Messire Trinquamelle had just heard the witnesses. Then, blowing his nose sonorously like a canon, he enquired of the sorcerer: 'What do you say, scoundrel?'

"The sorcerer, belling like a stag at bay, began to respond: 'Yes, it's true; I've sold myself body and soul to the Evil Spirit, for a thousand *écus au soleil*; he paid me them dishonestly by the heritage of my cousin, passed away last night. I've caused the death of one of my relatives, yes, but Heaven is my witness that I did not intend that to happen; I only wanted a thousand *écus au soleil* to marry Marie, Marie whom I love so much!"

"At that moment I raised myself up in order to see the face of the poor fellow more easily.

"At the sight of me he fell in a faint. 'There he is!' he said. 'There's the Devil who bought my soul! He's hiding behind the provost…I saw him in the wood... he was following a white phantom... Have mercy on me! He's come to carry me off to Hell!'

"Everyone started looking at me and laughing, for, thank God, François Rabelais is known to be a devil of a fellow, impish perhaps, but not a buyer of souls. As that genteel page behind You Majesty, who was at the tribunal, observed, if I had a thousand *écus au soleil* in my wallet, I wouldn't be lying in wait in a wood to buy souls; the wine merchant would have the lot.

"Messire Trinquamelle shrugged his shoulders, invited me to supper for today, which I refused; then, as if he intended to corner water to prevent anyone else serving it at table, he hastened to render his verdict in order that the meal wouldn't be cold when he arrived.

"Henriot Maurepain was condemned to be hanged the same day, at vespers, after which his body would be burned and the ashes thrown to the wind.

"I went out feeling sorry for the so-celled sorcerer, who could be taken, at the worst, for an unhinged mind. But why had he recognized me as the Devil? That was what intrigued me. Suddenly, I remembered. That was the man I had encountered in the forest the previous night with Mathurine...curse my tongue! My secret's out!

"The innocent cause of the poor fellow's misfortune, I had, in all conscience, to remedy it. You know, Sire, how his mercy was granted to me benevolently by Your Majesty, on the intercession of Madame la Duchesse. You'll remember also by what means I received recompense for my good deed, if one can call recompense a fiery memory that will prevent me from sleeping for more than three nights; a memory that will cost me, in order to be forgotten, more than thirty bottles of Lacryma Christi. If it pleases the one who caused the malady to procure the remedy, she would be very welcome. Amen."

"My cellarman will bring them to your house, Master Rabelais," the beautiful Diane put in, whose cheeks were still covered, this time by a modest blush.

"Oyez, oyez, for here comes the most marvelous. On emerging from the château, I encountered my friend the great cantor Bonneau, who was as pale and distraught as if he had been drinking nothing but pure water for two full weeks. He had woken up at daybreak in the middle of the wood, where he had been asleep since the night before, at the same spot where he had fallen down dead drunk.

"I began to see the story clearly. 'Come with me,' I said. 'Come and do a merciful deed: extracting a poor fellow from the claws of justice.'

"'Right!' he replied. 'What's the prisoner's name?'

"'You'll soon find out.'

"We went into the prison. At the sight of us, Henriot uttered loud screams. 'Oh, mercy! The Devil! The Devil! The soul of my dead cousin!'

"Everything was explained; the poor fool had seen me and...the white phantom...in the wood at the moment when he was summoning the Devil; in the morning he had tripped over his cousin, profoundly asleep from good wine and amour, which are two famous soporifics if ever there was one. I recommend them as such, as a physician, to these noble Seigneurs, and to you as well, Mesdames. If your heart bids you, you'll always find the latter of those drugs in my laboratory, always provided that you're neither ugly nor ill-tempered, for then it loses its virtue."

There is no need to add that Henriot Maurepain was liberated, and that he married Marie, endowed by the Duchesse de Valentinois. The noble lady did not forget, either, to send Rabelais the same evening the thirty bottles of Lacryma Christi she had promised.

There were, however, many people, and the Lord Provost Trinquamelle was of that number, who claimed that the Devil had had a good deal to do with that affair. "Satan might well," he said, "have resuscitated Grégoire, as he had killed him. The intervention of Rabelais, which certainly cannot pass for very orthodox, gives a great deal of weight to my suspicions. In any case, the judgment might have been rendered in error without it being necessary to overturn it; one cannot have too much respect for the sentences passed by men of the law, especially the Lord Provost."

Fortunately, a few days later there was a fine execution of heretics and sorcerers, among whom was the old sinner Mathias. That satisfied the zeal of the malcontents, and the young bridegroom and Rabelais were left in peace.

THE EGLANTINE;

or, The Death of Hugues, Sire d'Ostremont
1598

Undoubtedly, there can be no pure and unalloyed good
fortune in this world; for frightful examples of its
fragility spoil the delight of the happy, as the sword
suspended over his head by Dionysius, tyrant of
Syracuse, informed a certain Damocles.
(Sermon delivered by the Rev. Père Laurent
in the monastery of Notre-Dame on the first Sunday
in Advent of the year 1521.)

Nothing but tears could be heard in the palace of good
King René. That Prince had departed in mid-morning to go
hunting, having with him for an escort only a small number of
hunters, and although the night was well-advanced, he had not
yet returned.

Prey to the keenest anxieties, the officers of his house,
the pages and the varlets, gathered in the vestibule, were deploring the fruitlessness of their searches. A few were reciting
prayers, which they interrupted at the slightest sound, for immediately, they believed that the good King had finally returned.

The almoner Marini, an austere priest who possessed all
René's confidence, strove in vain to dissimulate the dread that
his agitation and pallor revealed. Sometimes he advanced toward the desolate group, as if he had a question to ask, and
then withdrew abruptly without speaking, marching at a rapid
pace; sometimes, he proffered a few inconsequential words in
a low voice.

In the meantime, a man appeared remarkable for his ro-
tundity and his grotesque attire; he wore a tiny cutlass sus-

pended on a large gold chain. "Well, Courcou," exclaimed Marini, in the impatient tone of a man demanding good news although he knows only too well the impossibility of learning any, "Has your research finally been fortunate? Have the sounds of the horn been heard?"

"May God protect our god King," relied that singular individual in a grave and capable tone. "Some misfortune has surely overtaken him. His gracious Majesty said to me as he left: 'Prince of cooks, we shall bring you back, before the angelus chimes, roe deer, partridges, or even a boar, although the poachers scarcely leave me any...'"

"Fatal imprudence," murmured the priest, drawing away from Courcou—who, in spite of the dolor he was experiencing, was no less sensible to the abrupt manner in which a conversation not calculated to flatter his vanity had terminated. "We've warned him many a time of the attempts at seduction that the treacherous Louis never ceases to make with regard to all of us. Too good, too confident, he didn't want to believe us; and now he's fallen into the ambush of his mortal enemy! Great God! It will be the same with Provence as with Anjou, then!"[17]

As he launched himself outside the vestibule in his distress, however, he heard the cries of the people whom anxiety had gathered outside the palace:

"Joy! Joy! The King! The King!"

---

[17] Author's note: "Louis XI had expelled René from Anjou at the moment when the overconfident old man had least expected that perfidy. 'Where is the hand,' said a chronicler of the epoch, 'that could satisfactorily describe the plaints, regrets and lamentations of the poor folk at the departure of the easy-going King of Sicily, so curious and such a vigilant tutor of the land, amorous of pace and concord, sustainer of the poor, director and support of honorable Ladies and Damoiselles, and all benign and merciful brothers?'"

And René, only having for an escort a hermit armed with a knotty stick, advanced surrounded by an immense crowd expressing its joy by noisy acclamations.

"Sire!" cried Marini, carried away by his impetuous zeal. "In what affliction you have plunged your faithful subjects! Is he a King to trouble and entire town for a frivolous pleasure? To expose his liberty and the salvation of the kingdom thus?"[18]

"Marini," the King replied, mildly, "You attachment almost gives bitterness to your remonstrations. At any rate," he added, turning toward two venerable old men who were advancing toward him weeping with joy, we're grateful to you for it, and we shall take it into account, like that if our loyal and faithful servants Jéhan Binée and Jehan Cossa.[19] But by Saint Hubert, it's necessary to admit that no peril as great ever menaced our royal head. If this courageous hermit had not come to my rescue, my traitorous hunters, in spite of my cries and futile efforts, would have delivered me to my cousin the

---

[18] Author's note: "These bold words of Marini's ought not to astonish; that preacher dared, one day, from the pulpit, to reproach René for his liking for ballads. The good King was not annoyed. See L'Hist. de René d'Anjou by M. le Vicomte L. F. De Villeneuve Bargemont."

[19] Author's note: "Jean Binée refused an honorable and important position that the king had offered him. The letter has been conserved in which he enters into details full of candor and naivety to prove to René that he would fulfill the functions of the post poorly and does not have the qualities necessary to acquit it worthily. 'So I simply cannot serve you,' he says, 'at least as the estate and office require.' Jehan Cossa was René's ambassador to Louis XI when that Prince took possession of Anjou. The faithful servant trued to protest against that infraction of all human rights. 'If the ambassador of the King of Sicily does not withdraw in all haste,' said Louis XI coldly, turning to his satellites, let someone sow him up in a sack and throw him in the river.'"

King of France. He would doubtless not have failed to lodge me in his black towers, which scarcely please anyone but him, apart from the fact that in order to get out it's necessary to pay such huge ransoms!"

Stifling a sigh, he went on: "Come on, Courcou, serve us supper; we'll do honor to it, for this venerable hermit and I, although both old, have acted like young men today, me in exposing myself with such scant prudence, and him in striking as I would have been able to do when I fought next to my uncle the Cardinal de Bar with my brave brother-in-arms the Bishop of Amiens."[20]

The stranger replied to these words by making a respectful bow. Although he seemed to be as old as René, everything in him announced a more than ordinary strength. The melancholy expression of his features inspired an interest that could not be defined; and his noble manners, full of ease, seemed to announce that he was highly-born. In those times it was not extraordinary to see seigneurs who, suddenly renouncing the world, went to seek in a pious solitude the calm and happiness that they had been unable to find in the milieu of courts.

They went into the banqueting hall, preceded by Master Courcou. The latter filled with wine a golden goblet that René emptied in a single draught; after which he presented to the king a small bunch of silver keys, with which the Prince opened the padlocks of the closed the immense lockers with which the table was covered. They contained forty-eight different dishes; there were storks, roasted herons, partridges and pheasants; in the middle, a peacock rose up artistically orna-

---

[20] Author's note: "Cardinal de Bar, René's uncle, gave him an entirely martial education, for in that era, prelates often took up arms. 'And on the battlefield," says Monstrelet, 'they were obliged to wear a basinet for a miter, a piece of steel for a chasuble and a battle-ax for a cross.' The Bishop of Amiens was Conrad Brayer de Boppau, who always remained linked to René by narrow amity."

mented with its rich plumage and its long tail, which was as marvelous to see as it was delicious to savor.

While Courcou took from its sheath the little cutlass that he wore suspended from a golden chain, and sliced with ease and skill, and showed by means of a smile of satisfaction how highly he esteemed the high functions that he acquitted, René's eye suddenly filled with tears.

"Alas!" he cried, with bitterness, "I find no one at my table but a cenobite. Even he has only sat down out of obedience; and yet, I was once surrounded by my son Antoine d'Anjou and his brother Nicolas; their sisters Marguerite and Yolande and my noble son-in-law Ferry de Vendemour...[21] Not a single one of my grandsons remains to me, whose joyous caresses could still charm my distressed soul! Oh, if God had conserved them for me, I would not have been expelled from my estates, a feeble old man."

Wiping away his tears after a moment's pause he added: "But let God's will be done!"

The meal was silent. As Marini was saying grace, a child of about fifteen came in precipitately and ran to embrace the Prince with the effusion of joy that only belongs to that age of innocence.

"Oh, there you are, my dear Bertrand,"[22] said the King, passing his hand through the blond hair. "By your redness and

---

[21] Author's note: "Antoine d'Anjou, the elder son of the good King, perished at Barcelonne in the midst of the most splendid triumphs, mourned by the Aragonnais, who adored him. Nicolas d'Anjou, his sister Yolande and Ferry Vendemour did not long survive their brother. Marguerite married Henri VI of England and reestablished that weak King devoid of courage to the throne twice. Her husband and son perished before her eyes; she retired to France, 'where she died,' says Voltaire, 'the unhappiest of queens, wives and mothers.'"

[22] Author's note: "Bertrand d'Alamanon, born in Aix. This is the translation of one of his songs, full of grace and naivety: 'You want to know why I am making a demi-song; it's be-

153

your fatigue I see that you have been searching for me too, in great anxiety." And using his royal hand to serve him food, he seemed to take pleasure in seeing the appetite with which Bertrand did honor to his repast.

"This child," said René to the hermit, "is an orphan; he's a legacy given to me by his father, Claude Alamanon, who died poor in the service of my son-in-law Vendemour. Endowed with an extraordinary and precocious talent for poetry, he does not cede to any troubadour for composing and singing ballads. But what I appreciate most in him is the rare qualities of his heart. He loves me with a tender amity; he seems to forget the tastes of his age to yield to all the weaknesses of mine; if I want to tell stories, he is always ready to listen. If I remember my misfortunes, he weeps with me; one might think that he had no other pleasures but mine, no other troubles but mine."

The child then came to sit down beside the prince.

"Fetch your mandolin, Bertrand," René said to him, and sing us one of your ballads—the one you composed during our last voyage to Navarre, the subject of which you borrowed from an event of the region."

The child obeyed, and, taking off the light blue mantle that covered his shoulders, he began the following ballad:

"Interred in a prison in Burgundy, the brave sire Vadales incessantly reported his thoughts to the pleasant land of Navarre.

---

cause I only have a demi-subject to sing; there is only love on my part; the lady I love does not love me; but for lack of the ayes that she refuses me I take the nays that she lavishes upon me. Hope next to her is better than enjoyment next to another, and, unable to resist the Empire of Amour, I know no means to soothe my troubles but thinking that one day she might perhaps love me.' (see *Le Dict. des Poètes franc.*, by M. Philippon de la Madelaine, and *L'Hist. des Troub.* by Abbé Millot."

"'Traitor Commercy,' he was heard to cry, may Heaven punish you, for if you had not betrayed our valiant warriors, King René would not be groaning in irons. Barbezan[23] would be defending him still and I would be with Marguerite, my beloved daughter.

"In the morning her kisses would come to wake her father; in the evening she would sing the ballad that I sang to her mother, and bitter and delicious tears would flow over my cheeks, at the memory of the one whose cherished image would be retraced by the grace and ingenuousness of Marguerite.

---

[23] Author's note: "The celebrated Barbezan made every effort to defer a battle that would decide René's fate. 'He who is afraid retreats!' said young de Commercy. 'Let's march to combat!' cried the old warrior. 'I'll attack enemies so forcefully that those who insult me will not dare to place the head of their horse where the tail of mine will be.' The battle was lost and Barbezan was killed after prodigies of valor. Lying on the battlefield bathing in his own blood, but still breathing, he sees de Commercy passing, spurring his horse to flee as quickly as possible. Full of indignation, Barbezan lifts his dying head and reanimates his strength in order to address reproaches to the unworthy knight. 'I promised my darling,' replied the latter, coldly. 'In fact,' says an old chronicler, 'the youth had to go, at vespers, to see a certain Agathe, whom he had promised that he would quit the battle and come to her bedroom—which is better, she said, than a field where there is nothing but blows and pikes.' The place where Barbezan fell and died, marked by two elms hollowed out by time, is still celebrated and sacred. A rustic bridge and a small hill bear his name, which is not forgotten by the simple villagers, who still repeat it today with veneration." The reference is to Arnaud de Barbazan, "le chevalier sans reproche," who was René d'Anjou's most faithful supporter and became a model of knightly loyalty in consequence.

"More than one young knight would come to ask me for her hand; but neither the splendor of his birth nor the wealth of his possessions would decide my choice; if a simple troubadour made Marguerite's heart beat faster, a simple troubadour would be her spouse.

"But where is my spirit straying? I am dreaming of my daughter's betrothal, and perhaps she is groaning, oppressed by some cowardly suzerain, for she has no point of support, no protector. Her father is captive, far away from her.

"One day, the doors of his prison opened noisily. Someone said to him: 'Take up your sword and lance; mount your horse.'

"He is free, he departs. He soon reaches the end of his journey; he has scarcely paused on the way, for he is going to see his daughter again.

"Already he perceives the Château de Vadales, but O surprise! It is not the banner with the azure field and the silver hind that floats over the towers of his fortress; it is the sinister flag of the coward de Commercy.

"What has become of Marguerite? At that thought he feels faint and the reins of his horse escape his hands. Suddenly he hears the sounds of the clarion and the hoofbeats of a hundred men-at-arms.

"At their head is young Hugues d'Ostremont, a Cambrésian seigneur. 'Warrior,' he shouts to Vadales, 'come fight with us against the man who has stolen the orphan's domain.' The signal for the assault is given, and Vadales and Hugues d'Oisy cast down the sinister flag of Commercy.

"'Brave knight,' said Vadales, mounted on the breach, 'noble and valiant Hugues, you have protected the poor orphan, and her father, on this breach, offers you Marguerite's hand.'

"What was Marguerite's joy when she saw her father again! What sudden blush covered her cheeks, what soft tears shone in her eyes when he said to her: 'Marguerite, here is your husband!'

"Soon the rumor of the noble marriage spread through the land. It was celebrated by a brilliant tourney; for the subjects of the good King liked their forefathers' games; only those of the grim Louis of France are as grim as their master.

"The bride was led to the altar, and when the chaplain had said: 'Baron Hugues d'Ostremont, noble seigneur de Cambrésis, Marguerite is yours…Damoiselle, Hugues d'Ostremont is your husband,' the vassals uttered cries of joy, and magnificent feasts and noisy dances commenced everywhere.

"Fleeing those importunate festivities, it is under a pure sky, to the mountain that neighbors the château, that the two spouses go to deliver themselves without witnesses to tender caresses and tender conversation.

"They shelter from the fires of the sun beneath a steep rock that extends menacingly above their heads. An eglantine-bush crowns it, and on raising her eyes, Marguerite perceives flowers swaying softly in the breath of the wind.

"She points them out to her spouse. Hugues has already climbed the mountain; he picks the charming flowers, and Marguerite, under the rock, lifts her hands to receive the roses.

"O terror! The rock, with a horrible din, comes away, rolls, bounds, and the unfortunate couple have disappeared under its enormous debris.

"Marguerite! Marguerite! That plaintive cry resounds all night in the gorges of the mountain, sparkling with torchlight. Finally, what a spectacle for a father! Vadales discovers his daughter; she is lying, bloody, next to her spouse, her hand still holding the fatal eglantine."

Suddenly, the hermit, who has covered his face with his hands, utters a cry and falls down, pale and unconscious. People gather around him, and water is sprinkled on his face. But a reliquary concealed on his bosom escapes and rolls to the feet of the King; it contains a desiccated rose and two locks of hair, one blonde the other black, enlaced in two rings such as those a priest gives to spouses whose union he is blessing.

Vadales—for it was him—returned to his hermitage in spite of René's efforts to retain him in his court. But the Prince and the troubadour often went to visit him, and more than once, during the winter, in those pleasant places sheltered from the wind, the monarch was seen warming himself in the mild sun of Provence, chatting familiarly with his young favorite and the pious old man. He often held his court of justice there, and his humblest subjects came to approach him without dread and implore his benefits or his protection. Travelers are still show the debris of the hermitage; they are known in the locale as "good King René's hearth."

A STORY HEARD WHILE LISTENING AT DOORS
1824

> There is more poetry than one thinks in the ordinary
> events of life. Unfortunately, habit prevents us from
> understanding it; it is like a man who is envied
> universally for an income of a hundred thousand écus,
> but who finds no enjoyment in his fortune, because he
> has been habituated since the cradle to the wellbeing it
> procures, and the pleasures that another would find
> therein have become for him needs as necessary as
> drinking, sleeping and eating.
> (*Contes misanthropiques*,
> unpublished work by the author.)[24]

I experience a happiness that I cannot describe when, sunk in my large armchair of antique form, I start leafing through the books scattered on my old oak desk.

The silence, the solitude and physical wellbeing distract me insensibly from my reading, gradually stimulating my imagination, and causing my ideas to flow. Sparse and vague at first, they wander amid I know not how many different things; then, suddenly, inspiration springs forth unexpectedly, forceful and imperious. Subjugated by a sort of mechanical ecstasy that partakes simultaneously of somnolence and fever, I write and write and write without pausing; and, more than once, I have surprised myself writing in spite of the darkness and without

---

[24] Berthoud did publish a collection called *Contes misanthropiques* (tr. as *Misanthropic Tales*) in 1832, but it does not contain the quotation reproduced here. It might be from a story belatedly omitted from the collection, but it is more likely that Berthoud simply improvised it *ad hoc* for the purposes of the present story, as he often did.

perceiving the energetic remonstrations of my stomach, fasting since I got out of bed.

When such sensations eventually cease I experience fatigue and distaste; everything around me seems cold, deserted and arid.

Oh, how I would like then to see a young woman's smile, to hear her speak, to sit down next to her, holding a hand that she would abandon to me. How she would see my forehead blossom under the youthful kisses of a little boy who would climb up on my knees and say the naïve words to me that a father shivers on hearing.

But I'm alone, in the world, alone! And I stay there, sadly sitting next to my half-extinct hearth, while the tempest howls or the rain resonates on my windows, which is its lashing.

Nevertheless, when a beautiful sky encourages me, I sometimes overcome that collapse; I wrap myself in a cloak and I go to wander through the poorest and most solitary streets.

There is in that silent obscurity, in the solitude of an entire city, I know not what poetry, which relaxes and soothes.

And then, at long intervals, one sees a vacillating lantern, the yellow-gray light of which is reflected her and there like a luminous fog. Then one hears resounding on the pavement, and dying away further on, the hasty footsteps of furtive couples, whose double shadow looms up on a wall illuminated by a street-lamp, and suddenly disappears. And then the two-part song of a few drinkers, to whose hoarse voices distance lends a harmony full of charm; and then the guttural sounds of a hurdy-gurdy, a few notes of which the wind brings, comes to add further to the spells I am recounting.

I have not told you yet all the pleasures of a night-prowler.

On the curtains, or the panes of the majority of lighted windows, bizarre or gracious silhouettes are designed; sometimes the crooked profile of an old man, sometimes the slim figure of a young woman who, semi-naked with her arms raised, is gathering and putting up her hair.

A luminous beam that escapes a poorly-closed shutter is another stroke of good fortune; I put my eye to it avidly and, almost always, a scene full of naivety is offered to me, such as our old Flemish painters take pleasure in reproducing.

There is an indescribable charm in surprising, by that means, people who believe that they are devoting themselves without witnesses to the ordinary actions of life: an entire family gathered around a big table, at which a grandmother in a Flemish bonnet fulfills the function of steward; a young seamstress half-bent over her work-frame, entirely intent on the narrow hem that is extending under her fingers; or lovers who are chatting close—very close—beside one another; or spouses delivering themselves to the altercations to which the shrill character of our housewives is so well-adapted.

Once, among others, I saw an old shoemaker working next to a cast iron stove while his wife, a septuagenarian at least, was turning one of those large spinning-wheels with a handle, known only in Flanders, I believe. A young woman was kneeling in front of the stove in order to warm herself more comfortably; she had just come home, for her cheeks were still chapped by cold.

At every moment that group, disposed as Teniers would have wanted them, and whom a flickering lamp left in semi-obscurity, was animated by the play of the light, in the most picturesque fashion; those effects were produced by false gleams that escaped the cracks in the stove, and which cast their red and sudden reflections on the pale physiognomy of the young woman, the stunted features of the old woman and the shiny bald head of the shoemaker.

"Holy Virgin!" said the good woman. "What are you telling us, my daughter?"

"It's a very horrible death," said the shoemaker, in a dogmatic tone, "but it doesn't astonish me at all, for the family has always been unlucky, and I know, on the account of the talion,[25] his great-grandfather, and his grandfather, things that are not good to know. I had them from my father, who was a porter at the Abbaye du Saint-Aubert, and he learned them on good authority, for it was monsieur the prior who told him. You know, Marthe, that while my mother was alive, that monsieur the prior often came to chat with her, for he was not proud and did not deny his cousin, who was not a near relative, but not so very distant.

"I'll tell you about it. Listen.

"One day, when his talion, a good gardener, was working in his suburban garden and he was grafting a pear-tree, an old woman arrived at his gate and asked him for alms.

"Pierre, as Philippe's talion was called, replied to her: 'There's nothing to give; let the good Lord assist you.' And he resumed grafting his pear-tree.

"The old woman did not go away, but set about begging more insistently, saying that she was dying of hunger and that she had had nothing to eat for two days.

"Finally, Pierre, sick of those jeremiads, shouted at her brutally to go away or that she'd regret it.

"The beggar woman did not do as she as bid, and asked more insistently. Then Pierre went to her, pushed her away and caused her to fall.

"In her fall she struck her head against the block of stone in the middle of the threshold that stopped the two battens of the gate, and the impact was so rude that she had a large wound on the forehead.

"When he saw the blood flowing, Pierre repented of his harshness and tried to bandage her and give her money, but the old woman did not want to receive any or to allow herself to be bandaged and drew away, covering the ground with her blood.

---

[25] Berthoud's use of the term "talion" here is enigmatic, and seems to have no warrant in any dictionary, but it is possible that it is a contraction of "tabellion," meaning scrivener or clerk, usually in a legal context.

"When she reached the end of the path, she turned round, made a grand gesture as if to threaten Pierre, and shouted something. He only heard the word 'pear-tree' repeated twice, and he resumed grafting his tree without paying much heed to the beggar-woman's words.

"Seven or eight years later, Pierre's tree had become a large and handsome pear-tress, the best in the neighborhood and the most renowned for its excellent Saint-Germain pears.

"Now, the habit of drinking more than was reasonable had become stronger than ever for Pierre. Having gone to the abbey in an indecent state, a monk made him sage remonstrations. Pierre, who, as I have said, was brutal, did not take it in good part, as he should have done, and insulted the monk grossly. The latter had him thrown out, saying that he would sell nothing more at the abbey. Pierre, beside himself on hearing such words, made the most horrible threats against the monk and swore that he would extract from him, before long, a vengeance such as had never been seen.

"But the night brings counsel, as they say, and the following day, Pierre wanted to go and apologize to the monks and try to get the custom of the abbey back. With that aim, he took a basket of his most beautiful pears and went to offer them to the monk, begging him to forget the previous day. The monk, to show Pierre that he did not bear a grudge, took a pear from the basket he was holding and bit into it; but scarcely did he have a morsel in his mouth than he went very red, writhed like a dying man, and fell unconscious.

"The people who saw that remembered the threats that Pierre had made the day before and believed that he had poisoned the monk. Without going deeper into the matter they took him to prison, calling him scoundrel and poisoner, and promising that he would be broken n the wheel.

"When Pierre found himself alone in his cell with irons on his feet and hands, he remembered the menaces of the old beggar-woman, who had predicted that the pear-tree he was grafting would bring him bad luck. He understood then that there was no hope of escaping it, and, in a movement of rage—for as I've told you, he had a very violent character—he smashed his head against the wall and died within the hour.

"Meanwhile, a physician had been summoned to the Abbaye de Saint-Aubert. The latter, perceiving that the monk was choking and not poisoned, extracted a large pear-pip from his throat, which was suffocating him, and the monk found himself almost as well as before eating the pear.

"They ran to Pierre's prison in order to release him, but it was too late, and the monk, very sad, as you can imagine, made an oath to celebrate, throughout his life, a mass for the dead in Pierre's intention."

After finishing his story, the shoemaker looked at the small audience that surrounded him, and formed a somewhat proud smile, on seeing the extent to which he had interested them. In his expression there was the joy of an author who is being begged to continue the second chapter of a work he is reading when the young woman asked him: "And the story of Philippe's grandfather? Tell us that, Father."

"Oh, that one," said the shoemaker, nodding his head, "is even more terrible to hear."

After that oratory precaution, the worthy man started to speak, and I know not what bizarre accompaniment to his nasal voice was formed by the repeated blows of his hammer and the rhythmic hum of his wife's spinning-wheel.

"Mathias, Philippe's grandfather, had held over the baptismal font the sin of the gravedigger of the parish of Saint-Waast. One evening, when he went to enquire how his godson and his friend were, he found the latter trembling with fever and in a pitiful state.

"'I'm very ill,' the gravedigger said to him, 'and see what bad luck I have—it's necessary now, cold as it is, to get up and go dig a grave.'

"Mathias kindly offered to take his friend's place, and the gravedigger accepted gratefully.

"It must have been between half past eleven and midnight when, after having had an appropriate drink in a tavern—in order, as they saying has it, to armor the breast against the cold—Mathias went to the cemetery with his spade on his shoulder. He set to work ardently, and he had finished the grave when he saw a procession of people coming in, clad in white, whose faces could not be seen. They were each holding a lighted candle, but their hands were covered by a large sheet that enveloped them, and that sheet did not even allow the ends of their feet to be seen.

"After having made a tour of the cemetery, they came to pass very close to Mathias, and dropped the candles they were holding at his feet. The last person in the procession threw down a kind of large ball of wax, in the middle of which two wicks were burning.

"That was the day of All Saints, and Mathias was not astonished to see monks making a procession in the cemetery, but he was amazed that they were gratifying him with such a quantity of wax.

"*Why*, he thought, as he picked up the candles and put them in a sack, *didn't my friend the gravedigger mention this rich windfall? In any case, I won't mention it to him either, and in truth, since I've done the work, I want to have the profit. It's mine alone! I'll go and hide the sack under my bed, and in a month or two when my friend will no longer be thinking about the manner in which I obtained them, I'll simply sell the candles, and I'll have a small sum of money, about which I won't say anything to my wife; it'll allow me to spend a joyous evening at the tavern.*

"He did as he had said, and the sack was carefully hidden under Mathias' bed.

"The following day was the day of the dead.

"At midnight, while Mathias was asleep, as is appropriate, beside his wife, three raps on the door were heard. Mathias, still half-asleep, went to open it.

"Great was his surprise on seeing the previous evening's procession; his wife's alarm was even greater.

"The procession made a tour of the room silently, and then came to stand around the bed, into which Mathias had fallen back at the sight of such a spectacle in his house.

165

"Then, all of a sudden, all of the sheets that enveloped the people that Mathias had taken for monks from head to toe fell at the same time, and Mathias and his wife saw a frightful series of skeletons.

"They were not entire; some lacked an arm, others a leg, some ribs and others a backbone.

"The last had no head.

"Then the packet of candles hidden under Mathias' bed the previous night came into the middle of the room of its own accord. Instead of candles, it no longer held anything but dead men's bones.

"And each of the skeletons started to say:

"'Mathias, my arm.'

"'Mathias, my leg.'

"'Mathias, my backbone.'

"'Mathias, my thighbone.'

"'Mathias, my ribs.'

"And it was necessary for Mathias to return to each of the skeletons the bone that it was demanding.

"Finally, nothing remained in the sack but a skull, the one that had appeared to Mathias the previous evening to be a large ball of wax with two wicks.

The last skeleton came forward, hopping, and Mathias replaced its head on its shoulders.

"It's necessary to tell you that Mathias played the violin, and that that instrument was hanging on the wall.

"A skeleton detached the violin, put it in Mathias' hands, and made him a sign to play, after which it stood behind Mathias with the long bones of its arms lifted in the air.

All the skeletons joined hands and commenced the most frightful dance that has ever been seen. And when Mathias tried to stop, the arms of the skeleton that was standing behind him struck him relentlessly in order to make him continue.

"Daylight finally appeared, and the skeletons covered themselves again with their large sheets and went away.

"After that night, neither Mathias nor his wife ever recovered their sanity. It was necessary to put them in a hospital where people were kept out of pity and where they did not say a word until the hour of their death. It was only before rendering his last sigh that they recounted what had happened to them."

The shoemaker fell silent, and his story was succeeded by an almost terrible silence. The old woman's spinning-wheel had stopped and the young woman was listening with her mouth open.

Finally, she said: "What you've told us, Father, is terrible, but Philippe's death was even more terrible.

"To leave home cheerful and well, in order to go and dance in the village at his sister's wedding.

"Then to fall, alive, into an abandoned quarry and to stay there for a week with nothing to drink or eat.

"To scratch the earth with his fingernails, and to wear away his fingers in such movements of range and despair.

"And finally to be taken out, after such a long time.

"To suffer for three days as no one has ever suffered. To die after that, leaving nine children and a pregnant wife!"

"My daughter," said the shoemaker, reinforcing his voice, "When bad luck is in a family, things don't go as one would wish, and it only remains to say: 'Let God's will be done.'

"Come on, wife, serve the supper."

THE SOUL IN PURGATORY
A Flemish Legend
1825

> And what do despair, opprobrium and death matter
> to me? what does the wrath of an outraged master
> matter? What do captivity and poverty matter? Yes, it's
> for you, my sweet love, that I suffer all that?
> That madwoman importunes me with her amour.
> (*Elle et lui*.)[26]

It was six years since Henri had seen his birthplace.

But that evening he found himself once again in his mother's bedroom, sprawling in the large armchair of which he had once been so fond. Two large logs were burning in the tall Gothic fireplace and casting into the room a light that was reflected, ruddy and flickering, from the old family portraits, the gilded leather wall-hangings, and the old-fashioned fluted oak furniture.

It was just as in the times of his childhood. Nothing in the place had changed, nothing was missing, except the good and saintly woman who resided there, his mother—his mother, who had been no more for three years, alas.

He rediscovers there his cousin, then the pretty Lisette, delightful and mischievous, with floating black hair, her malicious and naïve repartee; his cousin, now the pensive Elise, a young woman with a tender gaze and a soft voice, which makes him shiver.

And both of them, separated for such a long time, take pleasure in the memory of their childhood, a happy time gone

---

[26] There is an 1813 vaudeville entitled *Elle et Lui*, but the quoted lines do not appear in it.

forever: excursions in the country, foolishness, naïve games, trivia, a bouquet of flowers, idle chatter, a rattle; they find a soft, sweet, inexpressible charm in all that; tears fill their eyes and emotion interrupts their voices.

It was so good; he was so well able to become a child again to please her: him, a grave and passionate young man. The young woman's amusements were his. He surrounded her with pleasures and games; for then, nothing was required but games to be happy!

And there were those marvelous stories that he loved so much telling her in the evening, when night began to fall, just as it is now. Oh, she has not forgotten a single one of them. They are all present in her memory, as if she had heard them related yesterday.

There is one, above all, that she has not forgotten, one that charmed her while making her feel sad: the story of a soul retained in purgatory. He will have to tell her that one again; it will be as in the time of their childhood.

Except that she cannot, as in those days, climb up on Henri's knees, huddle there and listen to him, motionless, scarcely breathing, raising herself up slightly at the saddest part, when tears flowed from her eyes and the voice of the storyteller faltered itself.

Henri sighed, and, taking Elise's hand in his own, he commenced the story that the young woman had demanded of him.

"In those days, the angel Eloim made audible in Paradise a song so sweet and so pure that it obtained the recompense that the Lord sometimes accords to his angels: permission to go to console, by his divine appearance, the souls retained in Purgatory.

"Eloim immediately delayed his white wings with blue tips, and, taking flight, descended from the abode of the blissful to the obscure and cold dwelling of suffering souls.

"As soon as he appeared, as soon as the aureole that emanated from his beautiful hair had illuminated limbo, a canticle of actions of grace was sung by thousands of voices that blessed the messenger of the Lord.

"'Oh, tell us, divine spirit, tell us what the ineffable joys of Paradise are. Console us by the narration of the marvels that we are called upon to see when the day of the Lord's mercy comes.'

"That is what the souls in purgatory requested. And the handsome Eloim responded to them with marvelous words and consolations that made them forget the sad place in which they were.

"There was only one soul—a woman—whose tears did not dry up, and who repeated in despair the name of a man: 'Paul! Paul! Unfortunate Paul!'

"At the sight of the dolor that the unfortunate was showing, Eloim felt gripped by a profound sadness, and he forgot all the other souls in order to go to console that one.

"But she could not be consoled, even by the angel's gentle words, and although he talked to her about the Lord's mercy, and promised to intercede on her behalf with the mother of God, so powerful with regard to her divine son, the unfortunate woman kept repeating: 'Paul! Paul! Unfortunate Paul!'

"Eloim them enquired of the woman as to the cause of such profound despair, and enveloped her with his wings to prevent her confidences reaching the other souls. He listened to her so attentively that she interrupted her sobbing and made her plaintive voice heard.

"The divine spirit knew that there is no greater consolation for those who are suffering without hope than to hear them relate their dolors and to sympathize and commiserate with them. And more than once during the soul's story, tears flowed from the angel's eyes.

"She was a young woman named Beatrix, married when still a child to Sire Hugues de Noyelles in Cambrésis.

"For two years she fulfilled her wifely duties as best she could in Christian dignity, having respect and submission for her seigneur and husband, a crafty old man, hard-living, with no loyalty in regard to poor Beatrix. Then the nephew of the

170

Sire de Noyelles, Paul de Quièvy, came to Sire Hugues' manse.

"The said Messire Paul fell in love with Dame Beatrix and spoke to her tenderly. Beatrix resisted for a long time as best she could, but finally the poor girl yielded to Messire Paul's soft words and they exchanged their faith, swearing to wait for better days, and making an oath to marry if Heaven granted Beatrix the good fortune to become free, and if not, to die faithful to one another.

"But the Sire de Noyelles had overheard those culpable voices, and without revealing the extent of his outrage, he made it known that Madame Beatrix's father, a seigneur of the estates of our holy father the Pope, was on his deathbed and desired to see his daughter again before departing this world. In order to do that, he took four men-at-arms who were to escort Madame Beatrix's litter, and accompanied them part of the way.

"He came back two months later, and since that time no one ever heard mention of Madame Beatrix again. Paul dared not enquire as to what had become of her, because the Sire de Noyelles only responded to such questions with a frightful anger, and curses.

"Alas, he had struck Madame Beatrix in the heart with his dagger and sent the men-at-arms and their varlets to the Holy Land, buying their silence and their departure with a large sum of money.

"The soul of Beatrix had flown to the terrible judge who was to decide its fate. Her guardian angel hid his consternated face with his wings, and the demons rejoiced, crying: "Adulteress!! Adulteress! Make way, the damned, make way! Here comes a new companion."

"But the Lord had shown mercy on earth to Mary Magdalen, and he had forgiven her a great deal because she had loved greatly.

"And the Lord showed himself merciful in Heaven toward Beatrix, and forgave her a great deal because she had loved a great deal.

"The demons howled with rage on seeing descend into Purgatory one they had regarded as they prey, but those cries of distress soon turned into cries of jubilation, for another soul soon arrived, the Sire de Noyelles, who had been slain by leprosy.

"The terrible judge of men opened the divine book and read: *Thou shalt do no murder*. The angels wept, turning their heads away, the demons hurled themselves upon the Sire de Noyelles, and the frightful laughter of all the damned saluted the arrival of the Sire de Noyelles among them.

"'O good angel,' said Beatrix, when she had finished her story, "my Paul is ignorant of these terrible events; he only knows of the death of the Sire de Noyelles, and every day is dragging by for him in long and dolorous expectation, for he is saying to himself: *I have the promise of Beatrix, and she must come back to fulfill the oath she made to me*.

"'And every hour, every week, every day, every month, passes in that fashion without him seeing me come.

"'And he is tormenting himself, and accuses me, saying: she has broken her sacred promise.

"'Good angel, grant my return to earth for a single day, in order to be able to say to him: I have died for you, and the last word on my lips was the name of my Paul. Cease, therefore, to wait for me, my beloved, for I am no longer on earth and we shall only see ne another again in Heaven. Seek consolation in other, and, if possible, sweet and perennial amours. Only, in the name of the salvation of our soul by the sufferings that I have endure for you, recite in my intention the occasional *de profundis*. It would be so sweet for me to owe your prayers, my Paul, one day fewer in Purgatory, not because of the suffering avoided, but because it would come from you.'

"The angel Eloim wept, for he had never seen such love. And he said to Beatrix: 'Do you know, Christian soul, that to obtain such a favor as a return to earth, it will be necessary for you to suffer a thousand years more in Purgatory?'

"'Oh, I consent to that, I consent to that!' cried the soul of Beatrix 'Immediately, good angel, immediately!'

"Eloim pronounced the name of Jehovah, and the soul of Beatrix returned to earth, to the castellany of Quièvy.

"It was near the hour of midnight, but no one was asleep in that place, for there was joyous feasting in which nothing was lacking: delicate dishes, fine wines, joyous clamors and beautiful young woman.

"Sire Paul de Quièvy was shouting louder than all the rest, for drunkenness had reddened his face, and his head was reposing on the knees of a young woman frantic in her body and almost naked.

"And he said to her: 'Give me a kiss, darling, and anther, and another; you never give me enough. Sing the song for me again that I taught you and which made you blush this morning; it's a beautiful song, that one. Isn't it true, my friends? It has made a prostitute blush.

'Come on, come on, take off that mantle, take off that collaret. I've never liked fashions of restraint. By my word, it was necessary, for that Beatrix I mentioned to you just now, to play the hypocrite and feign virtue for three long months! So I hope that she's in the utmost depths of Hell to punish the ennui she caused me. Wherever she is, I'll be damned if any prayer of mine ever extracts her.'

"The desolate soul of Beatrix returned to Purgatory.

"And the angel Eloim was waiting for her on the threshold of Purgatory, and he took her to Paradise, for she had suffered more in the hour that she had spent on earth that during a thousand years in purgatory."

Throughout that legend, Elise's hand had remained in Henri's hands, and she did not take it away when he had finished, and did not remove her head, which she had leaned on the shoulder of her childhood friend.

To tell you what tender words they repeated to one another and what other memories they evoked, is impossible for human words, for there are sensations that words cannot express; gazes and embraces are necessary for that.

Those sensation and those memories were delectable, however, for now that Elise and Henri are old, their children often hear them remembering, emotionally, the evening when they saw one another again, after six years of absence, and when Henri recounted to Elise the legend of the soul in Purgatory.

THE DELATION

A French Adventure
1826

> The Judge: Accused, reveal your accomplices
> and the law will send you away absolved.
> The Forger: Condemn me. I prefer the blade
> of the guillotine to the infamous name of Delator.
> (S. Henry Berthoud, *Angoisses*.)[27]

To see her again!

That was an idea that burned his brain, an idea that made him agitate and writhe in the post-chaise.

To see her again! When he has been far away six months for six months; when for six months he has not even heard her name: Clarisse!

If, at least, before quitting her, she had said to him: "Paul, I love you!"

He knows full well that she loves him, that she loves him as no angel in heaven has ever loved; he has read it in her moist yes, in her emotional voice, in the indecisive pressure of hr tremulous hand; but she never made him that confession: "Paul, I love you!"

Before hearing those words, the words for which he would have paid a year of his life, it was necessary for him to leave, to depart on a long voyage, to depart without seeing her once more.

But it was a matter of the life of a brother; for his brother would not have survived the dishonor, and without Paul's prompt arrival, without the sacrifice of a part of his fortune, his brother would have been dishonored. He could not hesi-

---

[27] The reference appears to be fictitious.

tate, therefore, and he had quit everything, his life as an artist, his old mother, and perhaps even more: Clarisse.

But he is going to see her again, and she will love him more than on his departure, for her generous soul can appreciate such a sacrifice. He is going to see her again! Oh, the sensations that he experiences at that idea almost make him bless the absence.

And the dusty vehicle traverses Lille rapidly. A door opens before it; cries: "My son! My dear Paul!" His mother is in his arms.

She weeps with joy; she hugs her son; she hugs him again; she blesses him, she calls him her only consolation, the sole joy that she has in the world.

And she has not wanted to be alone in rejoicing. Oh no! Of all those who came every evening to say: "Is he coming back?" all those who repeated: "In a month, in a week, in a day, we'll see him again!" not one is lacking this evening. She is giving a ball, and it is necessary that Paul dance, in spite of his three nights spent in a carriage. His friends are so joyful: his friend, whom she enumerates with a child-like complaisance, and among whom she names Clarisse's husband, and Clarisse herself.

That overflowing of a mother's tenderness, that celebration of his return, those illuminated drawing rooms, the noise of carriages, the guests who are arriving, the sounds of the instruments tuning up, and then the waiting, the waiting with the palpitating heart, searching among the women coming in: all of that produces an intoxicating exaltation in him, a delightful anguish.

There she is! There she is!

He runs. She stops him with a cold smile, devoid of amour.

She has done well to stop him, for without that smile, his emotion might perhaps have compromised her.

She has done well; oh, yes—and yet, he is saddened by such a great prudence; a vague anxiety grips his heart.

What folly!

Finally, now, he can approach her without imprudence. A young man gets in ahead to him; he invites her to dance, and she smiles at him as he would have given anything in the world for her to smile at him on seeing him again.

How long he takes before going away... Finally, he goes.

Clarisse! Again that icy smile, and then indifferent words, a hand that no longer responds to his grip.

She no longer loves him; it is that young man she loves.

So much the better that she no longer loves him, so much the better that she has not deceived him any longer. After all, such an amour is not to be regretted; it will soon be consoled. To love a woman who does not comprehend your love would be horrible, it would depreciate it. It's necessary to take revenge for such inconstancy by a cold scorn; that will not be difficulty.

Ah! The young man isn't quitting her; she only has words for him, smiles for him.

They're only dancing with one another. Now he's leaning toward her ear; she's blushing, she's looking at him tenderly. Malediction! Malediction!

And his fists clench, and his teeth grind.

That fit of despair is succeeded by an even worse joy; an anxious malaise full of agitation and dejection; an excessive lassitude mingled with an imperious need for movement; his eyes are burning, his lungs are burning; his head is burning.

When two o'clock chimes, he has to leave the ball. It's stifling there.

He searches in vain for a chair in which to sit down. Not one can be found in the antechamber; it's in vain that he orders the domestics to bring him one. They don't obey him, because twenty new orders from the mistress of the house make them forget Paul's.

He remembers then that there is an old sofa at the end of a long corridor directly opposite the room where everyone is dancing, and he goes to sit down there.

Soon, he experienced strange sensations.

He could no longer hear the music; only the vague murmur of voices reached him at long intervals, and then came a great calm, to be interrupted again, a few moments later, by one of those instinct rumors.

An extreme fatigue, the warm and heavy atmosphere of the corridor, its obscurity, the murmurs of the drawing room, after so much stifling warmth, agitation and hubbub, the moving crowd talking soundlessly, the dancing devoid of music that were perceptible through the embrasure of a distant door as if through the undulations of a transparent gauze, plunged Paul into a sort of nightmare, the torpor of which blunted neither the anguish of the soul not the faculties of the senses, but which compressed everything with its iron hand and formed I know not what execrable assemblage thereof, with which a suffocation of the chest and an insipid aftertaste were combined.

He was suffering, in such a state, beyond what can be described, and yet he could not find the strength get out of it, and even found a sort of inexplicable charm in it. Someone walked around him, someone came to sit down beside him, without him paying any heed to it, without him making a movement that might have put an end to that cruel anguish.

That is what he was experiencing when a clear, guttural voice began to speak to Paul's left, and to proffer him confused words that he heard without understanding them, and which added further to the strangeness if his sensations.

It even seemed to him that the voice was one of the tricks of his dream, for there was a mockery in its bizarrely articulated words that associated itself with his memories and reawakened his pain in a cruel fashion.

"Ha ha!" said the voice. "How that young woman dressed in pink is abandoning herself softly in the arms of her waltzer. Do you know her? Excuse me, Monsieur, I don't live in Lille. What gazes they're exchanging! Either I don't know anything, or, upon my word, she's just reached the point of imprudence that precipitates into the abyss of dishonor."

As soon as the man spoke, Paul thought that he had glimpsed in the shadows the features of Clarisse's husband, and he understood the urgency of making the voice shut up that was revealing the young woman's fatal secret; but he experienced such a strange sort of enjoyment on hearing that denunciation, and had so little energy in his numb organs, that he could not find sufficient will-power to emerge from his horrible state, and he let the voice continue.

"Now she's passing in front of us again—how her breast is palpitating! How her hand is pressing her lover's! Now she's taking a piece of paper from her bosom; she's giving it to him."

And specters assembled around Paul; and they turned their icy gazes toward him; and there was a young woman there who was trying to lift up with her hands the brain matter that was spreading from her broken skull; and there was a young man who was covering his heart with his hand, and that hand was raised up by the force of the blood that was spurting from a large wound; and that woman was Clarisse, and the young man was her lover.

In the meantime, the voice continued: "How they're devouring one another with their gazes! How he's gripping her waist! Their disturbance is at its peak: they're doomed! They're doomed forever, I'm sure of it! Now their lips are meeting!"

A sudden, terrible noise woke Paul from his nightmare. A man, Clarisse's husband, ran with great strides and seized Paul's traveling pistols from the mantelpiece.

Two detonations, and the crowd rushed out of the drawing rooms.

And Clarisse hid her bloody forehead with her hands, and her lover pressed, with a dying hand, the wound that he had in his heart.

THE SPELL

1829

> You would not believe all the evil results produced
> in Flanders by the belief in witches. Even recently, in a
> town in the vicinity of Valenciennes a poor old woman
> was nearly killed, who had been accused of purring a
> spell on a horse that had died of glanders. In addition,
> she had cast a spell on a child.
> (*Lettres flamandes.*)[28]

He had not seen the old woman for a long time. He was
surprised and afflicted by the change that had occurred in all
the unfortunate woman's features. An extreme thinness had
stripped the flesh from her pale face. There was something of
the cadaver in those bones jutting beneath a livid skin, in those
sunken and extinct eyes, and those hollow and withered
cheeks. Once her garments, of an extreme neatness, had been
disposed symmetrically; now their disorder revealed the apa-
thetic carelessness of misfortune.

Moved by that sad sight, he put more benevolence into
his welcome than was his custom. The old woman experienced a sort of consolation from that, for our woes become
less bitter if they win us the compassion or interest of people
who are above us by their moral superiority or their rank in
society.

---

[28] The references is presumably to *Lettres flamandes ou Histoire des variations et contradiction de la prétendue religion
naturelle*, published anonymously in Lille in 1752, allegedly
the work of Charles-Louis Richard and Joseph-Robert-
Alexandre Duhamel, but the quotation is fake.

He made her sit down next to him; he comforted her with good words, and then enquired as to the causes of her sadness. He had seen that her chagrins were of the kind for which only one consolation remains: that of being able to satisfy a need to recount them and hearing an emotional voice say thereafter: "Oh, you have a great deal of which to complain!"

Poor woman, her only daughter had died a fortnight before.

"If you knew, Monsieur," she said, wiping away the tears that filled her eyes, "how resigned she was! She died like a saint...

"Accursed witch, who made my child die!

"Yes, Monsieur, it as a spell that was cast upon her. One day, an old peasant woman come to bring us some handiwork. When it was finished we didn't want to give it to her before having received the payment, because, Monsieur, when one is poor and has nothing on which to live but one's handiwork, one can't give credit to strangers.

"The peasant begged us for a long time to permit her to take away the work my daughter had done for her. Holy Virgin! Why didn't I give it to her; then I would only have lost a week's income...but we didn't want to yield. My daughter, especially, opposed it overtly; for myself, I admit, I would have consented.

"That made the peasant angry. If you had seen the treble way she looked at my daughter! 'You don't want to?' she said. "Adieu.' She struck my daughter's chest lightly, who took no account of it, and she went away, muttering threats in a hoarse voice, which I couldn't comprehend.

"The next day my daughter got up with a violent fever, feeling great pains in the chest. What she had liked the best before caused her disgust, and, ordinarily so cheerful, she no longer said a word to me, and always sat there motionless.

"That lasted six weeks.

"The physicians could not understand it at all. It cost me large sums every day to pay for drugs. The drugs were ineffective; the malady only got worse.

"One evening I told my chagrins to one of my neighbors, a woman of great sense. 'Look,' she said to me, 'I'm certain of it—someone has cast a spell on your daughter.'

"That was an idea that had come to my mind more than once.

"That unknown old peasant woman to whom we hadn't wanted to give credit, who went away full of anger, who had touched my daughter on the chest where she was suffering the most... There was no longer any doubt; she was a witch, and the cause of my daughter's illness.

"I had heard talk of a shepherd, a savant man, if they exist, who knew medicine better than a physician. He possesses admirable secrets for curing all sorts of ills, and at one time, it was him that had lifted the spell cast on one of my cousins, to whom someone had given epilepsy.

"I begged him to come and see my daughter. When he had seen her he shook his head and said: 'It's a spell, but a spell I can't lift. She'll die of it. In any case, you'll know who has cast the spell, for the witch will come to your house on the day when your daughter renders her last sigh.'

"The shepherd had spoken only too true in saying that she would die. The next day..."

At that point the poor woman's sobs burst forth in spite of her efforts to suppress them.

When she had recovered slightly, she continued in these terms:

"She had just been buried, and I was praying on my knees for the repose of her soul when someone knocked softly on the door. 'Come,' someone said. Oh, Monsieur, I saw the witch appear!

"'Go away!' I shouted. 'Go away, scoundrel, you who have caused my child to perish.'

"If you had seen the infernal creature's feigned surprise! Beside myself, I threw myself upon her to strangle her. One of my neighbors held me back.

"The hypocritical witch! She swore on her great gods that she did not know what we wanted her to say...she was as innocent as a newborn babe…she had simply come in search of the handiwork that she had given to be done.

"I took that handiwork in order to throw it in the fire, but strength abandoned me and I fell down inert.

"When I came round, she had gone. She had left the money she owed me on the table. I would not touch that money for all the gold in the world. It served to have masses said for the soul of my poor child, may God grant her peace and mercy."

He listened to that story with the respect that is owed to misfortune, and when the mother had finished he did not seek to demonstrate to her that spells and witchcraft are absurd superstitions. The most accurate and convincing reasoning would have remained futile before the belief and prejudices with which she had been surrounded since the cradle.

He consoled the old woman as best he could, and when she had gone he sighed bitterly. He thought about the strange and absurd contradictions that one finds among people deprived of the enlightenment of education, among people who believe in witches and who deny the benefits of vaccine. Everything that degrades, everything that debases the human species is welcomed eagerly; people are only incredulous regarding the truth.

THE BEGGAR'S SOU

1827

> *The Pauper*: Poor blind man,
> if you please, my good lady.
> *The Innkeeper's Wife*: There's nothing to give,
> my worthy man; may God assist you.
> *The Pauper*: May the Devil take you,
> damned woman, confirmed miser.
> *The Innkeeper's Wife*: When will it please God
> to deliver us from this rabble of beggars?

If you have traveled in Flanders you have encountered—it cannot be otherwise—some vagabond of tall stature clad in a ragged smock, with stout stick in his hand, and whose heavy tread is forcefully emphasized by a heavy pair of clogs. The pains of the heart and the burning thoughts of ambition had never impoverished his long, stiff, thick and bushy hair. Gall would have accused his low and narrow brow of incapacity; according to Lavater, his physiognomy did not lack cunning and his dull eyes and features degraded by ignoble habits revealed a being withered since youth by idleness, poverty and contagious examples.

That man is typical of the Flemish beggar. Every village and hamlet is afflicted by at least one such wretch. Full of insolence in his prayers, preserving to the point of obstinacy, he comes regularly, every week, to receive alms that he regards as his legal entitlement. "It's my day," he cries, after having murmured an unintelligible prayer in which it is difficult to recognize the primitive language. "I didn't come last week, so you owe me my last alms."

He stops in that fashion at every door, collects his tribute, and when evening comes he presents himself at a farm, where they hasten to shelter him in the barn, one a fresh bale of hay, sometimes better than the proprietor's bed.

There is not in all of Flanders a farmer resolute enough to refuse alms or hospitality to a beggar. Woe to him if he does, for soon the red flames of a conflagration will escape in swirls from the roof of his barn and the dome of his wheatmill; his cadaver will soon be found lying on a path with his head fractured by a terrible blow from a knotty staff.

Furthermore, a beggar, in Flanders, is a redoubtable individual, on whom is reflected all the evil renown of sorcerers and spell-casters.

Substitute maledictions for their murmured prayers, magic words whose occult power strikes with affliction those who refuse to help them, fascinate livestock with a stare and cause the labors of the farm to fail: that is of what they are accused by old women and the majority of the inhabitants of the countryside. There is no farmer who does not reply in an amicable voice, in the evening, to the taciturn salute of a beggar, and who does not hasten to make the sign of the cross as a preservative against the spell that might have been cast on him.

But what is feared most in the country is the aid of a beggar in any fashion whatsoever, or, worse still, the possession of an object belonging to an individual of that dangerous class. A terrible misfortune is always attached to it; so the robust maidservant, the farm-worker and the plowman carefully refrain, not only from requesting aid for a beggar, but from receiving the slightest service from him. Finally, if the smallest of object of value falls from his wallet, one hastens to restore it to him, for it will assuredly bring bad luck to anyone who keeps it, even unintentionally.

Beggars encourage such prejudices, which ensure that their idleness is respected and gave them the power of dread that Tiberius did not think purchased too dearly when he paid the price of hatred for it.

185

During my sickly childhood the physicians told my family that only the pure and salubrious air of the country could render me a health that the excessive cares and exaggerated precautions of an idolatrous mother had rendered frail and languishing. It was therefore resolved, not without difficulty, that I would spend a few months in the home of one of my father's farmers, a worthy man who enjoyed an honest ease.

On arriving at my destination, I found a child of my own age there, the worthy Hubert, taller than me by a head, with blond hair, a dark complexion and large blue eyes.

You will understand that I rejoiced in seeing myself associated with such a companion, that I was happy to find myself liberated from the tender captivity in which the fearful solicitude of my mother had previously held me. It was marvelous to see us, Hubert and me, running around all day in the ardor of the sum, without any surveillance.

Ten times as robust as me and proud of his physical superiority, Hubert watched over his little comrade with a tender solicitude. No child in the village would have dared to offer me the slightest insult; my protector's fists would have chastised him for it immediately. If I was fatigued, Hubert carried me in his arms. If it was necessary to climb a hill, Hubert took me by the hand. When I hesitated to set foot in some muddy pool he hoisted me up on his shoulders and started running gaily, and whistling, as if to offer further evidence that he was not rendered breathless by his burden.

Then too, he supported my caprices of a spoiled child with an angelic patience. Nothing fatigued him, nothing discouraged him, nothing irritated him; either his friendship for me gave that child the patience of a mature man, or he loved me like a precious toy, whose springs one fears to break by compressing them.

One day, when we had built a kind of little chapel with braches and we were ecstasizing over that marvelous work, a merchant of primitive images passed by. The same idea struck my comrade and me: that we could decorate our chapel with some ornament. But for that, we needed a sou, and we did not possess one

From that moment on, our chapel, constructed with so much difficulty and previously so perfect in our eyes, appeared sad and poor. Discouraged, we sat down on a stone a few paces away, and it was in a loud voice that we built fanciful castles in Spain, ardently desired, which we only needed a sou in order to realize.

A tall man, of unattractive appearance, whose ragged accoutrement, stout staff and beggar's wallet clearly indicated his profession, heard our naïve plants. He doubtless found it piquant, poor fellow, to accomplish the desires of two individuals, and, holding a handful of small coins, he chose a sou therefrom and gratified Hubert with it.

We immediately started running after the merchant of images, but it was impossible for us to catch up with him and it was necessary to come back without having spent our petty treasure.

When my companion's grandmother saw us playing with a coin, and learned from what hand we had obtained it, the good woman gave evidence of the sharpest anxieties.

"Dear children," she said, "return as quickly as possible to the place where you left the beggar and return his accursed coin. If he has gone, if it's impossible for you to catch him—utterly impossible, you understand, my children—throw it in the first ditch you come to…no, wait; it's better to slide it into the tree-trunk at the foot of the Calvary."

You can imagine that the old woman's discourse filled us with fear, and we ran in search of the beggar immediately, but it was quite impossible for us to find him.

During our travels and investigations, the panic and anxiety that had been inspired in us by what Hubert's grandmother had said gradually eased, and gave way to a cheerfulness that one never loses for long at the age we were.

Soon, the coin at which we had scarcely dared look before, served us as a plaything. Hubert made it bounce and roll on the pavement of the road. We tried to catch it in our little hands. Our bursts of laughter redoubled at each new course of the sou, and our pleasure was unequaled when the coin struck the axle of a cart and fell alongside the wheel. Hubert tried to pick up our plaything. Oh! My poor Hubert was seized by the wheel. It fractured his skull.

His grandmother reminded me about that terrible adventure not long ago, and she asked with sobs of despair why the good God granted beggars such a terrible power to do evil and to take away children from their mothers in that fashion.

THE SEMINARIST
1830

There is no place that I would not like better with you,
my sweet Henri, than the most beautiful palace in the
world. Yes, my friend, it seems to me that I would prefer
and eternity of dolor with you to Paradise without you.
That is because, for me, you are more than repose, than
happiness, than all the world. It is because I love you
more than I can say, that I love you as you can love.
(*Lettres d'amour.*)

Is it not true that we shall not longer be apart?
"Is the tomb not there?"
(Maurice Pteuginter, *Contes allemands*.)[29]

I want to make a bet of four gold pieces with you.

I want to bet that none of you, good people of Paris,
knows clearly and exactly what a collector of direct contributions does in a commune of two thousand souls under the min-
istries of Messieurs Villèle and Polignac.

Form a circle around me, then, and lend me your ears.
I'll tell you simply and in my own fashion.

A rural tax-collector is a man to whom one gives fifty
francs a year.

In order to obtain that large sum, he is enjoined to do
various things, among which is collecting thirty or forty thousand francs in three hamlets, in which the richest of house-
holds never has two silver coins to rub together. If, on the ap-
pointed day, the said collector has not assembled the required

---

[29] Fake, unsurprisingly.

sum in good coin, too bad for him; it's necessary that he put his hand in his pocket.

It's marvelous, also, to see a collector depart from his residence at daybreak, coiffed in a broad-brimmed hat if the weather is sunny, or wrapped up in a cloak if there is rain, wind, hail or snow.

As soon as he arrives in a village, woe betide the taxpayers—as he calls them—who are not "in measure," that being the official term. First he issues them with a summons without expenses, then a summons with expenses, and then threatens a collective garnishing.

It does them not good to protest: "I have nothing; I'm in the grip of poverty." The garnisher does not take long to come to their home, a brutal, devouring biped animal, drunk without ever losing his reason. The law, as you see, is delicate and good, squandering the meager possessions of its debtor recklessly, in order to assist him to pay.

Now, the man about whom I am speaking was a collector of contributions in a commune of three thousand souls. No one administered as well, or as honestly; never—and I mean never—was he ever found in remiss of a centime when the day came to transmit the funds to the receiver.

So, when evening came, he remained quietly at home, only daring to go out secretly, and equipped with loaded pistols. That did not always prevent him, nevertheless, from hearing whistles or feeling some large stone thrown by some unknown hand falling on his back.

Every Sunday, moreover, he was punctual in going reverently to hear mass, always at the moment when the sub-prefect came to say his prayers. A miscreant would have felt edified to see the worthy Christian on his knees, turning the pages of a Book of Hours and reciting litanies and psalms while moving his lips—not to mention the good *mea culpas* with which he struck his breast, and the white eyes that he turned to the heavens when the elevation bell rang.

One day, one of the sub-prefect's domestics brought the tax-collector a letter, and the collector omitted to gratify him

190

with a tip. He had, however, traveled two leagues; it was election time, and in order to obtain goodwill, no one, as you know, neglects either the messages or the good care of tax-collectors.

Three days later, the same motive brought the said domestic back to the said tax-collector's abode. While awaiting a response, he went into the kitchen, where the lady of the house, good housekeeper as she was, was preparing a pullet of appetizing appearance.

At the sudden and unwelcome appearance of the administrative domestic, the pullet was immediately hidden, for it was Friday. But a glance had been sufficient for that benign individual; and even though the lady, when he left, doubled the usual tip, the sub-prefect nevertheless showed the poor tax-collector the most severe expression the following day.

The honest father of four did not get a wink of sleep that night.

The following day he went to confession and took communion solemnly; and as there was a procession he followed it bare-headed, singing high and clear, neither more nor less than a cantor, and responded more loudly that any other of the faithful *ora pro nobis* or *libera nos, Domine*.

Apparently, the work of piety, like the wood of Sganarelle, is salted by all the devils. For he, so orderly and of such edifying mores, spent the rest of the day in the café, drinking alone and in small sips a bottle of Burgundy wine.

Someone, by chance, uttered the celebrated word "consequent," then much in fashion.

The tax-collector—the Burgundy wine must have troubled his reason; God alone knows how he could have thought of such a thing—told the man that he was talking through his hat.

Alas, he realized instantly the immense error that he had just made. In order to recover his composure he picked up a newspaper, mechanically. Mercy! It was the *Courrier Français*.

He dropped it as if it were a fragment of red hot iron.

But it was too late. An honest Jesuit, who had long had his eye on the tax-collector's position for his own nephew, had seen everything. And without losing a moment he ran to ring the doorbell of the sub-prefect, whose house was opposite the café. He only came out again an hour later, so long had his report been, and listened to at leisure, and he went straight to vespers. You can imagine how ill the jubilation of that honest man made the tax-collector feel.

His destitution was infallible.

With death in his heart he slowly resumed the route to his village, and had no sooner arrived there than it was necessary for him to go to bed, for he was shivering with fever. His family, rendered anxious by the distress in his features, asked about the reasons that had produced it, but he attributed it to a sudden illness.

Alas, he thought, *the unfortunates will learn only too soon about the blow that will cast them into poverty.*

That day, I had been hunting since daybreak, and, more fatigued than I can say, I was doing my best to return to my village, from which two long leagues still separated me, when the village in which Monsieur Lefebre resides—that being the name of the tax-collector about whom I am talking—appeared to me, with its gray steeple, in the middle of a little wood.

Without intending to, I stopped walking, and my fatigue seemed greater than ever.

Then, I started thinking about a benevolent and jovial welcome, a large armchair next to a crackling fire, an abundant supper and a soft warm bed.

Madame de Staël has said that "the best means of getting rid of a temptation is to succumb to it." I followed Madame de Staël's advice, and I took the small side-path that began at my feet and which led to Monsieur Lefebre's house.

Having arrived at his door, I knocked on it with the butt of my rifle and shouted joyfully: "Hey! I've come to ask you for shelter." The door opened; Madame Lefebre gave me a good welcome, but, in spite of that, it as easy for me to see at the first glance that my arrival was an inconvenience.

I would have given anything in the world to get out of that false position and to be able to retrace my steps, but it was too late.

The good Madame Lefebre read in my face what I was thinking, for she hastened to explain the cause of her embarrassment.

"My husband fell ill on returning from the village," she said. "I fear that he has learned something troubling, for I believe that the malady is more anxiety than fever."

I asked to see him; I was taken to the bedroom where he was lying, and we were left alone. At the sight of me the poor fellow held out his hand, gripped mine convulsively and started to weep.

Then he told me what had happened to him and the fears that he had.

"Oh, my dear Monsieur," he added, as he concluded, "how frightful it is to have no other means of subsistence, for oneself and one's family, than a wretched position for which it is necessary to dread the loss incessantly, for which it is necessary to make the sacrifice of one's beliefs, opinions and honor every day. Better than anyone else, you know what I have done. Wretch! I have gone so far as to let my son, my poor Étienne, become a priest, drawn by an irreflective devotion and subjugated by insidious advice. Alas, how many chagrins that career is preparing for his weakness of character, his inconstant enthusiasms and his Romantic sensibility! I would have liked to oppose my paternal authority to that foolish resolution, but it was made known to me that if I opposed the slightest obstacle to what they called my son's vocation, I would immediately be destitute; it was necessary for me to curb my head and remain silent. Tomorrow he will be a priest.

"Ought I confess to you my weakness, and let you see the extremity to which poverty has reduced me? I have been cowardly enough to rejoice, in spite of myself, in that insensate resolution of my son, in the hope that its accomplishment might prevent my ruination. My God! What execrable thoughts poverty gives!"

I cannot tell you what I was caused to experience by that struggle of an honest man in the perpetual alternative of either offending his conscience or ruining his family.

I encouraged him as best I could; I enabled him to envisage things from a less depressing point of view, and succeeded in rendering him a measure of calm, and almost of hope.

His wife came to interrupt us, and I was very glad, for the heavy and unhealthy air that one respired in the invalid's little bedroom, combined with my extreme fatigue and the emotion caused by the tax-collector's confidences, was making my head ache severely and my depriving heart of vigor.

I hastened to go out into the fresh air, but it brought no relief to my malaise.

Black clouds had accumulated in the sky; flashes of lightning succeeded one another so promptly that my vision was fatigued by them; I could scarcely breathe, and there was I know not what impatience in all my nerves, mingled with agitation and depression.

I sat down at the entrance to a little shed at the bottom of the garden.

There, what the unfortunate collector had told me about his son Étienne returned to my imagination and took possession of it forcefully.

Étienne had been my comrade at school; for six years we had been inseparable; both sickly, both fonder of a work of fiction than a dance, we had not taken long to be united in the tender intimacy that takes such forceful possession of two young adolescents. Of a character weaker than mine, Étienne had allowed himself to be led, most of the time, by my advice, and his confidence in me was limitless. My affection for the excellent Étienne was no less, and I lent myself obligingly to the sidesteps of his strange and sometimes delirious imagination. Another might have mocked his bizarre ideas for their exaggeration and their eccentric impetuosity; exceedingly fond of everything related to the marvelous, I found in Étienne's conversation the attraction that one finds in a tale that makes one shiver.

194

It was eventually necessary for us to separate; and when, after ten years of absence, we met up again, I had become indolent, skeptical and disenchanted, while he was about to receive the tonsure.

I made a few observations to him; he responded bitterly, and since then we had seen one another rarely, and coldly, for we no longer understood one another. Nevertheless, my relations with his family had not suffered, as you can see, and from time to time, as on that day, when hunting drew me too far, I went to seek shelter with Monsieur Lefebvre.

I was entirely occupied with those childhood memories; I was wondering, with no less anxiety than his father, what Étienne's despair might soon become in finding himself enchained by mystical vows that were so little in accord with his character when I saw a man dressed in black advancing toward me precipitately, with a gesture of mystery.

It was Étienne.

His clothing was in disorder, his head bare, and he attached a distraught gaze to me. He sat down beside me, covered his face with his hands, and made no response to my questions.

"Henri," he said, eventually, "I'm going to make you a strange confidence; I'm going to die soon." He placed a burning and fleshless hand on me. "Shh! Don't interrupt me, let me speak. I'm going to die soon, and I'm damned."

It was easy to see that it was a madman that was talking to me, and yet I could not help shivering.

"I wanted to visit my father's house once more," he continued, without noticing that movement. "I wanted to place my pale and hollow cheeks against the panes of his room, and see him, my mother and my sisters, but without them perceiving me, without saying a word to them, for my moments are counted, and their despair will commence only too soon.

"I'm damned, Henri, damned for eternity. I have given my soul to an infernal spirit; it will only return it to me when I prefer Hell to Paradise; for I love it, that demon, and I love it more than an eternity of happiness. For it I have renounced the

195

sacred character of a priest of Jesus Christ, I have renounced the happiness of giving alms, of reconciling sinners with God, the ecstasies of prayer! I am going to die today in order to be with it more quickly, in order never to quit it again.

"Listen, Henri. Two months ago, I was reciting my breviary; at first I prayed with fervor, but gradually, other thoughts preoccupied my imagination and drew it far away.

"I started thinking about a soul that responds to every thought to our soul, to the transports and tenderness of amour, to a burning bond of sublime affection that nothing can weaken or break. A sigh escaped me.

"I heard, beside me, a sigh respond to mine.

"There was a being there the sight of which made me feel ill and delighted, a being such as the most tender and fecund mind cannot imagine.

"Forms more ingenuous, more voluptuous, more delicate than those of a young woman; bare breasts, over which flowed long black hair; eyes simultaneously sparkling, soft and timid, whose gaze penetrated my soul.

"I dared not make a movement, I dared not let my breath escape. The apparition might have vanished!

"She sighed again, and the tears that were flowing from her eyes trickled down her cheeks like those of a sick child and came to fall upon her breast; and then she lowered her head as if she were afraid to show it to my gaze.

"'Étienne,' she murmured, finally, in a low voice full of emotion. 'Étienne!'

"I was beside myself; I extended my arms toward her.

"But she knelt down at my feet and said to me, in the tone of a young woman trying in vain to retain her sobs: 'Étienne, make the sign of the cross in order that I shall vanish.'

"'Oh, no! Stay, stay! Always! Always! You're so beautiful!'

"'Make it, the redoubtable sign, in order that I might return to the abode of malediction without having accomplished

196

what Satan has demanded of me. Make it, I beg you, for I'm an angel of darkness sent to earth to doom your soul.'

"She still remained there at my feet, her beautiful eyes raised toward me, her imploring hands joined together.

"'Étienne,' she continued, 'only tell me that you forgive me; tell me before I leave and I shall go without a murmur to offer myself to the chastisement of my irritated master; I shall not curse the horrible blows of his fiery whip, for you will not hate me, Étienne.

"'And then I will retain a sweet and sincere memory of you, a memory that will make me dream under the immense vaults reddened by the reflection of the eternal flames. Listen, I shall try to hide a drop of water, which I shall pour on to the lips of one of the damned. I shall say to him: *It's for love of Étienne that I'm soothing you*; and Hell will wax ecstatic on hearing its sad echoes repeat a benediction, for the damned soul will repeat: *Blessed be Étienne, forever*.

"'When you are in Paradise—for, Étienne, you have only a few days to live—when you are in Paradise, I shall try to approach its divine vaults; perhaps, in the midst of the eternal canticles, I shall be able to distinguish your voice. Then I shall return to my prison, and I shall say to myself: *I am alone, alone and unhappy for eternity, but Étienne is happy!*

"'Make the sign of the cross, Étienne, make it, that I might disappear.'

"And I, Henri, I listened, in an ineffable delight; I would have given my soul for her not to stop speaking.

"'Étienne,' she resumed, 'I imagined a kind of happiness for myself with you, but I no longer want it; it would cost me too dear, I would buy it at your expense. I said to myself: We will never be separated, a mysterious and indissoluble marriage will unite us for eternity, he and I, who will henceforth only be one. I shall carry him tenderly on my wings, in order that he does not feel the bite of the flames; with my breath I shall refresh his forehead; with my soft embrace, I shall cradle him softly in order that his eyes will be able to close in sleep. And while he alone is asleep in Hell, I shall repeat in whispers words of love and songs that will suspend the sufferings and cries of the reproved.'

"Henri, I could not resist those words; I surrounded the fallen angel with my arms and hugged her to my bosom. 'I want to be yours,' I said to her. 'I want to be yours, for you are able to love, as I am able to love, as I imagined love in the insensate dreams of my youth.'

'No! Make the sign of the cross,' she interrupted me, 'there is also love in Paradise, and you will be loved by a cherub with a heart of flame. The torments of Asraelle will be increased by your happiness, but what does it matter? You will be happy.'

"'I want to be yours, to belong to you, who bear the sweet name of Asraelle, to be yours for eternity. I deny my God for you, I deny for you the salvation of my soul. Asraelle, Étienne belongs to you.'

"The naked arms of the angel were enlaced with mine; our lips met...and when I returned from a long ecstasy of amour, Asraelle started to weep, for I was damned.

"Every night, she has come to visit her husband; every night, she has come to rest her head on my shoulder, and surround me with her caressant arms.

"Yesterday, she seemed sad, and instead of covering my forehead with kisses, she folded her arms sadly over her breast and said: 'Étienne, tomorrow we shall no longer be apart.'

"I understood her meaning.

"'Tomorrow, Asraelle,' I replied, 'yes tomorrow, I consent to that; but let me see my mother and my sisters once more; let me see my father once more.'

"'You shall see them again' she said, 'but without speaking to them.'

"This morning, I fled the seminary, and I hid in this garden, and just now I have seen them all. At present, Asraelle is waiting for me,"

The storm had begun to rage violently, the wind was roaring, the rain falling in torrents, and the precipitate claps of thunder scarcely allowed me to hear Étienne's voice.

I cannot tell you the terror I experienced during my unfortunate friend's strange story.

"Don't allow yourself to be carried away like this by the whims of your imagination," I said to him, without paying overmuch heed to what I was saying.

A flash of lightning suddenly burst forth, and by its light I saw Étienne smile sadly; then he listened attentively, as if he had heard a noise. "Asraelle, my Asraelle," he cried, "there you are, my beloved. Come, come, I'm eager..."

The lightning fell at my feet, and when I recovered my senses, Étienne's cadaver was lying there.

Étienne's father has been rendered destitute, for having, according to the sub-prefect, engaged his son to flee the seminary.

The village curé, a young priest of twenty-five, preached a sermon, in which he proved clearly that God had struck Étienne with lightning to punish his apostasy.

Étienne's mother lost her reason. I'm assured that within his family, two other persons have also been afflicted by mental alienation.

THE ANGEL ASRAEL
1150

I. The Three Damned Souls

Thus God has wished it: in the torments of Hell there are moments of relaxation, and almost of repose. The flames cease to spring forth then, folding into themselves, fading no longer exhaling anything more than a smoke as pale as the mists of Flanders at sunset. The lightning ceases to bristle then, no longer throwing forth sparkling darts. The cries cease then, the plaints expire, the howls fall silent, and in the eternal abysms there is a sad obscurity and a bleak silence. One might think that Hell and its victims have sunk into a profound slumber.

But sleep, by means of which one forgets the pains of the body and the distress of the soul, the mysterious benefit given by the Almighty to humans in exchange for the miseries of this base world, is not made for the reproved. A numbness replete with malaise grips their limbs, stiffened by tortures; a glacial cold penetrates their bones, semi-calcined by the flames; an anguish compounded of stupor and impatience weighs upon their heads, and without thought being entirely annihilated by it, mingles a dolorous uncertainty therein.

Nevertheless, a kind of joy shines in the fatigued eyes of the damned souls and the devils, simultaneously torturers and companions in torment of the damned, when the shadow of the hand of God, extending over Hell, casts that cruel appeasement over it. Yes, a kind of joy shines in their eyes, and, in order to understand it, it would be necessary to know how horrible the suffering of Hell are—but no mortal thought is able to comprehend what such sufferings are, none! And yet, the imagination of humans, so poor and so imperfect in creating for itself an image of happiness, becomes rich and fecund in order to invent horrible torments.

St Paul has said: "The flames of the earth, compared with the flames of Hell, are only painted flames. And if the rich man whose foot drove poor Lazarus from his table could obtain from that pauper a single drop of water to refresh his burning tongue, he would change his clamors of despair into benedictions and transports of joy."

Now, it is not for a frail motive that benedictions and joy would be able to penetrate such an abode.

For a few hours, Hell had been plunged into the appeasement that God only deigns to accord at long intervals, when a piercing scream suddenly burst forth beneath those mute vaults, an expression of both triumph and dolor. Suddenly, the flames were reignited, and their roaring sheaves woke up and bit the damned. The demons resumed their own torments and their duties as torturers, and Satan raised his hands despairingly to his forehead, on which the iron crown was red and resplendent, like an aureole.

Devils and damned souls raised their eyes, and saw above their heads a demon who was flying in circles, with wings extended, repeating the cry that had reawakened Hell, and holding two men and a young woman in his claws, by their hair. At a sign from Satan he furled his wings and knelt down before the infernal throne, without releasing his triple prey, who, upright and panting with terror, dared not raise their eyes to look upon the horrible face of the master to whom they belonged forever.

First there was an old man. His balding forehead attested that he had worn a helmet more than once and hidden his face beneath the plates of his visor. Beside him stood a youth whose gaze was seeking a pale and beautiful woman, whose arms were striving modestly to veil her breasts, and who was blushing at the lubricious gazes and impure laughter of the demons.

Never had such merriment contracted the lips of fallen angels. To begin with, they enjoyed the poor woman's embarrassment, at length and with pleasure; afterwards, they lifted up her hair, which veiled her shoulders slightly; they parted her hands, and ran their filthy claws over her delicate limbs, amused on seeing them tremble convulsively at that frightful contact.

The old man and the youth could not contain their indignation and their jealousy. The demons understood that, with an inexpressible joy. Placing them facing the young woman, holding their heads in order that they could not turn away and placing iron fingers on their eyelids in order that they could not be lowered, they continued the cruel game for a long time, which amused the accused cohorts greatly. The damned souls, surprised, sat up on the ardent couches of the abyss in order to watch their executioners' frolics.

That lasted for several hours.

But ennui is the finest chastisement imposed by God on the reproved, and ennui did not take long to contract the diabolical brows: ennui, the deadliest evil of the eternal fires; the ennui that does not permit an idea to unfurrow the brow and nourish the activity of thought. Soon, therefore, the persecutions that had previously enthused them to such a degree fatigued them.

They sought hard to reanimate them by refinements, but nothing could do it. In vain they took the young woman in their black arms, covered her with noxious kisses and then passed her on to another; in vain they knotted their claws in her long hair and whirled the poor bewildered victim over their heads; their blasé enjoyment was not reanimated. Folding their fatigued arms over their chests, they interrogated with their eyes and in silence the orders of Satan.

The sovereign demon had already turned his head away a long time ago, and he was parading his indecisive and aimless gaze hither and yon. In the end, he brought them back to the three souls standing in his presence, and, after having considered them with a distracted attention, he spoke to them.

"Who are you, old man with a harsh and boastful expression?"

"Jacques, Seigneur de Crèvecoeur."

"And you, honeyed youth who is playing timid?"

"Daniel de Cantaing, seigneur of the village of that name,

"And you, tearful beauty, who have taken it into your head to ape modesty here, where there is truly no place for it? Speak, and quickly, else..."

The blow followed, or rather accompanied, the threat, for Satan struck the young woman violently with his iron scepter. She shivered under the rude impact.

"My name is Jeanne de Beaumetz, and this is my very noble and very redoubtable lord, husband and master."

"Good, I understand. Your sins are more of those sins that all resemble one another, the monotony of which is a torture for me. Stupid human race! You only know how to march in the tracks of others. Is it impossible for you, then, to put your feet anywhere but where those who preceded you placed theirs? Wretched fools, who are caught in traps still fully garnished with remains, whom example does not render wary, and who have the pretention to be wicked when they are merely imbeciles bound by routine! Your imagination must be very poor not to be able to invent some new crime.

"If you want to be damned, at least don't be damned foe a ridiculous peccadillo to which too much honor is done in charging the infernal spirits with chastising it. We live in Hell ourselves, but at least it's for having almost conquered Heaven. It's for having shaken the one who presently calls himself the Almighty on his throne. We reached as high as him, though! But for traitors, but for cowards, but for hazard, above all—hazard, even more powerful than Jehovah!—yes, I would be God at present, and it's Jehovah who would be wearing the iron crown! Mine would be Heaven, mine the angels, mine the choirs of Seraphim, mine the hymns of virgins, mine the universe, and mine nature!

"No matter; I did not triumph, but I march as his equal. Those adorations, of which he is so proud, I have troubled; that worship, in which he contemplates himself, I share with him, I receive more of it than him. Seven legions of angels took part in my revolt. Let him count his elect, and he will see whether he finds them as numerous as my reproved.

"You see, stupid mortals, that in order to damn myself, I raised myself up to be the equal of God. And you, what have you done? You, handsome youth, received a kiss from a woman; you, brutal old man, gave two thrusts of a dagger; this madwoman preferred Hell to Paradise, and that in order not to be separated from a lover she will quit for eternity. Imbecile creatures, is that not your story? The same as that of all the others...

But it's necessary that I hear it with its futile details; I have to submit to that tedium. Come on, Astaroth, don't strut so much on account of these three souls conquered for my kingdom; don't brag about such a little thing as a splendid victory. Certainly, it wasn't worth the trouble of waking me up with your boastful cry just now. It wouldn't take much for me to plunge you into the most profound abysms of my realm for three centuries, reducing you to the condition and torments of a simple mortal.

"Tell me for what reasons these three creatures are damned; tell me, since it's necessary that you tell me, alas, and so that I can decide the genre of torture to which it's appropriate to subject them."

II. Jeanne de Beaumetz

That speech by the King of the Abyss wounded Astaroth's pride profoundly. Nevertheless, he enclosed his wound within himself, for the demons surrounding him were directing piercing and mocking gazes at him, rejoicing in the humiliation to which their rival had been subjected in his triumph.

Feigning an insouciant indifference, therefore, he lay down nonchalantly at the foot of the throne, propped himself up on one elbow, and started speaking in these terms:

"Satan knows that about two years ago, the efforts of the spirits of the infernal empire to doom humans were obtaining no other result than bringing Christians who, sooner or later, could not fail to become the prey of Hell. No soul predestined for Heaven, no soul that was an object of predilection for the angelic slaves of Satan's rival, were deserting the road of salvation to enter that of perdition. Paradise was triumphant over Hell, and every time that one of us, following the terrible conditions that you have laid down, exposed his spiritual nature and attempted, under the penalty of losing it, to seduce a privileged soul, he returned alone after the expiration of the term of his voyage. Then you stripped him of his wings and relegated him disdainfully among the souls of mortals suffering in our gulfs.

"No demon any longer wanted to run such dangerous risks; I smiled with pity at their pusillanimity and the incompetence of those whom the example frightened so much, and I departed. You gave me three years to accomplish the work of the conquest of one human, and now, scarcely two years after I left, I am bringing you three victims. But as you have said, the work was so facile that truly, I admit, I was wrong to bring them with so much racket. I should have thrown them myself, without notifying you, into some obscure corner of Hell, and waited until hazard enabled me to talk to you and inform you of my success.

"Two years ago, scarcely had I quit Hell and reached the atmosphere of the terrestrial globe than I sensed myself embalmed by a pure and sweet perfume of virtue, a perfume whose divine impressions human organs only experience vaguely, but which the rebel angels cannot mistake. In spite of my demonic wisdom, which makes me appreciate good and evil at their true value—which is to say, to comprehend that both are vain distinctions—that perfume of virtue produced in me a dolorous vertigo, which nevertheless did not lack a sort of charm. I immediately headed for the region from which it was exhaled, and I found myself above the Château de Beaumetz.

"There, my eyes, whose rays do not know the obstacles that limit the sight of terrestrial creatures, perceived a young woman of rare beauty, who was on her knees reciting prayers. Three times I ought to have drawn away, quivering with rage, for three times she made the sign of the cross; and there were above her two angels who, with their white tunics, their blond hair and their sanctimonious manner, were receiving those prayers and bearing them to the feet of the master whose servile slaves they are.

"That young woman was named Jeanne de Beaumetz.

"She was expecting, in a few days' time, her father, the old Sire Hugues de Beaumetz, who had departed ten years before for the Holy Land with the Sire de Crèvecoeur. Jeanne was thanking the mother of Jesus, "the Holy Virgin," as she put it, for having finally returned her father to her, a poor orphan, whose dear mother, the chatelaine Catherine, had been lying in the tomb since the feast of the Kings. Now, the feast of All Saints was approaching. Poor mother! How tender she had been! With what bounty she had been kind enough to encourage the amour of her daughter and the young sire Daniel de Cantaing. Daniel had generously taken the side of Catherine de Beaumetz, defenseless and persecuted in a cowardly manner by the avid seigneurs of the vicinity, who had ravaged and pillaged her domain. Daniel, polite, timid and gentle, showed himself to be such a loving suitor, such a good Christian and, above all—which does no harm—a becoming youth skilful at playing the sistrum; he even composed virelays like a professional troubadour.

"In three days, her father would return to the château; and in three days, the chaplain would hand to the Sire de Crèvecoeur a written document made by order of Dame Catherine de Beaumont on her death-bed. In that document, she recommended her noble spouse, if ever he returned from the Holy Land, to have the marriage celebrated of her daughter Jeanne to Sire Daniel de Cantaing, in consideration of their chaste love and the services that the said sire had rendered to his fiancée's family. For, without him, not one stone would remain atop another of the Château de Beaumetz, and the veritable seigneur of that domain, on his return, would have searched in vain for its vast lands and high towers. He would no longer have found anything but vassals submissive to various sires and naked lands divided between avid predators.

"Immediately after that discovery, which I owed to the chatter of the angels who were glorifying themselves in bearing such ingenuous prayers to their God and who repeated them joyfully, I planned the means of winning for Hell that woman, whose soul they were so certain of guiding to Paradise after having led an edifying life on Earth. I took flight in the direction from which the sires de Beaumetz and de Crèvecoeur were coming.

"Truly, it is something to see, the manner in which God recompense his own. The two imbecilic knights, reduced by the sermon of I know not what bald Capuchin, who is roasting here among so many others of his species condemned to the fire, and inflamed with a fine zeal, melted down their gold and silver vessels, pledged four years of their income, removed from the exploitation of their lands the youngest and most capable vassals, and left their mothers, wives and daughters behind to go and deliver the tomb of their God—who does not care about it—by making war on the Saracens, who had never done them the slightest harm.

"Six years later they were coming back without having liberated the Holy Land. In vain they had put on their banners: *God wishes it!* In vain they had battled like fanatics; in vain they had had themselves blessed and reblessed by the Pope, by bishops, by priests; in vain they had charged themselves with relics from the crest of their helmet to the guard of their sword. The Saracens, those heretics, remained the stronger, and the knights of the Almighty obtained nothing from their fine zeal but wounds, misery, fatigue and leprosy. Oh, I forgot something else: their domains were pillaged and their wives had gone off with a few handsome sires who were not such fervent Christians.

207

"Is that not your story, Jacques de Crèvecoeur? On setting foot on the soil of Flanders, did you not learn that nothing in the world remained to you? That your château had been dismantled, that your wife had been seduced by Nicolas d'Oisy three years before, and that, on the news if your return, discarded by her seducer, she had thrown herself in the Escaut?

"When he learned of the misadventures of his companion in peril, the old Sire de Beaumetz felt deeply moved, and began to shed warm tears. I took advantage of that ridiculous tenderness to slide into his soul a project no less ridiculous, and I had all the more influence of him because that morning, at breakfast, he had eaten an enormous piece of roast pork and emptied a large bottle of wine without taking the trouble to enquire as to what day of the week it was and whether it might not be Friday. I therefore set about breathing into him a spirit of vertigo that greatly troubled and obscured his ideas, which were already not very clear.

"I caused him to recall, although he had had nothing to do with it, that the sire de Crèvecoeur had only taken up the cross for the crusade in accordance with his advice, that of the sire de Beaumetz. I caused to pass before his eyes a host of so-called services and so-called proofs of devotion that the sire de Crèvecoeur had lavished upon him, so effectively that the dull-witted dupe took that old warrior by the hand and said: 'Jacques, we have fought side by side for a year; we have shared our bread more than once; we have supported the same sufferings for the same cause, and on your return you have found neither a wife nor a fortune. I want, my brother in arms, to render you a wife and a fortune. Therefore, within three weeks you shall espouse in legitimate marriage my daughter Jeanne, and I shall share with you, in equal parts my castellany of Crèvecoeur. In addition, I'll aid you to combat the wretched felons who have profited from your absence to invade your property, and we'll treat them as we did the Saracens.'

"Jacques de Crèvecoeur, who was dying of the desire to accept—'Say no if you dare, old hypocrite!'—feigned generosity and obstinately refused such fine offers.

"Then the sire de Beaumetz took his dagger, in the hilt of which there was a fragment of the true cross—at least, he thought so, although it was only an old splinter of oak taken from the forest of Mormal; a monk, a fabricator of relics, had found it more convenient to pick up the fragment of the true cross there than to go and look for one in Judea—kneeling before the relic, swore this oath: 'On my share of Paradise and on the holy fragment of thee true cross that I am holding, I make an oath that what I have said will be accomplished, whatever might happen. May the Holy Virgin aid me to bring it to the end, and the Devil take me if I fail!'

"Assured of my prey and having nothing more to do henceforth than let the results of my ruse unfold, I set about furnishing opportunities for mortal sin to fifteen or twenty Christians who could not fail to arrive among us sooner or later. Among that number it is necessary to count seven fornicating monks, four obscure honest men suddenly summoned to the delicate functions of judges or collectors of taxes, and a few other misdeeds that I no longer remember. As they were not men to repent but, on the contrary, to sink more deeply into sin and impenitence every day, I paid no more heed to them and am sure that not one of those who are dead is missing from here; the others will arrive at their leisure, I guarantee it.

"Two days later, therefore, I went to the Château de Beaumetz, where a brilliant reception was being prepared for the seigneur who was coming back, after such a long absence and so many perils. I saw Jeanne everywhere, running around, going up and downstairs, and never leaving Messire Daniel far from her side, who was aiding her briskly, and divined her desires before she had formulated them fully.

"Perched on the summit of a turret, I could not help laughing at their confidence in the future and a happiness that had escaped them forever. My bursts of laughter became so forceful that the tower shook and I had to fly away, else it would have collapsed. At any other time, crushing a few hundred peasants and sending them to another world without confession would have appeared to be quite a good joke, but the terror of such an accident would have spoiled the little joy that remained for our two lovers of savor, and I needed the blow already raised above their heads to strike them in the midst of a complete happiness; otherwise they would not have felt the impact as much.

"Finally, the cries of vassals and their crowd, which ran precipitately out of the avenue of the château, informed me of the arrival of the sire de Beaumetz. Jeanne, her eyes full of tears, threw herself into the old man's arms, covered him with kisses, and could not weary of clutching to her heart the father that Haven had returned to her...and who would give the name of son-in-law to the young and handsome sire de Cantaing.

So, how the damsel longed to see drawing away from that father the knight with the gray beard and the face scarred by blows of the lance and sword, who no more quit the Seigneur de Beaumetz than his shadow quit him—a shadow that rendered so apparent a beautiful yellow sun, such as there are in the region of Flanders in winter. But the importunate old man, encased in his armor, remained there, marching in measured step, sniffing the castellany and the young woman and, so to speak, digesting them in advance. To the one he gave a smile, a veritable grimace apt to terrify the poor thing; he looked at the other from the corner of his eye, saying to himself: *It appears to me to be in a good state, and there's the high forest that it's necessary to sell at a price of lovely golden angelots.*

"Already he saw himself as the father of a line of children and the possessor of a rich domain. For myself, I stood there laughing, jubilant at all the hopes and all the joys that were about to be disappointed.

"When the crowd of vassals had shouted enough and testified to enough delights, they were given twelve or fifteen

210

barrels of beer to slake their thirst and drink to the health of the lord and master. I took a drop of sweat from my brow and cast it among those drunkards, and they fought ne another so fiercely that twenty-nine fell in the melee and the next day the provost hanged four of those who had struck most rudely, one of them at his own brother and another at his son.

"While they were drinking and building up to that battle, the sire de Beaumetz summoned his richest tenants to appear before him. When they had gathered, he set his fist on his hip, spoke for half an hour without saying anything, and concluded in these terms: 'Now, then, there will be recompense for those who have done well during the crusade, and punishment, such as fines and confiscations, for the others who have acted as faithless vassals devoid of loyalty. In addition, I make it known that three weeks from today, on the day of the Feast of Saint André, our beloved daughter Jeanne will marry this noble knight here, Messire Jacques de Crèvecoeur.'

"At those words, Jeanne, who, her eyes sparkling with joy, had expected to see her father's speech conclude with the name of Daniel de Cantaing, uttered a piercing scream and fell unconscious. Daniel, more dead than alive, threw himself back into the crowd. As for this gross seigneur here, Jacques de Crèvecoeur, he strove to reanimate the damsel, whom his presence rendered sicker than ever. She might even have died of dolor, but as that would not have suited my plan at all, since she could be that means have gone straight to Paradise, I approached her ear and whispered into it mysterious words that attenuate the power of death. Jeanne therefore returned to life, and was carried away to her apartments.

"While that was happening, the chaplain handed the sire de Crèvecoeur the parchment that he had written on the orders of Jeanne's mother, which contained the lady's last will. The seigneur had the contents of the vellum explained to him, and the almoner told him at length, after which the sieur de Beaumetz replied:

"'Master, I have made a vow on my share of Paradise, and I have sworn to accomplish it while kissing the pommel of

211

my dagger, in which a holy and precious relic of the wood of the true cross is contained. There is no power either in Heaven or on earth that can release me from such an oath. It is therefore necessary that I accomplish it. In consequence, I am throwing this vellum in the fire. In order that my worthy and defunct spouse, who is, I hope, in Heaven, will not hold it against me that I cannot execute her last will, you will celebrate a mass every day for two years, for the repose of her soul, accompanied by appropriate prayers.'

"'Now, go tell my daughter Jeanne to be ready to obey me with good grace; otherwise I will give her my paternal malediction and, if necessary, will drag her to the altar myself. Finally, the sire de Crèvecoeur must know nothing of this secret; you will answer to me for that with your head. Remember that I have the right of high and low justice, and that your title of cleric will be worthless in this instance.

"'The sire de Cantaing was here a little while ago. Hey, young squire, will you not go in quest of him for me? Look, there he is, mounting his horse, and thinking of leaving us. Tell him that your master needs to speak to him for a few moments.'

"Daniel came at a slow pace, and nevertheless with a sort of hope that I amused myself by inspiring in him. But he no longer retained that hope when he heard Jeanne's father say: 'Messire Daniel, seigneur de Cantaing, my very honored and defunct spouse Catherine de Cisoing, dame de Beaumetz, had resolved to unite you in legitimate marriage with my daughter Jeanne, but I have made a vow on the pommel of my sword, which contains a relic of the true cross, and no power on earth or in Heaven can release me from that oath. I have come, therefore to require you, as the good and loyal knight that you are, no longer to present yourself before my daughter and not to confide to any person in the world what had been resolved in her regard between my wife and you. In doing that, you will acquire unlimited rights to the esteem of an old knight who has fought for years to deliver the Holy Sepulcher from its infidel oppressors.'

"Daniel promised all that the sire de Beaumetz wished and departed in an inexpressible dolor. I leapt on to the rump of his horse as he quit the château and whispered a thousand confused projects of despair and vengeance to him."

At this point the angel of darkness suspended his story briefly and attached to his three victims, and particularly to Jeanne, a gaze full of pride. In fact, few young women as beautiful and endowed with so much candor had fallen until then into the gulfs of Hell. In spite of the terror that distressed her pure and naive physiognomy, and in spite of the despair that contracted her face, it was necessary to inhabit Hell to consider without pity the frail creature destined for the flames that are to burn forever.

The unfortunate Jeanne shuddered under Astaroth's gaze like a bird before the fascinating eye of a snake. Freed from the persecutions of the evil angel and not yet being marked with the seal of the reproved, the seal of ineffaceable fire that is attached to the forehead and endures forever, Jeanne experienced a sort of charm recalling the happiness of the early days of her amour. In spite of the sarcasms of the demon who was the cause of her doom, and in spite of the sardonic tone of his voice, which grated like the bite of a rasp, she allowed herself to lapse into prestigious memories; and in the face of damnation she dreamed again of tenderness. Love is so powerful! Hell itself cannot prevail against amour!

Astaroth, after having considered his prey proudly again, resumed his story in these terms:

"As I was saying, mounted on the rump of Daniel's horse, I escorted him back to his château, where I left him to agitate a thousand confused thoughts, beside himself, devoured by jealousy, burning to avenge himself, and resolved, at no matter what price, to snatch Jeanne from his rival. Daniel already belonged to me body and soul; I therefore returned to Beaumetz, where I found Jeanne in complete prostration, annihilated by resignation and despair.

"I tried in vain once again the power of the magic words that had succeeded so well the previous day. Those words could do nothing for organs broken by an excessively violent shock. Only one means remained to me of reanimating Jeanne, and that was to summon hope to my aid.

"Then I gradually reassembled around her the memories of her childhood; I showed her images of her father playing with her; her father unhappy at a slight illness she had; her father complaisant to her slightest girlish caprices. With those memories, I led her insensibly and without difficulty to believe that the influence she had exercised in those days over the sire de Beaumetz she could still exercise today, and that he could not resist his daughter's pleas. One conversation with him, caresses and sobs, and the old man, far from persisting in his cruel resolution, would criticize himself for his child's dolor, and would deem it a crime to wait any longer to console her.

"One easily believes what ne desires; soon, therefore, from a frail and implausible hope, Jeanne passed to the certainty of success; and, almost reassured as to the future, she went to the ramparts that her father was visiting, resolved as she was to open her heart to him, to make him change his plan and persuade him to recall Daniel to the château.

"Seeing Jeanne in the state of mind in which I wanted her, I drove away the clouds that were obscuring the sky with a heavy gray vapor. The mild rays of the sun came to caress nature; their voluptuous warmth reanimated Jeanne's limbs and completed the blossoming of her ideas. The wellbeing of physical sensations spread over her mental sensations, and with a smile on her lips and a heart that was almost light she headed in the direction in which her father the castellan was walking alone.

"In the ten years since the sire de Beaumetz had quit the soft life of the château to take up the rude métier of warrior, by dint of suffering, he had become pitiless to the suffering of others. The man who had once ceded his firmest will to his daughter's slightest smile now made everyone tremble under his imperious gaze. It was necessary for everyone to obey him as his men-at-arms had obeyed him in Palestine—which is to say, in the days when he had had men-at-arms, for, having departed with fifty lances, he had come back alone on a charger stolen from I know not where. All hail the God of the Christians, for recompensing so well the simpletons who devote themselves to serving him!

"Jeanne's confidence vanished like her smile at the sight of the old sire's forbidding physiognomy. The poor girl stood there alone for some time, mute and downcast. The castellan demanded of her, in a tone that was scarcely of a nature to reassure her: 'How comes it, damoiselle de Beaumetz, that you are wandering on these ramparts at this hour without a matron to accompany you? That is unbecoming and must no longer happen in future. I forbid it—take heed!'

"Jeanne, frightened by the old man's severe tone, did not reply, and felt ready to turn round without saying a word to her father. In the end, however, love prevailed over fear and, advancing toward the seigneur, she tried to take his hand and raise it to her lips. The latter who was meditating I know not what changes to effect in a defective tower, and who had found his château in a state of dilapidation that would have put a less sullen man in a bad mood, was not disposed to listen to jeremiads or to receive the young woman's caresses. He therefore withdrew his hand brutally, and demanded, in a voice in harmony with the gesture: 'What do you want with me? Speak quickly; I'm in haste to finish my visit to the castellany.'

"'Father, father! Permit me to go into a cloister!'

"'Jeanne, what does this mean? Tell me, do you believe that you are able to shake my will and cause me to break my word? You're strangely mistaken, my girl. I will not sacrifice to the caprices of a few days and tears of which no trace will remain in an hour, the honor of my name in this world and my salvation in the next. Be ready to obey me; I wish it.'

"She remained there, as if struck by death, watching her father draw away and know knowing to what saint to pray.

"I set about fluttering above her head, fascinating her with my breath, warming her forehead with the beat of my fiery wings, and then, running after Daniel, whom I had seen prowling around the château, I found him climbing along a half-ruined wall, making a ladder of his belt and his dagger, about to reach the summit of the rampart not far from the place where Jeanne had met her father, and where distress and despair still caused her to remain

"If they had seen one another, adieu all me efforts and all my pains, for Daniel would easily have persuaded Jeanne to go with him and Hell would have lost its prey. The God of the Christians, in favor and in memory of the beautiful sinner Madeleine, forgives many of those who have loved a great deal, and he would not have punished very severely a young woman yielding to an amour that her mother had nurtured and encouraged. I therefore rushed at Daniel, seized him by the hair and dragged him to the foot of the wall. He thought he had been afflicted by vertigo, and soon wanted to recommence climbing the cracked wall, but I deceived him with a vision that showed him the ramparts garnished with men-at-arms; it was therefore necessary for him to retire. That disappointment, moreover, far from calming his despair, only rendered it more exasperated and more enterprising.

"That was what I wanted, and, far from appeasing the youth, I excited his rage twenty times more. Nevertheless, it was necessary that the marriage be accomplished, and, in order that the young fellow would not raise any obstacle to it, I hugged him in my arms and gave him a kiss on the lips. Immediately, a devouring fever gripped him; it troubled his reason and a few peasants found him, more dead than alive, in the middle of the high road, where I had left him. A physician was summoned, and I blurred the reason of that man so well—nothing much remained to do—that the old donkey in a black robe would have made the malady last more than six months but for the plant juices that I put without his knowledge into the beverages he prepared.

"Thus, after having had the pleasure of seeing Daniel suffering, cursing and despairing in his bed for six months, I allowed his fever to be cured. As soon as he was able to go out, he headed for the castellany of Beaumetz. To amuse myself, I let him wander in that was for several weeks without permitting him to see a pleat of Jeanne's veil. Finally, one day when he fell down in a thicket, overcome by fatigue and despair, I caused the sire de Crèvecoeur to pass by with his mournful spouse, whom he was heaping with caresses, unable to comprehend her chagrin and her decline. He was cooing amorously, making me burst out laughing and making Daniel, a witness to that tenderness and words of love, weep

"Twenty times the young man felt ready to run at the sire de Crèvecoeur immediately and kill him, but I wanted more than that, and I did not take my hand from the shoulder of the desperate fellow, who told his confidant the Vicomte de Sars that evening that he could not comprehend what unknown force had prevented him from getting up and striking the old man. 'The will was there but the power was lacking,' he said.

"Well, handsome sire, now you know that force. You were a miserable plaything who were obeying me—nothing more.

"I had also made sure that Jeanne glimpsed Daniel. The sire de Crèvecoeur's wife went for a week without going into the wood, for, now that she bore the title of another man's wife, she wanted to fulfill her duties, and if not to forget Daniel, at least to try not to see him again. But all her efforts only ended up reviving the memory of Daniel and rendering him more present to the imagination.

"She wept; she invoked the aid of all the saints; but the saints and their God himself exercise no power over the human passions; too stupidly scrupulous to excite them, they are unable to tame them, even feebly. Quite the reverse: it is to us, the demons, that the domain of human passions belongs; we give birth to them, develop them, foment them and augment them. They are ignited by our breath, and our breath caused

217

them to spring forth in terrible floods. They erupt, they devastate, and hurl millions of slaves into our empire.

"The saints and the angels were therefore limited to saying to Jeanne: *it is necessary not to love Daniel any longer; it is necessary not to think about him, because that is a sin.*

"For myself, I murmured in her ear: 'Love him! Love him! Was he not the companion of your childhood? Has your mother not blessed your saintly love? On her death-bed did she not say: I want you to be husband and wife, united forever on earth and then in Heaven? And now you have been abruptly separated! What was once duty and virtue has become crime. Oh, no, that cannot be! The crime belongs to those who have disunited souls that the will of a dying mother had united,'

"'What! It is necessary for you not to see Daniel again? No longer to hear his soft and tender voice? No longer to feel your hand pressed by his? It is necessary to efface his memory and replace it with tenderness for an old man who speaks coldly of a love of which he is incapable and which makes the least vassal smile when he is seen, trembling with old age, turning his extinct gaze toward his young wife...

"'No, oh, no, that cannot be!'

"Or at least, since it must be, since honor and duty, cruel duty, demand it, let her at least see her fiancé, her lover, her Daniel, one or more time! Can it be a crime to see him again without speaking to him, without him knowing? To glimpse him through a thick bush or from the height of a turret? Yes, tomorrow morning, she will go into the forest, and doubtless Daniel will be there, as usual; for she is quite sure that Daniel comes there every day. The sire de Crèvecoeur has gone to his château, recaptured from the pillagers who had stolen it from him. Well, she will profit from his absence to see Daniel one last time, to weep at the sight of his sadness. And then, after that, with God's help, she will not forget him or cease to love him, for that cannot be, but she will resign herself to her unhappiness with the hope that death will soon put an end to it.

"Thanks to my secret influence, such were Jeanne's thoughts during the night, when the door of her bedroom opened cautiously, and Daniel, pale and trembling, appeared to her, saying: 'Jeanne, you must come with me! I have reached you at the peril of my life; I scaled the rampart, I've killed three men-at-arms. Come, come; one moment more might doom us!'

"'Go with you, Daniel! Me? Another man's wife? Soil the nuptial bed! Oh, my God, my God, what is he daring to propose to me? Go, go away, or I'll call for help!'

"'Do it, then!' cried Daniel, folding his arms and sitting down with a frightful calm. Do it, then, and let me be stabbed before your eyes. Infidel, belier of the love that you had sworn to me, do it. I shall wait. Is it necessary to call for you?'

"'Daniel! Daniel!,

"'Here is your silver whistle; go on, call!'

"'Daniel, oh, my Daniel, stop! My God, will you abandon me in such peril? Daniel, Daniel, listen! Flee, out of pity for a poor woman; she asks it of you on her knees. Flee, flee!'

"'I will not flee without you! It's necessary for you to come with me, if not out of love, at least to save your life. They will know that those men-at-arms have been killed, the ramparts scaled by a man and the arrival of that man in your bedroom. You will not be excused; they will not listen to your justifications, for your father knows about our love and your tears. Come, then: flight with me, or opprobrium and death here.'

"Jeanne covered her face with her two hands; prey to a horrible agitation, she did not know what decision to make, when the sire de Crèvecoeur burst into the apartment, rushed upon Jeanne, pierced her with a dagger-thrust and began a battle with Daniel, the conclusion of which was death for both of them. Then I, who had thrown the suspicion of jealousy into the old man's heart, who had inspired the idea of a false journey in order better to spy on his wife, seized the souls of my three victims and I took flight toward Hell.

"Angels stopped me, and cried: 'Take the sire de Crèvecoeur and Daniel; they belong to you, they are murderers; but Jeanne is ours, Jeanne has not sinned.'

"Oh, despair! Already they were snatching her from my hands, already they were flying with her toward Heaven, when, by a sudden inspiration, I cried out, imitating Daniel's voice: 'Jeanne! Jeanne! We shall be separated, then, for all eternity!'

"At that plaintive tone, that adieu, Jeanne appealed to her lover with loud cries, quit the angels and came to throw herself into the young man's arms. It was into mine that she fell, and, laughing uproariously at the disappointment of the angels, who veiled their faces with their wings, I arrived and I brought these three souls."

As he concluded, the fallen spirit directed a proud and satisfied glance around him. The demons applauded in chorus; the groans of the damned responded to them, and the flames of Hell roared and launched toward the vault with more violence.

III. The Condemnation

Satan made a gesture and everything returned to silence. Nothing was heard any longer but the dull moan of the flames, rumbling like the last furies of a storm that is drawing away.

"This old man will be cast among the jealous, and this young man among the adulterous. As for Jeanne, let her be taken to the other extremity of Hell; let the name of Daniel never be pronounced before her; let her never learn what sufferings he is enduring, nor whether he retains any memory of her.

"Go! That is for eternity!"

At those terrible words, pronounced in a loud voice, magnified by all the echoes of Hell, the three souls were taken up by demons and carried to the places assigned for their torment. And in the meantime, thousands of groaning voices repeated:

"That is for eternity! That is for eternity!"

IV. Asrael

Among the reproved angels who had listened with most attention to Astaroth's story there was once who still conserved I know not what vestige of his forfeited splendor. His soiled wings still shone with a residue of gold and azure; his forehead, branded by the reproving seal, tilted over his left shoulder with a meditative sadness, and he usually found himself the butt of the derision of the evil spirits, who had only drawn him into their revolt by means of a trap.

Before the revolt of the angels against the Almighty, Asrael, as he was named, had been part of the legion of cherubim. Sitting facing the throne of the Eternal, he mingled his voice with the ineffable choirs that celebrated the glory of the Almighty. Next to him sat the most beautiful of all the divine creatures, the angel Nephta, with whim the mysterious knots of a celestial hymen united him. With arms and wings enlaced, they inebriated themselves together with the bliss of paradise; together they expressed the transports and the ecstasies of divine love.

If some message sent Asrael to direct the course of a planet or reestablish the divine harmony that rules the universe, Nephta, immediately knotting her tunic, accompanied him and aided him to support the ennui that angels experience far from the presence of God. When fatigue stiffened the cherub's wings, Nephta surrounded him with soft embraces and, fortified by love, carried him through space. On the other hand, when sleep came to weigh down Nephta's eyelids, she would have been unable to sleep if her Asrael's shoulder had not received her head, if her breath had not mingled, during repose, with her Asrael's breath.

The mystic bond that united them with one another recalled both the chaste devotion of a sister and the ardent tenderness of a husband. It was the most holy amity, the most sacred marriage, the most passionate amour. Never any jealousy, never satiety: a pure and suave calm; incessantly re-

221

newed transports, a happiness of which the imagination of mortals can dream, but which they have never tasted. For the need for amour and happiness, always so imperious and always so disappointed among humans, is nothing but a reflection of the celestial life in the life on earth, an instinct that causes the desire for Heaven, a vague perfume that reveals Paradise, as the perfume of a flower reveals the flower's stem and corolla.

Such was the fate of the cherubim Asrael and Nephta when Satan raised the standard of revolt against God. Faithful to their master, they were taking refuge in the enclosure of the good angels when a horde of rebels suddenly precipitated upon them. The shock of the horrible battle separated Asrael and Nephta and, after the combat, Asrael, alone, his eyes full of tears, called to his companion with loud cries—but no voice responded to him. The unfortunate cherub was sinking into despair when a demon approached him.

"Don't weep, Asrael," he said. "Don't weep, for I can take you to Nephta. Nephta is among us, she has joined the ranks of the angels who are combating our oppressors; she has asked me to come to console you and invite you to rejoin her."

"Evil angel," Asrael replied to him, "you're deceiving me. Nephta has remained faithful to God; Nephta cannot be a rebel. Gone astray during the battle, she has drawn away from the celestial refuge. I want to bring her back and I shall. Nephta! Nephta! Hear the voice of your Asrael!"

But Nephta did not reply.

"Ingrate," said the demon, "since you require proof, since you don't want to believe me, who has come to this place, amid the greatest perils, to bring a message from your Nephta; ingrate, recognize then this veil, which she gave me for you, and which covered her forehead and her shoulders. Adieu! I shall reply to her that Asrael, a coward devoid of amour, prefers the tedious wellbeing of Heaven to the inebriating transports of Nephta's tenderness. Adieu! It's up to me to console her for your abandonment; up to me to love her henceforth and to make her forget your tenderness by means of mine."

"If you were speaking the truth, I wouldn't hesitate—but no, you're lying, you're abusing me."

"Well, will you at least believe my oath? By my immortal life, by Heaven and by the earth, by the universe and by the firmament, I swear that Nephta is among the angels who follow the standards of Satan!"

At that perjury, the first that had been proffered to him, Asrael, unable to suppose that anyone would dare to profane the sanctity of oaths to that extent, believed the evil angel and followed him. But when he found himself among the revels and he asked: "Nephta, tell me where Nephta is!" a group of perverted angels, their eyes sparkling with lubricity, surrounded the handsome cherub and said to him: "Nephta is not here, but we will love you in her stead." And they enlaced him with their caresses, covered him with their kisses, and surrounded him with a thousand intoxicating and lascivious spells.

Stunned by their seductions, Asrael fell into the arms of one of them, making her repeat that she would love him forever. The next day, his perfidious lover laughed at the promises she had made him, and ran to lavish her transports on another.

After that fatal day, Asrael, alone among the fallen spirits, wept with bitterness over the horrible existence to which he found himself condemned. The horror and the tortures of Hell mattered little to him; what he regretted, the evil that consumed him, was the memory of Nephta, and of her tenderness; that was an unbearable isolation, a void that human words cannot express. As he once had in Heaven, he experienced imperiously the need for love, but alas, he no longer had Nephta to love him, as in Heaven. To speak of love to the sisters of demons only resulted in exciting their ridicule and mockery. Saint Theresa depicted the torture of the rebel spirits very well in saying: "The unfortunates, they are unable to love!"

The adventures of Daniel and Jeanne awoke in Asrael I know not what vague hope of finding on earth a love to respond to his love. The devotion of that young woman and the partial resemblance of his own misfortunes to those of the unfortunate woman excited his interest to the highest degree. In spite of Satan's orders he took pleasure in conveying from Daniel to Jeanne and from Jeanne to Daniel their words of love. He consoled them by his active protection, and, for the price of so many benefits, he asked them to tell him the story of their amours in earth.

"Those impetuous and passionate accounts exalted him to such a point that he resolved, no matter what the cost, to be loved once again. With that design, he asked Satan for permission to spend two years on the earth, making a pact either to bring him a privileged soul, or, in the contrary case, to lose his wings and his title of angel, and to be eternally relegated to live among the simple mortals condemned to the fire.

Satan accorded him that pact, and Asrael took flight for earth.

V. The Chatelaine

On emerging from the somber and burning gulfs of Hell, Asrael felt himself assailed by numerous sensations that were simultaneously energetic and confused. The pure air inebriated him with vertigo; his dazzled eyes closed under the radiant floods of daylight, and the profound calm of nature produced a sort of numbness replete with emptiness in the angel accustomed to the execrable tumult of the eternal abysms.

That astonishment was gradually succeeded by an indescribable wellbeing, such as Asrael had not experienced since his fall. It seemed to him that a heavy burden had been removed from his breast, and that a new existence was beginning for him. Yielding to a child-like joy, he played for a long time in the atmosphere, warmed by the first rays of the rising sun. Everything became, for the cherub, ineffable and unalloyed enjoyment. The dew of the clouds bathed his limbs soiled by the filthy smoke of Hell, and rendered them flexibility and freshness. The wind blew through his hair and came to caress his forehead softly. Finally, a sad and soft smile parted his lips, contracted for so many centuries by the shriveling of despair.

Then he smoothed the plumage of his wings voluptuously, effacing the remains of the mud that still tarnished them. Afterwards, he flew and soared beneath the most vivid rays of the sun, in order to gild those wings with the brilliant and rich reflections of the star's rays.

The songs of birds, the murmur of waves, the quivering of trees whose crowns were swayed by the morning breeze, the thousand harmonious voices of nature that rose toward the sky like a hymn of gratitude for the Creator, made the angel feel better, as the kiss of the only woman who has remained faithful to him in his distress makes an unfortunate man feel better, as the cares of a mother make a sick child feel better, and as a naïve memory of the time of his youth makes a man disillusioned by disappointment and experience feel better.

Nevertheless, when the coolness of the evening came to penetrate the cherub's limbs and make them shiver, he felt returned to himself, to the sentiment of his misery and the memory of the motives that had brought him to the abode of men. Fulfilling the pact contracted with Satan was of scant importance to him—oh, no importance at all. What he wanted, for which he did not believe his demotion from an angel of darkness to the torture and slavery of simple damned souls, to be too high a price to pay, was amour, to be loved, to experience once again the sensations that he recalled, at least vaguely, of the sublime inebriations of divine amour and the tenderness of Nephta.

Then the angel remembered Heaven, and began to weep. And all night long his tears flowed, and all night long he blessed those tears, for he had not, alas, been able to weep for a very long time.

The power of the reproved angels over humans is one of the deadly consequences of the sin of our first fathers. From the fatal day when the seductions of Eve, the victim of the serpent, drew the excessively weak Adam into disobedience, mortals became slaves of demons, and demons received the power to tempt them and to use all means to succeed in doming them. They could, at their whim, remain invisible while extending their traps, or put on human appearances, or even take on the features of living individuals, and by that means lessen the guard mounted by the prey around whom, according to the holy Scriptures, they circle and roar like hungry lions.

Before using that mysterious faculty, Asrael quit the oak in the branches of which he had nestled until dawn and, deploying his wings, flew toward a château whose high towers surged forth on the summit of a hill. The castellan was about to go hunting; horses were waiting at the foot of the perron, and the varlets and the lords, falcons on their wrists or dogs on the leash, were standing there awaiting their master. The latter soon appeared; although already old, age did not seem to have depleted his strength; he leapt lightly on to his charger, and then, looking toward the perron and being astonished only to see pages there come to enjoy their seigneur's departure, he called out two or three times, urgently:

"Lydorie! Lydorie!"

Then a young woman appeared, a young woman whose features offered to the gaze something bold and imposing. Pale, but with a pallor that suited her noble physiognomy, her eyebrows and her great dark eyes, her hair bound and raised on to the top of her head, her tall stature was imprisoned in a robe that designed her gracious and severe figure. She came out, smiling at the old man's impatience, putting no less slowness into disposing the pleats of her robe and knotting the cords of her girdle. Certain of the power that she exercised over her father, and proud of abusing it, she spent a long time examining her mount's harness, adjusting it several times. Finally, she sat down nonchalantly in the high saddle. Then the horn sang, the voices of the beaters rag out, and the barking of the dogs and the bellicose whinnying of the horses replied to them.

At that tumult, Lydorie's eyes sparkled and a vivid redness animated her cheeks. Raising her hand, she repeated the clamors of the hunt, struck the hack stamping its feet beneath her with her crop, and, without waiting to see whether the others were ready, she departed at the gallop, drawing after her a flood of horsemen and dogs.

No obstacle stopped her, not the ditches to be leapt, the thickets to be penetrated or the steep slopes to be scaled. The stag, the stag—that was the sole idea that dominated her. It was necessary that she be there when the hunter, setting foot on the ground, struck the animal at bay. Halloo! Halloo! This way! This way! You're following a false trail! You're going wrong! To me! To me! Victory. Horn sound and resound! Victory! Victory!

How beautiful she is, thought the angel, *and how that fiery soul, passionate for frivolous pleasures, would burn with a veritable amour! She consumes all the activity of her senses in the emotions of the hunt; but when a heart comes to comprehend her heart, a voice will come that says: "Love me and I will give you my amour. Love me and I will reveal to you what the fire is that is devouring you, the fire you do not know how to direct, or upon what object. Love me and we shall have long days of delight and ecstasy; you will quiver with transports unknown to your virginal soul; one idea will dominate you, one idea will no longer quit you. What importance henceforth will chagrins, anxieties, tears and despair itself have to you? You will not longer have a void in your soul; you will love, you will be loved."*

Yes, that is the one that ought to belong to him, that is the one who ought to console him for the loss of Nephta, the one who ought to share with him the eternity of Hell, the Hell that will cease to be redoubtable, since amour will have penetrated it. It is necessary that he set to work straight away, without delay! Where could he find a more beautiful and more passionate creature?

Immediately, Asrael assembled a few of the primitive atoms of which nature is composed, and which the production and destruction of beings combine in thousands and thousands of different forms. He mixed those atoms; he fecundated them

227

with his breath; he penetrated them with the creative heat of the Sun; of that mixture and that heat, precious stones did not take long to be born, and the matter that the alchemists have sought in vain to produce with their search for the philosopher's stone: gold.

Furling his wings then, and dressing himself with the tunic and hat of a seigneur of aristocratic appearance, Asrael came to sound a horn before the drawbridge of the manor and request the hospitality that is owed to every sire of good lineage gone astray at the approach of nightfall.

VI. Hospitality

Scarcely had the angel sounded the horn for the third time than the drawbridge was lowered and two men-at-arms, spears in hand, came to recognize the newcomer and enquire as to what he wanted. At the sight of the unknown seigneur's elegant costume and magnificent charger, they bowed respectfully and said to him:

"God and Saint Julien be blessed. You will find good shelter, a good table and a good welcome here."

A squire took the angel's horse by the bridle and led it into the court of honor. There, a page held the stirrup in order that Asrael could descend without encumbrance. Then he marched straight to the reception hall and announced:

"The guest of Messire le Chevalier de Saint-Hylaire."

The sire de Saint-Hylaire received Asrael with an almost theatrical gravity, without getting up and without saying a word.

Lydorie came to present him with a cup of fuming hippocras, and two varlets announced that a bath was being prepared for him, and that their master's guest would soon begin to refresh himself there after the fatigues of the road.

Such were the rules of Flemish hospitality in those days that the person admitted to a manor was only designated by the name of guest. Such a custom was also observed among the ancient Greeks; they would have thought it lacking in decorum to ask the name of the person who had recourse to their hospitality.

If politeness imposed that discretion, however, it did not prevent curiosity from forming conjectures and seeking to divine the name, the title or at least the homeland of the stranger, and Lydorie and her women neglected nothing in that regard.

That was, moreover, quite natural. Recluses in the narrow circle of the castellany in which they had been born, women, in the epoch of which we are speaking, led an existence of claustral monotony. Praying to God, supervising domestic labors, working on detailed embroideries, masterpieces of skill and even more of perseverance, sometimes running after a deer or hunting a wild boar—that was everything to which their way of life was limited. So you can imagine that the arrival of a stranger was good fortune for them.

In exchange for the hospitality he received, the guest, moreover, did not fail to recount what he had seen during his voyages or following his route. Even if he had only come from five leagues away, he would find an attentive audience whom he could inform of new and unknown details. Without commerce, almost without maintaining any relations with one another, without any high roads to connect them, the Flemings, especially the Flemings of the Middle Ages lived, for the most part, in complete isolation. They nourished themselves on the wheat they cultivated and livestock they bred; local hops and barley gave them beer. They had flax to make vestments, wool to fashion the cloth of their coats.

In that era of simple mores, in which a man was born, lived and died in the same place, like a plant, for what wellbeing would they have gone in search by traveling or trading? Without fear for the future, they were marvelously content in the present. Less sophisticated in their habits than their descendants would become, they possessed in exchange the absence of anxieties, the joy of the soul and the happiness of existing from day to day, glad when an unexpected episode came to create a diversion from that good monotony and re-

229

place the banal interest of the fantastic legends of old and stories of feats of arms told and retold twenty times over, if not more.

All that can, therefore, explain the urgency with which Lydorie and the women of her entourage put into seeking to divine who the sire was who was receiving hospitality at the château that evening.

"He has a bronzed complexion and dark eyes," said one. "He must have come from the Holy Land; it's the African sun that has burned his face and hands in that fashion."

"Nevertheless," observed another, "he seems to be too young for you to have guessed correctly; his hands are so frail and delicate that they prove their lack of habitude in handling the lance. Look at the hands of the sire de Saint-Hylaire and the men-at-arms, even the youngest, and you'll confess that I'm right."

"I know the coats of arms of all the Seigneurs of Cambrésis," Lydorie objected, "but I've never heard mention of those with which his tunic is divided: two golden arrows on a sable field, with the device: *I must succeed*."

"I've heard tell that Eustache de Nivernois, nephew of Monseigneur the Bishop of Cambrai, Messire Jean de Béthune, arrived at his uncle's house not long ago; the young sire might well be him."

"He's going to emerge from the bath, Dame Berthe, and you can mention Monseigneur Jean de Béthune as if by chance; we'll see what he says."

"Shh! Here he comes."

And the group of ladies resumed their needlework actively, in such a fashion as to create the impression that the work in question had never ceased to preoccupy them intensely. Nevertheless, they were not plying the needle so hard that they did not dart surreptitious glances at the young sire, who was advancing toward them with a marvelous grace. Already he was pronouncing the fulsome words, of an exaggerated gallantry, that characterized courtesy and good education in those days, when the sire de Saint-Hylaire came back into the hall and ordered the varlets and maidservants to set out the supper.

"It will soon be curfew, my guest, and it is necessary that it does not surprise us at table. It's always better not to depart from the established order; so, come this way. Sit down in the place of honor, at the end of the table here, to my right and facing my daughter. Hats off now, hats off, everyone, and let our worthy chaplain recite the *benedicite*.

The chaplain obeyed, and everyone spoke the responses to the prayer with fervor, with their eyes lowered. When the orison was concluded, the chaplain and the entire assembly made the sign of the cross. To general surprise, the stranger was pale and almost dying in his chair; sweat was running down his face, and a convulsive agitation as shaking his limbs.

People hastened round him and wanted to give him aid.

"It's nothing," he said, "it's nothing. I've just experienced the afflictions of a malady to which I've been subject since childhood. You'll see them dissipate, and calm restored to my visage."

In fact, the symptoms that were agitating him gradually disappeared; his features became serene again, and nothing any longer remained but a gracious pallor, at least in the opinion of the ladies of the entourage. All were in accord, moreover, in singing the praises of the young man, who deployed a mild affability full of charm. They had never heard tales told with such artistry; no pilgrim or crusader had ever been able to rival him in describing the habits of different lands, the costumes that were worn there and the usages observed there. The towers of Notre-Dame de Paris, the beautiful manuscripts of the King of France, the camel-hair tents of the Sudan, the lands where people have thick lips and black skin as thick as an ox-hide breastplate, countries inhabited by dwarfs where it as daylight for six months of the year, and thousands of things of which they had only heard vague mention, well, he had seen them, or he knew voyagers who had told him about them.

Lydorie, her women, the varlets and even the old sire de Saint-Hylaire listened to him with an attention so great that no

231

one heard the curfew rung, and the belfry chimed midnight to everyone's great surprise.

Then the almoner, one the castellan's orders, commenced the evening prayer; but at the first sign of the cross, the stranger was seized once again by the afflictions of is malady. The chaplain exhorted him to retire, saying to him that fatigue sometimes causes such accidents, that, in view of his unhealthy constitution, he was not required to take part in the prayer, and that a brief mental orison would substitute for it. To that effect, he cited the canons of the Church and a papal bull.

The stranger yielded to such good reasons, and two varlets escorted him to the room where he was to spend the night.

VII. The Ruse

In spite of their organism being far superior to the organism of mortals, demons are not, like the angels who remained faithful, initiates to the mysteries of human thought. They can only read thoughts by means of conjectures and with the aid of surprise or study.

In order to divine the thoughts and sensations of a young woman devoid of suspicion who thinks she has nothing to hide, however, that celestial gift is unnecessary.

Asrael understood easily what a profound impression had been produced in Lydorie by his discourse, honeyed with courtesy, and specially the mystery with which he was enveloped; a mystery beneath which, adroitly, he allowed a high lineage and rich domains to be glimpsed. The young woman's pride was already vaguely caressing, without her admitting it to herself, the hope that the young chevalier might fall in love with her. Upon that hope—improbable, she knew—she devoted herself to a thousand brilliant thoughts that were only, she told herself, vain dreams devoid of reality; vain dreams to which she surrendered because they were pure folly, because their charming and sweet spell was merely a suave perfume that embalmed everything around her, that would evaporate forever, and without leaving any trace.

Tourneys in which the handsome knight broke lances in honor of his lady and wore on the crest of his helmet a pledge of amour given to him by Lydorie, groups of ladies of the bedchamber, varlets, richly-clad pages and numerous vassals delighted Lydorie imagination in that fashion all night long, and were reproduced in her dreams. She amused herself with them as if with a book of chivalry, like a romance that communicates melancholy, and sad and tender thoughts. She laughed at the fragility of the seductive scenes that she created and took pleasure in setting out before her imagination; but she never ceased creating new ones and intoxicating herself with their charms. Like those imprudent children who amuse themselves with firebrands, she had ignited a blaze while she thought she was still only playing.

That is what the fallen angel understood, who, stripped of his terrestrial appearances, had come to sit down beside Lydorie's bed. Undoubtedly, he recognized, pride and ambition had been solely dominant thus far in the damsel's soul, but pride and ambition might lead there to amour. And the young woman, whose heart was beating so rapidly at the idea of adorning her head with the crown of a duchesse, would perhaps not recoil one day before the idea of changing existence and sitting down on a demon's fiery throne. Oh, how much less frightful Hell would then become for Asrael! What would his dolor and despair matter to him then? He would have a friend to listen to and console his suffering, a voice to encourage him and sustain him.

To work, then! To work!

Profiting from the rest of the night, he created, with the aid of magical means, rich carriages and a numerous retinue. He enjoined his new servants, subaltern spirits at the orders of demons, to come and join him toward evening at the castellany of Saint-Hylaire, and, at daybreak, he was back in the bedroom to which the pages had conducted him the previous evening.

233

Soon, a varlet came to inform him that, after the break-fast that was already served, everyone was going hunting.

The hunt was animated and joyful. An enormous wild boar had been discovered in the nearby marsh. They headed in that direction. Lydorie, at the head of the most ardent, and Asrael, always by her side, did not quit the tracks of the ferocious beast for a moment, and showed an unparalleled boldness. Twice she struck the monster with the short spear she was holding, and twice, without the aid of Asrael, who attacked the boar, she would have been unhorsed and exposed to the direst peril. In the end, she delivered a thrust with so much dexterity that the boar, struck dead, fell like a mass and did not get up again.

The commonalty of the dangers that they had run together established from then on between Asrael and Lydorie a kind of intimacy full of confidence and abandon. They continued throughout the rest of the hunt to ride side by side, talking about a hundred different things and putting a price the least of those things by making them seem important, speaking of them as if they were secrets. So, however frivolous their conversation was, they suspended it when a third person arrived and resumed it thereafter in low voices, not without looking several times to see whether the importunate individuals might be coming back.

The day passed in that fashion; when they had returned to the foot of the perron, Asrael, who had arrogated the exclusive right to render Lydorie all the petty cares that, without apparent importance, nevertheless say and are worth so much, launched himself from his horse in order to hold the damsel's stirrup, and it was on his shoulder that she leaned in order to descend from the hack.

Leaning over the balustrade of the perron, the daughter of the seigneur de Saint-Hylaire was making sure, before going back inside the château, that the grooms were not neglecting to care for her favorite mount, covered in sweat, when the sound of a horn was heard. The drawbridge was lowered, and a magnificent hunting-carriage came into the court of honor.

"Monseigneur," said one of the squires, approaching Asrael, "we have been trying to catch up with you since this morning, but while we were searching the forest one of the sire de Saint-Hylaire's men-at-arms came to tell us that you were in this château; we've come here to receive your orders."

Asrael turned his head as if to hide a tear.

"It only remains for me, then," he said, "to take my leave of my worthy host, and you, noble demoiselle." Leaning toward Lydorie he added, in a low voice: "I shall long retain a sweet memory of this day."

"Do you think so, my guest?" exclaimed the old seigneur. "No, upon my soul, you shall not depart today. You are too trusty and too merry a companion for that. No; unless you have some complaint to make about my hospitality, you'll stay in this château for a few more days, or weeks, not to say months, if that doesn't bore you too much. One doesn't often have the opportunity to encounter knights of your worth. Give me your hand, and promise me that you'll stay."

Asrael alleged a few excuses.

"I don't want to listen to you. It's necessary to obey me, or you'll leave an ill renown here for docility and courtesy."

"True!" said Lydorie. "And we'll all think badly of you."

"That would be a very harsh punishment and very unjust, but perhaps it's better to submit to it than expose oneself to assured chagrins and penalties without remedy."

"I don't believe," Lydorie interjected, feigning not to understand him, but whose burning cheeks and lowered gaze revealed her emotion, "that staying a few days more at my father's château would be an assured chagrin and a penalty without remedy for you."

"Oh! Why do you not want to understand me, damoiselle?"

Lydorie did not reply.

"It's necessary that I leave. It's necessary that I escape the peril, if there's still time—and perhaps, alas, there isn't! Oh, why was I separated from my retinue? Why did Monseigneur your father welcome me to his domain?"

Without raising her eyes to look at Asrael, Lydorie still kept silent.

"Now that you understand me, now that you know my secret, you can see that it's necessary for me to leave. You won't retain me any longer, will you? If I stayed, it would be necessary for you to see me, it would be necessary for you to hear me, for I wouldn't be able to hide my amour from you any longer. It's necessary that I leave, you see. Squires, make everything ready for my departure; and you, servants of the noble sire de Saint-Hylaire, receive this guerdon to thank you for your kind attentions and to help you remember me."

So saying, he threw them a purse containing more than a hundred gold coins.

Suddenly, while Asrael, leaning over the balustrade of the balcony, was giving a few orders to his servants, the young woman marched toward him, and, placing her hand on the arm of the individual she believed to be a knight, she said to him with an inexpressible inflection of her voice, full of emotion:

"Stay!"

VIII. Deception

For a month Asrael stayed at the Château de Saint-Hylaire, and no one gave any thought to seeing him leave, much less being astonished at such a long sojourn. Far from it, he found that he had entered to such a point into the habits and good graces of everyone, that no one did anything except by or for Monseigneur Asrael, and the latter formed the center at which all tender attentions and almost all ideas ended up. For one thing, the grace of his manners and the charm of his discourse had won hearts; secondly, his love for Lydorie and Lydorie's love for him seemed to be tacitly recognized and adopted as an absolute article of faith. It was something received by all, even by interested parties: a mute accord, but of such an irrefutable authenticity that everyone acted as if it had been proclaimed aloud.

So, a benevolent complicity with that amour showed itself incessantly and everywhere attentive to favor it and caress it. In order to please Lydorie, people obliged Monseigneur Asrael; in order to please Monseigneur Asrael, everyone obliged Lydorie. If they were seen chatting together, people refrained from coming between the two of them and withdrew discreetly. While hunting, the hunters allowed them to progress together, and if they saw them heading for an indirect path, all of them, without even exchanging a knowing glance, without even smiling, out of habit and because the tenderness of the two lovers was so solemnly known, turned their bridles and took another direction. Finally, if vassals had a favor to obtain, they addressed themselves without hesitation to Monseigneur Asrael, for their young mistress could not refuse Monseigneur Asrael anything, and Monseigneur Saint-Hylaire had no other will than that of his daughter. Asrael, Lydorie and the sire de Saint-Hylaire found nothing strange or inappropriate about that mode of intervention, for they shared, as we have already said, that intimate consciousness of the reality and authenticity of their amour.

However, Asrael has not yet asked the sire de Saint-Hylaire for the hand of his daughter Lydorie, and the old seigneur did not yet know by any other name than Asrael the man whom he already loved as a son-in-law. Confident as a man whom no one dared deceive can be, little accustomed and perhaps scantly capable of reflection, and most of all dominated by the indolent bonhomie of the Flemish, he knew that his daughter was loved by a rich young lord, courteous, becoming and nobly born; that was sufficient for him and it would never have occurred to him to enquire about Asrael's homeland, his family or a thousand other items of information that prudence would have necessitated. He liked Asrael, Asrael loved his daughter; the rest therefore seemed to the worthy seigneur to be unimportant accessories that could not impede a marriage that was in his eyes, inevitable.

As for the possibility that anyone might love his daughter and aspire to make her love him without being of noble lineage, that appeared to him to be so absurd that the idea never crossed his mind.

Without sharing that blind confidence entirely, Lydorie found so much charm in Asrael's tenderness that a vague anxiety rarely appeared to her, which she immediately drove away. Nevertheless, from time to time, that anxiety returned to assail her and mingle her happiness with I know not what sentiments of bitterness and dread. Often, in Asrael's absence, she promised herself to dispel the doubt, to address positive questions to him and to provoke satisfactory explanations. Once in Asrael's presence, however, a modest embarrassment took hold of her and struggled against her resolution to speak; soon, at her lover's soft words and the spell of his gaze, she forgot her designs and only any longer experienced one idea, or rather one sensation: the love of Asrael.

The fallen angel abandoned himself wantonly to the charm of such a situation. Not that the terrestrial passion he experienced could compare to the delights and transports of cherubim, for amour down here is only a poor reflection of the amour of Heaven, but, cast for so many centuries among demons full of hatred, he felt as glad of the emotions he was experiencing as an exile at the distant sight of his lost homeland. Hell and the pact made with Satan only appeared to him to be like a painful dream devoid of reality. Entirely committed to the present moment, he forgot the past and the future. Loved! Loved! He, who was been stamped with eternal reprobation, was loved by an adorable creature who had even sacrificed her pride for him, for she did not know his homeland, his rank or any name but Asrael, and she loved him.

"Oh, it is not true, demoiselle," he said to her once when, sitting on a high turret, they were savoring together the calm of a beautiful autumn night, "that for a veritable love, rank and obscurity, fortune and poverty, fortune and misfortune are vain distinctions that amour cannot admit? Is it not true that, if you love, you will not recoil before the greatest sacrifices and nothing can diminish our tenderness?"

"Yes. If I had given my heart, I would always love the one who has received it; I would associate myself with his misfortune; I would console him in his dolors; I would share his suffering without a murmur—what am I saying?—gladly."

"What! Nothing would discourage you? You'd renounce your peaceful life for difficulties and poverty?"

"What would it matter? Would not the glory of my lover, my husband, be a wealth, a treasure, happiness?"

"But what if that lover, that husband, had nothing to offer you but despair and an eternity of dolor?"

"What would it matter? I would be proud of his illustrious name, and everyone would still envy me."

"So, even if the man you love had deceived you, even if he had put on deceptive appearances, even if he had promised you the crown of a duchesse and..."

"Ah!" said Lydorie.

And she lifted the head that as resting on Asrael's shoulder and removed from Asrael's hand the hand that it was holding. And then, pale, she attached her gaze to him, which seemed to be darting flames.

"Why pretend any longer, Lydorie?" the angel continued. "Why hide the truth from you any longer? I'm not what I appear to be; I'm not a Duc, I'm not a knight; I'm..."

He stopped raising his eyes to look at Lydorie, and he saw so much anger in the damsel's features that he thought his fatal secret had been divined,

And that anger did not leave him any hope; for, he could not be mistaken; indignation and scorn were the sole cause of it; indignation and scorn alone, without any residue of love.

To annihilate her tenderness instantly, he thought, *it can only be the terrible aspect of Hell. Nothing else could have prevailed.*

Courage failed the cherub, and, in order to make his happiness last a few seconds more, since he still had a year and a half to spend on earth, he interrupted his deadly confidence and said, making use of the first idea that presented itself to his troubled imagination:

239

"I'm only the son of a merchant."

"And you raised your amour as far as me, wretch!" cried Lydorie, standing up and stamping her foot. "Insolent! It needs a creature of your species to insult a noble family thus!"

"Listen to me, Lydorie. To reach as far as you, to see you, for you alone, I have sold my father's patrimony, I have spent in three months the wealth that he had gained by labor throughout his life. I have destroyed my future—and all that for love of you. Oh, tell me, would a noble lord have loved you to that extent?"

But she was not listening.

"Men-at-arms, come here! Seize this wretch and throw him from the height of the postern. He has just outraged me in a cowardly fashion. Do it, or, on the salvation of my soul, it will cost you dear!"

Asrael threw himself on his knees. "Oh for pity's sake! In the name of the amour that you had for me, in the name of my old mother who has only me to console her, have pity! Mercy!"

She only responded with an imperious gesture to the men-at-arms. They seized Asrael, dragged him to the edge of the postern and let him fall into the profound ditch. But the angel of darkness, deploying his wings and causing his crown of fire to spring forth, immediately reappeared before Lydorie.

"My turn!" he said. "Follow me, murderess!"

"Mercy!" she cried. "Mercy! Pity!"

Asrael did not reply.

"My father! My father!"

"I begged you for a mother; you did not even listen to me."

"Oh, who can save me?"

"Nothing. It will be done to you as you have done. You have been devoid of pity; no one will have pity for you. You have not loved; you will be thrown into the abyss of hatred. Come."

He seized her in his arms and, flying through space, he presented his victim to Satan.

But Satan responded to him with a bitter laugh.

"Lydorie de Saint-Hylaire belonged to us already by virtue of pride; this is not a privileged soul."

And Asrael returned to earth, discouraged and desperate, and resolved to act as a demon and to drag pure souls into Hell, not this time in order to be loved, but solely for the pleasure of dooming them and associating their misery with his own.

IX. The Boatmen

Asrael directed his flight toward other countries. He traveled Artois and Hainaut by turns, but without ever descending to earth and always cursing the fatal deception that had made him quit Hell and risk the almost certain degradation of his power as an infernal spirit. The discouragement and the disgust weighed upon his imagination and almost produced in him the execrable somnolence that sometimes suspends the dolors of the region of Hell.

He went forth aimlessly and came back the same way; sometimes he hovered over a village, and his eyes gazed without seeing; sometimes he wanted to return to the abyss, but a mysterious force rejected him and made him remain on earth. His sadness appeared so great and his dejection so complete that once, one of the good angels charged with standing sentinel at the entrance to Heaven opened the door slightly, in order that the harmony of celestial singing might console and reanimate his fallen brother.

On hearing that divine music, Asrael could not hold back his tears, and he struck his breast in despair.

"Oh, what have I done? What have I done? Cursed be the traitor who drew me into the abyss! Cursed be my weakness that enabled me to listen to him! Cursed be the hour when I was born! Why did the supreme Will not leave me in oblivion? I was fortunate, for one is fortunate not to feel, not to exist! Yes, I would bless oblivion if I were able to return there; because for me, there is no happiness and repose except in oblivion. O my former brothers, you who were able to resist the traps of the rebel angels, you who are still admitted to the sight of the Lord, tell me: can your divine prayers not soften his wrath and obtain the clemency of death for Asrael, for Asrael who detests his immortality? Oh, I am not as guilty as the other rebel angels. If they had not said to me: 'Nephta is among us, Nephta is weeping for her Asrael to come and share her fate,' alas, the lightning of the Almighty would not have furrowed my brow."

"Unfortunate, we can only shed tears with you. Why these plaints? Why these prayers? They are futile. Nothing can change the immutable will of God."

"But at least speak to me about Nephta, tell me that she is faithful to me; tell me that a memory of me sometimes summons a tear to her eye, and that the love of another cherub has not replaced the love of Asrael in Nephta's heart...

"You're not replying to me; you're veiling your faces and drawing away. Does a demon horrify you? Alas, it's not fear, it's pity that I ought to inspire. Adieu, then, beautiful children of Heaven, adieu forever! Adieu! For the sight of your happiness and your glory causes me a torture more cruel than the flames of Hell; it makes me remember the wealth that I have lost forever, lost without hope of ever possessing them again. Adieu! Adieu!"

After that he resumed his errant life, incessantly pursued by the memory of the singing he had heard, which still seemed to be resonating in his ears. The sentiment of his misfortune was revealed more cruelly and more forcefully than ever, as on the day of his fall, when the laughter of the demons had told him that he was the victim of a perfidious lie.

One evening when he delivered himself to such dolors and was mechanically following the banks of the Escaut, which, a feeble stream at first, gradually became a river, and then a veritable sea, he perceived near the shore one of those long flat boats named bilanders that navigate on the pure and fecund waters of the beautiful river. He drew nearer to the boat and saw a numerous company of people sitting on their folded knees, who were forming a circle, in order to listen to the story that an old boatman was getting ready to tell them.

The bilander offered a truly singular scene. All of those who were there, by their strange garments and their no less strange physiognomy, seemed to be a class of beings apart, cast among the Flemings. Their blond and curly hair formed a bizarre contrast with their bronzed complexion, like the complexion of the inhabitants of India. Their ears were laden with large silver rings, embroideries covered their woolen jackets, and heir bare feet stuck out of breeches of an extreme width.

The women presented an admirable perfection in their forms; they combined the slightly slender flexibility of Egyptian women with the nervous grace of the daughters of Italy. Their hair, put up and knotted at the top of the head, allowed a vast forehead to be seen in all its beauty and a profile worthy of Greek regularity. The sleeves of their narrow corset showed their arms, naked to the shoulders, and a skirt what descended a little below the knee, attested to the voluptuous proportions of their similarly bare legs. Finally, their voice, soft and accented like the voices of the Midi, sang rather than spoke the modulated language of Flanders, and rendered it even more harmonious.

That race of boatmen was then the same as it still is today. Ten centuries have scarcely modified a few of its habits and softened a few of the prominent features of their primitive character. Dressed as in the thirteenth century, they live as in the thirteenth century, apart, without mingling with the inhabitants of the land they traverse. They retain their terrible passions and indolence of old; they spend more than they possess and never direct a prudent gaze toward the future. Sensual to the point of libertinage, jealous to the extent of murder, civilization has neither ameliorated nor bastardized them; it has not touched them. Their boat is their fatherland, the river their domain, their laws the will of the patriarch of their race.

When evening comes they assemble on the largest of their boats that is in harbor; there, in order to occupy the interest of their fiery imagination, incessantly stimulated by idle-

243

ness and solitude, it is necessary that they hear stories; the marvelous alone pleases them, the marvelous whose glare strikes, dazzles and causes shivers. Avid for strong emotions, they understand nothing of a story of mild and scantly pronounced interest. No, give them the catastrophes that cause weeping, the memory of which displays phantoms during slumber and makes one look behind in terror when one finds oneself alone; give them the thrill caused by a mysterious turn of events, and the expectation of a terrible denouement. Yes, those men who reach for their daggers and gaze at the waters of the river at the thought of a rival, those men require stories that stir them, that shake them and make them stand up with astonishment and fear.

After having gazed for some time at his silent audience, which attached to him gazes full of attention, an old man lit the wick of a lamp that the wind caused to flicker, and which projected a red light and mobile, capricious shadows over the boatmen.

Then he passed his coarse hand over his suntanned forehead two or three times, and he began to speak:

"It only happened to me once in my life to spend the hour of midnight in the vicinity of Mont Brûlé; I shall never spend another there...

"Yes, even if Monseigneur le Duc de Flandre promised me as a reward the castellany of his finest city, even if our Holy Father the Pope were to grant me a relic of the tree of the true cross with an indulgence of an entire year! For I would surely die, even before seeing again what I saw in that accursed place; my soul would depart from my body merely at the panic of expectation...

"I saw on Mont Brûlé what no human eyes have ever seen.

"I was coming back placidly from the village of Flesquières, and riding as fast as I could toward Estrées, spurring my horse with sharp thrusts of my heels, for it is scarcely good to find oneself outside one's shelter at such an hour, on a black night with a cold north wind.

"Now, when I had just passed close to Mont Brûlé, which, in broad daylight, merits that vile name only too well by virtue of its ruins of I know not what olden time, and its pitiful and sterile flanks, I felt anxious on seeing a red light shining there, reminiscent of a spearhead glinting in the moonlight. Although I took the light to be some shepherd's lantern, I made use of the protective sign of our salvation just in case.

"It was as well I did, for if, in spite of such a shield, I received such rude blows, what would have happened to a miscreant with no safeguard?

"Suddenly, the little red light flared up, extended and, in the midst of a torrent of flame, allowed me to see a château of beautiful appearance, where men-at-arms, varlets and hunters were moaning piteously, not to mention damoiselles and chatelaines; their keening generated shivers, and there was enough to cause faintness in hearing them.

"Little curious to see such a spectacle, I pressed my mount hard with my spurs, but it refused to take another step forward and remained motionless, as if retained by a magical and supernatural force.

I began to commend my soul to God, for I believed that my last hour had sounded.

"I believed that even more when I perceived, coming toward me as fast as his legs could carry him, a knight clad in armor as red as iron emerging from the forge.

"He was holding a large loaf of bread in his hands, and from as far away as he could he shouted to me: 'Take it! Take it!'

"I only replied with urgent signs of the cross, but instead of being frightened, he approached more rapidly and fell to his knees before me, still holding out his loaf of bread to me and saying:

"'Take it! Take it!'

"He remained there, at my knees, until daybreak.

"Then the crow of a cock was heard in the distance; the flames of the château were extinguished incontinently. I saw the turrets and the ramparts vanish; then the voice of the specter with the red armor became feeble, and he sank into the ground.

"My horse, covered with sweat and in a state of strange agitation, departed then at a fast gallop, and only stopped at the door of my lodgings.

"My wife and my children were waiting for me in great emotion. When they saw me pale and distressed, they thought that I had been ambushed by thieves, and expected to find me wounded by some dagger-thrust.

"Without telling them what I had seen, though, and offering the pretext of I know not what adventure, I sent in all haste for the saintly hermit Mathias, who lived in a grotto on Mont d'Arleux.

"The holy man, believing that there was a risk to the salvation of a soul in peril of passing from this world to the other came running with the holy oils and the sacrament, surrounded by faithful followers carrying candles and holy box-wood, preceded by a petty cleric with a hand-bell.

"I had the women and the young people withdraw and, in the presence of Père Mathias and the old men, I recounted the frightful things that I had seen.

"The hermit listened to me, his forehead supported on his hand, and when I had finished he spoke, as you will see, to the great edification of each of us.

"'Many years ago, there was on Mont Brûlé the château of a noble and powerful seigneur named the Vicomte de Sainte-Hermine. The said castellan was only hospitable to sires of high lineage.

"'One winter evening two hermits came to clamor piteously under the towers, saying that they had lost their way and would perish of hunger and cold if no one granted them a shelter and a loaf of bread.

"'The Vicomte de Sainte-Hermine did not care about their laments; he even started to laugh, and added indecorous insults, by the advice that he gave the hermits to dance and curse, as an infallible means of warming themselves.

"'The following day, when the Vicomte de Sainte-Hermine had the drawbridge lowered in order to go hunting, he found the rigid cadavers of the two hermits.

'Instead of feeling contrite, however and striking his breast with repentant *mea culpas*, he pricked his charger with his spurs in order to make it trample the bodies of the hermits underfoot.

"'At the same moment, two enormous serpents emerged from the ground hissing and enlaced the horseman with living knots, which he could not break.

"'And a terrible noise, like a tempest at sea, roared around him. Lightning flashed in all directions, the manor caught fire in a hundred different places, and soon, nothing any longer remained of it but ruins.

"'Then the great serpents released their prisoner, who stayed there, immobile, for three days, without making a movement, after which he died.

"'No one dared approach the place, and the cadaver of the Vicomte de Sainte-Hermine remained unburied, prey to the worms of the earth and the crows of the heavens.

"'The frightful spectacle that you have seen is surely nothing but the consequence of his punishment. Perhaps, if you had taken the bread that he offered you and you had recited a *de profundis* for the repose of his soul, he would have been delivered from punishment and admitted to purgatory, in order to reach from there the abode of the blissful.'

"A few days after what I have recounted, Père Mathias went to Mont Brûlé by night, and the people of the locality are sure that the frightful apparitions at the hour of midnight have ceased since that time.

"But how can one know whether that is true? For, since my misadventure, no one would dare to spend the night in the vicinity of Mont Brûlé.

"For myself, I wouldn't want to, as I said, even if Monseigneur le Duc de Flandre promised me as a reward the castellany of his finest city, even if our Holy Father the Pope were to grant me a relic of the tree of the true cross with an indulgence of an entire year!"

X. The Ballad Singer

The boatmen had listened to the old man's story with an extreme interest. Throughout the duration of his story no voice had spoken, no one had breathed deeply. Sitting on their heels, the chin supported by the hands and the elbows resting on the knees, they might have been taken for statues but for the emotions painted on their expressive features and the vague terror shining with a yellow gleam in the dark eyes attached to the storyteller.

When he had finished, they maintained for a few seconds more a silence produced by attention, a vague fear and a kind of expectation, which mingled with the regret of seeing the legend that had moved them so forcefully concluded.

Afterwards, one voice hazarded a few curt words articulated in a low voice, which hissed in the midst of that great silence. Gradually, other voices responded to it in the same manner; little by little the slight buzz became a confused and noisy conversation in which everyone was speaking at the same time. Commentaries were made, analogous adventures cited to confirm the marvelous events of Mont Brûlé. Everyone had got up, everyone had drawn closer. Scattered groups covered the deck of the boat intermittently, and a private conversation was held in each group.

At that point, the vague melody of a song became audible in the distance, of which a few feeble sounds arrived at intervals.

"It's Lorette! Here comes Lorette"" someone shouted. And that name produced a magical effect, for everyone immediately fell silent and pricked up their ears. Meanwhile the singer drew closer; her voice became more distinct, and the slow and melancholy rhythm of a popular ballad was already recognizable. Soon, it was even possible to distinguish the words of the ballad.

I

The Comte de Flandre Beauduin was known as Beauduin-à-la-Hache.[30] He was a noble and just seigneur, was Comte Beauduin-à-la-Hache.

II

With Comte Beauduin, prompt and good justice did not take long; it was delivered within the hour. Whether one wore the golden spurs of a knight, the trousers of a villain or the head-dress of a widow, justice was granted to all.

The Comte de Flandre Beauduin was known as Beauduin-à-la-Hache. He was a noble and just seigneur, was Comte Beauduin-à-la-Hache.

III

One day when the Comte à la Hache was returning alone to Winendale he met a poor woman weeping, sitting on the side of a ditch by the road. Her coat was in tatters, her hair unkempt, and lying beside her was a corpse slain by thrust of a sword, as could easily be seen.

The Comte de Flandre Beauduin was known as Beauduin-à-la-Hache. He was a noble and just seigneur, was Comte Beauduin-à-la-Hache.

---

[30] It is not obvious which of the five Comtes de Flandre with this name is referenced in the ballad, since none was conventionally credited with the nickname in question, but it is most probably the first, previously celebrated in the ballad "Beauduin Bras-de-Fer."

IV

Now the Comte à la Hache stopped his charger, which had been running at the gallop, and asked the weeping woman: "Woman, why are you weeping like that?

The Comte de Flandre Beauduin was known as Beauduin-à-la-Hache. He was a noble and just seigneur, was Comte Beauduin-à-la-Hache.

V

"Oh," she said, "nowhere in the land of Flanders is there woman who can shed tears worse than mine; for the first day of my marriage has been bloodied and if I do not lose my reason, the horrible memory will stay with me until the hour of my death.

The Comte de Flandre Beauduin was known as Beauduin-à-la-Hache. He was a noble and just seigneur, was Comte Beauduin-à-la-Hache.

VI

"This day I married my friend Pierre Mahormoudt, who loved me with a faithful and honest amour for four full years. I was coming back from the monastery with him, we had escaped the wedding party to talk alone at our leisure, and were here, sitting on the edge of this ditch, when eleven knights wearing escutcheons with your colors passed by and started saying: 'Here's a pretty girl; she must grant a kiss to each of us.'

The Comte de Flandre Beauduin was known as Beauduin-à-la-Hache. He was a noble and just seigneur, was Comte Beauduin-à-la-Hache.

VII

"'Go on your way, Messeigneurs, I said to them, and leave a poor village bride alone, who surely does not merit the ugly insult you have made.' But Pierre Mahormoudt did not take it so gently, and said to them, putting his hand on his dagger: 'Let my wife alone, or by God and Our Lady, it will not be said that I let you insult me.'

The Comte de Flandre Beauduin was known as Beauduin-à-la-Hache. He was a noble and just seigneur, was Comte Beauduin-à-la-Hache.

VIII

"The knights laughed in an insulting fashion and started striking Pierre Mahormoudt with their riding-crops, so long and hard that I saw him fall; for I was more dead than alive and did not even have the strength to flee. 'If you want to save his life,' one of them said to me, 'you must be mine.' At those uncouth words, Pierre got up and struck the knight with his dagger; eleven sword-thrusts immediately slew my husband."

The Comte de Flandre Beauduin was known as Beauduin-à-la-Hache. He was a noble and just seigneur, was Comte Beauduin-à-la-Hache.

IX

The Comte à la Hache asked the woman: "Would you recognize those knights."

"Yes, on my soul," she said.

"Then come with me right away."

And he walked slowly to his dwelling at Winendale, where he ordered all the seigneurs who answered to him to gather.

The Comte de Flandre Beauduin was known as Beauduin-à-la-Hache. He was a noble and just seigneur, was Comte Beauduin-à-la-Hache.

And he said to the poor woman: "Show me all eleven."

Without hesitation she pointed her finger at them one by one.

"Master Provost, put a rope around the neck of these disloyal men unworthy of the name of knights. Have them climb on to that table and attach the rope to the ceiling beam."

The Provost obeyed the Comte's orders.

The Comte de Flandre Beauduin was known as Beauduin-à-la-Hache. He was a noble and just seigneur, was Comte Beauduin-à-la-Hache.

XI

After that the Comte went on: "You are noble and do not have to blush at the hand that punishes you. To work!"

Then he took the table in his own hands and pulled it from beneath the feet of the eleven knights, who remained hanged until death ensued.

And everyone began to clamor: "God and the Holy Virgin aid the Comte à la Hache, for he does good and prompt justice!"

The Comte de Flandre Beauduin was known as Beauduin-à-la-Hache. He was a noble and just seigneur, was Comte Beauduin-à-la-Hache.

Lorette was still singing the last words of her refrain when she had already stopped her little boat alongside the larger vessel, and then, seizing the tiller, she climbed—or rather leapt—on to the deck. Immediately she found herself surrounded by all the young men, greeted with joyful acclamations.

"Welcome, pretty Lorette!"

"Welcome, pretty singer!"

"Her voice is as sweet as the voice of the nightingale, but she has no need to hide in the foliage like her, for where would one find a more charming girl than Lorette?"

Such were the words of the boatmen, for that strange race, in giving the Flemish language the poetic accentuation of the Midi has also given it numerous metaphors and almost the same exaggeration. In our day still they make use of impassioned images to express what they feel, and their gestures, like their words, reveal a southern origin transmitted purely during so many centuries and among people of a wholly opposed organization.

Lorette, pert in the middle of that adulatory group, without paying any heed to the honeyed tributes lavished upon her, in a fashion that proved that she was accustomed to such tributes, went to mingle with the young women, where her cheerful pleasantries soon excited a noisy merriment. All the young men drew nearer and were greeted with epigrams, to which the responded with the same playfulness.

Asrael, a witness to that scene, in which Lorette was playing the central role, could not help smiling in spite of his sadness, and vaguely envying the lot of the boatmen. Then he conceived the fantasy of living their life for a while, and trying to forget, for a few months, the Heaven he had lost and the Hell that had claimed him.

While he was indulging in such thoughts, his piercing gaze, that of a Spirit, perceived the cadaver of a young man some distance away, on the bed of the river. A few hours before, that young man had deliberately broken his head against a rock. Falling into the river he had been suddenly swallowed by the waves.

At the beginning of the evening someone had asked whether Mamert Delveau was there. "By God," someone had replied, "Mamert isn't a fellow like the rest, and you know his black humor. For a week he hasn't said a word to a single Christian."

Asrael immediately took on the features of Mamert Delveau, put on his costume and showed himself on the bank, imitating the cry with which the boatmen call to their comrades. A plank was rapidly thrown from the boat to the shore and Asrael sat down among the boatmen, who formed a circle again in order to listen to another story.

XI.

A few days thereafter, Lorette's boat was moored on a solitary stretch of the Escaut's bank. The young woman had climbed up from her little bedroom to the deck of the boat. She went back, and forth, tormented by a lack of occupation that she did not know how to employ. A review of the long, flat boat with no mast, a few reproaches to her two conductors and a ballad that she started to sing and interrupted in the middle of the second or third couplet did not calm her agitation. Then she went back down to her cabin, opened and closed the chest that contained her garments, took them out one by one, examined them, folded them up and put them back. Then she undid her hair, spread it out over her shoulders with a shake of the head and, putting it up again, arranged it with expertise. Then she gave the same care to the rest of her attire, washed her hands and feet in fresh water, went back on to the deck of the boat, and looked all around, as far as she could.

Still the most complete solitude.

Lorette folded her arms over her chest with the fatigue of ennui; her head gradually tilted forward, and her staring but sightless eyes betrayed the profound reverie into which the pretty young woman drifted. Pretty? Truly, for no boatwoman had ever worn the long corset and heavy silver earrings with more grace; no bilander had ever outlined the delicate proportions of such a dainty foot on its black planks.

Suddenly, an almost imperceptible sound extracted Lorette from her reverie. She raised her head, listened, and did not take long to distinguish an indecisive object on the river in the distance, and, in spite of the uncertain moonlight, she soon recognized it as a boat. That sudden apparition caused her features to expand.

Not that she knew either where that boat was coming from or who was steering it; but no matter, it was a boat; she would find a new face there; she would be able to exchange a few words, even indifferent ones; her emptiness and her ennui would cease, and that was sufficient...

In the meantime, the boat advanced and came to moor next to Lorette's boat. Then she was able to see Mamert Delveau standing near the poop. With one bound, the young man crossed the distance that separated the two bilanders and accosted the boatwoman with an ease and an urgency that she had never noticed in the taciturn boatman, for he lived in complete isolation, and a thousand various rumors ran around in his regard.

If some could be believed, the victim of a spell, he had never been permitted thus far either to be loved by a woman or become a father or bring a lucrative voyage to a successful conclusion. Some accursed witch had cast that abominable spell upon him.

Others said, in low voices, that such a sadness had to conceal a secret crime. When scarcely adolescent, Mamert had loved a young woman who disappeared one day, without anything ever being known of her fate. Perhaps Mamert's dagger had been the cause of that disappearance.

Finally, the third version, and the most accredited, consisted of a romance no less extraordinary than the first two: it was claimed that Mamert, by virtue of an unparalleled jealousy, kept that young woman imprisoned on his boat, and never let anyone see her.

The fact is that Mamert was quite simply afflicted by a malady of consumption, and that the romantic prestige with which his sadness had been adorned existed solely in the imagination of gossips and the curious.

Nevertheless, that romantic prestige had given Mamert an importance in the eyes of his comrades, and the young women took the same interest in him that a story recounted in the evening caused them to experience. Many a time, one of the former had tried to surprise Mamert's secret; many a time,

255

one of the latter had been furtively to visit Mamert's boat while he was absent; but none of them had discovered anything, because there was nothing to discover.

With his fine curly hair, his elegant figure, his pale face, and perhaps by the very fact that he did not share the urgency of the others in Lorette's regard, Mamert preoccupied the young woman's imagination greatly. Twenty times over she had put to work the most provocative enticements to attract the attention of the mysterious Mamert, and nothing had ever worked. Such disdain, the chagrin of her offended self-esteem and the ardent blood that ran in her veins had ended up inspiring in her a romantic passion for Mamert, a passion that knew no bounds, to which the boldest advances had attested many times over.

On recognizing Mamert's boat, on seeing the young man who had thus far been s cold and indifferent toward her come aboard with so much urgency, Lorette experienced a great disturbance that she tried to disguise by addressing a few insignificant words to Mamert. But she was trembling, and could scarcely articulate those words.

"In truth, I thought I would spend my entire evening here alone, without finding a Christian to talk to."

"And imagine my joy, Lorette, on finding you here when I expected to encounter nothing but solitude."

"I'm not sure whether you're telling the truth, for you like solitude; you like it more than the society of your comrades, and especially the society of young women."

"All of them, with only one exception."

"And what is her name?" asked Lorette, delighted to hear Mamert speak of amour, and sure that the boatman was about to speak her name.

"Her name is…but why tell you my secret?"

"Speak quickly! Speak, then! I want it…I beg you, Mamert."

Mamert continued to hesitate.

Poor fellow! Lorette thought. *How timid he is! Oh, it no longer astonishes me that he has kept silent for so long and has not dared to confess his love to me.*

"Well, Mamert, her name?"

"No, I can't say it; I want to keep my secret."

"You love her very much, then?"

"Judge for yourself, since I only live for her and by her; since, in order to receive the mysterious visits she makes me from time to time, I condemn myself to pass my life in the most complete isolation."

Lorette experienced a great disappointment on seeing all the illusions of her vanity and her amour dissolve and vanish.

"I have half your secret, Mamert," she said, finally and painfully, "and I'll have the other whether you like it or not."

"Oh, I don't believe so; I even defy you. Judge how scantly redoubtable your threat is; I have no fear of telling you that my mistress is coming to visit me this evening."

"And no one in the world can prevent you from being faithful to that rendezvous?" she demanded, while her lips laughed and her gaze attached itself to Mamert, full of disturbance and jealousy.

"No one," he replied, in a voice in which Lorette thought she could divine an imperceptible hesitation.

"You are a lover such as there has never been and never will be. You are linked to this woman, then, like death to a cadaver. But what if another loved you? What if she loved you as much, or more than your mysterious unknown woman?"

Mamert shook his head and smiled to signify doubt.

"What proof of such great love has she given you? Is her beauty perfect, then? What if another loved you, Mamert, if you read it in her eyes, if she even confessed it to you…?"

"I would try not to understand her."

"But if she took your hand in hers, if she looked at you with eyes full of tears, finally, if the emotion she experienced were so keen that the words could scarcely emerge from her lips…tell me, Mamert, what would you do?"

"Then..."

"Then, Mamert," she said, taking his hand in hers and making him shiver under her moist gaze. Well? *Then...?*"

"Oh, I think I would flee."

She let go of Mamert's hand, turned her head and wiped away a furtive tear.

"The love of which you speak is impossible," added Mamert, taking Lorette's hand again. "Who could love me, then? Me, with my sadness and my poverty?"

"Mamert!" cried the young woman, while this time, tears flowed abundantly from her eyes, and her hand squeezed the boatman's hand convulsively...

The next day, at dawn, Lorette, with her arm passed around Mamert's neck, asked him, with a malicious tenderness: "What about your rendezvous, Mamert?"

XII. Delights

Lorette could not detach herself from Mamert's side for a moment. If it was necessary to get down on the bank to hasten and direct the horses that were dragging the bilanders, she got down with him, marched arm in arm with him, her lover, and spoke words of love or considered him with a passionate gaze. If he went to make purchases in a nearby village, she took a veil to cover her face, put shoes on her habitually bare feet, and accompanied him.

"Oh, you don't know," she repeated to him incessantly, "you don't know how much I love you. Before loving you, I didn't exist, I was asleep. Now I'm awake, now I'm alive, for you're my life, you're my soul. Oh, Mamert, when you quit me, even for a moment, it immediately creates a profound solitude around me. If you knew how my blood freezes, how my ideas tarnish, when your hand is no longer in mine, when your voice is no longer intoxicating me! I'm cold; I feel ill; I'm desirous without knowing what it is that I desire; everything discontents me, and angry words contract my lips for no reason.

"On the contrary, when you're there, my sweet love, my ideas blossom; tears of joy fill my eyes; nothing matters, nothing can upset me or move me; I have you beside me, what can the rest matter!

"You'll love me forever, won't you? You'll never think with pleasure of anyone else but me? You'll never love anyone else? You, love another! What a horrible thought! How ill it makes me feel! It's impossible, for you love me so much. Well, only in thinking about it, see, my hands clench, my eyes light up, rage swells my heart and blood rushes to my face! No longer to be loved by you would mean: It's another he loves, it's no longer Lorette; he's disdained her, he's cast her aside. Oh, you see, you see, that can never be! Rather my death! Rather yours, yes yours! For I don't love, myself, like all those women who only love in part; me, I would rather kill you with my own hand than let a rival have you! Yes, with my own hand. And it wouldn't be with poison, it wouldn't be an obscure murder. No, in broad daylight, a dagger that one plunges slowly, and allows the enjoyment of the terrors sand tortures of the infidel; a dagger that one twists in the wound, a dagger that cannot be stopped by prayers, by tears or by screams.

"And if ever I come to that, nothing in the world would prevent me from avenging myself. You might be a man, young and strong; I, whose arm is so frail compared with yours—look, it is only half as thick—if I have said I will kill you, it's necessary that you are killed. But where am I going? Where am I being carried by the fear of a woe that can never arrive, since you love me? Oh, forgive me, forgive my delirium! It's because I love you so much. It's because there's something so frightful in the idea of losing Mamert's love."

Asrael experienced an indescribable joy on listening to Lorette's discourse. He had found in her and with her a fanatical passion, not the chaste and ineffable amour of Heaven but an amour that at least occupied all the faculties of his soul, an amour that filled the insupportable void left in him by the eternal absence of Nephta.

"And me?" he replied. "And me? Do you believe that I love you with less force than you love me? Am I happy anywhere but in your arms? Have our boats not become for me a world, a fatherland, a family? When we approach a shore that is not solitary, do you not see me seize the tiller and shout to the conductor of the horses: 'March, march more rapidly!' Are not you, and you alone, my pleasure, my joy, my happiness?"

Then they recalled the slightest details of their amours; they made one another long confidences of their thoughts and their sensations before they knew one another. They consecrated their memories thus, they caused them to be reborn; they embellished the present with them; they exchanged and made one another a gift of their previous existence.

One summer evening, after one of those stifling days that precede and prepare a storm, Lorette and her lover were sitting under a light tent formed by a sail suspended with the aid of a few stakes. It had been necessary for them to quit the interior of the boat, for the heat that had been concentrated there and the lack of air rendered its habitation impossible. Leaning against the tall unique mast of the bilander—a mast that can be erected or folded up according to the boatman's caprice, and seems more like a luxury ornament than an object of real utility—Lorette supported her fatigued lover's head on her knees.

Parodying the tender cares of a mother for a son still very small, she invited Mamert to sleep by means of those naïve words, imprinted with an inexpressible grace, which cannot be proffered by any other mouth than a maternal one; for their charm does not reside in the thought they express, not only in the inflection of the voice that pronounces them, the emotional gaze and the caressant gestures that accompany them. Amour, as if by a tacit confession of the superiority of maternal tenderness over the other affections of the soul, amour, in its most naïve and truest phases, only borrows those delicious words.

Lorette balanced Asrael's head softly, passing her fingers through his black hair, and said to him, in a child-like voice:

"Go on, my child, sleep; for you ought to be so comfortable, lying as you are upon my bosom. Sleep, I want you to;

sleep, for the storm is coming; sleep, and during the storm, your mother will watch over you; sleep, you have nothing to fear from the demons that take little children, especially little children who are not good."

Asrael smiled at Lorette as a child smiles at his mother, and there was in the abandon of their childish frolics a magic, a pure joy, a complete forgetfulness of everything, as one experiences at the happy age that they were feigning in their lovers' caprices.

"Oh, you don't want to go to sleep, bad boy, you don't want to! I've threatened you with my finger, I've said to you: 'Sleep, sleep!' but you don't do it. Far from it, you're raising yourself up to give me a kiss." Go on, be good, and then go to sleep. Go to sleep, and to put you to sleep—for I want you to sleep—I'll sing you one of my most beautiful ballads: a ballad that I don't sing every day, at least. Be good, put your head on my knees; listen, my child, for I'm going to sing the ballad of Simon Brade-vie.

I

Who wants to hear, who wants to know, the adventures of Monseigneur Simon Brade-vie?[31]

He was a brave knight, a knight such as Flanders counts in large numbers, a night at whom ladies smiled and before whose strong lance the bravest warriors fled.

Who wants to hear, who wants to know, the adventures of Monseigneur Simon Brade-vie?

---

[31] Simon Brade-vie was Simon de Marlis, who died in 1305, and whose presence in the present story is therefore anachronistic. An account of him is given in Le Carpentier's *Histoire de Cambrai et de Cambrésis* (1664), previously mentioned as key source from which Berthoud drew raw materials.

II

He had taken part in seventy battles and received a hundred and twenty-two wounds, but he never received a single one in the heart, for he was as faithful to his lady as to honor, and his lady was the beautiful Agnès de Saveuse.

Who wants to hear, who wants to know, the adventures of Monseigneur Simon Brade-vie?

III

One day, the brave sire encountered a weeping damsel, who was lamenting with her hair in the wind and her white shoulders half-naked, for in her dolor she had forgotten to adjust her mantle and her gorget. Now, her shoulders were white and beautiful, and her hair was as long as the cloak of a queen.

Who wants to hear, who wants to know, the adventures of Monseigneur Simon Brade-vie?

IV

"Handsome sire," she said. "Help me, handsome sire. A felon knight, if he is still permitted to give himself the holy title of knight, a coward, after having stolen my litter as I was returning to my father's château, has left me in the road like this, and gone away repeating that he has had the grace of my amour.

Who wants to hear, who wants to know, the adventures of Monseigneur Simon Brade-vie?

V

"Now, he lies, my good seigneur," she said, "I have borne in my heart for a long time the image of a handsome knight whom I love and whom I once saw vanquish in a tourney."

Who wants to hear, who wants to know, the adventures of Monseigneur Simon Brade-vie?

VI

"What knight has such good fortune, noble lady?" enquired Simon Brade-vie.

The lady covered her blushing face with both hands, like a rose hiding its flower in a large bouquet of foliage. It could not be easily glimpsed between her fingers.

Who wants to hear, who wants to know, the adventures of Monseigneur Simon Brade-vie?

VII

"Tell me at least in which tourney," said Simon.

"I will tell you that soon."

"Well than, climb on to the rump of my horse, Madame, and let's run in pursuit of your ravisher."

The lady leapt nimbly on to the rump and embraced the knight's breastplate with her beautiful arms, who soon felt it warm up as if the lady's hands were on fire.

Who wants to hear, who wants to know, the adventures of Monseigneur Simon Brade-vie?

VIII

They did not take long to catch up with the knight of whom the lady had spoken, and who, far from fleeing, was standing calmly in the middle of a clearing. As soon as he saw Simon and the lady coming he stated to laugh so loudly that he nearly fell down in the grass.

Who wants to hear, who wants to know, the adventures of Monseigneur Simon Brade-vie?

IX

Simon Brade-vie raised his lance as if to strike him, but that fit of anger increased the other's hilarity further, who said: "Do you know, Simon, against whom you have come to fight? Against Satan in person. Do you know what lady it is whose cause you have taken up? A chatelaine of the stewardship of Hell."

Who wants to hear, who wants to know, the adventures of Monseigneur Simon Brade-vie?

X

"False or true, it matters little to me. I have sworn to serve this lady against you, To horse, lance at the ready, for I want to keep my promise, and I shall not be seen to replace on my horse's neck the shield that I have raised to fight, my beautiful golden shield which the anchored sable cross. Let's go, take the field, and may victory be to the best!"

Who wants to hear, who wants to know, the adventures of Monseigneur Simon Brade-vie?

XI

The demon, for it really was a demon, whistled in a strange manner, and a horse as hideous as its master suddenly appeared; he bestrode it, uprooted an oak to make a lance of it, and rushed upon the brave knight at a great gallop.

Who wants to hear, who wants to know, the adventures of Monseigneur Simon Brade-vie?

XII

Simon avoided the terrible thrust, and struck his enemy so well in the middle of the breast that the lance emerged from the middle of the back more than ten handspans. Instead of falling, the demon laughed more loudly than ever, for he had never ceased laughing, and he stated capering and maneuvering his horse, as if the lance had not traversed his torso.

Who wants to hear, who wants to know, the adventures of Monseigneur Simon Brade-vie?

XIII

Then, drawing his sword, he ran at Simon, and both started cutting and thrusting at one another with their swords. The forest resounded with the terrible blows they delivered. But the contest was not equal, for the demon's were effective and broke Simon's armor, while the armor of the demon was unaffected.

Who wants to hear, who wants to know, the adventures of Monseigneur Simon Brade-vie?

XIV

Addressing a mental prayer to God, Simon suddenly envisaged a means that succeeded for him; he gripped his sword by the point and started striking the demon with the hilt, where there were relics of Saint Géry and a fragment of the true cross.

Who wants to hear, who wants to know, the adventures of Monseigneur Simon Brade-vie?

XV

If you had seen the demon writhe under those blows! If you had heard his clamors! Oh, he was no longer laughing this time, I can answer for that.

"Mercy, mercy! Oh, I beg you, brave knight, mercy! Have pity on my suffering, each of those blows is burning and killing me!"

Who wants to hear, who wants to know, the adventures of Monseigneur Simon Brade-vie?

XVI

"Will you liberate that lady and rehabilitate her honor?" demanded the knight.

"Yes, yes, but cease your thrusts, I beg you."

"And do you swear never tempt or induce any of my family to evil?"

"I swear it," cried the demon, "but cease your thrusts!"

Who wants to hear, who wants to know, the adventures of Monseigneur Simon Brade-vie?

XVII

"And you, whom I have aided and served on this occasion, are you veritably a chatelaine of the stewardship of Hell?"

"Alas, yes," said the lady, "but since I have known you, brave knight, I would like to be an angel, for perhaps you might love me."

Who wants to hear, who wants to know, the adventures of Monseigneur Simon Brade-vie?

XVIII

"I can only love my lady, the beautiful and good Agnès de Saveuse," the knight replied, "so cease these accolades and genuflections, and if my aid is no longer necessary to you, go wherever you please."

Who wants to hear, who wants to know, the adventures of Monseigneur Simon Brade-vie?

XIX

"You are a brave knight, and the boldest one could see," said the chatelaine of Hell. "I am the wife of Lucifer, prince of the somber empire; if it ever comes about that one of yours dies in a state of mortal sin, and falls into the gulfs of Hell in consequence, let him implore me by saying your name, and the eternal flames will be less dolorous for him than any other. I will be less unhappy too, for I shall have had someone speak to me of Simon Brade-vie.

Who wants to hear, who wants to know, the adventures of Monseigneur Simon Brade-vie?

XIII. The Apparition

While Lorette commenced the ballad of Simon Brade-vie, Asrael, sustained by the knees of his mistress and his eyes closed in a voluptuous languor, continued idly to deliver himself to the puerile and tender joys of before, but as the boat-woman sang and the legend unfolded, he opened his eyes, lifted his head, raised himself up on his knees and, folding his arms over his chest, he started listening gravely and sadly. That song, which spoke of Hell, of the amour of a demon, had awakened his dreams, rendering him the memory of his present situation.

When Lorette had finished the song, she was very surprised to see Mamert with is head bowed over his breast, and his eyes filled with tears.

"Poor chatelaine of Hell!" he murmured, finally.

"I like your pity, Mamert, truly! Your pity for an evil angel! For a demon! Fie!"

"Why, then have less compassion for the amorous sufferings of a demon than the amorous sufferings of a human? Is it because he is condemned to eternal punishment? Is it because there can be no more hope for him? Is it because he is an object of fear and that it is necessary for him to live in an isolation even more frightful that the eternal fires? What! When, after having let himself fall into a very mild error, when, after having thought that a mortal might love him and help him to support existence with less despair, when, after so much imaginary happiness he finds himself rejected into all the bitterness of his punishment, you do not want anyone to feel compassion for him!"

"If he were a Christian, yes—but a demon!"

So, then, if I were a demon, Lorette, you would immediately take back the love that you have given me? My tears and my despair would not matter to you? You would summon your priests and their rites to drive me away? You would thank Heaven for having been liberated from me?"

"Oh, Mamert, you, that would be quite different; any anyway, you're not a demon."

"But what if I were? What if I had renounced for you the attributes of the infernal angels? What if, in order to see you, to receive your caresses, I were incurring perils without number and a torture that lasts not years but an eternity? You would reject me fearfully? You would curse me?"

"What would it matter to me what you are? Would you be any less my Mamert, my happiness, my joy, my soul, my life? Would not Hell with you be better than Paradise in losing you?"

"You're deceiving me, Lorette, and you're allowing yourself to be deceived by the illusions of your love. If it were necessary to swear an oath to accomplish the promises you make, alas, you would soon be seen to recoil and to recant."

"Ingrate! You don't know, then, how much I love you? Well then, since you still doubt me, become a demon if you really are one; assume your terrible face and your fork, and you'll see whether I love you any less!"

"Lorette, my Lorette!" cried Asrael, in a voice whose melody no longer had anything mortal about it.

The young woman went pale and shivered, for it was no longer Mamert that she was holding in her arms. It was a creature of supernatural beauty who was waving two azure and gold wings in the air. A circle of fire ringed his forehead with a dazzling band, and the gracious form of his limbs revealed a celestial origin.

"Do you still love me, Lorette? Tell me, do you still love me?" demanded the infernal angel, kneeling at the boatwoman's feet.

She threw herself into his arms, crying: "Yours forever!"

"Be my companion for eternity, then. I will change your mortal nature into an immortal essence; you will become an infernal spirit; you will have the elements in your power; nature will obey you; at the slightest sign from your hand, thunder would rumble; at the slightest word from your mouth, the waves would roar and rise up to form tempests."

Lorette's eyes sparkled with surprise, pride and amour.

"Persevere in your tenderness for me, and all those marvels will be accomplished. One more year on earth, and you will quit it to share my power, to wear the immortal ring that circles my head."

"Oh! This isn't a dream?"

"It's a dream that will last throughout eternity!" replied Asrael, passing an iron ring over her finger.

XIV. The Shepherd

Happiness is only found in heaven. What is named happiness on earth only offers a pale and icy reflection of the ineffable joys with which the elect intoxicate themselves; their transports succeed one anther endlessly, without lassitude, always renascent, always more vivid and sweeter. God is there, who inundates them with sublime ecstasies and immutable joys.

Among humans, the transports of delight and the bliss of affections deteriorates, weakens, wearies and dies away, and even their memory, alas, often ends up becoming a burden. Satiety, an incurable evil, satiety, a chill that numbs and kills, always waits close to happiness, which it soon stifles with its embrace; it blows over the human heart, and the blood that vivifies that heart with a generous warmth slows down, contracts, and scarcely flows.

After six months of amour with Asrael, Lorette felt that satiety. To begin with, on seeing her, nothing seemed to have changed in her; she surrounded Asrael with the same caresses, she spoke the same amorous words to him. But there were on her forehead I know not what wrinkles formed by a mysterious ennui; her gaze no longer shone, and through the soft intonations of her voice a constraint was revealed.

The reproved angel understood that change without feeling it himself, and that change made his despair. In vain he tried to reawaken in Lorette's soul the amour that had been extinguished; his efforts, his reproaches, his tears and his cares only ended up provoking impatience and hastening distaste.

And the distaste came; it had come; the distaste that causes one to curse what had once made one pant with delight; the distaste that struggles against habit and against the decency that prevents one from breaking the bonds one has assumed; the distaste that is the harsh expiation of temporary human joys, the deadly evidence of their poverty and their annihilation. The boatwoman's imagination, ardent and hence full of inconstancy, surrendered to the force of sensations; and those sensations were rapidly consumed and extinguished. Lightning hurls an immense flame that sets the entire horizon alight, but lightning only flashes, and dies.

Now, she no longer wept if Asrael went away; now, she no longer went up on deck in order to see him coming from further away. When he sang out to announce his return, she no longer ran to him. Far from it; she listened with indifference when he said: "Lorette, it's necessary that I leave, that I leave you for a day, a week, a month..." When she had seen him draw away, she experienced satisfaction; it seemed to her that she had become freer, and that she could breathe more easily.

But inconstancy is a sentiment that causes remorse, or at least shame. One blushes at such mobility of affection, one criticizes oneself, or rather seeks to justify it, and sometimes succeeds in that by means of some paradox with which one dupes oneself. Thus, Lorette attributed her felony in amour to a laudable sentiment of piety and the fear of Hell. She even ended up persuading herself that if Mamert had always remained Mamert, that without the fatal night on which he had shown himself adorned with his demonic attributes, she would have continued to love him faithfully forever.

Once that interpretation was found, she convinced herself of it, and her indifference to Asrael was embittered and envenomed by all the hatreds of a deceptive devotion—so thoroughly that an idea took possession of her, dominated her, exalted her, and became her only idea: to get away from Asrael and then to doom Asrael.

But she feared that; a pact bound her to him; it was necessary to break it, that terrible pact. How? What power could do it? None...

Would not God take pity on her? Would he snatch her away from the demon that held her, from the wretch that had cast her into an infamous trap? For, after all, it was not a demon that she had believed that she loved; it was a man. She had been deceived in a cowardly fashion, unworthily deceived!

My God, what had she done to be deceived in that fashion? She had loved him so much, had found so much happiness in loving him! She had surrendered herself to her love with such a great abandon! And him! He had been thinking of nothing but dooming her. He had looked out for her most tender words, he had troubled her in order better to receive her. In sum, was it not in the midst of the most intoxicating ecstasy, was it not when she no longer retained enough reason to know what she was doing, that he had obliged her to contract that infamous pact? That he had damned her!

Damned? No, she would not be. God would not permit an angel of darkness to triumph. God would suggest to her the means of becoming free again; for, after all, means must exist. A Christian soul cannot find itself delivered, without defense, to the mercy of a demon.

She had loved him, however, she had loved him when he precipitated her thus into the abyss. That is a crime too odious to remain unpunished. It cries out for vengeance, and it is necessary that the vengeance come. It would come!

Yes—and it is God, there was no doubt about it, that has given her the thought—certain shepherds know means of warding off demons and defeating all their ruses. It is necessary that she consult one. After all, what is she risking? She will still remain free to take the resolution that suits her. Indeed, there is, not far from the shore where her boat is moored, an old shepherd who enjoys a great renown for wisdom in magic. A little while ago she saw him directing his flock toward a field not far away. Come on; it's necessary to go find him, and perhaps he will render poor Lorette a means of salvation.

Lorette wrapped her head in a large veil of woolen cloth such as women of her caste wore in those days, and headed for the field in which the shepherd had parked his flock.

She saw the mysterious individual standing in the distance, at the corner of a copse, his eyes raised to the sky, and, according to every appearance, absorbed by a profound meditation. From beneath the gray cloak that covered him, a large pleat of which revealed the right shoulder, a thin and semi-naked arm emerged, holding an oak staff. Two dogs were coming and going around the ewes, holding them in respect, and turning toward their master from time to time a gaze that seemed to be interrogating his desire. But the shepherd remained impassive, and nothing could extract him from his reverie, not even the barking of the two animals, which, as soon as they perceived Lorette, hurtled toward her and prevented her from advancing.

She remained thus, frightened, not daring to take another step, and appealing to the shepherd with loud cries. He finally deigned to hear her and lowered the eyes that had been fixed on the heavens toward her. He whistled in a shrill manner; immediately, the dogs, humble and submissive, fell silent and returned as quickly as possible to huddle against their master's feet.

Lorette, recovering somewhat from her fright, advanced toward the shepherd, who received her with an imperturbable gravity.

"Shepherd," she said, in a voice slightly distorted by the emotion she felt, "here are two gold coins, in order for you to give me some good advice.

The shepherd took the boatwoman's gift and put them in the fold of a sleeve of his cloak. Then, still without saying a word, he looked at Lorette again.

"Tell me, shepherd—it's not for my own account, by the way, that I'm consulting you—when one has made a pact with a demon, is there any means of breaking it?"

"Has the person that you wish to serve ever received any infernal object as a gift?"

"Yes, only one," Lorette replied, her face reddening, and who, by means of a small movement of her left hand hid that hand beneath the pleats of her veil. "Yes, a ring."

"How is that ring fashioned?"

"Of iron, but it shines with a very particular gleam."

"Yes, in such a manner that it can even be seen through a veil," said the shepherd, taking Lorette's left hand.

In so doing he attached a piercing gaze to her, under which the boatwoman shivered. Then he said: "Woman, a demon is your lover!"

She only replied with a dull groan.

The shepherd removed the ring from Lorette's finger; he examined it with a attentive curiosity, and, depositing it in the fold of the sleeve that served him as a pocket, he went into the a cabin mounted on two wheels, the ordinary habitation of people of his estate. He soon came back holding an exactly similar ring and a little bottle filled with a clear liquid.

"Here is a ring that it is necessary not to take off again. So long as you wear it, the demon can do nothing against you. As for this liquid, if you are able to make use of it, it will deliver you from the power of your enemy and render him miserable forever.

"There is in Italy a marble Christ that weeps on the holy day of Good Friday. This liquid is composed in part of the tears of the miraculous Christ. I have combined them with Holy Water; the almost imperceptible fragment that is floating in the bottle is a splinter of the wood of true cross. I have proffered the most powerful words over this liquid; I have saturated it with the light of the moon and it has been submitted to the influence of the stars. Sprinkle that philter over the demon and he will instantly lose his power; he will become a simple mortal submissive to misery and suffering. Far from being redoubtable, he will remain an object of pity. Go, and if you value the salvation of your soul, if Hell frightens you, don't delay for one day, for tomorrow it might be too late.

With an imperious gesture he ordered Lorette to go away, and, resuming his profound meditation, he turned his gaze once again toward the sky.

XV. Jealousy

Almost always, after having pursued an extreme end for a long time, passionately desired but which one is in despair of attaining, if one suddenly finds oneself face to face with that objective, one recoils in a sort of surprise, mingled with uncertainty and dread. Partly abstracted from the deceptive spells of desire, and glimpsing the consequences of what one is about to do, one goes on, but it is with apprehension, by virtue of an almost mechanical rigidity of the will, and even more so by the force of circumstances.

Lorette, at the moment of seeing herself liberated from the demon for whom she had wanted to remove herself for such a long time, who finally possessed an infallible philter to break the bonds rendered insupportable by satiety and terror, now felt hesitant, and her breast and heart squeezed by apprehension and doubt, asked herself: "Will it be today?"

As she approached the boat, her panic and doubt increased.

"It's necessary to wait until tomorrow," she said to herself.

Then, soon, it was no longer for the next day but for the next week, and then the next month, for a term even longer.

What need have I for haste? Do I not have the philter in my possession? When I want to strike, will it not be praiseworthy to strike? Would it not be better to wait for some new misdeed on Asrael's part?

274

And, by a bizarrerie of the human imagination, the memory of the happy times of her first amours came to surround her and smile upon her, fresh and caressant. It was not Asrael that they showed her, it was Mamert, Mamert alone; Mamert with his beautiful pale face, his soft words; Mamert who knew how to love better than any other; Mamert who wept with joy simply on hearing Lorette sing one of the virelays that he had composed for her.

And, insensibly, and without being aware of it, the most tender words of those virelays took possession of her memory and she began to sing them almost without perceiving that she was singing.

I

Love is the only happiness there is on earth; remove amour from the surface of the earth and it would be better for a man to remain in oblivion.

II

If there is a truly happy man, it is the one who never quits a young woman with dark eyes and a moist gaze; it is the one who spends his life in the arms of an adored woman.

III

And I am the happiest of men, for I am the lover of a young woman with dark eyes; I never leave her, and at her smile alone, I tremble with intoxication and happiness.

IV

When she passes by, old men feel rejuvenated and say: "We have never admired one so beautiful! Fortunate is the man who sees such a young woman leaning over his funereal bed at the moment of his death; that sweet vision will efface the horrors of the demise.

V

When they see her pass by, young men forget to press against their chest the arm of the mistress who is leaning on their arm. They watch her draw away, they follow her with their eyes, they still seek to see her when she has disappeared, and that evening and the following days they will remain thoughtful beside their fiancée.

VI

But she is mine! She loves no one but me! She will love me forever! For she is my happiness, she is my soul, she is my life! Without her, without her love, I would have nothing more to do but die; without her, without her love, no smile would ever come to part my lips, and life would be an unbearable torment for me.

VII

She is mine, she loves no one but me, and she will love me forever. Love is the sole happiness that there is on earth. Take away love from above the earth and it would be better for humans to have remained in the void.

As Lorette sang, her hatred and her projects of vengeance weakened and disappeared from her mind with the satiety and the disgust; the magic of memories almost prevented her from glimpsing the through the thousands of cheerful images that she evoked. As in happier times, the young woman's heart beat, and her cheeks colored at the sight of the Escaut, where Mamert's bilander appeared in the distance as a black dot amid the waves resplendent with the while light of the moon.

276

Far from foreseeing the change that had taken place in Lorette's ideas, Asrael was delivering himself, in that bilander to the most dolorous thoughts. In putting on human appearance, his superior essence was shackled and almost reduced to the restricted limits of human intelligence, a mixture of light and darkness, subject to deceptions and reduced to conjectures and errors.

Now, only too convinced of Lorette's coldness and the loss of his love, he was deploring the inconstancy of the woman he loved with so much passion and forming a thousand confused projects for reawakening that amour. *Happiness and satiation have killed it*, he thought; *it is privation and jealousy that will cause it to be reborn. However precious it is, one only attaches a mediocre price to something whose loss one does not fear; dispossession and regret give an inestimable value to the most frivolous thing. Were Lorette to lose or think she has lost my tenderness, she would then regret that tenderness and seek to reconquer it.*

Following those ideas, therefore, he caused to arrive near to his bilander the bilander of a young boatwoman which, without her perceiving it, had covered several leagues in a moment by virtue of a magical and insensible force. She too had allowed herself to be gripped by sadness and the mystery of the handsome boatman; Asrael, fascinating her with his infernal breath, only developed within her an amorous seed that was already very powerful.

The young woman was in the angel's arms, trembling, ceding to irresistible emotions, only able to respond to his tender words with tender words when Lorette was able to begin to distinguish on Mamert's boat what was happening there. At first she doubted it; she believed that the mist and the moonlight were producing by their fantastic play an illusion that was deceiving her. Such was her confidence in the affection of her lover that, even at close range, she could hardly believe her eyes.

Asrael, who pretended not to see Lorette, applauded the success of his ruse and rejoiced in the wrath that was sparkling in the eyes of his mistress.

To describe the emotions that were bowling the latter over would not be easy. A fiery vertigo had engorged her face with a heavy blood. Her breast breathless, her legs giving way, her hands were closing and clenching with rage. She, who had once wanted at any price to remove herself from Asrael, who had just bought at a price of gold a means of killing him, accused him of perfidy, and she was dying of despair, because he was unfaithful to her. In her confused, broken, burning ideas, one idea alone was dominant: Vengeance! Vengeance!

With one bound Lorette launched herself on to the boat and poured the shepherd's philter, in its entirety, over the angel's head.

Asrael uttered a dolorous scream and threw himself into the river to extinguish the execrable fire that was consuming him. He stammered mystical words, which remained powerless. He summoned the aid of his brothers, the demons, but bursts of laughter came from all directions, and mocking voices said to him: "Asrael, you are no more than a human now; you have lost your Spiritual essence; you are no longer anything but a human subject to malady and death. Adieu, human!"

XVI. Sister Clotilde

The following day, two nuns were passing along the bank of the Escaut and stopped in fright before a cadaver that was lying in the middle of the path. Profound lesions furrowed his forehead and breast; his clothing, although soaked with water, seemed half-consumed by fire; the decomposition of his features and the force with which his fists still remained clenched, attested to the horrible dolors he had suffered.

The two brides of Christ knelt down in order to try to re-animate the unfortunate man. For a long time their cares remained ineffective; finally the older of the two exclaimed: "God be praised, Sister Clotilde; I can feel his heart beating!"

Sister Clotilde raised her head and allowed the sight, beneath her veil, of pale features, which her companion's exclamation animated with hope and joy. Then she redoubled her efforts, bandaged the sick man's wounds, and had him respire a balm that completed his return to life. Asrael opened his eyes, but, as if the glare of daylight had wounded them, he closed them immediately and let his head fall back.

"Hope, my brother," said Sister Clotilde. "You have suffered a great deal, but with God's help, it is not impossible to cure you."

"And if you cannot save your body," added the other nun, "At least you will have time to save your soul. The body is perishable, but the soul is immortal."

The sick man uttered a dull groan and made a gesture of despair.

"How can this unfortunate man be transported as far as our convent?" asked Sister Clotilde.

"I don't see any way."

"If some boatman were nearby, we could have recourse to his charity, and he could carry in his skiff, as far as our convent, the sick man that God and Saint Julien have caused us to encounter. But I've looked hard and I can only see on the Escaut, still far, far away, a single bilander, which seems to be no more than a dot, and which seems to be drawing away rapidly.

"What can we do?"

Sister Clotilde sought in vain, and started to weep at not being able to see any means.

"Well, let's try to carry him. God will give us the strength..."

And so saying, Sister Clotilde tried to lift the sick man up, but she was scarcely able to move him, and her tears flowed again.

"My God! My God! Won't you come to our aid?"

"What if one of us were to go as far as the leper-hospital to warn our sisters that a wounded man is lying here and that it's necessary to send men immediately to transport him?"

"Listen! I can hear the noise of a carriage. Oh, God be praised! He's saved!"

Sister Clotilde immediately ran in the direction from which the noise was coming; she perceived a cart laden with hay, drawn by six large Flemish horses led by a peasant, escorted by half a dozen men at arms. Her joy increased further when she recognized at the head of the men-at-arms an old soldier who had once been cared for in the leper-hospital after receiving a grave wound in the leg.

"Greetings to you, my sister! How hurriedly you're running in this direction! There must be some poor sick fellow there, for only a good deed could put so much haste into your stride."

"I have a favor to ask of you," she said, with a smile that filled the old soldier with ease.

"A favor! For you who cared for me with so much bounty for six months when I was suffering like a damned soul, without being able to budge from my bed. A favor! Jacques Levatois would have to be direly ingrate to refuse you that. He has his faults, it's true, but at least he does not have the fault of ingratitude.

"You're a worthy man, and you have a good heart too, Monsieur Levatois; it's for that reason that I have recourse to you. We've found a man over there struck by lightning last night, and we request from you the charity of having him transported as far as our leper-hospital.

"Is that all you want, Sister Clotilde? By Saint Jacques, my patron, I would have liked you to demand more of me. It will be done as you desire; two of my men-at-arms will transport the sick man on this hay-cart, where he will be couched like a Baron. The carriage will only proceed at a walk, in order that its jolts won't fatigue your protégé.

"Hola! Benoit and Philippe, go in quest of this man and handle him with as much delicacy as you can muster, clodhoppers that you are. By Saint Martin, woe betide you if he utters a single cry!"

In the meantime, the vehicle arrived near the dying man, who was placed on the hay in the vehicle. The two sisters, fearing to see the unfortunate man die if they abandoned him during the rest of the journey, took their places at his sides.

Levatois, out of respect for the holy women, and in spite of their pleas, made the little troop that he was commanding remain within bowshot all the way to the convent. Having arrived at the threshold of the pious house, he saluted the two nuns militarily, and continued on his route.

XVII. The Hymn to the Virgin

For three days, the sick man that Sister Clotilde and Sister Marthe had transported to the leprosarium remained unconscious, hovering between life and death. On the fourth day, at the beginning of matins, he emerged from the annihilation that held him, and, opening his eyes, was astonished by the place where he found himself, and especially by the new and unfamiliar sensations of wellbeing that he felt. Fresh ideas were playing in his head, which was no longer gnawed by a dull pain; for the first time since his fall from Heaven the fatal thought "damnation for eternity," did not make him tremble with terror.

Next to the bed where he was lying, a kneeling nun was praying, and mingling her fervent prayer with a hymn full of melody that was being sung in the distance, in chorus, by female voices. That hymn, in which the name of the Almighty was repeated incessantly, in which the mercy and the power of Jesus was celebrated, far from agitating Asrael dolorously, threw him into a reverie full of charm. He raised himself up on his bed, and, his eyes moist with tears, considered the chapel from which those voices were coming: the chapel that, resplendent with candles, appeared luminous in the depths of the vaults and somber arcades of the leprosarium, plunged in a profound obscurity.

The voices sang:

"Holy Mother of God, Holy Mother of God, you who guide the fisherman and who render him hope as a star guides the sailor and renders him hope, listen to our supplicant prayers and come to our aid.

"Celestial creature, holy and pure virgin, mother of mercy, intercede for us, poor fishers, for without you, what would become of us in the presence of God's wrath?

"You are the beneficent mother who tempers the flamboyant glare of the sun. You are the gentle dew that comes to refresh and fecundate the field that the heat of the day has dried out.

"You are the Queen of Heaven, you are the Queen of the Angels; the cherubim bow down before you with respect, and the endless choirs unite your name with the thrice holy and thrice redoubtable name of Jehovah!

"You are the Mother of the Savior of men; one alone of your gazes disarms his wrath, you take that crown, among all your crowns; it permits you to sustain the weak, to console the afflicted, and to spare the guilty punishment.

"That is why young mothers consecrate their children to you, and dress them in white tunics and blue belts, in order that the demons will spare them and dare not set traps for those young souls placed under your protection.

"That is why sailors raise chapels on the shore to you, and kneel down there before exposing themselves to the perils of the sea; they come back there barefoot after a fortunate crossing, or when they have escaped a shipwreck.

"Mediating saint, you always maintain yourself between heaven and earth. At the first cry of repentance you raise your hands toward your divine Son and you cry: 'Mercy!' When an angel descends to the earth in order to enable an irresolute soul to persevere in the good path, it is you who order that message.

"You are there to aid chaste amours, you are there to aid virtuous hopes; no repentance ever finds you deaf to its lamentations. So you are blessed on the earth as in Heaven; so no

Christian ever prays without combining your name with the name of the Eternal, the Savior and the Holy Spirit.

"Be our aid too, those of us who, like the dove that builds its nest far from the vulture, have taken refuge in these places in order to pray and to bless you forever. Be our aid! Oh, be our aid, Holy Mother of the Savior!"

Alas, thought Asrael, *those hymns delight me, make me weep, and yet what are thy compared with the hymns my brothers the cherubim sang? The transports of pious love of these nuns cause me envy, and yet, what are they compared with the divine ecstasies of Heaven? Alas, I have lost them without return!*

Such were his thoughts during the office of matins; when the hymns ceased, when the candles were extinguished, when everything became silent and somber again, he uttered a sigh, became sad and bemoaned the dolors that his wounds were causing him, dolors that preoccupation had suspended almost entirely.

At the cry that he uttered, Sister Clotilde interrupted the prayer that she was saying and drew closer to the invalid.

"My brother, are you suffering a little less?" she asked him, with an ineffable pity.

Asrael looked at her without responding, for the charm that he had experienced at the chants of the nuns, the sight of Sister Clotilde caused him to experience again. He had never seen those blue eyes, that calm forehead, that white and regular physiognomy; he had never heard that ingenuous voice; never had that frail and soft hand sustained his sick forehead as it was sustaining it at that moment. Nevertheless, he felt at the sight of Sister Clotilde the intimate joy that one senses on rediscovering a childhood friend, on seeing once again the place where one came into the world.

"Are you suffering a little less, my brother?" Sister Clotilde asked again, in her soft voice.

"Oh! Yes, I'm suffering less! Much less than just now, a little while ago, before losing consciousness."

"Just now? A little while ago? But it's four days since we found you on the bank of the Escaut."

"Four days? I've been able, for four days, to abstract myself from the despair I endure!"

"Are you very unhappy, then, with much to lament?"

"Unhappy, yes! To lament! Alas, I've never heard a word of compassion, never received a gaze of pity since the fatal moment...since my birth, I mean."

"My brother, you're still very weak, and so much agitation might augment your illness."

"No, no. Look, I'm no longer suffering as I have suffered, as I was suffering still four days ago! See, I'm breathing easily; a fatal imprint is no longer there on my brow. The gnawing worm that was devouring my heart has ceased to make itself felt, and benedictions come in spite of me to wander over my lips. Benedictions! Oh, you don't know, my sister—my sister! alas, that name is sweet to give—you don't know how much joy one experiences in no longer being accursed and no longer hearing oneself accursed. Is it not the case that you are not cursing me? Is it not the case that I don't inspire horror in you? Is it not the case that you feel sorry for me and that I move you to pity?"

"It's a duty for me to feel sorry for you and to love you. Are you not my brother in Jesus Christ?"

A shiver agitated all Asrael's limbs; he hid his head in his hands, and when he lifted it again, his eyes were red and his cheeks bathed with tears.

"A word from you has destroyed all my illusions and has returned me to reality, the deadly reality. Alas, without that cruel word I might almost have allowed myself to hope. Hope! What dolor, what tortures would be redoubtable with that idea; hope! But no, it will never calm my fear, it will never sustain me in my torments. Two abysms surround me: behind, the crime and the sentence: "Eternity!" before, the punishment: "Eternity!"

"My sister," said an old nun, "The sick man is talking too much; he's delirious."

284

Sister Clotilde wept.

The old nun went on: "It's necessary not to be moved to pity, Clotilde, by capricious words, which don't even make sense... But after all, I'm wrong to scold you, and my scolding will achieve nothing," she added, indulgently, almost repenting her slight reprimand. "Like you, I've been compassionate, weeping at the slightest thing; habit, and perhaps, even more, the insensibility that age produces, have cured me of that weakness."

Sister Clotilde smiled at the nun, wiped away her tears, and was preparing to quit the sick man's bed when the latter called her back.

"In the name of God, in the name of all that is most sacred, don't go away! My illness is appeased next to you, and I no longer feel it. Stay here, stay there; I'm as glad as in the times when I could pray."

The nun recoiled in an involuntary movement of fear, for the poor girl could not conceive that there existed on earth creatures sufficiently abandoned not to pray. Nevertheless, she immediately drew closer to Asrael and said to him:

"Why despair of divine mercy? It is great and infinite. Whatever your crimes might be—for crimes alone can prevent one from praying—ask for God's forgiveness."

"There is no more forgiveness for me."

"Hope."

"Hope is a word banished from my memory, a thought stifled in my heart."

"Believe me, try!"

"There are judgments of God, terrible judgments, for which it is not permissible to have recourse to mercy."

"Well, if the justice of God frightens you, have recourse to the intercession of his divine mother; pray to her; she will request your pardon from her son, our Redeemer; I will unite my voice with yours."

"I'm not able to pray!"

"Don't deliver yourself to such despair. If prayer cannot spare you entirely from punishment, at least it can abridge its duration."

"Alas, what would thousands of years of expiations matter to me, if I could at least glimpse, after so much suffering, the faintest hope of salvation!"

At that moment the office of sext began, and the choir of nuns chanted these terrible words:

"The Lord is just; he crushes the heads of the wicked. Let all those who hate Sion be confounded and put to flight!

"Let them be similar to the grass that grows on rooftops, to the grass that dries out before it is torn up.

"To the grass that never fills either the hand of the reaper nor the bosom of the one who collects the sheaves."

Asrael uttered a loud cry.

"Never hope for me, never!"

XVII. The Prayer

The invalid's cry of despair caused Sister Clotilde to shed new tears; she resumed praying with devotion, in order to obtain from God, for the poor sinner, the sweetest of celestial benefits: hope.

From that moment on, the young nun, allowing herself to yield to an indefinable charm, which gradually increased, hardly ever left the sick man's bed. With the delicacy innate in women, which ensures that no other mortal hand is able, like theirs, to bandage and soothe a wound and no other voice calm and console an affliction, she carefully refrained henceforth from confronting Asrael with the idea that caused him such great terrors. Not that she renounced in the slightest her project of bringing the invalid back to the right path; but another instinct, no less special to women, the instinct of perseverance, awakened and rendered stronger by the obstacles, had informed Sister Clotilde that it was by skill, and by dint of time and mildness, that she would be able to obtain such a success.

Using all her means of influence, therefore, including those that her sex and beauty gave her, she soon captivated Asrael to such a degree that his eyes, heavy with fever, could not close in slumber unless the nun was sitting there, beside the bed, praying or delivering herself to one of her dutiful tasks.

Accustomed to such caprices on the part of the unfortunates that Providence sent to their care, and taking to heart the salvation of the suffering soul that they had encountered, the other nuns, by a pious complaisance, favored Asrael's desires and hardly allowed the attendant he preferred to go far from his bed.

Sister Clotilde did not take long to divine the manner in which it was necessary to approach the secret dolors of the patient without aggravating them, and to give birth in him to the desire for a good life on earth and for paradise in the other world. She talked to him incessantly about the wellbeing and the calm that she experienced in the cloister.

"If you knew how happy I am!" she said. "I have no cares, for I live from day to day, confident in the bounty of the God who gives nourishment to little birds and who will no more abandon me than he abandons them. What cares do you expect me to experience? The wealth of the earth no longer concerns me. The life of the cloister is a foretaste of the life of heaven.

"Tell me, what greater happiness could one invent than praying to God from evening to morning and from morning to evening? than intoxicating oneself on the ecstasy of prayer? than putting oneself thus, like the blissful, face to face with the Lord? I only interrupt so many ineffable joys to care for the sick, to bandage their wounds, to soothe their miseries, to console their chagrins and render them confidence   in the Lord's mercy.

"You do not know what a good satisfaction refreshes the mind when one sees the eyebrows of a sinner, contracted with despair, relaxing and allowing less bitter gazes to shine. You do not know, my brother, how joyfully one goes to sleep, blessing the Lord, when one hears lips stigmatized by the habit of blasphemy expressing pious words of repentance. For, you see, God is always ready to accept repentance; no sin exists, no fault and no crime, that he does not forgive the repentant."

In saying that, Sister Clotilde forgot to prepare the strips of cloth that she was turning in her fingers, or strip rose-petals in order to prepare balms; her eyes shone with a divine gleam and fascinated Asrael.

Every day the nun's influence over Asrael became more powerful; every day her words penetrated more deeply into the unfortunate's heart and rendered his regrets at being excluded from Heaven more bitter. Oh, if it had only been necessary to repent...! Alas, for twenty centuries, and above all moment, he had experienced a very cruel repentance... But no, the word "never" stood between God and himself.

It was therefore necessary to limit himself to the happiness he enjoyed at that moment, the fugitive happiness of seeing and hearing Sister Clotilde, or receiving the care that she gave him, of hearing her call him "My brother," and of responding, in exchange for that cherished name, "My sister!"

However, in seeking to exert her influence on Asrael and bring him to her, Sister Clotilde was subject to Asrael's influence and went toward him. The image of the individual she wanted to convert no longer quit her; she was occupied with it all day long; by night she reproduced it in her dreams, and she pursued it when she awoke. The innocent creature was not alarmed by those symptoms and did not seek to put herself on guard against such a preoccupation. So the evil made rapid progress and the nun loved Asrael recklessly, although she still believed that she was only occupied so keenly with him because she wanted his conversion.

Asrael read within Sister Clotilde's heart, and saw with simultaneous joy and regret that celestial soul imprinted with terrestrial passions. The idea of dooming her, of dragging her with him into the eternal abysm, frightened him and horrified him, to such an extent that after several days of intimate struggles he resolved to distance himself from Sister Clotilde and save her from the peril that was menacing her without her being aware of it.

One morning, on arriving beside her patient, Sister Clotilde found him standing up, dressed, with a traveler's staff in his hand.

"You want to leave?" she asked, going pale. And she repeated: "You want to leave?"

And it was necessary for him to support her, as she felt faint.

"Receive my adieux, my sister," Asrael replied.

"But you're still too weak to leave the leprosarium so quickly. Your wounds are not scarred; fever scarcely leaves you. Stay for a few days more."

"It's necessary for me to leave, my sister—I must! It would be criminal for me to stay in this place any longer. Adieu, then, and be blessed for the good that you have done me, blessed for the happiness that you have given me, blessed for the memory that you have put into my heart, which will never leave it henceforth."

Tears flowed from Sister Clotilde's eyes, and her efforts could not stem those tears.

"Adieu, then," she said. "Adieu!"

And she hid her face in her hands.

Asrael drew away.

Suddenly, Sister Clotilde ran after him and brought him back.

"At least reconcile yourself with God before leaving. Leave me, in my chagrin, the sweet consolation that you are not lost for eternity and that I shall find you again in Heaven."

"Alas, any reconciliation between God and me is impossible. He could not forgive me."

"Well, at least pray! One single prayer, one single word of prayer! Oh, you won't refuse me that—me, who collected you, dying; me, who cared for you as a true sister would have cared for her brother; me, who is weeping in quitting you."

Asrael smiled sadly and turned his head away.

"Yes, pray! God is not inexorable; he will forgive you, for I have divined repentance in your heart. You repent of your sins, don't you?"

"Alas, if the greatest repentance would be worth my pardon, the gates of Heaven would not be closed to me for eternity."

"Pray, then, pray with me! For the sake of mercy, for the sake of pity, I ask you on my knees!"

And she took Asrael's hands and she drew him toward her, and she shed tears in torrents.

Asrael yielded and knelt down, but without confidence and solely to please Sister Clotilde.

The latter, after a short mental prayer, began saying one by one the words of an orison, and made Asrael repeat them, folding his joined hands in her own.

As he repeated the words, Asrael felt a kind of blindfold come undone from over his eyes; a sublime joy took possession of his heart; a celestial light inundated him, and his soul, stigmatized with the seal of damnation, resumed its ardent gleam and its imperious need for tenderness. His eyes, which he had kept lowered at first, soon rose up, and it seemed to him that in the midst of the clouds the angels received his prayer and carried it to the feet of the Eternal.

Suddenly, a feeble cry brought back to earth the dazzled gaze that he bore toward Heaven, to Sister Clotilde, who had fallen in a faint at his feet. At the sight of that adorable creature delivered to him, the demonic essence once again obtained the upper hand in Asrael's soul; he seized the young woman and was about to draw her outside the cloister when he suddenly stopped.

"Rather Hell than that!" he cried. "Rather Hell than Clotilde's doom. Satan, I am vanquished. Plunge me once again into the abysms of Hell!"

Scarcely had he proffered those last words, and at the very moment when he was ready to see the infernal abysms open before him, his angelic wings reappeared and deployed, as fresh and splendid as they had been in Heaven; the mystic aureole of the cherubim sprang forth around his head, and another angel—Nephta, his Nephta, Nephta, in whom he recognized all the features of Sister Clotilde—Nephta, rose with him into the heavens, and surrounded him with her fraternal arms.

And a choir of angels surrounded them, and those angels sang the following hymn:

How great is the mercy of the Lord, how mysterious and infinite are his ways!

The cherub Asrael took part in the revolt of the evil angels, the victim of an execrable demonic trap and drawn by an excess of love for his divine sister, the beautiful Nephta.

As a rebel, he had to suffer throughout eternity; as a rebel, he had to bear on his forehead the fatal seal of the reproved; as a rebel, he had to remain forever deprived of the presence of God.

But Jehovah, touched by the intercession of the Holy Virgin May, Jehovah, whose bounty equals his power, Jehovah permitted that Asrael, having come to Earth, fell into the traps of a woman!

And the traps of that woman broke the chain that bound Asrael to Hell; thanks to those traps, Asrael became a man, a simple mortal.

Then Heaven no longer remained closed to him, and Nephta reopened its door to him, in teaching him to pray again, the prayer that the cherubim sang before God, prior to the revolt of the demons.

Nephta had been employed on earth and condemned to take a human body, because she had wept incessantly in Heaven at the loss of her Asrael.

Thus, of a double punishment, a double happiness is born!

How great is the mercy of the Lord, how mysterious and infinite are his ways!

Asrael and Nephta have sought love on earth in vain. They only encountered it when their celestial souls found themselves united again.

Veritable amour does not exist on earth. If any mortals, any unfortunates, feel inflamed by a pure and durable amour, an amour that does not recoil before any sacrifice, which nothing can extinguish, they can only be angels strayed from their celestial sphere, angels who are weeping incessantly over the bitterest deceptions, and who will only see their tears dry up in Heaven.

Cambrai, January 1831.

SF & FANTASY

Adolphe Alhaiza. *Cybele*

Alphonse Allais. *The Adventures of Captain Cap*

Henri Allorge. *The Great Cataclysm*

Guy d'Armen. *Doc Ardan: The City of Gold and Lepers; The Troglodytes of Mount Everest/The Giants of Black Lake; The Abominable Snowman*

G.-J. Arnaud. *The Ice Company*

André Arnyvelde. *The Ark; The Mutilated Bacchus*

Charles Asselineau. *The Double Life*

Henri Austruy. *The Eupantophone; The Olotelepan; The Petitpaon Era*

Barillet-Lagargousse. *The Final War*

Cyprien Bérard. *The Vampire Lord Ruthwen*

S. Henry Berthoud. *Martyrs of Science; The Angel Asrael*

Aloysius Bertrand. *Gaspard de la Nuit*

Richard Bessière. *The Gardens of the Apocalypse; The Masters of Silence*

Chevalier de Béthune. *The World of Mercury*

Albert Bleunard. *Ever Smaller*

Félix Bodin. *The Novel of the Future*

Pierre Boitard. *Journey to the Sun*

Louis Boussenard. *Monsieur Synthesis*

Alphonse Brown. *City of Glass; The Conquest of the Air*

Émile Calvet. *In a Thousand Years*

André Caroff. *The Terror of Madame Atomos; Miss Atomos; The Return of Madame Atomos; The Mistake of Madame Atomos; The Monsters of Madame Atomos; The Revenge of Madame Atomos; The Resurrection of Madame Atomos; The Mark of Madame Atomos; The Spheres of Madame Atomos; The Wrath of Madame Atomos* (w/M. & Sylvie Stéphan)

Félicien Champsaur. *Homo-Deus; The Human Arrow; Nora, The Ape-Woman; Ouha, King of the Apes; Pharaoh's Wife*

Didier de Chousy. *Ignis*

Jules Clarétie. *Obsession*

Jacques Collin de Plancy. *Voyage to the Center of the Earth*

Michel Corday. *The Eternal Flame; The Lynx* (w/André Couvreur)

André Couvreur. *Caresco, Superman; The Exploits of Professor Tornada* (3 vols.); *The Necessary Evil*

Gaston Danville. *The Perfume of Lust*
Camille Debans. *The Misfortunes of John Bull*
Captain Danrit. *Undersea Odyssey*
C. I. Defontenay. *Star (Psi Cassiopeia)*
Charles Derennes. *The People of the Pole*
Georges Dodds (anthologist). *The Missing Link*
Charles Dodeman. *The Silent Bomb*
Harry Dickson. *The Heir of Dracula; Harry Dickson vs. The Spider*
Jules Dornay. *Lord Ruthven Begins*
Alfred Driou. *The Adventures of a Parisian Aeronaut*
Odette Dulac. *The War of the Sexes*
Alexandre Dumas. *The Return of Lord Ruthven; The Man who Married a Mermaid* (w/P. Lacroix)
Renée Dunan. *Baal; The Ultimate Pleasure*
J.-C. Dunyach. *The Night Orchid; The Thieves of Silence*
Henri Duvernois. *The Man Who Found Himself*
Achille Eyraud. *Voyage to Venus*
Henri Falk. *The Age of Lead*
Paul Féval. *Anne of the Isles; Knightshade; Revenants; Vampire City; The Vampire Countess; The Wandering Jew's Daughter*
Paul Féval, *fils. Felifax, the Tiger-Man*
Charles de Fieux. *Lamékis*
Fernand Fleuret. *Jim Click*
Charles-Marie Flor O'Squarr. *Phantoms*
Louis Forest. *Someone is Stealing Children in Paris*
Arnould Galopin. *Doctor Omega; Doctor Omega and the Shadowmen* (anthology)
Judith Gautier. *Isoline and the Serpent-Flower*
H. Gayar. *The Marvelous Adventures of Serge Myrandhal on Mars*
Louis Geoffroy. *The Apocryphal Napoleon*
G.L. Gick. *Harry Dickson and the Werewolf of Rutherford Grange*
Raoul Gineste. *The Second Life of Doctor Albin*
Delphine de Girardin. *Balzac's Cane*
Léon Gozlan. *The Vampire of the Val-de-Grâce*
Jules Gros. *The Fossil Man*
Jimmy Guieu. *The Polarian-Denebian War* (2 vols.)
Edmond Haraucourt. *Daah, the First Human; Illusions of Immortality*
Nathalie Henneberg. *The Green Gods*
Eugène Hennebert. *The Enchanted City*
Jules Hoche. *The Maker of Men and His Formula*
V. Hugo, P. Foucher & P. Meurice. *The Hunchback of Notre-Dame*

Romain d'Huissier. *Hexagon: Dark Matter*
Jules Janin. *The Magnetized Corpse*
Michel Jeury. *Chronolysis*
Gustave Kahn. *The Tale of Gold and Silence*
Gérard Klein. *The Mote in Time's Eye*
Fernand Kolney. *Love in 5000 Years*
Paul Lacroix. *Danse Macabre; The Man who Married a Mermaid* (w/Alexandre Dumas)
Louis-Guillaume de La Follie. *The Unpretentious Philosopher*
Jean de La Hire. *The Fiery Wheel; Enter the Nyctalope; The Nyctalope on Mars; The Nyctalope vs. Lucifer; The Nyctalope Steps In; Night of the Nyctalope; Return of the Nyctalope*
Etienne-Léon de Lamothe-Langon. *The Virgin Vampire*
André Laurie. *Spiridon*
Gabriel de Lautrec. *The Vengeance of the Oval Portrait*
Alain le Drimeur. *The Future City*
Georges Le Faure & Henri de Graffigny. *The Extraordinary Adventures of a Russian Scientist Across the Solar System* (2 vols.)
Gustave Le Rouge. *The Dominion of the World* (w/Gustave Guitton) (4 vols.); *The Mysterious Doctor Cornelius* (3 vols.); *The Vampires of Mars*
Jules Lermina. *The Battle of Strasbourg; Mysteryville; Panic in Paris; The Secret of Zippelius; To-Ho and the Gold Destroyers*
Maurice Level. *The Gates of Hell*
André Lichtenberger. *The Centaurs; The Children of the Crab*
Maurice Limat. *Mephista*
Listonai. *The Philosophical Voyager*
Jean-Marc & Randy Lofficier. *Edgar Allan Poe on Mars; The Katrina Protocol; Pacifica 1, 2; Robonocchio; Return of the Nyctalope;* (anthologists) *Tales of the Shadowmen 1-13; The Vampire Almanac* (2 vols.)
Ch. Lomon & P.-B. Gheuzi. *The Last Days of Atlantis*
Camille Mauclair. *The Virgin Orient*
Xavier Mauméjean. *The League of Heroes*
Joseph Méry. *The Tower of Destiny*
Hippolyte Mettais. *Paris Before the Deluge; The Year 5865*
Louise Michel. *The Human Microbes; The New World*
Tony Moilin. *Paris in the Year 2000*
Michael Moorcock's *Legends of the Multiverse*
José Moselli. *Illa's End*
John-Antoine Nau. *Enemy Force*

Marie Nizet. *Captain Vampire*
Charles Nodier. *Trilby and The Crumb Fairy*
C. Nodier, A. Beraud & Toussaint-Merle. *Frankenstein*
Henri de Parville. *An Inhabitant of the Planet Mars*
Gaston de Pawlowski. *Journey to the Land of the 4th Dimension*
Georges Pellerin. *The World in 2000 Years*
Ernest Pérochon. *The Frenetic People*
Pierre Pelot. *The Child Who Walked on the Sky*
Jean Petithuguenin. *An International Mission to the Moon*
J. Polidori, C. Nodier, E. Scribe. *Lord Ruthven the Vampire*
P.-A. Ponson du Terrail. *The Immortal Woman; The Vampire and the Devil's Son; The Police Agent*
Georges Price. *The Missing Men of the* Sirius
René Pujol. *The Chimerical Quest*
Edgar Quinet. *Ahasuerus; The Enchanter Merlin*
Henri de Régnier. *A Surfeit of Mirrors*
Maurice Renard. *The Blue Peril; Doctor Lerne; The Doctored Man; A Man Among the Microbes; The Master of Light*
Restif de la Bretonne. *The Discovery of the Austral Continent by a Flying Man; Posthumous Correspondence* (3 vols.); *The Fay Ouroucoucou* (2 vols.)
Jean Richepin. *The Crazy Corner; The Wing*
Albert Robida. *The Adventures of Saturnin Farandoul; Chalet in the Sky; The Clock of the Centuries; The Electric Life; The Engineer Von Satanas*
J.-H. Rosny Aîné. *Helgvor of the Blue River; The Givreuse Enigma; The Mysterious Force; The Navigators of Space; Vamireh; The World of the Variants; The Young Vampire*
Marcel Rouff. *Journey to the Inverted World*
Marie-Anne de Roumier-Robert. *The Voyage of Lord Seaton to the Seven Planets*
Léonie Rouzade. *The World Turned Upside Down*
Han Ryner. *The Human Ant; The Superhumans*
Louis-Claude de Saint-Martin. *The Crocodile*
Frank Schildiner. *The Quest of Frankenstein; The Triumph of Frankenstein*
Pierre de Selenes: *An Unknown World*
Norbert Sevestre. *Sâr Dubnotal: Vs. Jack the Ripper; The Astral Trail*
Angelo de Sorr. *The Vampires of London*

Brian Stableford. *The Empire of the Necromancers (1. The Shadow of Frankenstein; 2. Frankenstein and the Vampire Countess; 3. Frankenstein in London); The Wayward Muse; Eurydice's Lament; The Mirror of Dionysius; The New Faust at the Tragicomique; Sherlock Holmes and The Vampires of Eternity; The Stones of Camelot* (anthologist) *News from the Moon; The Germans on Venus; The Supreme Progress; The World Above the World; Nemoville; Investigations of the Future; The Conqueror of Death; The Revolt of the Machines; The Man With the Blue Face; The Aerial Valley; The New Moon; The Nickel Man; On the Brink of the World's End; The Mirror of Present Events; The Humanishere*
Jacques Spitz. *The Eye of Purgatory*
Kurt Steiner. *Ortog*
Eugène Thébault. *Radio-Terror*
C.-F. Tiphaigne de La Roche. *Amilec*
Simon Tyssot de Patot. *The Strange Voyages of Jacques Massé and Pierre de Mésange*
Louis Ulbach. *Prince Bonifacio*
Théo Varlet. *The Castaways of Eros; The Golden Rock.; The Martian Epic* (w/Octave Joncquel); *Timeslip Troopers* (w/André Blandin); *The Xenobiotic Invasion*
Pierre Véron. *The Merchants of Health*
Paul Vibert. *The Mysterious Fluid*
Villiers de l'Isle-Adam. *The Scaffold; The Vampire Soul*
Gaston de Wailly. *The Murderer of the World*
Philippe Ward. *Artahe; Manhattan Ghost* (w/Mickael Laguerre); *The Song of Montségur* (w/Sylvie Miller)

Victor Margueritte. *The Bacheloress; The Companion; The Couple*

MYSTERIES & THRILLERS

M. Allain & P. Souvestre. *The Daughter of Fantômas*
A. Anicet-Bourgeois & Lucien Dabril. *Rocambole* (stage plays)
Guy d'Armen. *Doc Ardan: The City of Gold and Lepers; The Troglodytes of Mount Everest/The Giants of Black Lake; Doc Ardan: The Abominable Snowman*
Cyprien Bérard. *The Vampire Lord Ruthwen*
A. Bernède. *Belphegor*; *Judex* (w/Louis Feuillade); *The Return of Judex* (w/Louis Feuillade); *The Shadow of Judex* (anthology)
A. Bisson & G. Livet. *Nick Carter vs. Fantômas* (stage play)

André Caroff. *The Terror of Madame Atomos; Miss Atomos; The Return of Madame Atomos; The Mistake of Madame Atomos; The Monsters of Madame Atomos; The Revenge of Madame Atomos; The Resurrection of Madame Atomos; The Mark of Madame Atomos; The Spheres of Madame Atomos; The Wrath of Madame Atomos* (w/M. & Sylvie Stéphan)

Félicien Champsaur. *Homo-Deus; Nora, The Ape-Woman; Ouha, King of the Apes*

Jules Clarétie. *Obsession*

V. Darlay & H. de Gorsse. *Arsène Lupin vs. Sherlock Holmes: The Stage Play* (stage play)

Harry Dickson. *Harry Dickson vs. The Heir of Dracula; Harry Dickson vs. The Spider*

Séamas Duffy. *Sherlock Holmes in Paris*

Alexandre Dumas. *The Return of Lord Ruthven* (stage play)

Paul Féval. *The Black Coats (The Parisian Jungle; Heart of Steel; The Sword-Swallower; 'Salem Street; The Invisible Weapon; The Companions of the Treasure; The Cadet Gang); Gentlemen of the Night; John Devil*

Paul Féval, *fils. Felifax, the Tiger-Man*

Louis Forest. *Someone is Stealing Children in Paris*

Émile Gaboriau. *Monsieur Lecoq; The Casebook of Monsieur Lecoq*

Arnould Galopin: *Harry Dickson: The Man in Grey; Harry Dickson: Tenebras*

Goron & Émile Gautier. *Spawn of the Penitentiary*

G.L. Gick. *Harry Dickson and The Werewolf of Rutherford Grange*

Léon Gozlan. *The Vampire of the Val-de-Grâce*

Georges Grison. *The Heads that fell in Paris*

Paul d'Ivoi. *Around the World on Five Sous* (w/Henri Chabrillat)

Paul Lacroix. *Danse Macabre*

Jean de La Hire. *Enter the Nyctalope; The Nyctalope on Mars; The Nyctalope vs. Lucifer; The Nyctalope Steps In; Night of the Nyctalope; Return of the Nyctalope*

Rick Lai. *Shadows of the Opera: Retribution in Blood; Sisters of the Shadows: The Curse of Cagliostro*

Etienne-Léon de Lamothe-Langon. *The Virgin Vampire*

Steve Leadley. *Sherlock Holmes and The Circle of Blood*

Maurice Leblanc. *Arsène Lupin vs. Countess Cagliostro; Arsène Lupin vs. Sherlock Holmes (1. The Blonde Phantom; 2. The Hollow Needle); The Island of the Thirty Coffin; 813; The Many Faces of Arsène Lupin* (anthology)

Gustave Lerouge: *The Mysterious Doctor Cornelius* (3 vols.)
Gaston Leroux. *Chéri-Bibi* (stage play)*; The Phantom of the Opera; Rouletabille & the Mystery of the Yellow Room; Rouletabille at Krupp's*
Maurice Limat. *Mephista*
Jean-Marc & Randy Lofficier. *The Katrina Protocol;* (anthologists) *Tales of the Shadowmen 1-13; The Vampire Almanac* (2 vols.)
Richard Marsh. *The Complete Adventures of Judith Lee*
William Patrick Maynard. *The Terror of Fu Manchu; The Destiny of Fu Manchu*
Frank J. Morlok. *Sherlock Holmes: The Grand Horizontals* (stage play)*; Sherlock Holmes vs Jack the Ripper* (stage play)*; Sherlock Holmes, Fantômas, Lupin, Raffles and More: The Spanish Plays* (stage plays)
Jean Petithuguenin. *The Adventures of Ethel King, The Female Nick Carter*
P.-A. Ponson du Terrail. *The Immortal Woman; The Vampire and the Devil's Son; The Police Agent*
Georges Price. *The Missing Men of the* Sirius
Charles Rabou: *The Secret Bureau: 1. The Secret Bureau; 2: The Brothers of Death*
Antonin Reschal. *The Adventures of Miss Boston, The First Female Detective*
Norbert Sevestre. *Sâr Dubnotal vs. Jack the Ripper; The Astral Trail*
Eugène Thébault. *Radio-Terror*
P. de Wattyne & Y. Walter. *Sherlock Holmes vs. Fantômas* (stage play)
David White. *Fantômas in America*
Pierre Yrondy. *The Adventures of Thérèse Arnaud of the French Secret Service*

NON-FICTION

Stephen R. Bissette. *Blur 1-5. Green Mountain Cinema 1; Teen Angels*
Win Scott Eckert. *Crossovers* (2 vols.)
Georges Grison. *The Heads that Fell in Paris*
Jean-Marc & Randy Lofficier. *Shadowmen* (2 vols.)
Randy Lofficier. *Over Here*
Brian Stableford. *The Plurality of Imaginary Worlds*